P9-BBO-541

THE ASSASSINATION OPTION

ALSO BY W.E.B. GRIFFIN

HONOR BOUND

HONOR BOUND
BLOOD AND HONOR
SECRET HONOR
DEATH AND HONOR
(and William E. Butterworth IV)
THE HONOR OF SPIES
(and William E. Butterworth IV)
VICTORY AND HONOR
(and William E. Butterworth IV)
EMPIRE AND HONOR
(and William E. Butterworth IV)

BROTHERHOOD OF WAR

BOOK I: THE LIEUTENANTS
BOOK II: THE CAPTAINS
BOOK III: THE MAJORS
BOOK IV: THE COLONELS
BOOK V: THE BERETS
BOOK VI: THE GENERALS
BOOK VII: THE NEW BREED
BOOK VIII: THE AVIATORS
BOOK IX: SPECIAL OPS

CLANDESTINE OPERATIONS

BOOK 1: TOP SECRET
(and William E. Butterworth IV)

THE CORPS

BOOK I: SEMPER FI
BOOK II: CALL TO ARMS
BOOK III: COUNTERATTACK
BOOK IV: BATTLEGROUND
BOOK V: LINE OF FIRE
BOOK VI: CLOSE COMBAT
BOOK VII: BEHIND THE LINES
BOOK VIII: IN DANGER'S PATH
BOOK IX: UNDER FIRE
BOOK X: RETREAT, HELL!

BADGE OF HONOR

BOOK I: MEN IN BLUE
BOOK II: SPECIAL OPERATIONS
BOOK III: THE VICTIM
BOOK IV: THE WITNESS
BOOK V: THE ASSASSIN
BOOK VI: THE MURDERERS
BOOK VII: THE INVESTIGATORS
BOOK VIII: FINAL JUSTICE
BOOK IX: THE TRAFFICKERS
(and William E. Butterworth IV)
BOOK X: THE VIGILANTES
(and William E. Butterworth IV)
BOOK XI: THE LAST WITNESS
(and William E. Butterworth IV)
BOOK XII: DEADLY ASSETS
(and William E. Butterworth IV)

MEN AT WAR

BOOK I: THE LAST HEROES
BOOK II: THE SECRET WARRIORS
BOOK III: THE SOLDIER SPIES
BOOK IV: THE FIGHTING AGENTS
BOOK V: THE SABOTEURS
(and William E. Butterworth IV)
BOOK VI: THE DOUBLE AGENTS
(and William E. Butterworth IV)
BOOK VII: THE SPYMASTERS
(and William E. Butterworth IV)

PRESIDENTIAL AGENT

BOOK I: BY ORDER OF THE PRESIDENT
BOOK II: THE HOSTAGE
BOOK III: THE HUNTERS
BOOK IV: THE SHOOTERS
BOOK V: BLACK OPS
BOOK VI: THE OUTLAWS
(and William E. Butterworth IV)
BOOK VII: COVERT WARRIORS
(and William E. Butterworth IV)
BOOK VIII: HAZARDOUS DUTY
(and William E. Butterworth IV)

THE ASSASSINATION OPTION

A CLANDESTINE OPERATIONS NOVEL

W.E.B. GRIFFIN

AND WILLIAM E. BUTTERWORTH IV

G. P. PUTNAM'S SONS
NEW YORK

PUTNAM

G. P. PUTNAM'S SONS
Publishers Since 1838
Published by the Penguin Group
Penguin Group (USA) LLC
375 Hudson Street
New York, New York 10014

USA · Canada · UK · Ireland · Australia
New Zealand · India · South Africa · China

penguin.com
A Penguin Random House Company

Library of Congress Cataloging-in-Publication Data

Griffin, W. E. B.
The assassination option : a clandestine operations novel / W.E.B. Griffin and William E. Butterworth.
p. cm.—(A clandestine operations novel ; 2)
ISBN 978-0-399-17124-6
1. Intelligence officers—United States—Fiction. I. Butterworth, William E. (William Edmund).
II. Title.
PS3557.R489137A94 2014b 2014040663
813'.54—dc23

Printed in the United States of America
1 3 5 7 9 10 8 6 4 2

26 July 1777

"The necessity of procuring good intelligence is apparent and need not be further urged."

George Washington
General and Commander in Chief
The Continental Army

FOR THE LATE

William E. Colby
An OSS Jedburgh First Lieutenant
who became director of the Central Intelligence Agency.

Aaron Bank
An OSS Jedburgh First Lieutenant
who became a colonel and the father of Special Forces.

William R. Corson
A legendary Marine intelligence officer
whom the KGB hated more than any other U.S. intelligence officer—
and not only because he wrote the definitive work on them.

René J. Défourneaux
A U.S. Army OSS Second Lieutenant
attached to the British SOE
who jumped into Occupied France alone
and later became a legendary U.S. Army intelligence officer.

FOR THE LIVING

Billy Waugh
A legendary Special Forces Command Sergeant Major
who retired and then went on to hunt down
the infamous Carlos the Jackal.
Billy could have terminated Osama bin Laden in the early 1990s
but could not get permission to do so.
After fifty years in the business, Billy is still going after the bad guys.

Johnny Reitzel
An Army Special Operations officer
who could have terminated the head terrorist
of the seized cruise ship *Achille Lauro* but could not
get permission to do so.

Ralph Peters
An Army intelligence officer
who has written the best analysis of our war against terrorists
and of our enemy that I have ever seen.

AND FOR THE NEW BREED

Marc L
A senior intelligence officer, despite his youth,
who reminds me of Bill Colby more and more each day.

Frank L
A legendary Defense Intelligence Agency officer
who retired and now follows in Billy Waugh's footsteps.

AND
In Loving Memory Of
Colonel José Manuel Menéndez
Cavalry, Argentine Army, Retired
He spent his life fighting Communism and Juan Domingo Perón

OUR NATION OWES THESE PATRIOTS
A DEBT BEYOND REPAYMENT.

THE ASSASSINATION OPTION

PROLOGUE

Early in 1943, at a time when victory was by no means certain, Great Britain, the Union of Soviet Socialist Republics, and the United States of America—"the Allies"—signed what became known as "the Moscow Declaration." It stated that the leaders of Germany, Italy, and Japan—"the Axis Powers"—would be held responsible for atrocities committed during the war.

In December of that year, the Allied leaders—Prime Minister Winston Churchill of England, General Secretary Joseph V. Stalin of the Soviet Union, and President Franklin D. Roosevelt of the United States—met secretly in Tehran, Iran, under the code name Project Eureka. The meeting later came to be known as the Tehran Conference.

At a dinner in Tehran on December 29, 1943, while discussing the Moscow Declaration, Stalin proposed the summary execution of fifty thousand to one hundred thousand German staff officers immediately following the defeat of the Thousand-Year Reich. Roosevelt thought he was joking, and asked if he would be satisfied with "the summary execution of a lesser number, say, forty-nine thousand."

Churchill took the Communist leader at his word, and angrily announced he would have nothing to do with "the cold-blooded execution of soldiers who fought for their country," adding that he'd "rather be taken out in the courtyard and shot myself" than partake in any such action.

The war in Europe ended on May 8, 1945, with the unconditional surrender of Germany.

In London, on August 8, 1945, the four Allied powers—France, after its liberation, had by then become sort of a junior member—signed "the Agreement for the Prosecution and Punishment of the Major War Criminals of the European Axis Powers."

"The London Agreement" proclaimed that the senior Nazi leaders would be tried on behalf of the newly formed United Nations at Nuremberg, and that lesser officials would be tried at trials to be held in each of the four zones of occupation into which Germany was to be divided.

The Soviet Union wanted the trials to be held in Berlin, but the other three Allies insisted they be held in Nuremberg, in Bavaria, in the American Zone of Occupation. Their public argument was that not only was Nuremberg the ceremonial birthplace of Nazism, but also that the Palace of Justice compound, which included a large prison, had come through the war relatively untouched and was an ideal site for the trials.

What the Western Allies—aware of the Soviet rape of Berlin and that to get the Russians out of the American Sector of Berlin, U.S. General I.D. White had to quite seriously threaten to shoot on sight any armed Russian soldiers he found in the American Sector—were not saying publicly was that they had no intention of letting the Soviet Union dominate the trials.

They threw a face-saving bone to the Russians by agreeing that Berlin would be the "official home" of the tribunal.

The London Agreement provided that the International Military Tribunal (IMT) would, on behalf of the newly formed United Nations, try the accused war criminals. It would consist of eight judges, two named by each of the four Allied powers. One judge from each country would preside at the trials. The others would sit as alternates.

Interpreters would translate the proceedings into French, German, Russian, and English, and written evidence submitted by the prosecution would be translated into the native language of each defendant. The IMT would not be bound by Anglo-American rules of evidence, and it would accept hearsay and other forms of evidence normally considered unreliable in the United States and Great Britain.

The IMT was given authority to hear four counts of criminal complaints: conspiracy, crimes against peace, war crimes, and crimes against humanity.

It has been argued that the Russians obliged the Western Allies by agreeing to hold the actual trials in Nuremberg in a spirit of cooperation. It has also been argued that there was a tit-for-tat arrangement. If the Russians agreed to Nuremberg, the Americans and the English would not bring up the Katyn Massacre.

What is known—provable beyond doubt—is that in 1943 the Germans took a number of captured American officers from their POW camp to the Katyn Forest, about twelve miles west of Smolensk, Russia.

The American officer prisoners were a mixed bag of Medical Corps officers, Judge Advocate General's Corps officers, and officers of the combat arms. In the latter group was Lieutenant Colonel John K. Waters, an Armor officer who had been captured in Tunisia. He was married to the former Beatrice Patton. His father-in-law was General George S. Patton. Waters later became a four-star general.

At Katyn, there were several recently reopened mass graves. As the Americans watched, other mass graves were reopened. They contained the bodies of thousands of Polish officers who had surrendered in 1940 to the Red Army when the Russians invaded Poland from the East and Germany from the West.

The Germans told the Americans that the Polish officers had been taken from the Kozelsk prisoner-of-war camp to the forest in 1940—shortly after the surrender—by the Soviet NKVD. There, after their hands had been wired behind them, they were executed by pistol shots into the back of their heads.

The Germans permitted the American doctors to examine the corpses and to remove from their brains the bullets that had killed them. It was the opinion of the American doctors that the bodies had in fact been so murdered and had been decomposing since 1940.

The Americans were then returned to their POW camp. The bullets removed from the brains of the murdered Polish officers were distributed among them.

It is now known that there was some communication, in both directions, between the Allies and American prisoners of war in Germany. It is credible to assume that the prisoners who had been taken to Hammelburg managed to tell Eisenhower's headquarters in London what they had seen in the Katyn Forest, and possible, if by no means certain, that they managed to get the bullets to London, as well.

Very late in the war, in March 1945, General Patton gave a very unusual assignment to one of his very best tank officers, Lieutenant Colonel Creighton W. Abrams, who then commanded Combat Command B of the 4th Armored Division. Abrams had broken through the German lines to rescue the surrounded 101st Airborne Division at Bastogne, and was later to become chief of staff of the U.S. Army. The U.S. Army's main battle tank today is the Abrams.

The official story was that Patton told Abrams he feared the Germans would execute the American POWs being held in Oflag XIII-B, in Hammelburg, Germany, then fifty miles behind the German lines, when it appeared they would be liberated by the Red Army.

Abrams was ordered to mount an immediate mission to get to Hammelburg before the Russians did and to liberate the Americans. In the late evening of March 26, 1945, Task Force Baum—a company of medium tanks, a platoon of light tanks, and a company of armored infantry, under Captain Abraham Baum—set out to do so.

The mission was not successful. It was mauled by the Germans. When word of it got out, Patton was severely criticized for staging a dangerous raid to rescue his son-in-law. He denied knowing Colonel Waters was in Oflag XIII-B. When, shortly afterward, Oflag XIII-B was liberated by the Red Army, Waters was not there.

It later came out that Waters and 101st Airborne Division Second Lieutenant Lory L. McCullough (an interesting character, who learned that he had been awarded a battlefield commission only after he had been captured during Operation Marketgarden) had escaped from captivity while the Germans had been marching the prisoners on foot toward Hammelburg and had made their escape to North Africa through the Russian port of Odessa on the Black Sea.

When this came out, there was some knowledgeable speculation that Patton had known Waters was in Oflag XIII-B, and had been worried, because of Waters's knowledge of the Katyn Forest massacre, that if the Red Army reached Hammelburg before the Americans, Waters would have been killed by the Red Army to keep his mouth shut.

Why else, this speculation asked, would Waters have elected his incredibly dangerous escape with McCullough rather than just stay where they were and wait in safety to be liberated?

The Katyn Forest Massacre was not unknown in the West. The Polish government in exile had proof of it as early as 1942. When they requested an investigation by the International Red Cross, Russia broke diplomatic relations with the Poles. Churchill had not wanted to annoy his Russian ally, and Roosevelt believed it was Nazi propaganda. The Russians wouldn't do anything like that.

And then, at the very end of the war, Major General Reinhard Gehlen, who had been chief of Abwehr Ost, the German military intelligence agency dealing with the Soviet Union, added some further light on the subject.

Gehlen had made a deal with Allen W. Dulles, who had been the Office of Strategic Services station chief in Berne, Switzerland, to turn over all of his assets—including agents in place in the Kremlin—to the OSS in return for the OSS protection of his officers and men, and their families, from the Red Army.

Among the documents turned over were some that Gehlen's agents had stolen from the Kremlin itself. They included photographic copies of NKVD chief Lavrentiy Beria's proposal, dated March 5, 1940, to execute all captured Polish officers. Gehlen also provided photographic copies of Stalin's personal approval of the proposal, signed by him on behalf of the Soviet Politburo, and reports from functionaries of the NKVD reporting in detail their execution of their orders. At least 21,768, and as many as 22,002, Poles had been murdered. Approximately 8,000 were military officers, approximately 6,000 were police officers, and the rest were members of the intelligentsia, landowners, factory owners, lawyers, officials, and priests.

The Americans could not raise this in the face of the Soviet Union, however, as they would have had to say where they got their information, and when the Nuremberg trials began, the Americans were denying any knowledge of the whereabouts of former Major General Reinhard Gehlen.

I

[ONE]

Walter Reed Army Medical Center
Washington, D.C.
0905 22 December 1945

The MP at the gate did not attempt to stop the Packard Clipper when it approached the gate. He had seen enough cars from the White House pool to know one when he saw one, and this one was also displaying a blue plate with two silver stars, indicating that it was carrying a rear admiral (upper half).

The MP waved the car through, saluted crisply, and then went quickly into the guard shack—which was actually a neat little tile-roofed brick structure, not a shack—and got on the phone.

"White House car with an admiral," he announced.

This caused activity at the main entrance. A Medical Corps lieutenant colonel, who was the Medical Officer of the Day—MOD—and a Rubenesque major of the Army Nurse Corps, who was the NOD—Nurse Officer of the Day—rushed to the lobby to greet the VIP admiral from the White House.

No Packard Clipper appeared.

"Where the hell did he go?" the MOD inquired finally.

"If it's who I think it is," the NOD said, "he's done this before.

He went in the side door to 233. The auto accident major they flew in from South America."

The MOD and the NOD hurried to the stairwell and quickly climbed it in hopes of greeting the VIP admiral from the White House to offer him any assistance he might require.

They succeeded in doing so. They caught up with Rear Admiral Sidney W. Souers and his aide-de-camp, Lieutenant James L. Allred, USN, as the latter reached to push open the door to room 233.

"Good morning, Admiral," the MOD said. "I'm Colonel Thrush, the Medical Officer of the day. May I be of service?"

"Just calling on a friend, Colonel," the admiral replied. "But thank you, nonetheless."

He nodded to his aide to open the door.

The NOD beat him to it, and went into the room.

There was no one in the hospital bed, whose back had been cranked nearly vertical. A bed tray to one side held a coffee thermos, a cup, and an ashtray, in which rested a partially smoked thick, dark brown cigar. The room was redolent of cigar smoke.

"He must be in the toilet," the nurse announced, adding righteously, "He's not supposed to do that unassisted."

Lieutenant Allred went to the toilet door, knocked, and asked, "You okay, Major?"

"I was until you knocked at the door," a muffled voice replied.

"Thank you for your interest, Colonel, Miss," Admiral Souers said.

They understood they were being dismissed, said, "Yes, sir," in chorus, and left the room.

"Who is he?" the MOD asked.

"You mean the admiral, or the major?"

"Both."

"All I know about the admiral is that the word is that he's a pal of President Truman. And all I know about the major is that he was medically evac'd from someplace in South America, maybe Argentina, someplace like that, and brought here. Broken leg, broken arm, broken ribs. And no papers. No Army papers. He told one of the nurses he was in a car accident."

"I wonder why here?" the MOD asked. "There are very good hospitals in the Canal Zone, and that's a lot closer to Argentina than Washington."

The NOD shrugged.

"And that admiral showed up an hour after he did," she said. "And shortly after that, the major's family started coming. He has a large family. I think they're Puerto Ricans. They were all speaking Spanish."

"Interesting," the MOD said.

Major Maxwell Ashton III, Cavalry, detail Military Intelligence, a tall, swarthy-skinned, six-foot-three twenty-six-year-old, tried to rise from the water closet in his toilet by using a chromed support mounted to the wall. The support was on the left wall. Major Ashton's left arm was in a cast and the cast was in a sling. Using his right arm, he managed to rise about eighteen inches from the toilet seat before his hand slipped and he dropped back down.

He cursed. Loudly, colorfully, obscenely, and profanely, in Spanish, and for perhaps thirty seconds.

He then attempted to rise using the crutch he had rested against the toilet wall. On the third try, he made it. With great difficulty, he managed to get his pajama trousers up from the floor and over his right leg, which was encased in plaster of paris, and to his waist.

"Oh, you clever fucking devil, you!" he proclaimed, in English.

He unlocked the door, held it open with his forehead, and then managed to get the crutch into his armpit, which permitted him to escape the small room.

He was halfway to the bed when Lieutenant Allred attempted to come to his aid.

Ashton impatiently waved him off, made it to the bed, and, with difficulty, got in.

"You should have asked a nurse to help you," Allred said.

"I'm sure it's different in the Navy, but in the Cavalry, we consider it unbecoming an officer and a gentleman to ask women with whom we are not intimately acquainted to assist us in moving our bowels," Ashton said.

Admiral Souers laughed.

"I'm delighted to find you in a good mood, Max," he said. "How's it going?"

"Sir, do you really want to know?"

"I really do."

"I am torn between that proverbial rock and that hard place. On one hand, I really want to get the hell out of here. I am told that when I can successfully stagger to the end of the hall and back on my crutches, I will be considered 'ambulatory.' I can do that. But if I do it officially, that will mean I will pass into the hands of my Aunt Florence, who is camped out in the Hay-Adams extolling my many virtues to the parents of every unmarried

Cuban female in her child-bearing years—of the proper bloodline, of course—between New York and Miami."

"That doesn't sound so awful to me," Allred said.

"What you don't understand, Jim—although I've told you this before—is that unmarried Cuban females of the proper bloodline do not fool around before marriage. And I am still in my fooling-around years."

"Or might be, anyway, when you get out of that cast," Admiral Souers said.

"Thank you, sir, for pointing that out to me," Ashton said.

Souers chuckled, and then asked, "What do you want first, the good news or the bad?"

"Let's start with the bad, sir. Then I will have something to look forward to."

"Okay. There's a long list of the former. Where do I start? Okay. General Patton died yesterday in Germany."

"I'm sorry to hear that. He always said he wanted to go out with the last bullet fired in the last battle."

"And a car wreck isn't the last battle, is it?" Souers replied.

"Unless it was an opening shot in the first of a series of new battles," Ashton said.

"We looked into that," Souers said. "General Greene—the European Command CIC chief? . . ."

Ashton nodded his understanding.

". . . was all over the accident. And he told me that's what it was, an accident. A truck pulled in front of Patton's limousine. His driver braked hard, but ran into the truck anyway. Patton slid off the seat and it got his neck, or his spine. He was paralyzed. Greene told me when he saw Patton in the hospital, they had him stretched out with weights. Greene said it looked like something from the Spanish Inquisition."

"And what does General Gehlen have to say about it?" Ashton asked.

"I think if he had anything to say, Cronley would have passed it on. Why do you think it could be something other than an accident?"

Before Ashton could reply, Admiral Souers added, "Dumb question. Sorry."

Ashton answered it anyway.

"Well, sir, there are automobile accidents and then there are automobile accidents."

"Accidents happen, Max," Souers said.

"Sir, what happened to me was no accident," Ashton said.

"No, I don't think it was. And Frade agrees. But accidents do happen."

Ashton's face showed, Souers decided, that he thought he was being patronized.

"For example, sort of close to home, do you know who Lieutenant Colonel Schumann is? Or was?"

Ashton shook his head.

"He was Greene's inspector general. I met him when I was over there. Good man."

Ashton said nothing, waiting for the admiral to continue.

"More than a very good IG," Souers continued, "a good intelligence officer. He was so curious about Kloster Grünau that Cronley had to blow the engine out of his staff car with a machine gun to keep him out."

"That's a story no one chose to share with me," Ashton said drily.

"Well, we didn't issue a press release. The only reason I'm telling you is to make my point about accidents happening. The day Patton died, Colonel Schumann went to his quarters to lunch with his wife. There was apparently a faulty gas water heater. It apparently leaked gas. Schumann got home just in time for the gas to blow up. It demolished the building."

"Jesus!"

"Literally blowing both of them away, to leave their two kids, a boy and a girl, as orphans."

"Jesus Christ!" Ashton said.

"Quickly changing the subject to the good news," Souers said. "Let's have the box, Jim."

"Yes, sir," Lieutenant Allred said, and handed the admiral a small blue box.

Souers snapped it open and extended it to Ashton.

"Would you like me to pin these to your jammies, Colonel, or would you rather do that yourself?"

"These are for real?" Ashton asked.

"Yes, Lieutenant Colonel Ashton, those are for real."

"In lieu of a Purple Heart?" Ashton asked.

"Prefacing this by saying I think you well deserve the promotion, the reason you have it is because I told the adjutant general I desperately needed you, and that the only way you would even consider staying in the Army would be if your services had been rewarded with a promotion."

Ashton didn't reply.

"Operative words, Colonel, 'would even *consider* staying.'"

Again, Ashton didn't reply.

"If nothing else, you can now, for the rest of your life, legitimately refer to yourself as 'colonel' when telling tales of your valiant service in World War Two to Cuban señoritas whom you wish to despoil before marriage."

"Sometimes it was really rough," Ashton said. "Either the steak would be overcooked, or the wine improperly chilled. Once, I even fell off my polo pony."

"Modesty becomes you, but we both know what you did in Argentina."

"And once I was struck by a hit-and-run driver while getting out of a taxi."

"That, too."

"I really wish, Admiral, that you meant what you said to the adjutant general."

"Excuse me?"

"That you desperately need me."

"They say, and I believe, that no man is indispensable. But that said, I really wish you weren't—what?—'champing at the bit' to hang up your uniform. With you and Frade both getting out—and Cletus wouldn't stay on active duty if they made him a major general—finding someone to run Operation Ost down there is going to be one hell of a problem."

Ashton raised his hand over his head.

When Souers looked at him in curiosity, he said, nodding toward the toilet, "No, sir. I am not asking permission to go back in there."

"This is what they call an 'unforeseen happenstance,'" Admiral

Souers said after a moment. "You're really willing to stay on active duty?"

Ashton nodded.

"Yes, sir."

"I have to ask why, Max."

"When I thought about it, I realized I really don't want to spend the rest of my life making rum, or growing sugarcane," Ashton said. "And I really would like to get the bastards who did this to me."

He raised both the en-casted arm resting on his chest and his en-casted broken leg.

"I was hoping you would say because you see it as your duty, or that you realize how important Operation Ost is, something along those lines."

"Who was it who said 'patriotism is the last refuge of the scoundrel'?"

"Samuel Johnson said it. I'm not sure I agree with it. And I won't insult you, Max, by suggesting you are unaware of the importance of Operation Ost. But I have to point out Romans 12:19." When he saw the confusion on Ashton's face, the admiral went on: "'Vengeance is mine, saith the Lord.' Or words to that effect."

"The Lord can have his after I have mine," Ashton said. "When do you become our nation's spymaster?"

"That title belongs to General Donovan, and always will," Souers said. "If you're asking when the President will issue his Executive Order establishing the United States Directorate of Central Intelligence, January first."

"Let me ask the rude question, sir," Ashton said. "And how does General Donovan feel about that?"

"Well, the Directorate will be pretty much what he recommended. Starting, of course, with that it will be a separate intelligence agency answering only to the President."

"I meant to ask, sir, how he feels about not being named director?"

Souers considered his reply before giving it.

"Not to go outside this room, I suspect he's deeply disappointed and probably regrets taking on J. Edgar Hoover. My personal feeling is that the President would have given General Donovan the Directorate if it wasn't for Hoover."

"The President is afraid of Hoover?"

"The President is a very smart, arguably brilliant, politician who has learned that it's almost always better to avoid a bitter confrontation. I think he may have decided that his establishing the Directorate of Central Intelligence over Hoover's objections was all the bitter confrontation he could handle."

"How does Hoover feel about you?"

"He would have preferred—would *really* have preferred—to have one of his own appointed director. Once the President told him that there would be a Directorate of Central Intelligence despite his objections to it, Hoover seriously proposed Clyde Tolson, his deputy, for the job. But even J. Edgar doesn't get everything he wants."

"That wasn't my question, sir."

"He's hoping he will be able to control me."

"What's General Donovan going to do now?"

"You know he's a lawyer? A very good one?"

"Yes, sir."

"Well, the President, citing that, asked him to go to Nuremberg as Number Two to Supreme Court Justice Robert Jackson, who's going to be the chief American prosecutor."

"He threw him a bone, in other words?"

"Now that you're a lieutenant colonel, Colonel, you're going to have to learn to control your tendency to ask out loud questions that should not be asked out loud."

"Admiral, you have a meeting with the President at ten forty-five," Allred said.

Souers walked to the bed, extending his hand.

"I'll be in touch, Max," he said. "Get yourself declared ambulatory. The sooner I can get you back to Argentina, the better."

"I was thinking, sir, that I would go to Germany first, to have a look at the Pullach compound, and get with Colonel Mattingly and Lieutenant Cronley, before I go back to Buenos Aires."

"I think that's a very good idea, if you think you're up to all that travel," he said.

"I'm up to it, sir."

"I hadn't planned to get into this with you. That was before you agreed to stay on. But now . . ."

"Yes, sir?"

"Now that you're going to have to have a commander-subordinate relationship with Captain . . . *Captain* . . . Cronley . . ."

"Sorry, sir. I knew that the President had promoted Cronley for grabbing the uranium oxide in Argentina."

"And for his behavior—all right, his 'valor above and beyond the call of duty.'"

"Yes, sir."

"Prefacing this by saying I think he fully deserved the promotion, and the Distinguished Service Medal that went with it, and that I personally happen to like him very much, I have to tell you what happened after he returned to Germany."

"Yes, sir?"

"Admiral," Lieutenant Allred said, as he tapped his wristwatch, "the President . . ."

"The world won't end if I'm ten minutes late," Admiral Souers said. "And if it looks as if we'll be late, get on the radio to the White House and tell them we're stuck in traffic."

"Yes, sir."

"You know about those Negro troops who have been guarding Kloster Grünau? Under that enormous first sergeant they call 'Tiny'? First Sergeant Dunwiddie?"

"Cronley talked about him. He said he comes from an Army family that goes way back. That they were Indian fighters, that two of his grandfathers beat Teddy Roosevelt up San Juan Hill in Cuba during the Spanish American War."

"Did he mention that he almost graduated from Norwich? That his father was a Norwich classmate of Major General I.D. White, who commanded the Second Armored Division?"

"No, sir."

"Well, when Cronley returned to Germany, to Kloster Grünau, he learned that those black soldiers—the ones he calls 'Tiny's Troopers'—had grabbed a man as he attempted to pass through—going outward—the barbed wire around Kloster Grünau. He had documents on him identifying him as Major Konstantin Orlovsky of the Soviet Liaison Mission. They have authority to be in the American Zone.

"On his person were three rosters. One of them was a complete roster of all of General Gehlen's men then inside Kloster Grünau. The second was a complete roster of all of Gehlen's men whom we have transported to Argentina, and the third was a listing of where in East Germany, Poland, Hungary, et cetera, that Gehlen believed his men who had not managed to get out were.

"It was clear that Orlovsky was an NKGB agent. It was equally clear there was at least one of Gehlen's men—and very likely more than one—whom the NKGB had turned and who had provided Orlovsky with the rosters.

"When he was told of this man, Colonel Mattingly did what I would have done. He ordered Dunwiddie to turn the man over to Gehlen. Gehlen—or one or more of his officers—would interrogate Orlovsky to see if he'd give them the names of Gehlen's traitors.

"Do I have to tell you what would happen to them if the interrogation was successful?"

"They would 'go missing.'"

"As would Major Orlovsky. As cold-blooded as that sounds, it was the only solution that Mattingly could see, and he ordered it carried out. And, to repeat, I would have given the same order had I been in his shoes.

"Enter James D. Cronley Junior, who had by then been a captain for seventy-two hours. When Dunwiddie told him what had happened, he went to see the Russian. He disapproved of the psychological techniques Gehlen's interrogator was using. Admittedly, they were nasty. They had confined him naked in a windowless cell under the Kloster Grünau chapel, no lights, suffering time disorientation and forced to smell the contents of a never-emptied canvas bucket which he was forced to use as a toilet.

"Cronley announced he was taking over the interrogation, and ordered Tiny's Troopers to clean the cell, empty the canvas bucket, and to keep any of Gehlen's men from having any contact whatsoever with Orlovsky."

"What did Gehlen do about that? Mattingly?"

Souers did not answer the question.

"Cronley and Dunwiddie then began their own interrogation of Major Orlovsky. As Colonel Mattingly pointed out to me later, Orlovsky was the first Russian that either Dunwiddie or Cronley had ever seen."

"Sir, when did Colonel Mattingly learn about this? Did General Gehlen go to him?"

After a just perceptible hesitation, Souers answered the question.

"Colonel Mattingly didn't learn what Captain Cronley was up to until after Orlovsky was in Argentina."

"What?" Ashton asked, shocked.

"Cronley got on the SIGABA and convinced Colonel Frade that if he got Orlovsky to Argentina, he was convinced he would be a very valuable intelligence asset in the future."

"And Cletus agreed with this wild hair?"

"Colonel Frade sent Father Welner, at Cronley's request, to Germany to try to convince Orlovsky that Cronley was telling the truth when he said they would not only set him up in a new life in Argentina, but that General Gehlen would make every effort to get Orlovsky's family out of the Soviet Union and to Argentina."

"Gehlen went along with this?"

"The officer whom many of his peers believe is a better intelligence officer than his former boss, Admiral Canaris, ever was, was in agreement with our Captain Cronley from the moment Cronley told him what he was thinking."

"So this Russian is now in Argentina?"

"Where he will become your responsibility once you get there. At the moment, he's in the Argerich military hospital in Buenos Aires, under the protection of the Argentine Bureau of Internal Security, recovering from injuries he received shortly after he arrived in Argentina."

"Injuries?"

"The car in which he was riding was attacked shortly after it left the airport by parties unknown. They used machine guns and Panzerfausts—"

"What?"

"German rocket-propelled grenades."

"Then they were Germans?"

"The BIS—and Cletus Frade—believes they were Paraguayan criminals hired by the Russians. So does Colonel Sergei Likharev of the NKGB."

"Who?"

"When Major Orlovsky realized that the NKGB was trying to kill him, and probably would do something very unpleasant to his wife and kids if General Gehlen could not get them out of the Soviet Union, he fessed up that his name is really Likharev and that he is—or was—an NKGB colonel. And gave up the names of Gehlen's traitors."

"What happened to them?"

"You don't want to know, Colonel Ashton."

"So Cronley did the right thing."

"I don't think that Colonel Mattingly would agree that the ends justify the means."

"But you do?"

"On one hand, it is inexcusable that Cronley went around Mattingly. On the other hand, we now have Colonel Likharev singing like that proverbial canary. And on the same side of that scale, General Gehlen has gone out of his way to let me know in what high regard he holds Cronley and Dunwiddie. But let me finish this."

"Yes, sir."

"After Frade informed me that he believed Likharev had truly seen the benefits of turning, and that he believed he would be of enormous value to us in the future, I was willing to overlook Cronley's unorthodoxy. Then Cronley got on the SIGABA and sent me a long message stating that he considered it absolutely essential that when he is transferred to the DCI that he have another commissioned officer to back him up, and that he wanted First Sergeant Dunwiddie commissioned as a captain—he said no one pays any attention to lieutenants—to fill that role.

"My first reaction to the message, frankly, was 'Just who the hell does he think he is?' I decided that it probably would be unwise to leave him in command of the Pullach compound. I then telephoned General Gehlen, to ask how he would feel about Major Harold Wallace—do you know who I mean?"

Shaking his head, Ashton said, "No, sir."

"He was Mattingly's deputy in OSS Forward . . ."

"Now I do, sir."

"And is now commanding the Twenty-seventh CIC, which is

the cover for the Twenty-third CIC, to which Cronley and Dunwiddie are assigned. You are familiar with all this?"

"Yes, sir."

"I asked General Gehlen how he would feel if I arranged for Major Wallace to take over command of the Pullach compound. He replied by asking if he could speak freely. I told him he could. He said that in the best of all possible worlds, he would prefer that Colonel Mattingly and Major Wallace have as little to do with Pullach as possible. When I asked why, he said that he regarded the greatest threat to the Pullach compound operation, in other words, to Operation Ost, was not the Russians but the U.S. Army bureaucracy.

"In case you don't know, the Pentagon—the deputy chief of staff for intelligence—has assigned two officers, a lieutenant colonel named Parsons and a major named Ashley—to liaise with Operation Ost at Pullach."

"Frade told me that, but not the names."

"DCS-G2 thinks they should be running Operation Ost. Both Parsons and Ashley outrank Captain Cronley. See the problem?"

"Yes, sir."

"I thought it could be dealt with, since Mattingly, in the Farben Building, is a full colonel and could handle Parsons, and further that Wallace could better stand up to Parsons and Ashley than Cronley could."

Ashton nodded his understanding.

"General Gehlen disagreed. He told me something I didn't know, that First Sergeant Dunwiddie's godfather is General White, and that in private Dunwiddie refers to General White as 'Uncle Isaac.' And he reminded me of something I already knew:

The President of the United States looks fondly upon Captain Cronley."

"How did Gehlen know that?"

"I don't know, but I have already learned not to underestimate General Reinhard Gehlen. Gehlen put it to me that he felt Parsons was under orders to somehow take control of Pullach, that Mattingly, who is interested in being taken into the Regular Army, is not going to defy the general staff of the U.S. Army.

"Gehlen put it to me that DCS-G2 taking over Operation Ost would be a disaster—reaching as far up as the President—inevitably about to happen. And I knew he was right."

"Jesus!"

"And he said he felt that because both Dunwiddie and Cronley had friends in high places, they would be the best people to defend Operation Ost from being swallowed by DCS-G2. And I realized Gehlen was right about that, too.

"General White is about to return to Germany from Fort Riley to assume command of the Army of Occupation police force, the U.S. Constabulary. I flew out to Fort Riley on Tuesday and talked this situation over with him. He's on board.

"On January second, the day after the Directorate of Central Intelligence is activated, certain military officers—you, for example, and Captains Cronley and Dunwiddie—"

"*Captain* Dunwiddie, sir?" Ashton interrupted.

"Sometime this week, First Sergeant Dunwiddie will be discharged for the convenience of the government for the purpose of accepting a commission as Captain, Cavalry, detail to Military Intelligence.

"As I was saying, Cronley and Dunwiddie—and now you—

will be transferred to the Directorate. Colonel Mattingly and Major Wallace will remain assigned to Counterintelligence Corps duties. I told General Greene that Colonel Frade suggested that for the time being they would be of greater use in the CIC and that I agreed with him."

When it looked as if Ashton was going to reply, Admiral Souers said, "Were you listening, Colonel, when I told you you're going to have to learn to control your tendency to ask questions out loud that should not be asked out loud?"

"Yes, sir. But may I ask a question?"

Souers nodded.

"It looks to me as if the effect of all this is that in addition to all the problems Cronley's going to have with Operation Ost, he's going to have to deal with Colonel Parsons—the Pentagon G2—and Colonel Mattingly, and maybe this CIC general, Greene, all of whom are going to try to cut him off at the knees."

Souers did not reply either directly or immediately, but finally he said, "I hope what you have learned in our conversation will be useful both when you go to Germany and later in Buenos Aires."

"Yes, sir. It will be."

Souers met Ashton's eye for a long moment, then smiled and turned and started to walk out of the room.

[TWO]
Kloster Grünau
Schollbrunn, Bavaria
American Zone of Occupation, Germany
0330 22 December 1945

Senior Watch Chief Maksymilian Ostrowski, a tall, blond twenty-seven-year-old, who was chief supervisor of Detachment One, Company "A," 7002nd Provisional Security Organization, woke instantly when his wristwatch vibrated.

He had been sleeping, fully clothed in dyed-black U.S. Army "fatigues" and combat boots, atop Army olive-drab woolen blankets on his bed in his room in what had once been the priory of a medieval monastery and was now a . . . what?

Ostrowski wasn't sure exactly what Kloster Grünau should be called now. It was no longer a monastery and was now occupied by Americans. He had learned that the Americans were guarding—both at Kloster Grünau and in a village, Pullach, near Munich—nearly three hundred former Wehrmacht officers and enlisted men and their families. Both the monastery and the village were under the protection of a company of heavily armed American soldiers. All of them were Negroes, and they wore the shoulder insignia of the 2nd Armored Division.

Ostrowski was no stranger to military life, and he strongly suspected that it had to do with intelligence. Just what, he didn't know. What was important to him was his belief that if he did well what he was told to do, he wouldn't be rounded up and forced to return to what he was sure was at best imprisonment and most likely an unmarked mass grave in his native Poland.

He sometimes thought he had lived two previous lives and was on the cusp of a third. The first had been growing up in Poland as the son of a cavalry officer. He had graduated from the Szkola Rycerska military academy in 1939. He just had time to earn his pilot's wings in the Polish Air Force when Germany and Russia attacked Poland. That life had ended when his father died leading a heroically stupid cavalry charge against German tanks, and he and some other young pilots for whom there were no airplanes to fly had been flown to first France and then England.

Life Two had been World War II. By the time that ended, he was Kapitan Maksymilian Ostrowski, 404th Fighter Squadron, Free Polish Air Force. The watch that had woken him by vibrating on his wrist was a souvenir of that life. Fairly late in the war, he had been at a fighter base in France, waiting for the weather to clear so they could fly in support of the beleaguered 101st Airborne Division in Bastogne.

There had been a spectacular poker game with a mixed bag—Poles, Brits, and Americans—of fellow fighter pilots. He liked Americans, and not only because he could remind them that he wasn't the first Pole to come to the Americans' aid in a war. He'd tell them Casimir Pulaski was the first. He'd tell them Pulaski had been recruited by Benjamin Franklin in Paris, went to America, saved George Washington's life, and became a general in the Continental Army before dying of wounds suffered in battle.

This tale of Polish-American cooperation had not been of much consolation to one of the American pilots, who, convinced the cards he held were better than proved to be the case, had thrown a spectacular watch into the pot.

It was a gold-cased civilian—not Air Corps–issued—Hamilton chronograph. It had an easily settable alarm function that caused it to vibrate at the selected time.

Ostrowski's four jacks and a king had taken the pot.

On the flight line at daybreak the next morning, just before they took off, the American had come to him and asked, if he could come up with three hundred dollars, would Ostrowski sell him the watch?

Ostrowski was already in love with the chronograph, so he knew why the American pilot wanted it back. Reluctantly, he agreed to sell it. The pilot said he'd have the cash for him when they came back.

He didn't come back. The American had gone in—either shot down or pilot error—just outside Bastogne.

In Life Two, Ostrowski had worn an RAF uniform with the insignia of a captain and a "Poland" patch sewn to the shoulder. As what he thought of as Life Three began, he was wearing dyed-black U.S. Army "fatigues" with shoulder patches reading *Wachmann* sewed to each shoulder. There was no insignia of rank, as the U.S. Army had not so far come up with rank insignia for the Provisional Security Organization.

The Provisional Security Organization was new. It had been created by the European Command for several reasons, primary among them that EUCOM had a pressing need for manpower to guard its installations—especially supply depots—against theft by the German people, and the millions of displaced persons—"DPs"—who were on the edge of starvation.

There were not enough American soldiers available for such duties. Germans could not be used, as this would have meant putting weapons in the hands of the just defeated enemy. Neither, with one significant exception, could guards be recruited from the DPs.

That exception was former members of the Free Polish Army and Air Force. When they were hastily discharged after the war, so they could be returned to Poland, many—most—of them refused to go. The officers, especially, were familiar with what had happened to the Polish officer corps in the Katyn Forest. They had no intention of placing themselves at the mercy of the Red Army. So they joined the hordes of displaced persons.

When, at the demand of the Soviets, several hundred of them had been rounded up for forcible repatriation, some broke out of the transfer compounds and more than two hundred of them committed suicide. This enraged General Eisenhower, who decreed there would be no more forcible repatriations, and ordered that former Free Polish soldiers and airmen being held be released.

Then someone in the Farben Building realized that the thousands of former Free Polish military men who refused to be repatriated were the solution to the problem of providing guards for EUCOM's supply depots.

Over the bitter objections of the State Department, which Eisenhower ignored, the Provisional Security Organization was quickly formed. Although nothing was promised but U.S. Army rations and quarters, the dyed-black fatigues and U.S. Army "combat boots," and a small salary—paid in reichsmarks, which were all but worthless—there were so many applicants for the PSO that the recruiters could be choosy.

Training of the first batch of guards—in whose ranks was former Kapitan Maksymilian Ostrowski—was conducted by the 508th Parachute Infantry Regiment in a former Wehrmacht *kaserne* in Griesheim, near Frankfurt am Main.

It consisted primarily in instruction in the use of the U.S. Carbine, Cal. .30 and the Model 1911A1 Pistol, caliber .45 ACP with which the PSO would be armed. There were lectures concerning the limits of their authority, the wearing of the uniform, and that sort of thing. The instruction syllabus called for seventy-four hours of classes. The classes took two weeks. There were 238 students in Class One-45.

Officers and non-coms were obviously going to be required for the PSO, and ranks were established, and then filled from the ranks of the students in the first class. Ostrowski was appointed a "watch chief"—which roughly corresponded to second lieutenant—more, he thought, because he spoke English well, rather than because he had been a captain in the Free Polish Air Force.

Company "A," 7002nd Provisional Security Organization had then been loaded on U.S. Army six-by-six trucks and driven down the autobahn to Munich, and then along winding country roads to the village of Pullach.

There Ostrowski learned that the entire village had been commandeered by the U.S. Army for unspecified purposes. Army Engineers were installing a triple fence, topped by concertina barbed wire. The fence and the guard towers made the village look like a prison camp.

It was there that he had first seen the Negro troops assigned to guard whatever it was that needed guarding. They all seemed to be enormous. That they were really guarding something was evident. They constantly circled the village in jeeps that carried ready-to-fire .50 caliber machine guns, and there were similar weapons in the guard towers.

The initial mission of Company "A" had nothing to do with the security of the village—which the Americans called "the compound"—but rather the protection of the Engineers' supplies—of which there were mountains—and equipment.

Company "A" was provided with U.S. Army twelve-man squad tents, a mobile mess, and went to work.

Ostrowski was not happy with his new duties—he saw himself as sergeant of the guard, which was quite a comedown from being a captain flying Spitfires and Hurricanes—but he had food to eat, clean sheets, and he thought it highly unlikely he would be rounded up for forcible repatriation.

Then, a week after they had moved to Pullach—the day he saw a GI sign painter preparing a sign that read GENERAL-BÜROS SÜD-DEUTSCHE INDUSTRIELLE ENTWICKLUNGSORGANISATION and wondered what the South German Industrial Development Organization might be—it was announced that Company "A" had been given the additional duty of guarding a monastery in Schollbrunn, in the Bavarian Alps. Promoted to senior watch chief, Ostrowski was put in charge of a sixty-man detachment, which was then trucked to Kloster Grünau.

There, he reported to the American in charge, a Mr. Cronley, who appeared to be in his early twenties, and his staff. These were two enormous black men wearing 2nd Armored Division shoulder patches. One wore the sleeve insignia of a first sergeant and the other that of a technical sergeant. There was also a plump little man who was introduced as Mr. Hessinger.

Ostrowski had thought he had solved the mystery of what was

going on. Both Mr. Cronley and Mr. Hessinger were in civilian attire. That is, they were wearing U.S. Army uniforms—Cronley the standard olive-drab Ike jacket and trousers, and Hessinger the more elegant officer's green tunic and pink trousers—but carrying no insignia of rank or branch of service. Instead, sewn to their lapels were small embroidered triangles around the letters *US*.

They were military policemen, Ostrowski quickly decided. More specifically, they were CID, which stood for Criminal Investigation Division, and who were, so to speak, the plainclothes detectives of the Military Police Force. What was being constructed at Pullach was to be a military prison. It all fit. The three lines of fences, the guard towers, the floodlights, and as absolute proof, all those enormous Negro troops. They practically had "Prison Guard" tattooed on their foreheads.

"If you don't speak English," Mr. Cronley had begun the meeting, "I'm going to have a problem telling you what's going on here."

"I speak English, sir," Ostrowski said.

"And German, maybe?" the chubby little man asked in German.

He was, Ostrowski guessed, a German Jew who had somehow avoided the death camps and somehow become an American.

"Yes. And Russian. And of course, Polish."

"That problem out of the way, what do we call you?" Mr. Cronley asked.

"My name is Maksymilian Ostrowski, sir."

"That's an unworkable mouthful," Cronley said. "It says here you're a senior watch chief. What the hell is that?"

"I believe it is equivalent to U.S. Army first lieutenant, sir."

Cronley had raised his right hand as a priest giving a blessing does, and announced, "Since I can pronounce this, I christen thee Lieutenant Max. Go and sin no more."

"Jesus, Jim!" the enormous black first sergeant protested. But he was smiling.

"Any objections?" Cronley asked.

"No, sir."

"Any other officers in your organization?"

"Yes, sir. There is one who served as a tank lieutenant with the Free French."

"Okay. Then you and he will bunk and mess with us," Cronley said. "Sergeant Tedworth"—Cronley pointed to the technical sergeant—"who is Number Two to First Sergeant Dunwiddie"—Cronley pointed to the first sergeant—"who is my Number Two, will show you where your men will be quartered. I hope you brought somebody who can cook with you?"

"Yes, sir."

"You will answer to Sergeant Tedworth," Cronley went on. "You have any problems with that?"

Does he mean because I'm an officer?

"No, sir."

"Okay. Freddy, you go with Tedworth and Lieutenant Max and show them where they'll be. Then send Lieutenant Max back here. If you find someone who can translate for Tedworth . . . Abraham Lincoln speaks German, Max, but not Polish . . ."

"Abraham Lincoln"? Oh, he means Sergeant Tedworth.

". . . Hessinger speaks Russian and tells me that's close to Polish. If there are no translation problems, Freddy, you come back. If there are, stay and translate. But send Lieutenant Max back. I need to bring him up to speed on what's going on around here ten minutes ago."

Mr. Hessinger nodded.

Twenty minutes later, Hessinger and Ostrowski had come back into what Ostrowski was to learn was called the "officers' mess." Cronley and Dunwiddie were sitting at a bar drinking beer.

"No translation problems?" Cronley asked.

"Between the Poles who speak German and Tedworth's guys who do likewise, no problem," Hessinger reported.

"Do you drink beer, Max?" Cronley asked.

"Yes, sir."

"Then you better have one before I tell you how close you'll be to getting shot working here."

What did he say?

Cronley gestured to Hessinger, who went behind the bar, found bottles of Löwenbräu and mugs, and handed one of each to Ostrowski.

"Tell me, Max, how you came to speak the King's English?"

"I spent the war years in England."

"Doing what?"

"I was in the Free Polish Air Force."

"Doing what?"

"Flying. Mostly Spitfires and Hurricanes."

"And then they wanted you to go back to Poland and you didn't want to go, and became a DP. Is that about it?"

"Yes, sir."

"How do you feel about Germans, Max? Straight answer, please."

"I fought a war against them, Mr. Cronley."

"In other words, you don't like them very much?"

"Yes, sir."

"And the Russians? How do feel about them?"

"I like them even less than the Germans."

"You ever hear of the Katyn Forest?"

"That's one of the reasons I didn't think it was wise for me to go home."

"What we're running here is a classified—a highly classified—operation. I'm not supposed to tell someone like yourself anything at all about it. But I don't see how you can do your job at all, much less well, until I tell you something about it."

"Yes, sir."

"So I'm going to tell you some things about it. Prefacing what I'm going to tell you by saying we're authorized to protect the security of this operation by any means, including the taking of life. Do you understand what I'm saying? And if you do, should I continue, or would you prefer to be sent back to Pullach? There would be no shame, or whatever, if you don't want to stay. I personally guarantee that you won't be forcibly repatriated if you choose to go back to Pullach. Think it over carefully."

My God, he's serious! What the hell is going on here? What am I letting myself in for?

After a long moment, Ostrowski came to attention and said, "I am at your orders, sir."

"Anybody got anything to say before I start this?" Cronley asked.

No one did.

"What we're doing here is protecting a substantial number of former German officers and enlisted men from the Russians, and from those Germans and others sympathetic to the Soviet Union," Cronley said.

When there was no reply, he went on: "Eventually, just about all of them will be moved to the Pullach compound. That process is already under way. Any questions so far?"

"May I ask why you're protecting them from the Russians?"

"No. And don't ask again. And make sure your men understand that asking that sort of question is something they just are not allowed to do. If they do, that will ensure immediate and drastic punishment. You can consider that your first order. Get that done as soon as possible."

"Tedworth's probably already done that," Hessinger said.

"Even if Sergeant Tedworth has already gotten into the subject, I want the warning to come from Lieutenant Max."

"Yes, sir."

"I think I should tell you, Lieutenant," Dunwiddie said, "without getting into details, that there already have been a number of deaths . . ."

"Two yesterday," Hessinger chimed in.

Dunwiddie gave him a withering look and went on. ". . . directly related to security breaches, attempted and successful, of this operation," Dunwiddie finished.

"The Russians have a very good idea of what's going on in here," Cronley said. "We already have caught an NKGB colonel as he tried to sneak out of here with information given to him by German traitors. Your mission will be to augment the American soldiers—we call them 'Tiny's Troopers'—who have been guarding Kloster Grünau and are in the process of establishing security at the Pullach compound."

"Sir, may I ask a question?"

"Ask away, but don't be surprised if I reply you don't have the need to know."

"Sir, I understand. My question—questions, actually—are can we expect further attempts by the Reds to gain entrance to either place?"

"I think you can bet your ass they will," Cronley said.

"You said 'questions,' plural, Lieutenant?" Hessinger asked.

"Are there still the traitors inside you mentioned?"

Cronley answered carefully. "The NKGB colonel and the traitors he was dealing with are no longer a problem . . ."

My God, he means they have been "dealt with."

Which means killed.

". . . but we have to presume (a) there are more of them, and (b) that the NKGB will continue to attempt to contact them."

"I understand," Ostrowski said.

"I hope so," Cronley said.

Even as he spoke the word "understand" Ostrowski had thought that he not only understood what Cronley was telling him, but that his Third Life had really begun.

I've stumbled onto something important.

What I will be guarding here and at Pullach is not going to be what I expected—mountains of canned tomatoes and hundred-pound bags of rice in a Quartermaster Depot—but something of great importance to the U.S. Army and by inference, the United States itself.

And, whatever it is, it's just getting started.

And if I play my cards right, I can get my foot on the first step of that ladder of opportunity everybody's always talking about.

And the way to start playing my cards right is to become the best lieutenant of the guard not only in Detachment One, Company "A," 7002nd Provisional Security Organization, but in the entire goddamned Provisional Security Organization.

Each night, Senior Watch Chief Ostrowski set his Hamilton chronograph to vibrate at a different time between midnight and six in the morning. He selected the hour by throwing a die on his bedside table. The first roll last night had come up three. That meant three o'clock. The second roll had come up three again. That meant, since three-sixths of sixty minutes is thirty, that he should set the Hamilton to vibrate at 3:30.

Next came the question of whether to get undressed, and then dress when the watch vibrated, or to nap clothed on top of the blankets. He opted in favor of not getting undressed.

When he was wakened, he did not turn on the bedside lamp. He was absolutely sure that at least one, and probably three, of his guards were watching his window so they could alert the others that Maksymilian the Terrible was awake and about to inspect the guard posts.

Instead, he made his way into the bath he shared with First Sergeant Dunwiddie—they were now on a "Tiny and Max" basis—and dressed there. First he put on a dyed-black U.S. Army field jacket, around which he put on a web belt that supported a holstered Model 1911A1 pistol. Then, since it had been snowing earlier in the evening and the ground was white, he put on a white poncho.

Then, without turning on any lights, using a red-filtered U.S. Army flashlight, he made his way downstairs and out of the building.

The Poles were guarding the outer perimeter, and sharing the guarding of the area between it and the second line of fences with

Tiny's Troopers. The inner perimeter was guarded by the Americans only.

Twenty yards from the building, he saw the faint glow of another red-filtered flashlight, and quickly turned his own flashlight off. Fifty yards farther toward the inner fence, he saw that Technical Sergeant Tedworth, dressed as he was, was holding the other flashlight.

He wasn't surprised, as he knew Tedworth habitually checked the guards in the middle of the night. He also knew that Tedworth usually went to the outer perimeter to check the Poles first. It looked as if that's what he was up to now, so Ostrowski followed him.

If Tedworth found nothing wrong—one of the Poles, for example, hiding beside or inside something to get out of the icy winds—Ostrowski planned to do nothing. Tedworth would know the Poles were doing what they were supposed to do and that was enough.

If, however, Tedworth found a Pole seeking shelter from the cold—or worse, asleep—Ostrowski would then appear to take the proper disciplinary action himself. Tedworth would see not only that Ostrowski was on the job, but also that Maksymilian the Terrible could "eat ass" just about as well as Technical Sergeant Tedworth.

He had been following Tedworth for about ten minutes when the red glow of Tedworth's flashlight suddenly turned white. There was now a beam of white light pointed inward from the outer perimeter fence toward the second.

Ostrowski hurried to catch up.

He heard Tedworth bellow, "Halt! *Hände nach oben!*"

Ostrowski started running toward him, fumbling as he did to un-holster his pistol.

Another figure appeared, dressed in dark clothing, approaching Tedworth in a crouch. Before Ostrowski could shout a warning, the man was on Tedworth. Tedworth's flashlight went flying as the man pulled him back.

Ostrowski remembered, cursing, that he had not chambered a round in the .45, and stopped running just long enough to work the action.

He could now see three men, Tedworth, now flailing around on the ground, the man who had knocked him over . . .

He looped something around Tedworth's throat. Probably a wire garrote.

. . . and another man in dark clothing who had come from the second line of wire.

Ostrowski was now ten meters from them, and was sure they hadn't seen him. He dropped to a kneeling position and, holding the .45 with both hands, fired first at the man wrestling with Tedworth, hitting him, and then as the second man looked at him, let off a shot at his head, which missed, and then a second shot at his torso, which connected.

Then he ran the rest of the way to the three men on the ground.

The man who had been wrestling with Tedworth was now reaching for something in his clothing. Ostrowski shot him twice. The man he had shot in the torso looked up at him with surprise on his face. His eyes were open but they were no longer seeing anything.

Blood was spurting from Tedworth's neck, and as Ostrowski watched, Tedworth finally got his fingers under the wire that had been choking him and jerked it off his body.

Tedworth looked at Ostrowski.

"Jesus H. Christ!" he said, spewing blood from his mouth.

"You're bleeding. We've got to get a compress on your neck," Ostrowski said.

Tedworth reached for his neck again and again jerked something loose. It was a Cavalry yellow scarf.

"Use this," he said. "It probably kept me alive."

Then he added, disgust oozing from his voice, "If you hadn't showed up, these cocksuckers would have got me!"

"Just lie there," Ostrowski ordered. "Hold the scarf against your neck. I'll go for help."

That didn't prove to be necessary. As he stood up, he saw first the light from three flashlights heading toward him, and then the headlights of a jeep.

[ONE]
The South German Industrial Development Organization Compound
Pullach, Bavaria
The American Zone of Occupied Germany
1605 28 December 1945

A neat sign on the small snow-covered lawn of the small house identified it as the Military Government Liaison Office.

There were four rooms on the ground floor of the building and a large, single room on the second. The military government liaison officer—which was one of the cover titles Captain Cronley was going to use—lived there. A bathroom had been added to the second floor when the U.S. Army Corps of Engineers had hastily converted the village of Pullach into the South German Industrial Development Organization Compound.

The original bathroom on the ground floor and the kitchen had been upgraded to American standards at the same time. The main room on the ground floor held office furnishings. A smaller room provided a private office for the military government liaison officer. There was a small dining room next to the kitchen, and a smaller room with a sign reading LIBRARY held a substantial safe and a desk holding a SIGABA system. This was a communications device, the very existence of which was classified Secret. It provided secure, encrypted communication between Pullach, Kloster Grünau, Berlin, Washington, D.C., and Mendoza and Buenos Aires, Argentina.

There were five men in the downstairs office: Major Harold Wallace, a trim thirty-two-year-old wearing "pinks and greens"; James D. Cronley Jr.; First Sergeant Chauncey L. Dunwiddie, who like Cronley was wearing an olive-drab Ike jacket and trousers; Sergeant Friedrich Hessinger, in pinks and greens whose lapels bore small embroidered triangles with the letters *US* in their centers; and finally, a civilian, a slight, pale-faced forty-three-year-old with a prominent thin nose, piercing eyes, and a receding hairline. His name was Reinhard Gehlen, and he was wearing an ill-fitting, on-the-edge-of ragged suit. As a generalmajor of the Oberkommando of the Wehrmacht, Gehlen had been chief of

Abwehr Ost, the German intelligence agency dealing with the "Ost," which meant the East, and in turn the Union of Soviet Socialist Republics.

Gehlen and Cronley were sitting in upholstered chairs, drinking coffee. Major Wallace and First Sergeant Dunwiddie were seated at one of the desks as Hessinger hovered over them, like a schoolteacher tutoring backward students, as they signed sheafs of forms.

Finally, Hessinger proclaimed, "That's it. You are now a civilian and can no longer say cruel and unkind things to me."

He spoke with a thick, somewhat comical German accent. A German Jew, he had escaped Nazi Germany and went to the United States in 1938. Shortly after his graduation, summa cum laude, from Harvard College, he had been drafted. Physically unable to qualify for an officer's commission, he had been assigned to the Counterintelligence Corps and sent to Germany, where it was believed he would be very useful in running down Nazis and bringing them to trial.

He was now doing something quite different.

"Aw, come on, Fat Freddy, my little dumpling," Dunwiddie said, skillfully mocking Hessinger's thick accent, "when have I ever said anything cruel or unkind to you?"

Cronley laughed out loud. Major Wallace and General Gehlen tried, and failed, not to smile.

"Whenever have you not?" Hessinger said. "Now can I trust you to deliver these documents to General Greene's sergeant? Or am I going to have to send them by courier?"

"Freddy," Cronley asked, "why couldn't we have done what you just did tomorrow in the Farben Building? For that matter, why does this civilian have to go to Frankfurt to have Greene pin on his bars?"

"Because you can't be commissioned the day you get discharged as an enlisted man. That's what the regulations say. General Greene's sergeant was very specific about that, and when I checked, he was right. And he said General Greene thought it would be a nice thing for him to do."

And it will also serve to remind everybody that he's a general, and I'm a brand-new captain.

"Maybe Colonel Mattingly will be there," Cronley said. "Maybe we can ask him to pin on your bars. I'd love to see that."

"Let that go, Jim," Dunwiddie said. "If it doesn't bother me, why are you bothered?"

"Because I am a champion of the underdog, and in particular of the retarded underdog."

"You guys better get down to the *bahnhof* if you're going to catch the Blue Danube," Major Wallace said.

The Blue Danube was the military train that ran daily in each direction between Vienna and Berlin.

"We're not taking the Blue Danube," Cronley said.

"Why not?"

"Two reasons. One, I can't afford to take two days off just so this fat civilian can get his bars pinned on by General Greene."

"And two?"

"General Gehlen cannot ride the Blue Danube. Americans only."

"You're taking General Gehlen?"

"We're going to drive to Kloster Grünau, where I have some things to do. In the morning, we're going to fly to Eschborn. There, if I can trust Freddy, we will be met by a vehicle assigned to the 711th Quartermaster Mess Kit Repair Company, which will transport us to the Farben Building. That is set in concrete, right, Freddy?"

"The ambulance will be at Eschborn," Hessinger confirmed.

"You're asking for trouble with those mess kit repair bumper markings on those ambulances, Jim," Major Wallace said.

"The bumpers read MKRC. It's not spelled out."

"And if some MP gets first curious and then nasty?"

"Then I will dazzle him with my CIC credentials," Cronley said. "Which is another reason I'm going to Frankfurt. I want to ask General Greene about not only keeping the credentials after January second but getting more, so I can give them to half a dozen of Tiny's guys."

"Does Colonel Mattingly know you're bringing the general with you?"

"No, he doesn't," Cronley said simply. And then went on, "After Tiny becomes an officer, we will all get back in the ambulance, go back to Eschborn, get back in the Storch, and come back here. God willing, and if the creek don't rise, we should be back before it gets dark."

When Cronley, Gehlen, and Dunwiddie were in the car—an Opel Kapitän, now painted olive drab and bearing Army markings—Dunwiddie said, "You didn't tell Major Wallace about what happened at Kloster Grünau."

"You noticed, huh?"

"You going to tell me why not?"

"First of all, nothing happened at Kloster Grünau. Write that down."

"You mean two guys we strongly suspect were NKGB agents penetrated Kloster Grünau, tried to kill Tedworth, were killed by Ostrowski, and then buried in unmarked graves, that 'nothing'?"

"If I had told Wallace about that incident that never happened, he would have felt duty bound to tell Mattingly. Mattingly, to cover his ass, would have brought this to the attention of at least Greene, and maybe the EUCOM G2. A platoon of EUCOM brass, all with Top Secret clearances, all of whom are curious as hell about Kloster Grünau, would descend on our monastery to investigate the incident. It would be both a waste of time and would compromise Operation Ost. As Captain Cronley of the Twenty-third CIC, I can't tell them to butt out. So I didn't tell Wallace. Okay?"

"Okay. Incident closed."

"Not quite. I haven't figured out what to do with Ostrowski."

"Meaning?"

"That I haven't figured out what to do about . . . or with him."

"For example?"

"You do hang on like a starving dog does to a bone, don't you, Mr. Dunwiddie?"

"What are you thinking?"

"Among other things, he could fly one of our Storchs. He used to fly Spitfires."

"That would mean we would have an ex-Luftwaffe pilot and a Polish DP flying airplanes we're not supposed to have in the first place. And among what other things?"

"The OSS used to have civilian employees. Maybe the Directorate of Central Intelligence can."

"Interesting thought," General Gehlen said. "Ostrowski is an interesting man."

"With all respect, sir," Dunwiddie said, "whenever you and Captain Cronley agree on something, I worry."

[TWO]
Office of the Chief, Counterintelligence Corps
Headquarters, European Command
The I.G. Farben Building
Frankfurt am Main
American Zone of Occupation, Germany
1145 29 December 1945

Major Thomas J. Derwin, who was thirty-four, five feet ten, weighed 165 pounds, and to whose green tunic lapels were pinned the crossed rifles of Infantry and whose shoulder bore the embroidered insignia of Army Ground Forces, pushed open the door under the sign identifying the suite of offices of the chief, Counterintelligence Corps, European Command.

Derwin was carrying two canvas suitcases, called Valv-Paks. He set them down just inside the door and looked around the office. There were four people in it. One of them, sitting behind a desk, was a Women's Army Corps—WAC—chief warrant officer, an attractive woman in her late twenties. She was wearing the female version of pinks and greens—a green tunic over a pink skirt.

The three men were wearing OD Ike jackets and trousers. One of them was a stocky, nearly bald master sergeant. He was sitting behind a desk next to the WAC's desk. Sitting slumped in chairs before the master sergeant's desk were a captain—a good-looking young guy—and an enormous black man whose uniform was bare of any insignia of rank.

As they rose to their feet, Derwin realized he knew the captain.

Cronley, he thought. *James D. Cronley Jr. I had him in a Techniques of Surveillance class at Holabird. They were so short of officers in Germany that they pulled him out of school and sent him over here before he finished. Then I saw him again at the officers' club at Holabird a couple of months ago. He said he was in the States as an escort officer for some classified material.*

And then, immediately, Derwin knew he was wrong.

What the hell. I've just spent twenty-six hours flying over here. Brain-wise, I'm not functioning on all six cylinders. Which is not going to help me when I meet my new boss. First impressions do matter. That captain is not Cronley. Cronley's a second lieutenant. Amazing physical resemblance.

"May I help you, sir?" the master sergeant asked.

"I'm Major Derwin, Sergeant. Reporting for duty."

"Yes, sir, we've been expecting you," the WAC said. "I'll let the general know you're here."

She went to an interior door and pushed it open.

"General, Major Derwin is here."

"Captain," Derwin asked, "has anyone ever told you that you bear a striking resemblance to a second lieutenant named Cronley?"

"Yes, sir," the captain said, smiling. "I've heard that."

A stocky, forty-three-year-old officer with a crew cut appeared in the inner office door. His olive-drab uniform had the single star of a brigadier general on its epaulets.

That has to be my new boss, Brigadier General H. Paul Greene, chief, Counterintelligence, European Command.

And he looks like the tough sonofabitch everybody says he is.

General Greene looked at the WAC.

"Why didn't you tell me these two were here?"

The captain answered for her.

"We're waiting for General Gehlen, sir. He said he'd like to be present, and I thought it was a nice gesture on his part, so I brought him along."

Did he say "General Gehlen"? Not, certainly, Generalmajor Reinhard Gehlen?

"And where is General Gehlen?"

"As we tried to sneak in the back door, General Smith's convoy rolled up," Captain Cronley replied. "He asked the general if he had a few minutes for him, and of course General Gehlen did."

General Smith? General Walter Bedell Smith, chief of staff to General of the Army Dwight D. Eisenhower, commander in chief, European Command?

"And that surprised you?" General Greene said, chuckling.

"No, sir, it did not."

"You're Derwin?"

"Yes, sir, I'm Major Derwin."

The general's face showed he was thinking.

"Okay, everybody come in," he said finally. "They call that 'killing two birds with one stone.'"

He turned and they followed him into the office.

There was an elegantly turned out, handsome colonel of Armor slouched on a couch before a coffee table. He wore a green Ike jacket over pink trousers. His trousers were pulled up high enough to reveal highly polished Tanker boots.

The general went behind his desk.

Derwin marched up to it, came to attention, and saluted.

"Sir, Major Thomas G. Derwin reporting for duty."

The general returned the salute, said, "You may stand at ease," then extended his hand. "Welcome to EUCOM CIC, Major. How was the flight?"

The general gestured for the captain to sit, and he did so, in an armchair at one end of the coffee table.

"Long and noisy, sir."

"I am having symptoms of caffeine deficiency," the general said, raising his voice.

"Antidote on the way, General," a female voice called.

A moment later, the WAC chief warrant officer pushed a wheeled tray holding a silver coffee service into the room.

"We can pour our own coffee, Alice—or get Cronley to pour it . . ."

Did he say Cronley?

". . . and then no calls except from the Command Group. When General Gehlen appears, show him in."

"Yes, sir," the WAC officer said.

"Cronley, what's Gehlen doing here?" the Armor colonel asked, somewhat unpleasantly.

"He said that he'd like to be present, so I brought him along."

"Was that necessary?" the colonel asked.

"I thought it was appropriate," Cronley replied.

The colonel doesn't like Captain Cronley. And Cronley—twice—didn't append "sir" when replying to the colonel's questions.

But he—and Greene—let him get away with it.

"Bob, this is Major Derwin. Major, this is Colonel Robert Mattingly, my deputy," the general said.

"Welcome to EUCOM, Major," Mattingly said, and offered his hand.

"Coffee, Cronley, coffee," General Greene said.

"Yes, sir," Cronley said. He stood up and started pouring coffee for everybody.

When he got to Derwin, Derwin asked, "Have we met, Captain?"

"Yes, sir," Cronley said.

"At Holabird?"

"Yes, sir."

The sonofabitch is smiling. What's so funny?

The master sergeant appeared at the door.

"Sir," he announced, "Generals Smith and Gehlen."

General Smith, a tall, trim, erect officer who was in ODs, and General Gehlen walked into the office. Everyone rose and stood to attention.

I'll be damned, Derwin thought. *That is him, Generalmajor Reinhard Gehlen, former chief of Abwehr Ost, the intelligence agency of the German high command, dealing with the Ost . . . which meant the Russians.*

What the hell is he doing here?

With General Walter Bedell Smith, Ike's Number Two?

What's going on here?

"Rest, gentlemen, please," Smith said. "General Gehlen just told me what he was doing in Frankfurt, and I invited myself to the ceremony. I hope that's all right."

"Yes, sir, of course," General Greene said, not quite succeeding in concealing his surprise.

General Smith turned to Captain Cronley.

"Cronley, right?"

"Yes, sir."

"I had no idea who you were, Captain, just now at the rear entrance. Until General Eisenhower corrected me a few minutes ago, I thought the Captain Cronley who is to be chief, DCI-Europe, was going to be a barnacle-encrusted naval officer formerly on Admiral Souers's staff."

General Greene and Colonel Mattingly dutifully chuckled at General Smith's wit.

Major Derwin wondered, *What the hell is DCI-Europe? And who the hell is Admiral Souers?*

"No, sir. I'm just a simple, and junior, cavalryman."

"Well, you may be junior, Captain, but you're not simple. General Eisenhower also told me the circumstances of your recent promotion. I'm pleased to make your acquaintance."

He offered Cronley his hand.

"Yes, sir," Cronley said.

General Smith turned to the enormous black man.

"Now to the second case of mistaken identity," he said, and then asked, "Son, are you still a first sergeant?"

"Sir, at the moment I'm sort of in limbo. I was discharged yesterday."

He spoke softly in a very deep voice.

"Then I will call you what I used to call your father," General Smith said, "when, in the age of the dinosaurs, I was his company commander and your dad was one of my second lieutenants: Tiny."

"That's fine with me, sir."

"Tiny, I had no idea until just now, when General Gehlen told me, that you were even in the Army, much less what you've done and what you're about to do. Just as soon as things slow down a little, you're going to have to come to dinner. My wife remembers you as a tiny—well, maybe not tiny—infant."

"That's very kind of you, sir."

"Homer, where the hell is the photographer?"

A full colonel, wearing the insignia of an aide-de-camp to a four-star general, stepped into the office.

"Anytime you're ready for him, General," he said.

The general waved the photographer, a plump corporal carrying a Speed Graphic press camera, into the room.

"What's the protocol for this, Homer?" General Smith asked.

"First, the insignia is pinned to his epaulets, sir . . ."

"General Greene can do the left and I'll do the right," General Smith said.

"And then he takes the oath with his hand on a Bible."

"So then we need a Bible and a copy of the oath," General Smith said.

"I know the oath, sir," Dunwiddie said.

"And here's the Bible," the WAC officer said, "and the bars."

"And your role in this, Corporal," General Smith said, "is to take pictures. You ready?"

"Yes, sir."

"Which we will send to your parents, Tiny."

"Thank you, sir."

"And—I'm glad I thought of this—to General Isaac Davis White, your father's classmate at Norwich."

"That's a marvelous idea, General," Cronley said.

"Excuse me?"

"I understand, sir, that General White thought Tiny should have been commissioned a long time ago."

As he spoke, Cronley looked at Colonel Mattingly. Mattingly glared icily at him. Major Derwin picked up on it.

What the hell is that all about?

Flashbulbs exploded as Smith and Greene pinned the twin silver bars of a captain—known as "railroad tracks"—to Dunwiddie's epaulets.

"Who holds the Bible?" General Smith inquired. "What about that, Homer?"

"That's not prescribed, sir. Sometimes a wife, or a mother, or even somebody else."

"Sir," Dunwiddie asked, "what about Captain Cronley?"

"That'd work."

CWO Alice McGrory handed the Bible to Captain Cronley. He stood between Generals Smith and Greene and held the Bible up to him.

"Anytime you're ready, Tiny," General Smith said.

Dunwiddie laid his left hand on the Bible and raised his right.

"I, Chauncey Luther Dunwiddie," he boomed in a basso profundo voice, "having been appointed captain . . ."

He paused just perceptibly, and then continued slowly, pronouncing each syllable, ". . . in the United States Army, do solemnly swear that I will support and defend the Constitution of the United States against all enemies, foreign and domestic; that I will bear true faith and allegiance to the same; that I take this obligation freely, without any mental reservation or purpose of evasion; and that I will well and faithfully discharge the office upon which I am about to enter." He paused a final time, and then proclaimed, "So help me God!"

There was a moment's silence.

"I must have heard people take that oath a thousand times," General Smith said. "But never quite like that. Very impressive, Tiny. Moving." He paused. "Permit me to be first, Captain Dunwiddie, to welcome you into the officer corps of the United States Army."

He extended his hand, and Dunwiddie took it, said, "Thank you, sir." Then he asked, "Permission to speak, sir?"

Smith nodded and said, "Granted."

"Sir, as the general will understand, this moment is of great personal importance to the captain. The captain would very much like to have a memento of General Gehlen being here."

Smith's face tensed, and it was a long moment before he replied.

"Frankly, Captain, my initial reaction was to deny that request. But on reflection I realized that a photograph of us with General Gehlen among us ranks pretty low on the list of highly classified material with which you are already entrusted.

"General Gehlen, if you would, please stand here with us," General Smith went on. Then he turned to the photographer. "Corporal, the photograph you are about to take, the negatives and prints thereof, will be classified Top Secret–Presidential. You will personally develop the negative. You will then make four eight-by-ten-inch prints from the negative. You will then burn the negative. You will see that I get two of those prints, one of which I will send to Admiral Souers, and the other to General White. You will also give two prints to General Greene, who will get them to Captain Dunwiddie. You understand all that, son, or should I go over it again?"

Who the hell, Major Derwin again wondered, *is Admiral Souers?*

"I understand, sir."

"And I don't want you telling the boys in the photo lab anything about this. Clear?"

"Yes, sir."

"All right, gentlemen," General Smith said, "stand tall and say, 'Cheese.'"

Ninety seconds later, General Smith and his entourage were gone.

"Let me add my 'welcome to the officer corps of the United States Army' to General Smith's, Captain Dunwiddie," General Greene said.

"Thank you, sir."

"And mine," Colonel Mattingly said, without much enthusiasm.

"Thank you, sir," Dunwiddie repeated.

"What I'm going to do now is bring Major Derwin up to speed on what's going on around here. You're welcome to stay for that, of course."

"I think we can pass on that, sir," Captain Cronley said.

"It's always a pleasure to see you, General," Greene said.

"Thank you," Gehlen said.

Cronley stood to attention.

"Permission to withdraw, sir?"

"Post," Greene said.

Cronley saluted, did an about-face movement, and started for the door. He waved General Gehlen and Captain Dunwiddie ahead of him and then followed them out of the office.

Colonel Mattingly stood up.

"If you don't need me, sir?"

"I think it would be best if you stuck around for this, Bob," Greene said.

"Yes, sir. Of course," Colonel Mattingly said, and sat down.

"I suppose the best place to start, Major, is to tell you that what just transpired in here is classified. Twice. Maybe three times. First as Top Secret–Presidential. And as Top Secret–Lindbergh. And of course as simple Top Secret. You got that?"

"Yes, sir."

"All of that also applies to what I'm going to tell you now. And the best place to start that is at the beginning.

"On December twenty-first, Lieutenant Colonel Anthony Schumann, who was the inspector general of European Command CIC, and also of the Army Security Agency, Europe—which reports to the ASA in Washington through me, I think I should tell you—went home for lunch. Moments after he arrived, as well as we can put things together, there was an explosion. Apparently, the gas water heater had leaked, filled the house with gas, and something set it off. Maybe Mrs. Schumann lit the stove. We just don't know. There was a considerable explosion, which totally destroyed his quarters and severely damaged the houses on either side and across the street."

"My God!" Derwin said.

"And killed Colonel and Mrs. Schumann. Phrased as delicately as possible, there will have to be a closed-casket funeral. Tony Schumann was a fine officer and a close friend. A true tragedy.

"Obviously a replacement was necessary. There were several reasons why I had to go outside EUCOM CIC for a replacement. One is that, as I'm sure you know, we are very short of officers. We are even shorter of officers with the proper security clearances. A Top Secret clearance, dealing with what we're dealing with here, is as common as a Confidential clearance elsewhere.

"So I appointed Major James B. McClung, the ASA Europe Chief . . . you know who I mean?"

"Is that 'Iron Lung' McClung, sir?"

Greene nodded and went on.

". . . to temporarily add the duties of IG to all the other things on his plate. He was—is—the only officer available to me with the Top Secret–Lindbergh and Top Secret–Presidential clearances. Then I called Admiral Souers—"

"Excuse me, sir. Who?"

"Rear Admiral Sidney W. Souers," Greene answered, paused, and then said, "Well, let's deal with that. Have you heard the rumors that there will be a successor organization to the Office of Strategic Services?"

"Yes, sir."

"Well, let me give you the facts. Shortly after the President put the OSS out of business, he reconsidered the wisdom of that decision. There were certain operations of the OSS that had to be kept running, for one thing, and for another, Admiral Souers told me, he came to recognize the nation needed an intelligence organization, with covert and clandestine capabilities, that could not be tied down by putting it under either the Pentagon or the FBI. It had to report directly to him. More precisely, to the President.

"On January first, the President will sign an executive order establishing the Directorate of Central Intelligence, and name Admiral Souers as its director. Admiral Souers has been assigned to the Office of Naval Intelligence. But, he's been more than that. When the President realized that certain clandestine operations started by the OSS and which could not be turned off like a lightbulb needed someone to run them until he decided what to do about them, he turned to Admiral Soucrs. It is germane to note that the President and the admiral are close personal friends.

"Further, when the President realized there had to be a successor organization to the OSS, and that there were, for him, insurmountable problems in naming General Donovan to be its director, and that he did not want the Pentagon to have its man in that position, or someone who owed his allegiance to FBI Director J. Edgar Hoover, he again turned to Admiral Souers.

"Colonel Mattingly, would you like to add to, or comment upon, what I just told Major Derwin?"

"No, sir. I think you covered everything."

"Feel free to interrupt me at any time, Bob."

"Thank you, sir."

"As I was saying, when Colonel Schumann . . . was taken from us, I needed someone who could be given Presidential and Lindbergh clearances, and I needed him right away, so I called Admiral Souers and explained the problem. He said he would take the matter up personally with the G2 of the Army. He called back the next day, told me the G2 had proposed three officers, and given him access to their dossiers, and he felt you best met our requirements. He proposed sending you over here immediately to see if Colonel Mattingly and I agreed.

"Which brings us to Colonel Mattingly. Mattingly was OSS. In the last months of the war, he was chief, OSS Forward. When the OSS was put out of business, he was assigned to me, to EUCOM CIC, as my deputy."

"And now the colonel will be in this reconstituted OSS, the Directorate of Central Intelligence?"

"No. And please permit me to do the talking, Major," Greene said. "But since we have started down that road: At Admiral Souers's request—when he speaks, he speaks with the authority of the President—Headquarters, War Department, has tasked EUCOM CIC with providing the Directorate of Central Intelligence-Europe with whatever support, logistical and other, the chief, DCI-Europe, feels it needs. With me so far, Major?"

"I think so, sir. May I ask a question, sir?"

"Please do."

"Who will be the chief, DCI-Europe?"

"Captain James D. Cronley Junior. You just met him."

Major Derwin's face showed his surprise, or shock.

"There are reasons for this—"

"A couple of months ago he was a second lieutenant at Holabird!" Derwin blurted. "I had him in Techniques of Surveillance."

"I strongly suspect that as soon as Admiral Souers can find a more senior officer, say a colonel, or perhaps even a senior civilian, to appoint as chief, DCI-Europe, he will do so. But for the moment, it will be Captain Cronley."

"General, may I suggest we get into Operation Ost?" Mattingly said.

"This is the time, isn't it?" Greene said, and began to tell Major Derwin about Operation Ost.

Five minutes or so later, General Greene concluded the telling by saying, "I'm sure that you can understand, Major, since compromise of Operation Ost would not only be detrimental to the interests of the United States but would embarrass the highest officials of our government, why it behooves all of us to exert our maximum efforts to make sure it is not compromised."

"Yes, sir, I certainly can," Major Derwin said.

"And why any officer who does anything, even inadvertently, that causes any such compromise might as well put his head between his knees and kiss his ass goodbye? Because, even if his court-martial doesn't sentence him to spend twenty years polishing the linoleum in the solitary confinement wing of the Leavenworth Disciplinary Barracks, his military career is over."

"I understand, sir," Major Derwin said.

"I really hope you do," General Greene said. "We will now get into your duties with regard to the Pullach compound and Operation Ost. They can be summed up succinctly. They are invisible to you, unless it comes to your attention that someone is showing an unusual interest in them. If that happens, you will bring this immediately to the attention of Colonel Mattingly or myself. Or, of course, and preferably, to Captain Cronley or Captain Dunwiddie. You understand that?"

"Yes, sir."

"Any questions, Major?"

"Just one, sir."

"It is?"

"May I ask about Captain Cronley, sir?"

"What about Captain Cronley?"

"Sir, as I mentioned, two months ago, less, I saw him at Holabird as a second lieutenant—"

"If you are asking how did he become a captain so quickly, Major, I can tell you it was a reward for something he did."

"May I ask what, sir?"

"No," General Greene said. "But I can tell you—although his promotion order is classified Secret—that the promotion authority was 'Verbal Order of the President.'"

"Yes, sir."

"Unless you have something for Major Derwin, Colonel Mattingly?"

"No, sir."

"Then what I am going to do now, Major Derwin, is have the sergeant major put you in a car and send you over to see Major McClung. He will get you settled in quarters and then show you where you should begin your duties as inspector general."

"Yes, sir."

"That will be all, Major. You are dismissed."

[THREE]
The I.G. Farben Building
Frankfurt am Main
American Zone of Occupation, Germany
1225 29 December 1945

It took Captains Cronley and Dunwiddie and General Gehlen five minutes to get from General Greene's office to the "back door" of the huge building, which until the completion of the Pentagon in January 1943 had been the largest office building in the world.

The office of the chief, Counterintelligence Corps, European Command, was in the front of the extreme left wing (of six wings) in the curved five-story structure. The "back door" was in Sub-Level One between Wing Three and Wing Four.

First they had to walk down a long corridor to the connecting passageway between the wings.

There, Cronley and Dunwiddie had to "sign out" at a desk manned by two natty sergeants of the 508th Parachute Infantry Regiment, which was charged with both the internal and the external security of the building. The paratroopers wore white pistol belts, holsters, and spare magazine holders, and the white lacings in their glistening boots once had been parachute shroud lines.

The senior of the paratroop sergeants remembered that when the shabby Kraut civilian had passed in through their portal with

General Walter Bedell Smith's entourage, he had wisely not demanded that any of them sign in, or that he be permitted to examine the contents of the briefcases the Kraut and General Smith's aide-de-camp were carrying.

As a consequence, the sergeant not only passed General Gehlen out without examining the contents of his ancient and battered briefcase, but also gave him a pink slip, as he had given one to Cronley and Dunwiddie, which would permit them to exit the building.

Then the trio walked down the long corridor that connects the wings to the center, where they got on what most inhabitants of the Farben Building called the "dumbwaiter." Technically it was known as a "paternoster lift." It was a chain of open compartments, each large enough for two people, that moved slowly and continuously in a circle from Sub-Level Two to Floor Five. Passengers stepped into one of the compartments and rode it until they reached the desired floor, and then stepped off.

Cronley, Dunwiddie, and Gehlen got on the dumbwaiter and were carried down to Sub-Level One, where they got off.

Here there was another paratroop-manned checkpoint. The sergeant in charge here accepted the pink slips they had been given, but signaled to General Gehlen that he wanted to inspect his briefcase.

"Herr Schultz is with me, Sergeant," Cronley said, showing the sergeant the leather folder holding the ID card and badge that identified him as a special agent of the Counterintelligence Corps. "That won't be necessary."

The sergeant considered that a moment, and then said, "Yes,

sir," and motioned that Gehlen could leave the building. He did so, and Cronley followed him.

They were now in a narrow, below-ground-level, open-to-the-sky passageway.

There were three Packard Clippers parked against the wall. The "back door" to the Farben Building was also, so to speak, the VIP entrance. The Packards were the staff cars of Generals Eisenhower, Smith, and Lucius D. Clay, the military governor of the U.S. Occupied Zones. The Packards were, not surprisingly, highly polished.

There was also what had begun its military service as an ambulance, a three-quarter-ton 4×4. It was not polished, and the red crosses that had once been painted on the sides and roof had been painted over. Stenciled in white paint on the left of its bumpers was the legend 711 MKRC—which indicated that the vehicle was assigned to the—nonexistent—711th Quartermaster Mess Kit Repair Company—and on the right, the numeral 7, which signified that it was the seventh vehicle of its kind assigned to the 711th.

There were three paratroopers, one of them a sergeant, standing by the right front fender of the former ambulance, arguing with an enormous Negro soldier, a sergeant, who was leaning against the fender, his arms crossed over his chest. Even leaning against the fender, the sergeant towered over the paratroopers.

When the sergeant saw Cronley and the others approaching, he came to attention and saluted. Cronley returned the salute and asked, "Is there some problem?"

"You know about this vehicle, Captain?" the paratroop sergeant asked.

"Didn't they teach you it is customary for sergeants to salute officers before addressing them, Sergeant?"

"Yes, sir. Sorry, sir," the paratroop sergeant said, and saluted. Cronley returned it.

"Herr Schultz, if you'll get in the back with Captain Dunwiddie?" Cronley said, and then turned to the paratroop sergeant. "Is there a problem with this vehicle?"

"Sir, only the general's cars are allowed to park here."

"There are exceptions to every rule, Sergeant," Cronley said, and produced his CIC credentials. "In this case—it's an intelligence matter—I ordered the sergeant to wait here for me until I could bring Herr Schultz out. We didn't want him standing around where he could be seen. Weren't you here when General Smith passed him into the building?"

"Yes, sir."

"You did the right thing to question the vehicle, Sergeant."

"Thank you, sir."

"Carry on, Sergeant," Cronley ordered crisply. Then he turned to the black sergeant. "Well, Sergeant Phillips, what do you say we get out of here?"

"Yes, sir," Sergeant Phillips said. He got behind the wheel and Cronley got in the front seat beside him.

When they were rolling, Cronley said, "Those CIC credentials do come in handy, don't they?"

"Enjoy them while you can," Dunwiddie said. "I think we're about to lose them."

"I will bring up the subject of keeping them—and getting some more for some of your guys—to General Greene when there's an opportunity. I didn't want to do that when Mattingly was there—he can probably come up with a dozen reasons to take them away from us."

"I don't suppose it's occurred to you that making nice to Colonel Mattingly would be a good idea."

"I thought about that."

"And?"

"Mattingly is never going to forgive me for me, not him, being named chief, DCI-Europe," Cronley replied, "even though I had nothing to do with it. Or forgive you, Captain Dunwiddie, for those new bars on your epaulets."

"Speaking of which," Sergeant Phillips said, "they look real good on you, Tiny. Congratulations."

"Thanks, Tom," Dunwiddie said.

"Who's going to be the new Top Kick? Tedworth?" Phillips asked.

"Who else?" Dunwiddie said.

"General, can you tell me what General Smith wanted with you?"

"Of course," Gehlen said. "Two things. Once it was determined he had the right Captain Cronley—the Army one, not a naval officer—he asked if I 'was comfortable' with you being named chief, DCI-Europe. I assured him I was. And then he handed me this to give to you."

He handed Cronley a business-sized envelope. Cronley's name and the legend "By Officer Courier" was on it. When he opened it, he saw that it contained a second envelope. This one was addressed:

CAPTAIN JAMES D. CRONLEY JR.

CHIEF, DCI-EUROPE

C/O GENERAL WALTER B. SMITH

SUPREME HEADQUARTERS, EUROPEAN COMMAND

BY OFFICER COURIER

He tore the second envelope open and read the letter it contained.

TOP SECRET PRESIDENTIAL NUCLEAR

The White House

Washington, D.C.

Rear Admiral Sidney W. Souers, USN
Special Assistant to the President

December 24, 1945

Duplication Forbidden
Copy 1 Of 2
Page 1 of 8

Captain James D. Cronley Jr.

Chief, DCI-Europe

C/O General Walter B. Smith

Supreme Headquarters, European Command

By Officer Courier

TOP SECRET PRESIDENTIAL NUCLEAR

TOP SECRET PRESIDENTIAL NUCLEAR

RAdm Souers/Capt Cronley 24 Dec 1945

Copy 1 of 2

Page 2 of 8

Duplication Forbidden

Dear Jim:

The information herein, with which Lieutenant Colonel Ashton is familiar, is to be shared only with General Gehlen, General White, and Dunwiddie. It is to be hoped he will be Captain Dunwiddie by the time you get this. If his commission has not come through, let me know immediately.

This concerns the establishment of the Directorate of Central Intelligence and its operations in the near future.

Until the OSS's arrangement with General Gehlen provided the names of Soviet intelligence officers seeking to breach the secrecy of the Manhattan Project, and the names of Manhattan Project personnel who were in fact engaged in treasonous espionage on behalf of the USSR, it was J. Edgar Hoover's often announced position

TOP SECRET PRESIDENTIAL NUCLEAR

TOP SECRET PRESIDENTIAL NUCLEAR

RAdm Souers/Capt Cronley 24 Dec 1945

Copy 1 of 2

Page 3 of 8

Duplication Forbidden

that the FBI had been completely successful in maintaining the secrets of the Manhattan Project.

Hoover maintained this position, even after being given the aforementioned intelligence, up and until President Truman informed Marshal Stalin in Potsdam on July 18, 1945, that we possessed the atomic bomb, and from Stalin's reaction concluded he was telling Stalin something Stalin already knew.

Faced with the undeniable proof that the USSR had penetrated the Manhattan Project, Director Hoover said that what he had really meant to say was that of course the FBI had known all along of Soviet spies in the Manhattan Project, but that so far he had been unable to develop sufficient evidence that would stand up in court to arrest and indict the spies and traitors. He assured the President at that time that he would

TOP SECRET PRESIDENTIAL NUCLEAR

TOP SECRET PRESIDENTIAL NUCLEAR

RAdm Souers/Capt Cronley 24 Dec 1945

Copy 1 of 2

Page 4 of 8

Duplication Forbidden

order the FBI to redouble its efforts to obtain such evidence.

The President had taken me into his confidence about this even before Potsdam, and when he asked what I thought should be done, I recommended that he turn the investigation of Soviet espionage in the Manhattan Project over to General Donovan and the OSS. He replied that to do so would be tantamount to authorizing an "SS-like" secret police force in the United States, and he was absolutely unwilling to do anything like that. Furthermore, the President said, he had already decided to abolish the OSS.

There the situation lay dormant, until the President decided he had been too hasty in shutting down the OSS and had come to the conclusion that there was a great need for an organization with both covert and clandestine capabilities and answerable only to the chief executive.

TOP SECRET PRESIDENTIAL NUCLEAR

TOP SECRET PRESIDENTIAL NUCLEAR

RAdm Souers/Capt Cronley 24 Dec 1945

Copy 1 of 2

Page 5 of 8

Duplication Forbidden

In late November, the President told me that he had decided to establish by Executive Order the Directorate of Central Intelligence (DCI) as of January 1, 1946, and intended to name me as director. He told me one of the reasons for his decision was that he knew I found the notion of an American SS as repugnant as he did.

I told the President that unless the DCI was given authority to deal with significant Soviet intelligence efforts in the United States, such as the Manhattan Project, I would reluctantly have to decline the honor of becoming director, DCI.

The President said it was politically impossible for him to publicly or privately take any responsibility for counterintelligence activities within the United States from Mr. Hoover and the FBI and give it to the DCI. He then pointed out

TOP SECRET PRESIDENTIAL NUCLEAR

TOP SECRET PRESIDENTIAL NUCLEAR

RAdm Souers/Capt Cronley 24 Dec 1945

Copy 1 of 2

Page 6 of 8

Duplication Forbidden

in the draft of the Executive Order establishing the DCI the phrase "and perform such other activities as the President may order."

He said that if I were DDCI, he would order me to "investigate and deter any efforts by any foreign power to penetrate the Manhattan Project, or any such activity, and to report any findings and any actions taken, directly and only to him."

The President said that he did not feel that Mr. Hoover would have any need to know of these orders. The President also said that in none of his conversations with Director Hoover had the subject of "Operation OST" come up, either by name, or as a general subject such as the rumor that we have been sending Germans to Argentina. The President said he found this odd, as I had told him FBI agents were in Europe attempting to

TOP SECRET PRESIDENTIAL NUCLEAR

TOP SECRET PRESIDENTIAL NUCLEAR

RAdm Souers/Capt Cronley 24 Dec 1945

Copy 1 of 2

Page 7 of 8

Duplication Forbidden

question you, and others, on the subject. The President said he did not understand Mr. Hoover's particular interest in Operation OST, as it is none of the FBI's business.

At this point in our conversation the President again offered me the directorship of the DCI. I informed the President that if I could name Lieutenant Colonel Ashton as deputy director, DCI-Western Hemisphere, with overall responsibility for Operation OST, and you as DDDCI-Europe, with responsibility for Operation OST in Europe, I would accept the honor he offered.

The President told me to tell you and Colonel Ashton that he feels confident you both can establish an amicable, cooperative relationship between the DCI and the FBI while at the same

TOP SECRET PRESIDENTIAL NUCLEAR

TOP SECRET PRESIDENTIAL NUCLEAR

RAdm Souers/ Capt Cronley 24 Dec 1945

Copy 1 of 2

Page 8 of 8

Duplication Forbidden

time keeping secret those matters which do not fall within the FBI's areas of responsibility or interest.

He also said to send you his best wishes.

With best personal regards,

Sidney W. Souers

Sidney W. Souers

Rear Admiral, USN

Director, DCI

TOP SECRET PRESIDENTIAL NUCLEAR

Cronley handed the letter to Gehlen.

"Please give it to Captain Dunwiddie when you've read it, General," he said.

When Tiny had read the letter, Cronley said, "My take on that letter is that Truman is afraid of Hoover. Otherwise, he would just tell Hoover to butt out."

When no one replied, he asked, "Can I interpret the silence to mean you agree with me?"

"You can interpret my silence to mean I am obviously not in a position where I can presume to comment on anything the President of the United States does or does not do," Gehlen said. "I would, however, suggest that both President Truman and Admiral Souers seem to feel confident that both you and Colonel Ashton can deal with a very difficult situation."

"Shit," Cronley said, and looked at Dunwiddie. "And you?"

After a moment, Dunwiddie avoided the question, instead asking, "Lieutenant Colonel Ashton? I thought he was a major, and in Walter Reed with a broken leg?"

"In other words, no comment, right?" Cronley asked.

Dunwiddie said nothing.

"As to your question," Cronley said. "Applying my Sherlock Holmesian logic to it, I deduce Ashton (a) has been promoted, and (b) that he will shortly appear here, broken leg or not. Obviously, if he was in Walter Reed, we could not share this letter with him."

"Wiseass," Dunwiddie said.

Gehlen chuckled.

"I further deduce," Cronley went on, "that Lieutenant Colonel Ashton is coming over here to familiarize himself with his new underlings."

"Other than that Otto Niedermeyer speaks highly of him, I don't know much about Colonel Ashton," Gehlen said.

"All I really know about him is that he's a Cuban—an American whose family grows sugarcane and makes rum in Cuba—and that Clete likes him. The little I saw of him when I was in Argentina, I liked," Cronley said. "He's really . . . what's the word? 'Polished.' Or maybe 'suave.' He can charm the balls off a brass monkey."

"Now that's an interesting phrase," Gehlen said, chuckling.

"I have no idea what it means," Cronley confessed.

"Would you be surprised to hear it has nothing to do with the testicles of our simian cousins?" Dunwiddie asked.

Tiny has found a way to change the subject.

Well, what did I expect him to say? "I agree it looks like Truman is throwing us off the bus"?

"Pay attention, General," Cronley said. "Professor Dunwiddie's lecture is about to start."

"Until breech-loading rifled-barrel naval cannon came along," Dunwiddie began, "men-of-war, as warships were then called, fired round iron balls from their smooth-barreled cannon. These balls often contained a black powder charge, with a fuse that was lit just before the ball was rammed down the cannon muzzle. Is this too technical for you, Captain Cronley, sir, or should I continue?"

Gehlen chuckled.

"Carry on, Captain Dunwiddie," Cronley ordered.

"As you are aware, balls tend to roll around on flat surfaces," Dunwiddie continued. "They tend to roll around even more on flat surfaces which are themselves moving, as the deck of ships on the high seas tend to do. Since the balls the Navy was using weighed up to one hundred pounds, you can see where this was a problem. The problem was compounded by the explosive shells to which I previously referred.

"Phrased simply, if some of the black powder in the explosive shells came out of the touch hole—that's where they put the fuse—while it was rolling around on the deck, it made for a highly combustible environment. Even worse was the possibility that glowing embers—debris from previous firing of the cannon—would find the touch hole of the explosive ball as it rolled around the deck crushing feet and breaking ankles. Bang. Big bang.

"A solution had to be found, and one was. A clever sailor, one I like to think claimed my beloved Norwich as his alma mater, although I can't prove this—"

"General," Cronley asked, "has Captain Dunwiddie mentioned in passing that he went to Norwich University?"

"Not as often as Sergeant Hessinger has mentioned he went to Harvard, but yes, he has. No more than thirty or forty times," Gehlen replied.

"As I was saying," Dunwiddie went on, "a clever nautical person came up with a solution for the problem of cannonballs rolling and sometimes exploding on the deck. The balls, he concluded, had to be in some manner restrained from rolling around, and that the method of restraint had to permit getting the iron cannonballs from where they would be restrained into the mouth of the cannon quickly when that was required. And without causing the sparks which occur when steel and/or iron collide. Said sparks would tend to set off both the barrels of black powder and the explosive cannonballs.

"What he came up with were plates, into which he hammered depressions so that the cannonballs wouldn't roll around. He made the plates from brass so they wouldn't spark and set off the black powder. For reasons lost in the fog of history, he called these indented brass plates 'monkeys.' When they were getting ready to fight, they put the shells, the balls, on these monkeys until they were needed. Moving the balls, which weighed up to one hundred pounds, off the brass monkey was recognized to be very difficult. Any further questions?"

"Interesting," Gehlen said. "Now that you've brought it up, I remember seeing cannonballs stacked that way, forming sort of a pyramid, on your *Old Ironsides* in Boston Harbor." He paused, and corrected himself: "The USS *Constitution*."

"You've been on the *Constitution*?" Cronley blurted, in surprise.

"As a young officer," Gehlen said. "When it seemed that I was destined to serve as an intelligence officer, I was treated to a tour of the United States."

Sergeant Phillips announced, "We're here."

Cronley looked out the window and saw they were approaching the gate to the Eschborn Airfield.

"Great," Cronley said. "And now that Professor Dunwiddie's history lesson is over, we can return to our noble duties stemming the Red Tide. Maintaining as we do so an amicable relationship with the FBI."

He expected a chuckle from General Gehlen, but when he looked at him, he saw a look of concern.

Jesus, what did my automatic mouth blurt out now?

"Sir, if I said something . . ."

Gehlen shook his head. "No, Jim, you didn't say anything out of place. What popped back into my mind—I have a tendency to find a black lining in every silver cloud—when you said 'stemming the Red Tide' was something I thought when I was with General Smith earlier. You said it mockingly, but in fact—don't misunderstand me, please, I know you take it as seriously as I do—that's what we're trying to do. But there are so very few of us who really understand the problem. And so many clever Russians."

Cronley's mouth went on automatic again. He regretted what he was saying as the words came out of his mouth: "Not to worry, General. One of us went to Norwich."

There was no expression on Gehlen's face for a long moment, but just as Cronley was trying to frame an appropriate apology, Gehlen smiled and said, "That somehow slipped my mind, but now that you've brought it up, it certainly does wonders dispelling my clouds of impending disaster."

[ONE]
Kloster Grünau
Schollbrunn, Bavaria
American Zone of Occupation, Germany
1705 29 December 1945

When he took the Storch off from Eschborn, Cronley had been worried about the flight, although he said nothing to either General Gehlen or Tiny.

For one thing, the weather was iffy, and it gets dark early in Germany in December. If the weather got worse, he'd have to land somewhere short of Munich, which meant at an infantry regiment or artillery battalion airstrip somewhere. As far as the officers there would be concerned, in addition to wondering what he was doing flying a Kraut around in a former Luftwaffe airplane, they would be reluctant to house overnight or, for that matter, feed said seedy-looking Kraut.

Flashing the CIC credentials would overcome those problems, of course, but it would provide those officers with a great barroom story to share with the world.

You won't believe what flew into the strip yesterday. An ex-Luftwaffe Storch, with Army markings, and carrying two CIC cap-

tains and a Kraut. Wouldn't say what they were doing, of course. Makes you wonder.

And even if he could make it through the weather to Bavaria, by the time they got there, it might be too dark to land on the strip at the Pullach compound. That would mean he would have to go into Schleissheim—the Munich military post airfield—which had runway lights.

But there would be problems at Schleissheim, too. The Storch would attract unwanted attention, and so would General Gehlen. And they would have to ask the Schleissheim duty officer for a car to take them to the Vier Jahreszeiten as the Kapitän was at Kloster Grünau, and Major Wallace was sure to be off somewhere in their only other car, the Opel Admiral.

An hour out of Munich, the answer came: *Don't go to Munich. Go to Kloster Grünau. Have a couple of drinks and a steak. Go to bed. And in the morning, get in the Kapitän and drive to Pullach.*

He picked up the intercom microphone.

"General, would you have any problems if we spent the night at the monastery?"

"As far as I know, there's absolutely nothing waiting for me in Munich."

"Next stop, Kloster Grünau."

Technical Sergeant Tedworth, his cavalry-yellow scarf not quite concealing the bandages on his neck, was waiting for them in the ambulance. Cronley was not surprised to see Ostrowski was behind the wheel.

Cronley had something to tell him, and this was as good a time as any.

"Tedworth, Sergeant Hessinger—"

"Sir, he wants you to call him as soon as possible," Tedworth cut him off. "He says it's important."

"Sergeant, it's not polite to cut your commanding officer off in the middle of a sentence."

"Sorry, sir."

"Not only impolite, but the wrong thing to do, since what I was going to say had I not been rudely interrupted, was that Sergeant Hessinger has informed me that while I do not have promotion authority in normal circumstances, I do in extraordinary circumstances. I have decided that First Sergeant Dunwiddie, having created a vacant first sergeant position by becoming a commissioned officer, is such an extraordinary circumstance. I was about to tell you I am sure that Captain Dunwiddie will be happy to sell you the first sergeant chevrons he no longer needs at a reasonable price."

"I'll be damned," Tedworth said. "Thank you."

"You will of course be expected to pay for the intoxicants at your promotion party, which will commence just as soon as we get to the bar."

"First Sergeant Tedworth," Tedworth said wonderingly. "I will be damned!"

"You will be aware, I'm sure, First Sergeant Tedworth, that henceforth you will be marching in the footsteps of the superb non-commissioned officer who preceded you and will be expected to conduct yourself accordingly," Dunwiddie said solemnly.

"*Captain* Dunwiddie and *First Sergeant* Tedworth," Tedworth went on. "Who would have ever thought, Tiny, when we joined Company 'A'?"

And then he regained control.

"Captain, I think you better call Fat Freddy," he said. "He said it was really important."

"Immediately after I take a leak—my back teeth are floating—and I have a stiff drink of Scotland's finest," Cronley said.

"Twenty-third CIC, Special Agent Hessinger."

"And how are you, Freddy, on this miserable December evening?"

"When are you coming here?"

"That's one of the reasons I called, Freddy, to tell you Captain Dunwiddie and myself—plus two others whose names I would prefer not to say on this line while some FBI numbnuts are listening—will be celebrating First Sergeant Tedworth's promotion in the country and will not be returning to Munich until tomorrow."

"I don't think Colonel Parsons is going to like that."

"What? What business is it of his?"

"He called here and said General Greene had suggested he and Major Ashley take you to dinner to get to know you. He said he made reservations here in the Vier Jahreszeiten for eight o'clock and he expects to see you there."

That's disappointing. I thought Greene was going to maintain complete neutrality. But what he's obviously doing—or trying to do—is help this bastard Parsons take over Operation Ost for the Pentagon.

Why should that surprise me? Greene, ultimately, is under the Pentagon G2. They don't like the Directorate of Central Intelligence and they really don't want Operation Ost being run by a very junior captain. Greene knows on which side of the piece of toast the butter goes.

Wait a minute!

Do I detect the subtle hand of Colonel Robert Mattingly?

Oh, do I!

Mattingly thinks—and with good reason—that he should be chief, DCI-Europe. Instead, I am. But there's nothing he can do about it. Unless, of course, as a result of my youth and inexperience I get into a scrap with Parsons. Then he can step in—Greene would suggest Mattingly step in—to save something from the wreckage. For the good of the service.

I can see that sonofabitch suggesting to General Greene that Parsons take me to dinner "to get to know me." I can also see Parsons reasoning that Greene is on his side—otherwise why the "get to know him" suggestion—and interpreting "get to know him" to mean making it clear to the junior captain that this is still the Army, and in the Army, lieutenant colonels tell junior captains what to do, and junior captains say, "Yes, sir."

But I can't take orders from a lieutenant colonel whose mission it is to take over Operation Ost.

So what do I do?

"Would you be shocked to hear that I am not thrilled with the prospect of Colonel Parsons buying me dinner?"

"You not being thrilled doesn't matter. Colonel Mattingly called and said Colonel Parsons would probably call and invite you to dinner, and you had better go. Alone."

Well, there's the proof. I can hear Mattingly saying, "Parsons went out of his way, Admiral, to get along with Cronley. He even invited him to a private dinner. Cronley refused to go."

Making nice to Parsons tonight would be just delaying the inevitable confrontation. Mattingly—or maybe Parsons himself, he's clever—would make sure there was a confrontation.

Back to what do I do?

What I do is get this over with.

But as the soon-to-be chief, DCI-Europe, not as Junior Captain Cronley.

Which means I take off this Ike jacket with its brand-new captain's bars and put on the one with the civilian U.S. triangles.

"You know how to get Parsons on the phone, Freddy?"

"He's here in the hotel."

"Please call him back and tell him you've heard from Mister, repeat, Mister Cronley and he, General Gehlen, and Captain Dunwiddie, who had already planned to dine at the Vier Jahreszeiten at eight, would be delighted if he and Major Whatsisname could join us."

"You heard what I said about Colonel Mattingly saying you should go to dinner alone?"

"Anything else for me, Freddy?"

"Oberst Mannberg asked me when General Gehlen will be back. He says he has something to report."

"Whatever that might be, I don't think we want to share it with the FBI, do we?"

"So what do I tell Mannberg?"

"Tell him the general will be in your office just before we go to dinner with Colonel Parsons and Major Whatsisname."

[TWO]
Suite 507
Hotel Vier Jahreszeiten
Maximilianstrasse 178
Munich, American Zone of Occupation, Germany
1935 29 December 1945

Former Colonel Ludwig Mannberg was sitting with Sergeant Friedrich Hessinger at the latter's desk, both of them bent over a chessboard. They both stood when Cronley, followed by Gehlen and Dunwiddie, came into the room.

Mannberg was wearing a well-tailored suit and tie. Fat Freddy was in pinks and greens.

Cronley thought, more objectively than unkindly, *Looking at the two of them, you'd think Gehlen was a black marketeer caught dealing in cigarettes and Hershey bars and Mannberg was his lawyer. His English lawyer. I'm going to have to do something about getting the general some decent clothes.*

How am I going to do that? "Excuse me, General, but in that ratty suit, you look like an unsuccessful black marketeer."

"I just had one of my famous inspirations," Cronley announced. "Freddy, call the dining room and tell them there will be two more at dinner."

"Who?" Hessinger asked.

"You and Oberst Mannberg."

"Is that wise, Jim?" Dunwiddie asked. "Mattingly said you were to go alone."

"I know," Cronley said. "Do it, Freddy."

"General," Mannberg said, "we have heard from Seven-K."

Who the hell is "Seven-K"?

"And?" Gehlen asked.

"She reports Natalia Likharev and her sons, Sergei and Pavel, do in fact occupy a flat at Nevsky Prospekt 114 in Leningrad. It's a luxury apartment building reserved for senior officers of the NKGB."

Seven-K, you soaking-wet-behind-the-ears amateur intelligence officer, is obviously Gehlen's agent in Russia. If they said his name out loud, someone might hear. She?

"Which means," Gehlen said, "especially since the NKGB knows Colonel Likharev is now in Argentina, that they are watching them very carefully, and that it's just a matter of time before she is arrested. *Pour encourager les autres.*"

To encourage other NKGB officers not to change sides because the penalty is having your wife and kids sent to Siberia. Or shot. Or tortured. Or all of the above.

"Yes, sir," Mannberg agreed. "She also reports the Underground Railroad is in disarray."

"She"? That's twice Mannberg said "she." Seven-K is a woman?

Jesus, stupid! You should know the Russians have women spies. One of them made a horse's ass out of you. So why should Gehlen having female agents be such a surprise?

"Underground Railway"? As in the States? Getting slaves out of the South? Mannberg is obviously talking about this woman's setup to get the Likharevs out of Russia. Interesting that the Russians use a term from American history.

Gehlen said, "Send her 'Act at your discretion.'"

"Signed?" Mannberg asked.

Gehlen pointed his index finger at his chest.

I wonder what your code name is?

"*Jawohl*, Herr General," Mannberg said.

"Why don't we all go down to the bar and have a drink before we feed the nice men from the Pentagon?" Cronley asked.

"Once again," Dunwiddie said, "are you sure that's what you want to do, have us all there?"

"I don't want to face them all by my lonesome," Cronley replied.

But that's not the only reason I want everybody there.

In three days I will become chief, Directorate of Central Intelligence-Europe, which means essentially Operation Ost. I have zero, zilch qualifications to be given such an enormous responsibility. But I will have it, and I am about to compound the problem of the Pentagon's determination to take over control of Operation Ost from what they correctly believe to be a wholly unqualified—and very junior—officer by shifting into what Colonel Robert Mattingly has often referred to as my "loose-cannon" mode.

Specifically, I am going to apply what I was taught at my alma mater, Texas A&M: The best defense is a good offense.

If I told Tiny and Fat Freddy what I plan to do, they would conclude that I was once again going to do something monumentally stupid—and God knows I have quite a history of doing that. They would possibly, even probably, go along with me out of loyalty, but that's a two-way street.

If, as is likely, even probable, this blows up in my face, I want both Tiny and Freddy to be able to truthfully tell Mattingly, and/or Gen-

eral Greene—for that matter, Admiral Souers—that they had no idea how I planned to deal with Lieutenant Colonel Parsons and Major Ashley. So I can't tell them.

The same applies to General Gehlen. While my monumental ego suggests he would probably think it might be a good idea, I don't know that. So I can't tell him. If I did, and he suggested ever so politely that I was wrong, I would stop. And I can't stop, because it's the only way I can think of to deal with Parsons and Ashley.

[THREE]
The Main Dining Room
Hotel Vier Jahreszeiten
Maximilianstrasse 178
Munich, American Zone of Occupation, Germany
2000 29 December 1945

Lieutenant Colonel George H. Parsons and Major Warren W. Ashley were not in the dining room when Cronley, Gehlen, Mannberg, Dunwiddie, and Hessinger arrived, but the table was set with places for everyone.

Important people arrive last, right? Screw you, Parsons!

Cronley took the chair at the head of the table.

"General, why don't you sit here?" Cronley said, pointing to the first side chair. "So that when Colonel Parsons arrives, he can sit across from you."

Gehlen, his face expressionless, sat where Cronley suggested.

Cronley then pointed to people and chairs and everyone sat where he pointed.

Twenty minutes later, Colonel Parsons—a tall, trim forty-five-year-old—and Major Ashley—a shorter thirty-six-year-old version of Parsons—walked into the dining room. Both were in pinks and greens, and both of them wore the lapel insignia of the General Staff Corps and the shoulder insignia of the Military District of Washington.

Parsons marched on Cronley, who stood up but didn't put down his whisky glass.

"Glad to see you again, Cronley," Parsons said. "Sorry to be late. Tied up. Couldn't be helped."

"Good evening, Colonel," Cronley replied. "I was about to introduce you to General Gehlen, but he just told me he thinks you met when he was in Washington."

"No," Parsons said.

"My mistake," Gehlen said. "There was a Colonel Parsons at Fort Hunt, and I thought it might be you. But—"

"I don't have the pleasure of Herr Gehlen's acquaintance," Parsons said, and put out his hand.

"Herr Gehlen"? Okay, Colonel, if you want to go down that route, fine.

"And this is Oberst—Colonel—Mannberg, General Gehlen's deputy," Cronley said. "And Mr. Hessinger, who is my chief of staff, and Captain Dunwiddie, my deputy." He paused and then said, "And you're Major Ashburg, right?"

"Ashley, Captain Cronley, Ashley," Ashley corrected him.

"Right," Cronley said. "I'm bad with names. Well, gentlemen, I'm really glad you were free to join us. We're celebrating Captain Dunwiddie's commissioning."

"General Greene mentioned that you had been . . ." Parsons began.

Cronley interrupted him by calling for a waiter.

". . . in Frankfurt," Parsons went on, "for the promotion ceremony."

"Yes, we flew up when General Smith let it be known that (a) he would like to participate, and (b) that he wanted a word with General Gehlen."

"General Smith wanted to participate?" Major Ashley asked, either dubiously or in surprise.

Thank you for that question, Major Ashley.

"It turned out—Dunwiddie never told us—that when he was born—what did General Smith say, Tiny? 'In the age of the dinosaurs'?—his father's company commander was Captain Smith."

"Oh, so you're from an Army family, Captain?" Parsons asked.

"Yes, sir."

"And you, Captain Cronley?"

The waiter appeared, saving Cronley from having to answer. When the waiter had taken their orders, Parsons had a fresh question.

"Let me go off on a tangent," he said. "You said you flew up to Frankfurt, and presumably flew back. Is there reliable air service between here and Frankfurt? The reason I ask is that it's a long ride on the train, and I expect that I'll have to—myself and Major Ashley will have to—go up there often."

"You're asking about MATS? The Air Force Military Air Transport Service?"

"Yes, of course."

"I really have no idea."

"But you just said you flew back and forth to Frankfurt today. How did you do that?"

"I loaded the general and Dunwiddie into a Storch, wound up the rubber bands, and took off."

"What's a Storch?"

"It's a German airplane. Sort of a super Piper Cub. We have two of them."

"You're a pilot? An aviator?"

Cronley nodded.

"I don't remember seeing pilot's wings when I saw you in uniform at the Schlosshotel Kronberg," Parsons said. "And that raises another question in my mind. If you don't mind my asking."

"Ask away. Isn't that what this is all about? Finding out about each other?"

"Why is it you're not wearing your uniform now? I mean, isn't that civilian attire?"

"As a special agent of the CIC, I'm allowed to wear 'civilian attire' when I think it's necessary."

"But you're not a CIC special agent, are you?"

"Until January second, I am a special agent of the CIC, assigned to the Twenty-third CIC Detachment," Cronley said, and then indicated Dunwiddie and Hessinger. "We all are."

"And on January second?"

"Then we will all be transferred to DCI-Europe. I would have thought General Greene or Colonel Mattingly would have explained that."

"It's not clear in my mind," Parsons said.

"And after that, you and the sergeant here will have to wear your uniforms?" Major Ashley asked. His tone of voice made it a challenge.

"Who told you Special Agent Hessinger is a sergeant?"

"You don't use the term 'sir' often, do you, Captain?" Ashley snapped.

"I guess I don't. Sorry. Blame it on the OSS."

"'Blame it on the OSS'?" Ashley parroted sarcastically.

"The OSS was—and I suppose the DCI will be—a little lax about the finer points of military courtesy," Cronley said. "My question to you, Major, was who told you Special Agent Hessinger is a sergeant?"

"As a matter of fact, it was Colonel Mattingly."

"I'm surprised. He knows better."

"My question to you, Captain," Ashley snapped, "is whether after Two January you will wear the prescribed uniform."

"After Two January the chief, DCI-Europe, will prescribe what DCI-Europe personnel will wear," Cronley said. "Right now, I don't think that will often be a uniform revealing our ranks to the world."

Ashley opened his mouth to reply. Cronley saw Parsons just perceptibly shake his head, which silenced Ashley.

Two waiters appeared and handed out menus.

They ordered.

"You understand, of course, Mr. Cronley," Colonel Parsons said, "that Major Ashley was understandably curious."

"Mister Cronley"? Was that a slip of the tongue?

Or is he being nice?

If he's being nice, why is he being nice?

"Absolutely," Cronley said. "Curiosity's a common affliction of intelligence officers, isn't it?"

"Absolutely," Parsons agreed with a smile. "My wife says, aside from my drinking, it's my worst character flaw."

Everyone laughed dutifully.

"Truth to tell, I'm a little curious about what you're going to do after Two January."

"Do about what, Colonel?"

"Identifying yourself, yourselves."

"To whom?"

"Hypothetical situation?"

"Why not?"

"You and Mr. Hessinger and Captain Dunwiddie—in civilian attire—are riding down the super highway here—what's it called?"

"The autobahn."

"The *autobahn*, in that magnificent German automobile Major Wallace drives . . ."

"The Opel Admiral," Dunwiddie furnished.

"Thank you. And, deep in conversation about how to repel the Red Threat to all we hold dear, you let the Admiral get a little over the speed limit. The ever-vigilant military police pull you over."

"Don't let it get around, Colonel, but your hypothetical situation actually happened several times to Colonel Mattingly."

"Really?"

"He was driving me from Kloster Grünau to Rhine-Main to catch the plane to Buenos Aires. In his magnificent German automobile, his Horch. Have you ever seen his Horch? That's a really magnificent car."

"I don't think I'd recognize a Horch if one ran over me."

"Between the monastery and Rhine-Main, the MPs pulled him over three times for speeding. The last citation was for going three times the speed limit."

"You're pulling my leg."

"No, I am not. Three times the speed limit is a hundred and seventy KPH, or a little over a hundred miles an hour—"

"Cronley," Major Ashley interrupted him, "why don't you let the colonel continue with his hypothetical?"

"Sorry," Cronley said. "Go ahead, Colonel."

"So there you are, by the side of the road, and the MP says, 'Sir, let me see your identification, please.' What are you going to do?"

"Follow the example shown me by Colonel Mattingly," Cronley replied. "Dazzle him with my CIC special agent credentials. Telling him I am rushing somewhere in the line of duty."

"But you won't have CIC credentials after One January," Ashley said.

"Oh, but I will."

"No, you won't," Ashley snapped. "You'll then be in the Directorate of Central Intelligence, not the CIC."

"I'm sure Colonel Parsons has his reasons for not telling you about that," Cronley said.

"Not telling him what about that?" Parsons asked.

"Now I'm in a spot," Cronley said. "Maybe this hypothetical wasn't such a good idea after all."

"What are you talking about, Cronley?" Parsons asked.

Not only am I no longer "Mister Cronley," but he's using the tone of voice lieutenant colonels use when dealing with junior captains who have done something to annoy them.

"Colonel, I'm just surprised that General Greene—and especially Colonel Mattingly, after all, he did tell you Hessinger is a sergeant—didn't tell you about this. But they obviously had their reasons. But what the hell, they didn't ask me not to tell you, so I will."

Colonel Parsons gave Major Ashley another don't-say-anything shake of the head, but it was too late.

"*Ask* you not to tell us what?" Ashley snapped sarcastically.

Three waiters marched up to the table carrying their dinner.

Serving it was an elaborate ceremony, but finally everything was served and the waiters left.

I am now going to pretend I think the hypothetical is closed.

"Do you know the officers' clubs import this beef from Denmark?" Cronley asked. "It seems they're leaning over backwards to avoid any suggestion that the clubs are taking the best beef from the Quartermaster—"

"You were saying something, Mr. Cronley," Colonel Parsons interrupted him, "about General Greene not telling me something?"

"Right," Cronley said.

He paused before going on: "Oh, what the hell. I don't want to be stuffy about this—God knows there's a hell of a lot classified Secret and Top Secret that shouldn't be classified at all—but this is justifiably classified . . ."

"Meaning you're not going to tell us?" Ashley asked, rather nastily.

"No, Major, I've decided you have the need to know about this, so I'm going to tell you. But I also have to tell you this is classified Top Secret–Presidential."

"You are aware, Cronley, are you not, that both Colonel Parsons and myself hold Top Secret–Presidential clearances?" Ashley said, angrily sarcastic. "We're entitled to know."

Well, I finally got you to blow up, didn't I?

And I ain't through.

"What you and Colonel Parsons are entitled to know about the DCI, about Operation Ost, Major, is what I decide you have the need to know."

If that doesn't set Parsons off, nothing will.

Greatly surprising Cronley, it didn't.

"Warren, Mr. Cronley is right," Parsons said. "Why don't we let him tell us what he thinks we should know?"

I'll be damned.

But why is it that I don't think I've won?

"I'll tell you what I can, sir, about the DCI and the CIC," Cronley said. "The basic idea is, as you're fully aware, to hide Operation Ost from just about everybody who does not have a genuine need to know. Everybody, in this sense, includes the FBI and that part of the CIC engaged in looking for Nazis. As well, of course, as just about everybody else."

"Admiral Souers explained that to me in some detail," Parsons said.

"Yes, sir, he told me that he had. But what he didn't tell you, and what General Greene apparently hasn't told you—and I really wish he had—and what I'm going to tell you now, is how the admiral decided the concealment could best be accomplished."

"And how is that?" Ashley demanded.

"Warren," Colonel Parsons said warningly.

Now Parsons's on my side?

What the hell is going on?

"When Admiral Souers told me that, at his request, and with the President's approval, the Army was going to task EUCOM-CIC with the logistical support of DCI-Europe, I suggested to him that I'd like to use EUCOM-CIC for more than that."

"*You* suggested that *you'd* like?" Ashley demanded sarcastically.

"Warren, shut up!" Parsons ordered curtly.

Well, if nothing else, I really have Parsons's attention.

"I suggested to the admiral that we could conceal a great deal of DCI-Europe within the CIC," Cronley went on. "For example, if we let people think that the Pullach compound is a CIC installation, and that General Gehlen's people were being employed by the CIC to track down Nazis . . ."

"But you're calling it the South German Industrial Development Organization Compound," Parsons said.

"Admiral Souers raised the same objection, sir. I suggested that if the Pullach compound was actually being used by the CIC as a Nazi hunting center, they wouldn't put that on the sign. The sign would say something like the General-Büros Süd-Deutsche Industrielle Entwicklungsorganisation."

"Clever," Colonel Parsons said thoughtfully. "And, I gather, Admiral Souers and General Greene went along with your ideas?"

"Admiral Souers did. I don't think General Greene was unhappy with them."

"And, in any case," Parsons said, "what General Greene might think is moot, isn't it?"

"Colonel, I don't know this, but I think that if General Greene didn't like any of this, he would have told Admiral Souers, and I know the admiral would have listened. What I'm guessing is that General Greene didn't have any major objections."

Parsons considered that for a moment, and then said, "You're probably right. And now that I think about it, why should he have had problems with what the admiral asked him to do? Your suggestions make a lot of sense."

Yeah, I immodestly believe they do. But since your basic interest here is to get Operation Ost put under the deputy chief of staff for intelligence, and the only way you're going to be able to do that is to get me to fuck up royally, I don't think you're as pleased with my good suggestions as you're letting on.

"I find all of this fascinating," Parsons said. "And I suspect Warren does, too."

"Sir?"

"Warren and I have spent most of our careers in intelligence, Mr. Cronley, but just about all of it on the analytical side. Isn't that so, Warren?"

"Yes, sir."

"As opposed to the operational side is what I mean. What I suppose could be called the nitty-gritty side. So I find all these little operational details fascinating. I never would have thought of hiding a secret operation the way you're going to do it. A secret operation having absolutely nothing to do with the secret organization in which you're hiding it. Absolutely fascinating. Brilliant, even!"

Where the hell is he going with this?

"So I'd like to ask a favor of you, Mr. Cronley."

"Anything I can do for you, Colonel, of course."

"Cut me a little slack when we start working together."

"I don't think I follow you, Colonel."

"When I said, before, that my wife regards my curiosity as my worst character flaw, she was right on the money. And I know myself well enough to know that when we are working together I'll come across things that I know are none of my business, but which will cause my curiosity to shift into high gear.

"When that happens, and I ask you—or any of your people—questions that are out of bounds, I want you to feel perfectly free—and tell your people to feel absolutely free—to cut me off at the knees. Just say, 'That's none of your business,' and that will be the end of it. I won't take offense, and I'll stop asking questions. How does that sound, Mr. Cronley?"

Actually, you smooth sonofabitch, that's what I already decided to do if you and ol' Warren here got too curious. Cut you off at the knees.

"That's very gracious of you, Colonel," Cronley said. "Thank you. And I appreciate your understanding that there will be things going on around the Pullach compound that the fewer people know about, the better."

And I will now wait for the other shoe to drop.

Where's he going to go from here?

"Well, enough of this," Parsons said. "Why don't we change the subject?"

Cronley was so surprised at the other shoe that he blurted, "To what?"

"Women and politics are supposed to be forbidden subjects," Parsons said. "Either topic is fine with me."

He got the dutiful laughter he expected.

Then he grew serious.

"General Greene told me that he went to see General Patton shortly before he died. He said the scene was pretty grim."

Well, that's changing the subject, all right.

Where's he going with this?

"It just goes to show, doesn't it, that you never know what tomorrow will bring?" Parsons asked.

"Sir?"

"Losing your life, painfully, as a result of what General Greene said was really nothing but a fender-bender. And then your IG . . . or the CIC's . . . IG?"

Cronley felt his stomach tighten.

Jesus Christ, what does he know, what has he heard, about that?

"Sir?"

"The poor chap goes home for lunch, and his hot water heater blows up. Blows him and his wife up."

"I see what you mean," Cronley said.

And now where are you going to go?

"Let's get off those depressing subjects," Parsons said. "To what? Back to my curiosity, I suppose. I got the feeling, Mr. Cronley, from the way you rattled off 'General-Büros Süd-Deutsche,' et cetera, so smoothly that you're comfortable speaking German?"

"I speak German, Colonel."

"Fluently?"

"Yes, sir. My mother is a Strasbourgerin. A war bride from the First World War. I got my German from her. Colonel Mannberg tells me I could pass myself off as a Strasbourger."

"I'm jealous," Parsons said. "I got what little German I have from West Point, and I was not what you could call a brilliant student of languages. What about you, Captain Dunwiddie? How's your German?"

"I can get by, sir."

"You said before you're from an Army family. Do you also march in the Long Gray Line?"

"No, sir. I'm Norwich."

"Fine school. Did you know that General White, I.D. White, who commanded the 'Hell on Wheels'—the Second Armored Division—went to Norwich?"

"Yes, sir," Dunwiddie said. "I did."

"Warren, like General George Catlett Marshall, went to VMI," Parsons said. "That leaves only you, Mr. Hessinger. I'm not sure if I can ask General Gehlen or Colonel Mannberg, or whether that would be none of my business."

"I never had the privilege of a university education, Colonel," Gehlen said.

Cronley was surprised, both at that, and also that Gehlen had chosen to reply, to furnish information, however harmless it was, about himself.

"I wasn't bright enough to earn a scholarship," Gehlen went on. "My father, who owned a bookstore, couldn't afford to send me to school. Germany was impoverished after the First World War. So I got what education I could from the books in my father's store. And then, the day after I turned eighteen, I joined the Reichswehr as a recruit. My father hated the military, but he was glad to see me go. One less mouth to feed."

What the hell is Gehlen up to? He didn't deliver that personal history lesson just to be polite.

"The what? You joined the what?" Ashley asked.

"The Reichswehr, Major," Hessinger furnished, "was the armed forces of the Weimar Republic. It was limited by the Versailles treaty to eighty-five thousand soldiers and fifteen thousand sailors. No aircraft of any kind. It existed from 1919 to 1935, when Hitler absorbed it into the newly founded Wehrmacht."

Fat Freddy delivered that little lecture because Gehlen delivered his history lesson. Which means he's figured out why Gehlen suddenly decided to chime in.

Why can't I?

Because I'm not as smart as either of them, that's why.

"You seem very familiar with German history, Mr. Hessinger," Parsons said.

"It is the subject of my—interrupted by the draft—doctoral thesis, Colonel."

"And you were where when you were drafted?"

"Harvard, sir."

"But you're German, right?"

"I am an American citizen, sir, who was born in Germany."

"And that leaves you, Colonel Mannberg," Parsons said.

"My university is Philipps-Universität in Marburg an der Lahn, Colonel," Mannberg said.

"Well, truth being stranger than fiction," Parsons said, "I know something about your university, Colonel. Are you aware that your school has been training American intelligence officers since our Civil War? Maybe even before our Civil War? And that we plan to resume that just as soon as we can?"

"I didn't know that you were going to resume that program,

Colonel, but I knew about it. When we were at Philipps, your General Seidel and I were in the same *Brüderschaft*—fraternity."

Is that what Gehlen's been up to? Setting the stage for letting Parsons know that Mannberg and Seidel, the EUCOM G2, are old college fraternity buddies?

And how come Mannberg didn't tell me that?

"How interesting!" Parsons said. "And have you been in touch with General Seidel since the war ended?"

"Yes, I have," Mannberg said. "Actually, he tasked the CIC to find me. And, of course, they did."

And now I will sit here with bated breath waiting to see where all this goes.

It went nowhere.

As they talked, they had been eating.

When they had finished eating, they were through talking.

Parsons said something to the effect that while he hated to leave good company, he "and Warren have a lot on our plates for tomorrow" and that they were "reluctantly going to have to call it a night."

Hands were shaken all around, and thirty seconds later Colonel Parsons and Major Ashley had left.

When they were out of earshot, Gehlen asked, "Jim, would you think that talking this over while it's still fresh in our minds might be a good idea?"

Cronley nodded.

Gehlen, with his usual courtesy, is going to hand me my ass on a platter.

"Why don't we go upstairs to my room?" he said.

[FOUR]
Suite 527
Hotel Vier Jahreszeiten
Maximilianstrasse 178
Munich, American Zone of Occupation, Germany
2155 29 December 1945

Suite 527—an elegantly furnished bedroom, sitting room, bath, and small office—was Cronley's, although he rarely spent the night in it, or for that matter, used it at all.

He had inherited it, so to speak, from the OSS. When Colonel Robert Mattingly had commanded OSS Forward, he had requisitioned all of the fifth floor's right wing for the OSS when it had been decided to put—hide—General Gehlen's people at least temporarily in Kloster Grünau.

Mattingly had no intention of spending his nights on a GI cot in a cold, former, and until very recently, long-deserted former monastery in the middle of nowhere when the five-star Vier Jahreszeiten was available to him.

When the OSS was disbanded, and Mattingly became deputy chief, CIC-Europe, he had put Kloster Grünau under then Second Lieutenant Cronley. And turned Suite 527 over to him. At the time Cronley had thought it was a nice, if misguided, gesture. The very things that made the Vier Jahreszeiten appealing to Mattingly—it was a playground for senior officers and their wives and enforced a strict code of dress and decorum—made it unappealing to a young second lieutenant.

Cronley now believed that it was far less benevolence on Mattingly's part that gave him access to "the fifth floor" than Mattingly's desire to distance himself as far as possible from Kloster Grünau and what was going on there. There was a very good chance that Operation Ost was going to blow up in everyone's face, and Mattingly wanted to be far away when that happened.

"I don't know what's going on at Kloster Grünau. I turned the whole operation over to Cronley. I never went down there. Why, I even gave him my suite in the Vier Jahreszeiten because I never used it.

"Now, as far as FILL IN THE BLANK going so wildly wrong down there under his watch, I certainly don't want to belittle what Cronley did in Argentina, but the cold fact is that he was made a captain before he even had enough time in grade to be promoted to first lieutenant, and he really didn't have the qualifications and experience to properly handle something like Kloster Grünau."

Everyone filed into suite 527 and everyone but Cronley, who leaned against an inner wall, found seats.

The Louis XIV chair under Dunwiddie disappeared under his bulk.

If that collapses, it will add a bit of sorely needed levity to this gathering.

"Gentlemen," Cronley said in a serious tone, "if Captain Dunwiddie will forgo delivering the speech about the havoc a loose cannon can cause rolling about on a dinner table that he's been mentally rehearsing for the past hour, we can go directly to seeing if anything at all can be salvaged from that disastrous dinner."

Dunwiddie and Hessinger shook their heads. Mannberg and Gehlen smiled.

"I will admit, Jim," Gehlen said, "that if you had told us beforehand how you were going to confront Colonel Parsons, it might have gone a little better than it did. But it wasn't a disaster, by any means."

"As you may have noticed, General, I'm a little slow. You don't think that was a total disaster?"

Gehlen shook his head.

"'Know thine enemy,'" Hessinger quoted. "Sun Tzu, *The Art of War*."

"Precisely," Gehlen said.

"It looked to me like we gave him a lot of information about us. But what did we learn about him?" Cronley asked.

"We confirmed much of what we presumed about him," Gehlen said. "Most important, I suggest, we confirmed what I said a few days ago about the greatest danger posed to Operation Ost—that it will come from the Pentagon, not the Russians. And Colonel Parsons is going to be a formidable adversary."

"You think he's that smart, that dangerous?" Cronley asked.

"For several reasons, yes, I do. I presumed the Pentagon was going to send a highly intelligent officer as their liaison officer, since his purpose would go beyond a liaison function. His primary mission is to clip the just-born bud of the Directorate of Central Intelligence before it has a chance to blossom, and return it and its functions to where it belongs, under the assistant chief of staff for intelligence in the Pentagon.

"We saw that Parsons is highly intelligent—and I think Ashley, too, is not quite what he would wish us to believe. In other words,

I judge him to be far more intelligent and competent—and thus more dangerous—than a well-meaning, if not too bright, subordinate who has to be reined in when his enthusiasm gets the better of him."

"You think that 'Shut up, Warren' business was theater, rehearsed theater, sir?" Dunwiddie asked.

"Theater? Yes. Rehearsed? Not necessarily. I would judge the two of them have worked together before. They didn't, they thought, have to rehearse much to deal with a junior captain whom they thought would be facing them alone. That didn't happen. And then the junior captain proved a far more able adversary than they anticipated he would be."

Does he mean that? Or is he being nice? Or charming, for his own purposes?

"What makes Colonel Parsons and Major Ashley especially dangerous is that they believe passionately in their mission," Gehlen said. "Almost Mossad-like."

"Excuse me?" Cronley asked.

"The Zionist intelligence apparatus," Hessinger said.

"And once again, apparently, Hessinger knows all about something I never heard of," Cronley said. "Lecture on, professor."

Gehlen smiled and gestured to Hessinger to continue.

"The Zionists, the Jews," Hessinger explained, "want their own homeland, their own country, in what is now Palestine. Until they get it, they've got sort of a shadow government, *à la* the British. Including an intelligence service. It has many names, but most commonly, the Mossad."

"And are you planning to move to Palestine?" Cronley challenged.

"Not me. I'm an American," Hessinger replied. "I'll do what I can to help the Zionists, of course, but my plan for the future is to become a professor at Harvard."

"I'm glad you brought that up, Friedrich," Gehlen said.

"Sir?"

"'I'll do what I can to help, of course,'" Gehlen parroted. "There are two things that make the Mossad so good, Jim. And they are really good. Even better than the Vatican. One is that they really believe in their cause. The second is what Friedrich just said. Jews all over the world are willing to help them, even eager. Even when helping them violates the law.

"The same, I think, is true of Colonel Parsons and Major Ashley. Not only do they really believe Operation Ost, and the entire DCI, should be under the Pentagon, but as Jews all over, like our friend Friedrich here, are willing to help the Mossad, so will just about everybody in the Army support Parsons and Ashley."

"I got the feeling earlier today that General Smith is on our side," Cronley said.

"I'm sure he is. But I am not sure about every member of his staff who is in a position to help Colonel Parsons and hurt the DCI."

"For the good of the service," Dunwiddie said, drily sarcastic.

"Jesus Christ!" Cronley said. "So what it boils down to is that it's us against just about everybody."

"President Truman seems to be on our side. Or vice versa," Gehlen said.

"Even though we're the good guys," Cronley went on, "maybe what we should do is connect somehow with this Mossad. Maybe they could show us where we can get some help. Right now, I feel like Custer at the Little Big Horn. Where did all these Indians come from?"

He expected a chuckle, or at least a smile, from Gehlen and the others. Dunwiddie and Hessinger did in fact smile. But Gehlen's face was expressionless.

"You're a Jew, Freddy," Cronley went on. "How's chances you can get your co-religionists, the super spies of Mossad, to come galloping to our rescue before we're scalped?"

Hessinger, smiling, gave him the finger.

"Actually, in a sense, that's already happening," Gehlen said.

"Sir?"

What the hell is he talking about?

"Seven-K in Leningrad is a double agent. She's an NKGB officer and a Mossad agent," Gehlen said.

"My God!" Cronley said.

Gehlen smiled and nodded, and then went on: "One of the things Mossad is very good at is getting Jews out of Russia. When I realized getting Mrs. Likharev and her children out of Russia was really important, I asked her to help."

This is surreal. His agent—which means our agent—in Leningrad is an agent—a female agent—of this super Jewish intelligence organization—Mossad—that I never heard of?

"Why would she do that?" Hessinger asked before Cronley could open his mouth to ask the identical question.

"Over the years, we have been helpful to one another," Gehlen said. "I thought of that when Colonel Parsons told us he has had little experience with the 'nitty-gritty' side of intelligence. This is the nitty-gritty side."

"I'm lost," Cronley confessed.

"You're aware that middle-to-high-level swine in the Schutzstaffel grew rich by allowing foreign Jews—so-called *Ausländer Juden*—particularly those in the United States—to buy their relatives and friends out of the death camps and to safety in Argentina or Paraguay?"

"Cletus Frade told me," Cronley said.

"I hadn't heard about that," Dunwiddie said.

"Once the ransom money had been paid, Tiny," Gehlen explained, "SS officers would go to Dachau or Auschwitz or wherever and remove the prisoners 'for interrogation.' They were not questioned, because the camps were run by the SS. Nor were they questioned when they reported the prisoners had died during interrogation. That happened often during SS interrogation.

"What actually happened to the prisoners was that they were taken first to Spain, and then to Portugal, where they boarded vessels of neutral powers for transportation to South America.

"When this came to my attention, I knew I couldn't stop it. The corruption went right to the top of the Nazi hierarchy. If not to Heinrich Himmler himself, then to those very close to him. But the idea of getting people out of prison camps had a certain fascination for me. I didn't understand the fascination, but it was there. I told Ludwig here, and Oberst Niedermeyer—you met Otto in Argentina, right, Jim?"

"Yes, sir."

"I told them to think about it, and Otto came up with Mossad. We knew they had been active in the Soviet Union for a long time. The question then became what did we have that they wanted? And the corollary, what did they have that we wanted?"

"What was the Mossad doing in Russia?" Cronley asked.

"Zion's business," Mannberg said. "Somehow that had gone right over my head—and if I may say so, the general's."

"I don't know what that means," Cronley said.

"What they were interested in was this homeland they want in Palestine. It didn't really matter to them whether the Soviets won the war, or we did," Mannberg said, and then clarified, "*The Germans* did. What they wanted to do was get as many Zionist leaders out of Russia as they could. The Soviets, who didn't trust them, had jailed many of them, sent them to Siberia, or had them locked up in concentration camps."

"When Germany moved into Russia," Gehlen picked up Mannberg's narrative, "and took over the NKGB prison camps, the SS either killed all the Jews they found in them on the spot, or marched them off to become laborers. And among the people the SS marched off were many of the Zionist leaders Mossad wanted to get out of Russia and to Palestine.

"So, more than a little belatedly, I realized there was common cause between Abwehr Ost and Mossad. They had penetrated the highest levels of the Kremlin, far more successfully than we had. On the other hand, my people, especially those who were in the SS, could get into the SS prison and slave labor systems. And get people out of them with the same ease—actually far more ease—than the SS could take prisoners from the death camps.

"So I arranged to meet with the lady who was to become Seven-K."

"How did you know with whom to meet?"

"We knew who she was. Her given name is Rahil, by the way."

"What?"

"Rahil—Russian for Rachel," Gehlen said.

"Jesus!"

"I thought you would find that interesting," Gehlen said.

"Interesting?" Dunwiddie asked. "Fascinating! Two spies named Rachel."

"Fuck you, Tiny!" Cronley flared.

"Temper, temper, Captain, sir," Dunwiddie said.

"You're never going to forget that, are you?"

"Probably not, and I'm not going to let you forget Rachel, either."

"Now I don't know what anybody's talking about," Hessinger said. "Who the hell is Rachel? You're not talking about Colonel Schumann's wife . . . Or are—"

"Private joke, Freddy," Dunwiddie said. "Sorry."

"As I was saying," Gehlen said, "I arranged, with some difficulty, to meet with Seven-K in Vienna. In the Hotel Sacher. Before she met me, I had to turn Ludwig over to some of her people, to guarantee her safe return. But finally we met, and over Sachertorte and coffee—"

"Over what?" Cronley asked.

"A chocolate layer cake for which the Hotel Sacher is famous," Hessinger furnished. "I had my first when I was eight or nine, and still remember how delicious it was."

"Ours, unfortunately, was not," Gehlen said. "It was made with powdered eggs and ersatz sugar, and the coffee was made from acorns, but nevertheless, we struck our first deal.

"If she would get me certain information, I would try to get two people, two Zionists, out of the hands of the SS. She gave me the names, and Ludwig got them out of an SS-run factory in Hungary. I don't think they were Zionists, but she got me the information I asked for."

"How could you know it was the right information?"

"The general knew the answers before he posed the question," Mannberg said.

"You may have noticed, Ludwig, my tendency to ask stupid questions," Cronley said.

"Now that you mention it, Captain, sir . . ." Dunwiddie said.

Mannberg chuckled.

"I would suggest to the both of you," Gehlen said, on the edge of unpleasantness, "that Captain Cronley's ability to get his mind around all aspects of a statement, to question everything about a situation, not only is useful, but is far greater than your own. Jim, I hope you always ask whatever questions occur to you."

He let that sink in a moment, and then went on.

"I was impressed with her from the first. Her ability to get from Moscow, where she was then stationed, to Vienna proved that she was high-ranking. It required false identity documents, et cetera, and carried the real risk that it was an Abwehr Ost plan to seize her.

"I don't know this, but I suspect she told Nikolayevich Merkulov, the commissar of state security, or his deputy, Ivan Serov, that I had made overtures. They had to give her permission to go to Vienna. Why did they do so? For much the same reasons that I authorized Ludwig to meet with Mr. Dulles in Bern, when he first made overtures to me, to see what the head of OSS Europe had in mind.

"But what to keep in mind here is that what Rahil wanted to learn was what she might get from Abwehr Ost that would benefit Mossad, and only secondarily the NKGB.

"What is that phrase, Jim, you so often use? 'Cutting to the chase'? Cutting to the chase here, very slowly, very carefully, Rahil and I developed mutual trust. I was useful to her, and she was useful to me. Much of what I learned about the plans of the NKGB for Abwehr Ost personnel when they won the war, I learned from Rahil."

He paused for a moment and then went on.

"And much of what the NKGB initially learned about Mr. Dulles's postwar plans for Abwehr Ost, they learned from me. It was what you call a 'tough call,' but in the end I decided it was necessary to tell her. It further cemented both our relationship with her and hers with her superiors in the NKGB.

"But I was not in contact with her from the time I surrendered to Major Wallace until I decided the importance of getting Mrs. Likharev out of Russia justified the risk. I wasn't sure, when I told Ludwig to try to reestablish the link, that she was still alive, or more importantly would be willing to reestablish our relationship.

"Fortunately for us, she has apparently decided—and let me restate this—that the good the Süd-Deutsche Industrielle Entwicklungsorganisation can do *for the Mossad* justifies the risks entailed in getting the Likharevs out of Russia."

"What good can we do Mossad?" Cronley asked.

"Rahil will think of something," Gehlen said. "And if she manages to get the Likharevs out, we will be in her debt."

"Yes, we will," Cronley thought out loud.

"I don't think Colonel Parsons even suspects anything about the Likharev situation," Gehlen said. "And we have to keep it that way. It's just the sort of thing he's looking for."

"I don't see where that will be a problem," Cronley said.

"The problems that cause the most trouble are often the ones one doesn't suspect will happen," Gehlen said.

No one replied.

"If you don't have anything else for us, Jim," Gehlen went on, "may I suggest we're through here?"

"I'll drive you to Pullach, General," Hessinger said. "I'm going to need the Kapitän in the morning."

"I'll drive everybody to Pullach," Cronley said. "I have to go to Kloster Grünau. When do you need the car in the morning?"

"Nine. Nine-thirty. No later than ten."

"I'll either have one of Tiny's guys bring it back tonight, or I'll bring it back in the morning."

"You want me to go with you, Jim?"

"No. Thank you, but no."

"What do you have to do tonight at Kloster Grünau?" Dunwiddie asked.

"There's a problem with one of the Storchs. I promised Schröder I'd have a look at it."

"Tonight?"

"I promised him yesterday."

That's all bullshit. Schröder didn't say anything about a problem with a Storch.

What I want to do is have a little time to think, and I won't have it if I stay in Pullach, and I don't want to spend the night in the Vier Jahreszeiten.

But I didn't have to think about coming up with an excuse to go to Kloster Grünau. The excuse—the story, the bullshit, the lie—leapt to my lips.

Why am I surprised?

Everybody in this surreal world I'm now living in lies so often about everything, and I'm so used to that it never even occurred to me to tell the simple truth that I need some time to think.

[FIVE]
Kloster Grünau
Schollbrunn, Bavaria
American Zone of Occupation, Germany
0015 30 December 1945

The conclusion Cronley reached after thinking all the way to Kloster Grünau was that not only would he be way over his head when he became chief, DCI-Europe, but that Admiral Souers damned well knew it.

So why isn't there some grizzled full-bird colonel available to do what I'm clearly unqualified to do?

The non-availability of such a grizzled full-bird colonel—and Lieutenant Colonel Maxwell T. "Polo" Ashton would not qualify as even a grizzled lieutenant colonel even if he showed up here, which, considering his broken leg and other infirmities, I now think seems highly unlikely—was not a satisfactory answer to the question.

So what to do?

Face it that Gehlen has taken over Operation Ost.

Not for any political reasons, but because nature abhors a vacuum.

So how do I handle that?

Sit there with my ears open and my mouth shut?

It's already obvious that he and ol' Ludwig are only telling me what they think I can be trusted to know.

Not one word about Mata Hari, the super Mossad spy, until tonight.

A/K/A Rachel.

And didn't Fat Freddy pick up on that?

Does he suspect anything? Fat Freddy is pretty damned smart.

So what do I do about Gehlen not telling me what I should be told?

"See here, General, you and ol' Ludwig are going to have to tell me everything."

To which he would say, "Absolutely," and tell me not one goddamned thing he doesn't think I should know.

So what should I do?

Admit you don't have a fucking clue what to do, and place your faith in the truism that God takes care of fools and drunks and you fully qualify as both.

When he drove the Kapitän past the second barrier fence, Cronley saw that floodlights were on in the tent hangar built for the Storchs.

Maybe something is wrong with one of them. Truth being stranger than fiction.

He drove to the hangar.

Kurt Schröder was working on the vertical stabilizer assembly of one of them. And apparently being assisted by Lieutenant Max—whose name Cronley was wholly unsure he could ever pronounce.

Schröder seemed surprised to see him. Maksymilian Ostrowski looked as if he had been caught with his hand in the candy jar.

"We've got a frayed cable, not serious, but I thought I'd replace it," Schröder said.

"And drafted Lieutenant Max to help you?"

"I hope that's all right, sir," Ostrowski said.

"Fine with me, if it's okay with Kurt."

Cronley's half-formed wild idea about the Pole popped back into his mind.

Where the hell did that come from?

And now that it's back and I'm entirely sober, I can see it's really off the wall.

Or is it?

Why the hell not?

Who's going to tell me no?

None of us are supposed to be flying the Storchs, so what's the difference?

"Tell me, Max," Cronley said, "what's the name of your guy who served with the Free French?"

"Jaworski, Pawell Jaworski, sir."

"Could *Pawell Jaworski* take over the guard detachment?"

Ostrowski thought it over for a long moment.

"Yes, sir. I'm sure he could."

"Okay. On your way to bed, wake him up and tell him that as of 0600 tomorrow, that's what he'll be doing,"

"Yes, sir," Ostrowski said. "Captain, may I ask what this is about?"

"Oh, I guess I didn't get into that, did I?"

"No, sir, you did not."

"Presuming, of course, that Kurt can get that vertical stabilizer assembly back together and working, what he's going to do at 0600 is start checking you out on the Storch."

"Checking me out?"

"They didn't use that term in the Free Polish Air Force?"

"Yes, sir. I know what it means."

"Try not to bend my airplane, Max. I've grown rather fond of it."

Cronley turned and walked out of the tent hangar.

That was probably a stupid thing to do.

Colonel Mattingly would almost certainly think so.

But since I'll be running, as of January 2, DCI-Europe, I don't have to worry about what that bastard thinks.

That's my plan for the future.

Do whatever the hell I think will be good for Operation Ost, and keep doing it until somebody hands me my ass on a shovel.

Abraham Lincoln Tedworth, his sleeves now adorned with the first sergeant's chevrons to which he had been entitled since 1700 the previous day, was waiting for him when he walked into the bar.

"This came in about ten minutes ago, Captain."

He handed Cronley a SIGABA printout.

"Top, I just relieved Lieutenant Max as commander of the Polish Guard," Cronley announced.

"With all respect, sir, that was a dumb move."

That's what they call loyalty downward.

"I deeply appreciate your unfailing confidence in my command decisions, First Sergeant."

"Well, you better reconsider that one. Max is a damned good man."

"That's why I am transferring him to the Operation Ost Air Force. I told Schröder to check him out in a Storch."

Tedworth thought that over for a minute, and then announced, "Now that, sir, is a fine command decision."

"I'm glad you approve, First Sergeant," Cronley said, and then read the SIGABA printout:

PRIORITY

TOP SECRET LINDBERGH

DUPLICATION FORBIDDEN

FROM POLO

VIA VINT HILL TANGO NET

2210 GREENWICH 30 DECEMBER 1945

TO ALTARBOY

UNDERSIGNED WILL ARRIVE RHINE-MAIN MATS FLIGHT 343 ETA 0900 2 JANUARY 1946. USUAL HONORS WILL NOT BE REQUIRED. A SMALL BRASS BAND WILL SUFFICE.

POLO

END

TOP SECRET LINDBERGH

IV

[ONE]

Arriving Passenger Terminal
Rhine-Main USAF Base
Frankfurt am Main
American Zone, Occupied Germany
0915 2 January 1946

Cronley watched through the windows of the terminal building as the passengers debarked from the Military Air Transport Service Douglas C-54 "Skymaster," which had just flown—via Gander, Newfoundland, and Prestwick, Scotland—from Washington.

The procession down the ladder and into the terminal building was led by a major general, two brigadier generals, some other brass. Then came four senior non-coms, and finally a long line of women and children. They were "dependents" joining their husbands, called "sponsors," in the Army of Occupation.

When the dependents came into the terminal, they were emotionally greeted by the sponsors in a touching display of connubial affection.

Cronley's mind filled with the memory of his explaining the system to the Squirt at Camp Holabird the day they were married. The day before the drunken sonofabitch in the eighteen-wheeler ran head-on into her on US-1 in Washington.

He forced his mind off the subject.

No one was coming down the stairway.

What did you do, Polo? Miss the goddamn plane?

And then Lieutenant Colonel Maxwell Ashton III appeared in the door of the aircraft. In pinks and greens. He was on crutches. His right leg and left arm were in casts.

He stared down the stairs. Then, apparently deciding the crutches would be useless, he threw them down the stairs.

Jesus, he's going to try to hop down the stairs!

"Go get him, Tiny," Cronley ordered. "Before he breaks his other leg."

"They won't let me out there," Dunwiddie protested.

"Show them the goddamn CIC badge and go get him!"

"Right."

"And you go with him, and get the crutches," Cronley ordered.

"Yes, sir," Maksymilian Ostrowski said, and headed for the door.

Ostrowski was wearing, as Cronley was, a U.S. Army woolen olive-drab Ike jacket and trousers with "civilian" triangles sewn to the lapels. Dunwiddie was in pinks and greens.

Cronley, after thinking about it overnight, had decided to have Ostrowski fly the second Storch from Kloster Grünau to Rhine-Main to meet Ashton. For one thing, Schröder had reported—not surprisingly, since Ostrowski had been flying Spitfires and Hurricanes—that it had taken less than an hour for him to be convinced the Pole could fly a Storch. For another, Ostrowski spoke "British English" fluently. When he called the Rhine-Main control tower, that would not cause suspicion, as Schröder's heavily German-accented English would.

But the real reason he had ordered Ostrowski to fly the second Storch was to test his theory that he could—DCI-Europe could—get away with not only flying the Storchs that were supposed to be grounded, *but* having them flown by a German and a Pole, and hiding both behind CIC credentials to which they were not entitled.

It would either work or it wouldn't. If they suddenly found themselves being detained by outraged Air Force officers—or for that matter, outraged Army officers—calling for somebody's scalp, better to have that happen now, when Ashton was in Germany. A newly promoted lieutenant colonel might not be able to do much against the forces aligned against DCI-Europe, but he would have a lot more clout than a newly promoted captain.

Tiny, flashing his CIC wallet, and with Ostrowski on his heels, got past the Air Force sergeant keeping people from going onto the tarmac, and without trouble.

The young sergeant might have been dazzled by the CIC credentials, Cronley thought. But it was equally possible that he had been dazzled by an enormous, very black captain he knew he could not physically restrain from going anywhere he wanted to.

As Tiny started up the stairs, two at a time, another man appeared in the airplane door. A stocky, somewhat florid-faced man in his late forties, wearing the uniform of a U.S. Navy lieutenant.

He was somehow familiar.

Jesus Christ! That's El Jefe!

The last time Cronley had seen Lieutenant Oscar J. Schultz, USNR, he had been wearing the full regalia of an Argentine gaucho, a billowing white shirt over billowing black trousers; a gaily printed scarf; a wide-brimmed leather hat; knee-high black leather boots; a wide, silver-coin-adorned leather belt, and, tucked into the belt, the silver scabbard of a horn-handled knife the size of a cavalry saber.

El Jefe had once been Chief Radioman Oscar Schultz of the destroyer USS *Alfred Thomas*, DD-107, hence the reference *El Jefe*, the chief. Schultz had been drafted into the OSS by then-Captain Cletus Frade, USMCR, when the *Thomas* had sailed into Buenos Aires on a friendly visit to the neutral Argentine Republic. And also to surreptitiously put ashore a radar set and a SIGABA communications system for the OSS.

Frade thought he needed a highly skilled, Spanish-speaking (El Jefe had done two tours at the U.S. Navy base at Cavite in the Philippines) communications and radar expert more than the *Thomas* did, and General William Donovan, then head of the OSS, had not only agreed, but had had a word with the chief of naval operations.

Two days later, the *Thomas* had sailed from Buenos Aires without Chief Schultz. Schultz set up shop on Estancia San Pedro y San Pablo, Frade's enormous ranch, where Cronley had met him, and where he had quickly acquired both the regalia of a gaucho and a Rubenesque lady friend, who became known as "the other Dorotea," the first being Señora Dorotea Frade.

More importantly, he had become an important member of "Team Turtle," the code name for Frade's OSS operation in Argentina. So important that he had been given a direct commission as an officer.

What the hell is El Jefe doing here?

Before the question had run through his mind, Cronley knew the answer.

Admiral Souers, knowing that Polo would refuse the assistance of a nurse, even a male nurse, although he really needed it, had ordered Schultz up from Argentina so that he could assist and protect Polo while he traveled to Germany and then back to Argentina.

That noble idea seemed to be destined to become a spectacular disaster.

As Tiny bounded up the stairway, El Jefe, seeing an enormous black man headed for his charge, started bounding down them to defend him.

Cronley recalled Cletus Frade telling him that El Jefe enjoyed the deep respect of the gauchos of the estancia, despite his refusal to get on a horse, because he had become both the undisputed bare-knuckles pugilist of the estancia and the undisputed hand-wrestling champion. Gauchos add spice, Cletus had told him, to their hand-wrestling fun by holding hands over their unsheathed razor-sharp knives.

Captain Dunwiddie and Lieutenant Schultz had a brief conversation near the top of the stairs. Then, suddenly, as if they had practiced the action for months, they had Polo in a "handbasket" between them and were carrying him—like the bridegroom at a Hebrew wedding—down the stairs, across the tarmac, and into the passenger terminal.

Cronley was surprised that no one seemed to pay much attention.

"Welcome to occupied Germany," Cronley said, as Schultz and Dunwiddie set Ashton on his feet and Ostrowski handed him his crutches. "Please keep in mind that VD walks the streets tonight, and penicillin fails once in seven times."

Ashton shook his head.

"Thanks," he said to Dunwiddie, Schultz, and Ostrowski. "Where's the colonel?"

"Which colonel would that be?"

"Mattingly."

"I don't know. I hope he's far from here."

"The admiral said I should see him as soon as I got here. I've got a letter for him. What do you mean you hope he's far from here?"

A letter? From Souers to Mattingly? Why does that scare me?

"We're going to have to have a little chat before you see him," Cronley said. He gestured toward the door. "Your ambulance awaits."

"I don't need an ambulance."

"You do unless you want to walk all the way across Rhine-Main airfield."

"What's all the way across the field?"

"The Storchs in which we are going to fly to Kloster Grünau—the monastery—to have our little chat."

"How they hanging, kid?" Schultz demanded of Captain Cronley.

"One beside the other. How about yours?"

"I don't have to tell you, do I, about how lousy I feel about what happened to the Squirt?"

"No. But thank you."

"I really liked that little broad," Schultz said. "Mean as a snake, but nice, you know?"

"Yeah," Cronley said.

"You know, Jim, that you have my condolences," Max Ashton said. "Tragic!"

Cronley saw the sympathy, the compassion, in their eyes.

[TWO]
Kloster Grünau
Schollbrunn, Bavaria
American Zone of Occupation, Germany
1340 2 January 1946

Lieutenant Colonel Maxwell Ashton III tapped the remnants of his steak on his plate with his knife and fork and then announced, "Not too bad. Not grass-fed on the pampas, of course, and—not to look the gift horse in the mouth—this red wine frankly does not have the *je ne sais quoi* of an Estancia Don Guillermo Cabernet Sauvignon. But one must expect to make certain sacrifices when one goes off to battle the Red Menace on foreign shores, mustn't one?"

He got the dutiful chuckles he expected.

"Colonel Frade came to see me shortly before El Jefe and I got on the airplane—" Ashton began to go on.

"In Washington?" Cronley interrupted. "Cletus is in Washington?"

"He was there briefly en route to Pensacola, Florida, where he will be released from active service in the United States Marine Corps. I appreciate your interest, but I would appreciate even more your permitting me to continue."

"Sorry."

"Colonel Frade was kind enough to offer a few suggestions vis-à-vis my trip here. He recommended that should Colonel Mattingly not be able to find time in his busy schedule to meet me at Frankfurt, so that I might give him Admiral Souers's letter—"

"Why did he think Mattingly was going to meet you at Rhine-Main?" Cronley interrupted again.

Ashton ignored the interruption and went on, "I should ask whoever met us to take us to the Schlosshotel Kronberg, where we could rest in luxurious accommodations overnight, to recuperate from our journey. Then, the following morning, I could go to the I.G. Farben Building to meet with Colonel Mattingly, deliver the admiral's letter to him, and perhaps meet with General Greene and possibly even General Smith.

"Following that meeting, or meetings, Colonel Frade suggested we then reserve a compartment on a railroad train charmingly entitled 'the Blue Danube' and travel to Munich to meet with you, Captain Cronley, your staff, and General Gehlen, preferably at the Hotel Vier Jahreszeiten, which he assured me would provide El Jefe and myself luxury accommodations equal to those of the Schlosshotel Kronberg.

"Instead . . . as someone once said, 'the best-laid plans gang aft agley,' which I suspect means get royally fucked up . . . Captain Cronley meets us at the airport, tells me he has no idea where Colonel Mattingly is, but that he hopes wherever he is it is far away. He then stuffs me into the really uncomfortable backseat of a little airplane and flies me through every storm cloud he could find to a medieval monastery in the middle of fucking nowhere."

Cronley smiled, but he recalled seeing—a dozen times, more—Ashton wince with pain as the Storch had been tossed about by turbulence during the flight from Frankfurt.

"Now, one would suspect," Ashton went on, "that, in normal

circumstances, this deviation from the plan would annoy, perhaps even anger, your new commanding officer. These are not normal circumstances, however.

"I was given the opportunity, first while lying in my bed of pain in Walter Reed, and then whilst flying across the Atlantic, and finally as I flew here from Frankfurt, to consider what the circumstances really are.

"To start, let me go back to the beginning. The admiral came to see me at Walter Reed. Bearing my new silver oak leaves. He told me they were intended more as an inducement for me to stay on active duty than a recognition of my superior leadership characteristics.

"I then told him I didn't need an inducement to stay on active duty, as I was determined to get the bastards who did this to me."

He raised his broken arm.

"He immediately accepted my offer, which I thought surprised him more than a little. Not immediately, but right after he left, I began to wonder why. The cold facts seemed to be that not only was I going to have to hobble around on crutches for the next several months, but—more importantly—I was in fact no more qualified to take over Operation Ost from Colonel Frade than Jim was to handle Operation Ost in Germany.

"Certainly, I reasoned, although I had heard time and again that finding experienced people for the new DCI was going to be difficult, there had to be two or three or four experienced spooks—Colonel Mattingly–like senior spooks—who had joined the ranks of the unemployed when the OSS went out of business, who would be available. And Colonel Frade had made the point over and over that not all members, just an overwhelming majority of officers of the conventional intelligence operations, were unable to find their asses using both hands.

"I came up with a theory immediately, but dismissed it as really off the wall.

"And then I was given the letter—the carefully sealed letter in the double envelope—to deliver to Colonel Mattingly. 'What,' I wondered, 'does the admiral wish to tell Colonel Mattingly that he doesn't want me to know?'

"When I thought, at length, about this, my initial off-the-wall theory started coming back, and each time it did it made more sense.

"The conclusion I reached, after considering everything, is that Admiral Souers has decided that you and I, Jim—and of course Captain Dunwiddie—are expendable. I have also concluded that Colonel Frade—whatever his limitations are, no one has ever accused him of being slow—is, if not party to this, fully aware of it."

"How do you mean 'expendable,' Colonel?" Dunwiddie asked.

"Available for sacrifice for the greater good," Ashton said. "Consider this, please. To whom does Admiral Souers—with absolute justification—owe his primary loyalty?"

"The President," Cronley said softly. "Oh, Jesus!"

"Who must be protected whatever it takes," Ashton said.

"Why are you telling us this?" Dunwiddie asked.

"Well, after thinking it over, I decided that—as far as I'm concerned—it's all right. What we're doing is important. But I decided that it would be dishonest of me, now that I've figured it out, not to tell you. Before we go further, in other words, I wanted you to have the opportunity to opt out."

"'Before we go further'?" Dunwiddie parroted.

"What I've decided to do is live with the possibility, actually the probability, that Operation Ost is going to blow up in my face, and that when that happens, Souers, as he should, is going to throw me to the wolves to protect the President. And for that matter, Eisenhower and Smith. That's one of the things I've decided."

"And the others?" Cronley asked.

"That if Operation Ost blows up in my face, it's going to be because of a bad decision of mine. Not because Mattingly or General Greene 'suggest' something to me and I dutifully follow their suggestion to do—more importantly, not to do—something and it blows up."

"For instance?" Cronley asked softly.

"For instance, Colonel Frade suggested to me that I should act 'with great caution' in dealing with our traitor. I don't intend to heed that advice. My first priority is going to be finding out who the sonofabitch is, and then putting out his lights. I don't care if he spent three years holding Gehlen's hand on the Russian front, and has Joe Stalin's girlfriend's phone number, he's a dead man."

"By traitor, you mean the man who let the NKGB know we were sending Colonel Likharev to Argentina?" Cronley asked.

"With all the details of when and how," Ashton confirmed. "Gehlen has to be taught that he's working for us, and that our deal with him is to protect his people from the Russians. The deal didn't include protecting his people from us. He has to be taught, right now, that we won't tolerate a loose cannon."

"There are people in Gehlen's organization who are working for the NKGB—"

"You already had figured that out, huh?"

"And we're working on finding out who they are."

"'We're' meaning you and Gehlen, right? Isn't that what's called sending the fox into the chicken coop to see what happened to the hens? Frankly, Jim, I thought you had more sense than that."

"You will be astonished, Colonel, when I tell you how little sense I have had."

"What the hell does that mean?"

"Shortly after I returned from Argentina, I met a woman. The wife of the CIC-Europe IG. Shortly after that—"

"Wait a minute! You're talking about this woman whose water heater blew up?"

Cronley nodded.

"There has to be a point to this narrative of your sexual exploits."

"I told her about Colonel Sergei Likharev, then known to us as Major Konstantin Orlovsky, about whom she had heard from her husband and was curious. And the night I put him on the plane to Buenos Aires, I told her about that."

"And she ran her mouth?"

"I don't think they call it running the mouth when an NKGB agent reports to her superiors the intelligence she was sent to get."

Ashton looked at Cronley for a long moment.

"You're saying the wife of the CIC IG was an NKGB agent?" he asked incredulously.

"We're saying that both of them, the IG, too, were NKGB agents," Dunwiddie said.

"And the water heater explosion?"

"My orders from Colonel Frade, about finding and dealing with the leak, were to get out of General Gehlen's way when he was dealing with it. I complied with that order."

"And didn't tell Mattingly, or Greene—for that matter, Frade—about your suspicions?"

"They weren't suspicions. The only way the NKGB could have learned about our sending Likharev to Argentina, and when and how, was from my loving Rachel," Cronley said.

"And, as the general pointed out," Dunwiddie said, "a day or two after we caught Likharev sneaking out of here, Colonel Schumann showed up here and demanded to be let in. It took shooting his engine out with a .50 caliber Browning to keep him out. The general suggested Colonel Schumann's interest in Kloster Grünau was because he suspected we had Orlovsky/Likharev."

"My God!" Ashton said.

"Gehlen further suggested that how Jim planned to deal with the situation wasn't practical."

"He said it was childish," Cronley corrected him.

"And this impractical, childish situation was?" Ashton asked.

"I was going to shoot both of them and then go tell Mattingly why."

"General Gehlen said Jim going to the stockade . . ."

"Or the hangman's noose," Cronley interjected.

". . . made no sense."

"You didn't even consider going to Mattingly and telling him what you suspected? You just—"

"You're going to have to learn that when you tell Mattingly anything . . ." Cronley interrupted.

"I'm going to have to learn?" Ashton interrupted. "I don't think I like you telling me anything I *have* to do."

". . . Mattingly will look at it through the prism of what's good for Colonel Robert Mattingly," Cronley finished.

"Did you just hear what I said, Captain Cronley?"

"Yeah, Colonel Ashton, I heard. But you better get used to it. That won't be the last time I'll tell you what I think you have to do. Don't get blinded by those silver oak leaves. What the hell makes you think you can get off the plane and start telling us what to do? You don't know enough of what's going—"

"Enough," Tiny boomed. "Goddamn it! Both of you, stop right there!"

He sounded like the first sergeant he had so recently been, counseling two PFCs who were doing something really stupid.

And then, as if he had heard what he said, and was now cognizant that captains cannot talk to lieutenant colonels as if they are PFCs doing something really stupid, he went on jocularly, "In the immortal words of the great lover of our revolutionary era, the revered Benjamin Franklin, 'We must hang together, gentlemen, else, we shall most assuredly hang separately.'"

Ashton glowered at him for a long moment.

Finally he said, "Actually, Jim, I must admit the little fellow has a point."

"Every once in a great while, he's right about something," Cronley said, and then added, "I was out of line. I apologize."

"Apology rejected as absolutely unnecessary," Ashton said.

After a moment, he went on. "So what's next?"

"Before we get to what's next," El Jefe said, "I have a request."

"For what?"

"Is there a .45 around here that I can have?"

"Why do you want a .45?" Dunwiddie asked.

"Well, when people try to kill me, I like to have something to defend myself."

When there was no reply, El Jefe went on.

"This Colonel Mattingly of yours may think a gas leak took out this CIC colonel and his wife, but I don't think the NKGB is swallowing that line. I think they may want to come back here and play tit for tat."

"They already have," Cronley said. "A week ago, Ostrowski killed two of them. They already had a wire garrote around Sergeant Tedworth's neck."

"Correct me if I'm wrong," El Jefe said, "but following that, it was really heads-up around here, right? Double the guard, that sort of thing?"

Cronley and Dunwiddie nodded.

"So I think what these Communists will do is wait until you relax a little, and then try it again. At least that's what the Chinese Communists did."

"The Chinese?" Ashton and Cronley said on top of one another.

"When I was a young sailor, I did two hitches with the Yangtze River Patrol. The Chinese Communists were always trying to kill us. What they did was try. If that failed, they waited patiently until we relaxed a little and then tried again. And again. Most of the time, that worked. We used to say we got double time for retirement because the Navy knew most of us wouldn't live long enough to retire."

"Interesting," Dunwiddie said. "That's how the Apaches operated."

"Two things, Captain Cronley," Ashton said. "When you get Lieutenant Schultz a .45, would you get me one, too?"

"Yes, sir."

"And one last question. If you didn't want to go to Colonel Mattingly with it, why didn't you go to General Greene and tell him what you suspected—all right, knew—about Colonel Whatsisname and his wife?"

Dunwiddie answered for him: "General Gehlen said that the Schumanns were sure to have contingency plans—ranging from denial through disappearing—in case they were exposed. He said he didn't think we could afford to take the chance they were outwitting us. Jim and I agreed with him."

"So you went along with having Gehlen clip them," Ashton said.

"We don't *know* that Gehlen had them clipped," Cronley said.

"You don't know the sun will come up in the morning, either. But you would agree it's likely, right?"

When Cronley didn't reply, Ashton said, "I suggest, operative word, 'suggest,' that our next step is to meet with General Gehlen."

"I respectfully suggest our next step is getting the .45s," El Jefe said. "*Then* we can go talk to this general."

"Every once in a great while, the chief's right about something," Ashton said.

[THREE]
Kloster Grünau
Schollbrunn, Bavaria
American Zone of Occupation, Germany
1520 2 January 1946

CIC Special Agent Friedrich Hessinger and a very large, very black sergeant with a Thompson submachine gun cradled in his arms like a hunter's shotgun walked into the officers' mess.

Captain J. D. Cronley, Captain Chauncey L. Dunwiddie, First Sergeant Abraham Lincoln Tedworth, and a man in a naval officer's uniform were sitting at the bar drinking coffee. A lieutenant colonel sitting in a chair, with his en-casted leg resting on a small table, also held a coffee cup.

The sergeant smiled and, without disturbing the Thompson, saluted.

"Those captain's bars look good on you, Top," he said.

Dunwiddie returned the salute.

"Flattery will get you everywhere," he said. "Thanks, Eustis."

"And these stripes?" Tedworth asked, pointing to his chevrons. "How do they look on me?"

"Every once in a while, the Army makes a really big mistake," the sergeant said.

"That will cost you, Eustis. Sooner or later that will really cost you," Tedworth replied. "Now, get over to the motor pool and tell them to have an ambulance, with a couch, ready in ten minutes. We're going into Munich."

"And then come back here?"

"Wait there until I send for you."

"You got it, Top."

When he had gone, Cronley said, "Good man."

"Yes, he is," Dunwiddie agreed. "When he's told to do something, he does it. Not like some fat Kraut-Americans, like the one I'm looking at."

Hessinger held up both hands, a gesture that meant both that he didn't understand and that he surrendered.

"Captain Cronley, did you, or did you not, tell Fat Freddy to arm himself before driving out here?"

"I recall saying something along those lines to Special Agent Hessinger, yes," Cronley said.

"'Sorry, sir. No excuse, sir' will not be a satisfactory excuse, Sergeant Hessinger," Dunwiddie said.

Hessinger hoisted the skirt of his tunic. The butt of a Model 1911A1 .45 ACP pistol became visible above his hip.

"Say 'I apologize' to Freddy," Cronley said, laughing. And then he added, "Come here, Freddy, I want to see that holster."

Hessinger complied.

"Where the hell did you get that?"

"I had a shoemaker make half a dozen of them," Hessinger replied. "They call them 'Secret Service High Rise Cross Draw Holsters.' There was a schematic in one of the books on General Greene's sergeant major's shelf."

"Colonel Ashton, Lieutenant Schultz, meet Special Agent

Hessinger, sometimes known as 'One Surprise After Another Hessinger,'" Cronley said.

They shook hands.

"Your funny accent," El Jefe said. "What are you, German?"

"I was. Now I am an American."

"Can I have a look at that holster?" Ashton asked.

Hessinger hoisted the skirt of his tunic again and said, "They also work under an Ike jacket, Colonel."

Schultz took a good look, and then asked, "Who would I have to kill to get one of them?"

Hessinger didn't say anything, but he looked at Dunwiddie.

Cronley laughed.

"I have enough for everybody," Hessinger said. "I thought we would need more than one, so I had the extras made for us."

Cronley laughed again and then asked, "Freddy, how long have you been carrying a .45 in that Secret Service holster?"

"Ever since Tedworth caught the Russian," Hessinger said. "The first Russian. I thought the NKGB might try to kidnap one of us, and then try to make a swap. You didn't think about that?"

No, goddammit, I didn't.

One more entry in the stupid column.

Cronley saw El Jefe scribble something on a piece of paper and hand it to Ashton.

What the hell is that?

"Freddy," Cronley asked, "you just said 'we' and 'for us.' How strongly do you feel about that?"

"When I was growing up, my father told me you couldn't choose your parents, but you should choose your associates. Then

I was drafted and found out you can't choose either," Hessinger said. "Why do I think there is a question behind that question?"

"Because you're not nearly as dumb as you look?" Dunwiddie asked.

"Now that you're an officer, you're not supposed to insult junior enlisted men," Hessinger said. "Isn't that right, Captain Cronley?"

"Absolutely. That's two apologies you owe Fat Freddy, Captain Dunwiddie."

"And one, I would say, Captain Cronley, that you owe the sergeant," Ashton said.

"Excuse me, Colonel," Hessinger said. "We do this all the time. What it is is that they're jealous of my education."

"Did I mention that Hessinger is a Harvard graduate, Colonel?" Cronley asked.

"I'll try not to hold that against you, Sergeant Hessinger," Ashton said. "We all have a cross to bear, and your Harvard diploma must be a very heavy one."

There were chuckles all around. Even Hessinger smiled.

"Why did you ask me what you asked before?" he asked.

"Freddy, what if I told you Colonel Ashton believes, and so do Tiny and me, that if Operation Ost blows up in our face, everybody from Admiral Souers on down is going to throw us to the wolves?"

"That surprises you? In Russian literature there are many vignettes of the nobility throwing peasants out of troikas to save themselves from the wolves. Which is of course the etymological source of that expression."

"What's a troika?" El Jefe asked.

"A horse-drawn sleigh," Dunwiddie furnished.

"Three horses, side by side," Hessinger further amplified, using his hands to demonstrate.

"If we can turn from this fascinating lecture on Russian customs to the subject at hand, stemming the tide of the Red Menace?" Cronley asked. "Freddy, we've decided that if getting tossed from this three-horse buggy is the price that we have to pay for trying to protect Operation Ost and the President, okay, we'll take our lumps."

Hessinger was now paying close attention.

"And, further, we have decided that if we get tossed from the buggy, it will be because we fucked up somehow, not because we blindly followed the friendly suggestions of anybody—Mattingly, Greene, or even the admiral—on how to do the job.

"And, we have concluded that despite our best efforts, the odds are we're going to wind up over our asses in the snow with the wolves gnawing on our balls. Both the colonel and I have decided, with Captain Dunwiddie concurring, that we have to ask you whether or not you wish to join the lunatics or whether you should return to the bona fide CIC and chase Nazis."

"In other words, Tubby," El Jefe said, "there's no reason you should get your ass burned because these two nuts think they're Alan Ladd and Errol Flynn saving the world for Veronica Lake and Mom's apple pie. You want to take my advice, get as far away from this as soon as you can."

"Thank you just the same," Hessinger said, "but I don't want your advice. What I do want is for you, Jim, to tell me what I have done to make you think you had to ask me that question."

"What does that mean, Tubby?" El Jefe asked. "Are you in, or are you out?"

"Don't call me Tubby."

"Why not? It fits."

"They can call me 'Fat Freddy' or whatever they want. They're my friends. You're not. You can either call me 'Sergeant Hessinger' or 'Mr. Hessinger.' Got it, Popeye the Sailor Man?"

"Enlisted men aren't supposed to talk to officers like that, Freddy," Dunwiddie said.

"When I'm in my CIC suit," Hessinger said, pointing to the blue triangles on his lapels, "nobody's supposed to know I'm an enlisted man."

"Mr. Hessinger's got you, Captain Dunwiddie," Cronley said, and added, "Yet again."

"May I infer, Mr. Hessinger, that you wish to remain allied with us, despite the risks doing so entails?" Ashton asked.

"Yes, sir. He didn't have to ask me that."

"No offense intended, Freddy," Cronley said.

"Offense taken, thank you very much," Hessinger said.

"At this point, I would like to introduce an intelligence analysis I received a short time ago," Ashton said. "Would you read this aloud, Captain Dunwiddie?"

Ashton handed Dunwiddie a small sheet of paper.

That's what El Jefe handed him.

"'If Jim wants to let him go, overrule him. Trust me. We need this guy,'" Dunwiddie read.

Hessinger looked at El Jefe for a long moment, and then said, "Thank you, Lieutenant Schultz."

"Just the honest judgment of an old chief petty officer, Mr. Hessinger."

"You can call me Fat Freddy, if you like."

"Thank you. Fat Freddy, if you ever call me 'Popeye the Sailor Man' again, I will tear off one of your legs and shove it up your ass."

"Moving right along," Ashton said, "what I think we should do now is go to Munich and meet with General Gehlen."

"Stopping along the way wherever Fred has stashed the other five .45 holsters he said he has," El Jefe said. "I want one."

"They're in the Kapitän," Hessinger said. "I thought you would need them, so I brought them out here with me."

[FOUR]
Quarters of the U.S. Military Government Liaison Officer
The South German Industrial Development
Organization Compound
Pullach, Bavaria
The American Zone of Occupied Germany
1735 2 January 1946

Ashton had trouble getting off the couch, which had been bolted to the floor of the ambulance, and then had more trouble getting out of the ambulance and onto his crutches. The ground behind the ambulance's doors was covered with frozen snow ruts. Ashton looked to be in great danger of falling, but bluntly refused Schultz's and Dunwiddie's offer of "a ride": "When I need help, I'll ask for it."

So the others followed him very slowly as he hobbled on his

crutches through the snow from the curb to the small, tile-roofed building.

"Who is this guy?" Schultz demanded of Cronley, "and what's he got to do with us?"

"What guy?"

"The military government liaison officer."

Cronley motioned for El Jefe to come close, and then whispered in his ear, "We really can't afford this getting out, Popeye, it's something we really don't want Joe Stalin to find out. It's me. One more brilliant move to deceive and confuse our enemy."

"Wiseass."

Hessinger plodded through the snow and opened the door for Ashton. Then he held it for Cronley, Schultz, and Dunwiddie.

Former Major General Gehlen and former Colonel Mannberg were in the living room of the building, sitting in armchairs reading the *Stars and Stripes*. Both rose when they saw Ashton come in.

Ashton made his way to Mannberg and awkwardly held out his hand to him.

"General Gehlen, I am Lieutenant Colonel Ashton."

"I'm Reinhard Gehlen," Gehlen said. "This is Ludwig Mannberg, my deputy."

Cronley thought: *I would have made the same mistake. Good ol' Ludwig looks like what Hollywood movies have taught us senior German officers look like. And the general looks like a not-very-successful black marketeer.*

But that does it. Gehlen gets some decent clothes.

"Well, I hope that's not a harbinger of future confusion," Ashton said.

"Sometimes, Colonel, confusion in our profession is useful, wouldn't you agree?" Gehlen asked.

"Max," Cronley ordered, "sit down before you fall down."

"I'm sure you've noticed, General, that every once in a great while Captain Cronley does have a good idea."

He hobbled to an empty armchair and collapsed into it.

"This is Lieutenant Schultz," Cronley said.

"El Jefe?" Mannberg asked.

Schultz nodded.

"How did you know they call me that?" he asked, on the edge of unpleasantly.

"Otto Niedermeyer is one of your admirers," Mannberg said in Spanish. "He warned me not to arm-wrestle with you."

"Did he tell you I also cheat at chess?" El Jefe asked in Spanish.

"Not in so many words," Mannberg said in German.

"In English, Colonel," El Jefe said, in English, "we have a saying—'It takes one to know one.'"

Mannberg laughed.

Very clever, Cronley thought. *They haven't been together sixty seconds, and already they know how well the other speaks German, Spanish, and English. All of these guys are far more clever than I am.*

"Ludwig," Cronley said, "see if you can guess where Colonel Ashton got his Spanish. Say something in Spanish, Max."

"I have need of the bathroom. Where is it?" Ashton said in Spanish.

"Interesting accent," Mannberg said. "Not pure castellano, but close. Is that the Argentine version?"

El Jefe went to Ashton and pulled him out of the armchair.

"Through that door," Cronley said. "First door to the right."

"Actually, it's Cuban," Ashton said, and then switched to English. "If you will hand me my goddamn crutches, I can handle it from here. But while I'm communing with nature, see if Captain Cronley has any medicine."

"What kind of medicine?" Cronley asked, with concern in his voice.

"Almost anything that comes out of a bottle reading 'Distilled in Scotland' will do," Ashton said, as he began to lurch across the room.

When he was out of earshot, Gehlen said, "Interesting man. I like his sense of humor."

"Don't be too quick to judge him by that," Cronley said. "He's very good at what he does."

As the words came out of his mouth, Cronley thought, *What am I doing? Warning Gehlen about the man he's now working for? That's absolutely ass-backwards!*

"He would not have been selected as Cletus Frade's replacement if he was not very good at what he does," Gehlen said.

So what's the truth there?

Ashton is very good. That's true.

But it's also true that he was selected as an expendable who can be thrown to the wolves.

"That's true, of course," Cronley began. "But there is another, frankly unpleasant, possib—"

"Freddy," El Jefe interrupted him, "I'm not feeling too well myself, so while you're getting the colonel's medicine, how about making a dose for me?"

He looked at Cronley. "How about you? A little medicine for you?"

El Jefe didn't want me to get into that subject—for that matter, any subject—with Gehlen while Ashton is out of the room.

And he's right.

And Gehlen and ol' Ludwig certainly picked up on that.

And Tiny did.

And, of course, Fat Freddy.

I just had my wrist slapped in public.

And deserved it.

"A splendid idea," Cronley said. "I wonder why I didn't think of that myself?"

Because I'm stupid, that's why.

Ashton hobbled, far from nimbly, across the room and again collapsed into the armchair.

Hessinger handed him a glass of whisky, straight, and then offered a bowl of ice cubes. Ashton waved them away and took a healthy swallow of the scotch.

"Gentlemen," he said, "I had an idea just now. That sometimes happens to me when I am in that circumstance and have nothing to read while waiting for Mother Nature to turn her attention to me. And since I am drunk with the power with which Admiral Souers has invested me, we're going to try it. I ask your indulgence.

"There will be no briefing of Lieutenant Schultz and myself in the usual sense. Instead of each of you, junior first, taking turns telling El Jefe and me what has happened in the past—which of course the others already know—we are going to reverse the procedure . . ."

Where the hell is he going with this?

". . . specifically, General Gehlen is going to start by telling us of the most recent development in our noble crusade against the Red Menace—which not all of you, perhaps none of you, will know. Then, I will ask and all of you may ask, questions to fill in the blanks in our knowledge. This is known as 'reverse engineering.' General Gehlen, please tell us all what you would have told Captain Cronley had he walked in here just now, and Lieutenant Schultz and myself were nowhere around."

Gehlen, a slight smile on his lips, looked at Cronley, who shrugged.

"Very well," Gehlen said. "I would have said, 'Jim, we've heard again from Seven-K.'"

"Aha!" Ashton said. "We've already turned up something I know nothing about. What is Seven-K?"

"It's a her," Cronley said. "A/K/A Rahil."

"And who is Seven-K A/K/A Rahil?"

"An old acquaintance of the general's and Ludwig's," Cronley said, smiling at Gehlen.

Ashton picked up on the smile and, literally visibly, began to suspect that his leg was being pulled.

"Tell me about the lady," Ashton said.

"Tell you what about her?"

"Why was she sending you a message?"

"She wants fifty thousand dollars," Gehlen said. "*Another* fifty thousand dollars." He paused, and then, anticipating Ashton's next question, added: "She'd probably say for expenses."

"You've already given this woman fifty thousand dollars? For what?"

"Expenses," Cronley said, smiling.

"What's so goddamn funny?"

"Funny?"

"You're smiling."

"With pleasure, because your idea seems to be working so well," Cronley said.

"I told you to tell me about this woman."

"Well, for one thing, she's Jewish," Cronley said.

"What's that got to do with anything?"

"You ever heard of the Mossad?"

"This woman is Mossad? A Mossad agent?"

"And also a *Podpolkóvnik* of the NKGB," Gehlen said.

"A what?" Ashton asked.

"More probably, General, by now a *Polkóvnik*," Mannberg said. "That massive wave of promotions right after the war?"

"You're probably right, Ludwig," Gehlen said, and then, to Ashton, added: "The NKGB jokes that one either gets promoted or eliminated."

"What's that you said, General, 'Pod-pol' something?" Ashton asked.

"A *Podpolkóvnik* is a lieutenant colonel," Gehlen explained. "And a *Polkóvnik* a colonel."

Ashton, visibly, thought something over and then made a decision.

"Okay," he said. "I find it hard to believe that you're pulling my leg. On the other hand, with Cronley anything is possible. If you have been pulling my chain, the joke's over. Enough."

"We have not been pulling either your chain or your leg, Colonel," Cronley said.

"You have just heard from a woman who is both a Mossad agent and an NKGB colonel. She wants fifty thousand dollars—

in addition to the fifty thousand dollars you have already given her. Is that correct?"

Gehlen and Mannberg nodded. Cronley said, "Yes, sir."

"Where is this woman located?"

"The last we heard," Gehlen said, "in Leningrad. But there's a very good chance she's en route to Vienna."

"Why?" Ashton asked, and then interrupted himself. "First, tell me why you have given her fifty thousand dollars."

"Because she told us she would need at least that much money to get Polkóvnik Likharev's wife and sons out of Russia," Gehlen said.

"Jesus Christ!" Ashton exclaimed, and then asked, "You think she can?"

"We're hoping she can," Gehlen said.

"Where the hell did you get fifty thousand dollars to give to this woman?"

Gehlen didn't reply, but instead looked at Cronley.

"In Schultz's briefcase," Ashton said, "there is fifty thousand dollars. The admiral gave it to me just before we got on the plane. He called it 'start-up' money, and told me to tell you to use it sparingly because he didn't know how soon he could get you any more. That suggests to me that the admiral didn't think you had any money. Hence, my curiosity. Have you been concealing assets from the admiral? If not, where did this fifty thousand come from?"

"From me, Polo," Cronley said. "I came into some money when . . . my wife . . . passed on. A substantial amount of cash. Cletus pulled some strings with the judge of probate in Midland to settle the estate right away. I gave a power of attorney to Karl Boltitz—he's going to marry Beth, the Squirt's sister—and he got the cash, gave it to Clete, Clete took it to Buenos Aires, and then when he sent Father Welner over here, got him to carry it to me."

"Fifty thousand dollars?" Ashton asked incredulously.

"Just for the record, I'm loaning that fifty thousand, repeat, *loaning* it, to the DCI. I expect it back."

"Cletus didn't tell me anything about this."

"Maybe he thought you didn't have to know," Cronley replied.

"And now this woman wants another fifty thousand. What are you going to do about that?"

"Whatever General Gehlen thinks I should."

"You've got another fifty thousand?"

"Father Welner brought me something over two hundred twenty thousand."

"Does Mattingly . . . does anybody else . . . know about this?"

Cronley shook his head.

"Do you realize how deep you're in here?"

Cronley nodded.

"I asked before," Ashton said. "Do you think this woman can get Likharev's family out?"

"Nothing is ever sure in our profession," Gehlen replied.

Ashton made a *Come on* gesture.

Gehlen took a short moment to collect his thoughts.

"I've learned, over the years, when evaluating a situation like this," he said, "to temper my enthusiasm for a project by carefully considering the unpleasant possibilities. The worst of these here is the possibility that we are not dealing with Rahil at all. One of the reasons there was that wave of promotions to which Ludwig referred a moment ago was because there were a large number of vacancies. Fedotov purged the NKGB—"

"Who?" Ashton interrupted.

"Pyotr Vasileevich Fedotov, chief of counterintelligence. He purged the NKGB of everyone about whose loyalty he had the slightest doubt. Rahil certainly was someone at whom he looked carefully.

"Now, if she was purged, we have to presume that Fedotov learned of her relationship with me."

"Even if she was not purged, General," Mannberg said.

"Even if she was not purged," Gehlen agreed, "it is logical to presume that Fedotov knows of our past relationship."

"Which was?" Polo asked.

"We got Russian Zionists out of Schutzstaffel concentration camps for her, and in turn she performed certain services for Abwehr Ost. I doubt that Rahil told Fedotov the exact nature of our relationship, certainly not during the war, or even in any postwar interrogations, if she was purged. But we have to presume he knows there was a relationship.

"What I'm leading up to here is that even before the NKGB found us at Kloster Grünau, they suspected we were in American hands, under American protection, in other words . . ."

"I think they knew that was your intention, General," Mannberg said. "To place us under American protection. All they had to do was find out where we were. And I believe von Plat and Boss gave them both. We don't know when either von Plat or Boss were turned."

"Who are they?" Ashton asked.

"We're getting off the subject," Gehlen said.

"Who are you talking about?" Ashton pursued.

"Polo, are you sure you want to go there?" Cronley asked.

Ashton nodded.

Cronley looked at Gehlen.

"Jim," Ashton said, "you don't need General Gehlen's permission to answer any question I put to you."

Cronley shrugged.

"Oberstleutnant Gunther von Plat and Major Kurt Boss of Abwehr Ost surrendered to the OSS when the general did," Cronley replied. "Boss was SS, a dedicated Nazi. Von Plat was Wehrmacht. We were just about to load Boss on a plane for Buenos Aires when Cletus and Father Welner turned Polkóvnik Likharev. Likharev told Cletus these were the guys who'd given him the rosters he had when Tedworth caught him sneaking out of Kloster Grünau. Clete told us."

"Where are these guys now?" Ashton asked.

"No one seems to know," Cronley said.

"You mean they got away? Or that you took them out?"

Cronley didn't reply.

"Polo, the next time Cronley asks you if you want to go somewhere, why don't you turn off your automatic mouth and think carefully before you say yes?" Schultz asked.

Well, that's interesting, Cronley thought. *El Jefe just told Polo to shut up.*

Told. Not politely suggested.

And Polo took it. He looked as if he was about to say something, but then changed his mind.

And that suggests that Cletus sent El Jefe here to do more than help Polo get on and off the airplane.

And that raises the question what did El Jefe do for Clete in Argentina?

Once El Jefe got the SIGABA set up, it could have been maintained by some kid fresh from the ASA school. But El Jefe stayed in Argentina.

And was directly commissioned.

Just for running the SIGABA installation? That doesn't make sense.

If Clete had to take somebody out, or do something else really black, who would he ask to help?

A nice young Cuban American polo player who had never heard a shot fired in anger, much less fired one himself?

Or a grizzled old sailor who had served not only in the Philippines but also on the Yangtze River Patrol?

Why didn't Clete tell me what was El Jefe's actual function?

Because you don't talk about things like that to someone who doesn't have the need to know.

So what's El Jefe's mission here?

Whatever it is, it's not to keep his mouth shut when Polo does, or asks, something stupid.

He's here to keep Polo out of trouble.

No.

More than that. El Jefe is here to see—and probably to report to the admiral—what's going on here.

So what's he going to report?

That Captain James D. Cronley Jr. is indeed the loose cannon everyone says he is?

That I'm dealing with a Mossad/NKGB agent and haven't told the admiral anything about it?

"Returning to the worst possible scenario," Gehlen said, "there is a real possibility that what the NKGB decided when we contacted Seven-K was that it might give them a chance to get their hands on me."

"How would they do that?" El Jefe asked.

"In her—what we presume was her—last message, she twice referred to a Herr Weitz who was demanding more dollars."

"Who's he?" Ashton asked.

"I don't know anyone of that name, and neither does Oberst Mannberg. But in our previous relationship I met twice with Rahil in the Café Weitz in Vienna. That's why I suggested she may be headed for Vienna."

"Where Fedotov's people may be waiting for you at the Café Weitz when you go there to give her the fifty thousand dollars," Mannberg said.

"Where Fedotov's people may be waiting for me when I go there to give her the fifty thousand dollars," Gehlen parroted in confirmation.

"I'm just a simple sailor, General," El Jefe said. "You're going to have to explain that to me. Why couldn't you get her the money through an intermediary? How'd you get her the first fifty thousand?"

"Through an intermediary," Gehlen said. "But we can't do that again."

"Why not?"

"Because she wants to make sure, or at least that's what I'm expected to believe, that she is afraid this is a scheme to kidnap, or at least compromise, her. She said, to—in Jim's charming phrase—'cut to the chase'—"

"To hell with Jim's charming phrase," Schultz cut him off. "I just told you, I'm just a simple sailor. Take it slowly, step by step."

Has the general picked up that El Jefe is now giving the orders?

You can bet your ass he has!

Gehlen nodded.

"As I'm sure you know, one of the great advantages the Allies had over us was that you had broken our Enigma code. We—and I include myself in 'we'—were simply unable to believe you could do that. I had only heard rumors of your SIGABA system, rumors I discounted until Jim showed me the one installed at Kloster Grünau. And now here."

He pointed to a closed door.

"The Soviet systems are by no means as sophisticated as either," he went on. "They have therefore to presume that whenever they send an encrypted message, someone else is going to read it. So they use what could probably be called a personal code within the encrypted message. Making reference to something only the addressee will understand. 'Herr Weitz,' for example, immediately translated to 'Café Weitz' in my mind. Sometimes it takes a half dozen messages back and forth to clarify the message, but it works."

"I'm with you," El Jefe said.

"Rahil—or whoever is using her name—expressed concern that we might be trying to entrap her, and that the only proof she would accept that we were not would be for me to personally deliver to Herr Weitz the additional fifty thousand dollars he was demanding.

"Subsequent clarifying messages seem to confirm this interpretation. She wants me to meet with her, to give her the money, in the Café Weitz in Vienna."

"No way," Cronley heard himself saying.

"Excuse me?" Gehlen said.

Ashton and Schultz looked at him in mingled surprise and annoyance.

Is that my automatic mouth running away on me again?

Or am I doing what I'm supposed to be doing, commanding Operation Ost?

With overwhelming immodesty, the latter.

So I have to do this.

"The general is not going to meet with whoever's going to be waiting for him in the Café Weitz. I'm not going to take the chance that the Russians'll grab him."

"*You're* not?" Ashton asked, sarcastically incredulous. "Who the hell . . ."

El Jefe held up his hand, ordering Ashton to stop.

". . . do I think I am?" Cronley picked up. "Until you relieve me—and I'm not sure you have that authority—I'm chief, DCI-Europe . . ."

And probably out of my fucking mind!

". . . and as long as I am, I'm not going to take any chances of losing the general."

"So how, hotshot, are you going to get this Russian lady the fifty thousand she wants?" El Jefe asked.

"I'll take it to her," Cronley said.

And how the hell am I going to do that?

"How the hell are you going to do that?" Ashton demanded. "Have you ever even been to Vienna?"

"No. But I know where the *bahnhof* is, and that a train called the Blue Danube goes from there to Vienna every day at 1640."

"Oh, shit!" Ashton said disgustedly.

"Let him finish," El Jefe said. "Let's hear how the chief, DCI-Europe, wants to handle this."

"Ludwig, do you know what this lady looks like?"

"I know what she looked like in 1943," Mannberg said.

"Okay, so Ludwig, Lieutenant Max, and I go to Vienna," Cronley said.

And do what?

"Who is Max . . . what you said?" El Jefe asked. "That Polish-Englishman who flew us to the monastery?"

"Right."

"And what's he going to do?"

"Guard Colonel Mannberg. I don't want him grabbed by the Russians, either."

"Can he do that?" El Jefe asked. "More important, will he want to?"

"He killed the two NKGB guys who had the wire around Tedworth's neck," Cronley said. "Yeah, he can do it. And he wants to do more than he's doing right now."

"You mean, more than flying the Storch?"

"Actually, he's not supposed to be flying the Storch. Officially, he's in charge of the Polish guards at Kloster Grünau."

"Just so I have things straight in my mind, Captain Cronley," Ashton said. "You have this guy who's not in the service—technically, he's a displaced person, employed as a quasi–military watchman, right?"

"Right."

"Flying an airplane you're not supposed to have?"

"Right."

"And now you want to involve him in a delicate, top secret DCI operation?" Ashton asked. And then he went on, "Why are you smiling, Schultz? You think this is funny? Cronley doing this, doing any of this, on his own—which means absolutely no . . . authority? You think that's funny?"

"I was thinking it reminded me of when we were starting up in Argentina," Schultz said. "When Clete realized we needed some shooters to protect us from the Nazis, what he did was ask Colonel Graham to send some Marines down from the States. Graham told him to write up a formal request and send it to General Donovan.

"Clete never wrote a formal request, of course. What he did do was put gauchos—most of them had been in the cavalry, I'll admit—from Estancia San Pedro y San Pablo on the job. Then he sent the OSS a bill. Nine dollars a day, plus three dollars for rations and quarters, per man. The OSS paid without asking him a question. By the time the war was over, we had three hundred some gauchos in 'Frade's Private Army' on the payroll. If the OSS was willing to pay for hiring necessary civilian employees in Argentina, more than three hundred of them, I don't think the admiral will much care if Jim hires a few here."

"Are you telling me you're in agreement with what he's proposing?"

"I haven't heard everything he's proposing, but so far he's making a lot of sense," Schultz said. Then he turned to Cronley: "Okay, you, the colonel here, and that Polish-Englishman are in Vienna. Where did he learn English like that, by the way?"

"He was in England with the Free Polish Air Force. They were sort of in the RAF."

"So that's where he learned to fly?" El Jefe said. "So what do you do in Vienna?"

I'm making this up as I go along. Doesn't he see that?

"We go to the Café Weitz. Colonel Mannberg by himself, Max and me together."

"Why?"

"Mannberg so he can see Rahil, or she him. Max to protect Mannberg in case it is the NKGB waiting for him. After that, we play it by ear."

"Wrong," El Jefe said with finality.

Uh-oh.

Well, I got pretty far for somebody who is making it up as he goes along.

"You can't go, because by now the NKGB knows what you look like," El Jefe said. "I don't want to have to tell the admiral that you're on your way to Siberia. Or send you home in a body bag. So I'll tell you what we'll do. I'll go with the Polish-Englishman. Or the English-Polack. Whatever he is. And then we'll play it by ear."

"Oscar, I was there when the admiral told you he didn't want you getting into anything you shouldn't," Ashton said.

"Then you must have been there when he said I was running things but not to tell anybody unless I decided we had to," Schultz said. "And when the admiral said you were not to even think about running the whole operation until you were off those crutches. I'm going to Vienna. Period. Okay?"

"You know the admiral'll be furious when he hears about this."

"Then let's make sure he doesn't hear about it until after we pull it off, and Mrs. Whatsername and the kids are in Argentina. Then we'll tell him and maybe he won't be so furious."

"My God!" Ashton said.

"How do we get to Vienna?" Schultz asked.

"On the train," Cronley said.

"Is it too far to drive? I'd like to have wheels in Vienna."

"It's not far, Lieutenant Schultz," Gehlen said. "It's about a six-hour drive. The problem is—"

"Why don't you try calling me 'Chief,' General? I'm more comfortable with that."

"Certainly. Chief, the problem is crossing the borders. Austria has been divided among the Allies. The American Zone of Austria abuts the American Zone of Germany. Permission, even for Americans, is required to move across that border. And then, like Berlin, Vienna is an island within the Russian Zone of Austria. Permission is required to cross the Russian Zone."

"Permission from who?" El Jefe asked. "The Russians?"

"Freddy?" Cronley said.

"I don't know if this applies here," Hessinger said, "but if someone from the Twenty-third CIC wants to go to Vienna, I would cut travel orders. Major Wallace went there a couple of weeks ago. I cut travel orders for him, and then took them to Munich Military Post, who stamped them approved. You need that to get on the train. That would work for Captain Cronley, but Oberst Mannberg and Ostrowski?"

"Because they're not American, you mean?"

"Yes, sir."

"Not a problem," Schultz said.

"Not a problem?" Cronley parroted.

"I have goodies in my briefcase, in addition to the start-up money," Schultz said. He went into his briefcase and rummaged through it. He came up with a plastic-covered identity card and handed it to Cronley.

On one side was Schultz's photo. Above it were the letters *DCI.* Below it was the number 77, printed in red. On the other side was the legend:

Office of the President of the United States
Directorate of Central Intelligence
Washington, D.C.

The Bearer of This Identity Document

Oscar J. Schultz

Is acting with the authority of the President of the United States as an officer of the Directorate of Central Intelligence. Any questions regarding him or his activities should be addressed to the undersigned only.

Sidney W. Souers
Sidney W. Souers, Rear Admiral
Director, U.S. Directorate of Central Intelligence

"After we put Colonel Mannberg's—and the English-Polack's—pictures on one of these, do you think this Munich Military Post is going to ask them if they're American?" El Jefe asked.

"Very impressive," Cronley said. "Do I get one of these?"

He handed the card to Gehlen.

"I've got twenty-five of them," El Jefe said. "I can get more, but I thought that would be enough for now."

"If I may?" Gehlen said.

"Go ahead."

"I can make a small contribution. Seal the cards you brought in plastic."

"How are you going to do that?" Schultz asked.

"Abwehr Ost's special documents facility survived the war," Gehlen said. "Amazingly intact."

"Survived where?" Schultz asked.

"Here in Munich. In a sub-basement of the Paläontologisches Museum on Richard-Wagner Strasse."

"I thought that was pretty much destroyed," Hessinger said.

"Not the sub-basement," Mannberg said. "But just about everything else."

"We're back to getting something to drive in Vienna. What I'd like to have is a couple of cars—I'm too old to ride around in a jeep in this weather—and maybe a small truck—like that ambulance you had at the airport."

"That's no problem," Cronley said. "We have half a dozen of them. I don't know about cars. If we ask the Ordnance Depot for cars, they'll want to know why we want them."

"No, they won't," Schultz said. "I've got another letter from the admiral in my briefcase. This one directs all U.S. Army facilities to provide DCI-Europe with whatever support we ask for."

He produced the letter and passed it around.

"That'll do it," Hessinger pronounced. "I recommend you get Fords or Chevrolets, not German cars."

"Why would you recommend that?" Cronley asked.

"Because there's no spare parts for the German ones."

"So what's left to do?"

"Except for getting the cars, cutting the orders, and getting these ID cards filled out, I can't think of a thing," Hessinger said.

"Except wait to hear from Rahil," Gehlen said. "That would be useful."

"The one thing I didn't expect you to be, General, is a wiseass," Schultz said.

"Life is full of surprises, isn't it, Chief?" Gehlen said.

Cronley saw they were smiling at each other.

And that Mannberg and Ashton, seeing this, seemingly disapproved.

Screw the both of you!

V

[ONE]

Quarters of the U.S. Military Government Liaison Officer
The South German Industrial Development
Organization Compound
Pullach, Bavaria
The American Zone of Occupied Germany
1305 4 January 1946

"How'd you do at the Ordnance Depot, Freddy?" Cronley asked, when Hessinger, trailed by First Sergeant Tedworth, came into what they were now calling "the sitting room."

"I got us four 1942 Fords, one with three hundred miles on the odometer, one with forty-five thousand, and the other two somewhere between the extremes."

"I was hoping for at least one Packard Clipper," Cronley said.

"Even if you could get one, that would be stupid," Hessinger said.

"Stupid? What have you got against Packards?"

"A Packard would draw unwanted attention. As will painting 'Mess Kit Repair Company' on the bumpers of the Fords. I came to talk to you about that."

"Painting what on them?" Oscar Shultz asked.

He was sitting with Maksymilian Ostrowski at the bar. They were hunched over mugs of coffee and the *Stars and Stripes*. El Jefe had exchanged his naval uniform—and Ostrowski his dyed-black fatigues—for Army woolen OD Ike jackets and trousers. Civilian triangles were sewn to the lapels.

"You have to have your unit painted on the bumpers of your vehicles," Cronley explained. "Since I didn't want to paint CIC on them, and certainly don't want to paint HQ DCI-Europe on them, I told Freddy to have what we have on all the other vehicles—711th MKRC—painted on them."

"Which is?"

"It stands for the nonexistent 711th Mess Kit Repair Company," Cronley explained.

"Very funny, but one day some MP is going to get really curious," Hessinger said.

"What would you paint on them, Freddy?" El Jefe asked.

The question was unexpected, and it showed.

"Maybe some military government unit," he said after a moment.

"Freddy, when you don't like something, always be prepared to offer something better," Schultz said. "Write that on your forehead. It's up to Cronley, but I sort of like the sound of Seven-One-One-Em-Kay-Are-See."

"Yes, sir."

"And don't call me 'sir,' Freddy. I am trying to pass myself off as a civilian."

"I thought Captain Cronley would continue to be unreasonable," Hessinger said, "so I got him and Captain Dunwiddie these."

He handed each of them a small box.

"Oh, Freddy, you're sweet, but you shouldn't have!" Dunwiddie mocked.

"What the hell is this?" Cronley asked.

"Quartermaster Corps lapel insignia," Hessinger said. "It is possible that when you are stopped by the MPs, they will be less suspicious if they think you're in the Quartermaster Corps. Those swords you're wearing now . . ."

"Sabers, Freddy," Cronley corrected him. "Cavalry *sabers*."

". . . might make them curious."

"He's right," El Jefe said.

"Again. That's why I hate him. He's right too often," Cronley said. "Thanks, Freddy."

"I will be disowned if anybody in my family hears I'm trying to pass myself off as a Quartermaster Corps officer," Dunwiddie said.

"Say, 'Thank you, Freddy,'" Cronley ordered.

"Thank you, Freddy," Dunwiddie said.

One of the three telephones on the bar rang. The ring sound told them it was a leather-cased Signal Corps EE-8 field telephone connected to the guardhouse on the outer ring of fences.

Ostrowski picked it up, thumbed the TALK switch, answered it in Polish, listened, and then turned to Cronley.

"Captain, there are two CIC agents at the checkpoint. They have packages and letters for Lieutenant Cronley."

"What?"

Ostrowski repeated what he had announced.

"Pass them in," Dunwiddie ordered. "Have them report to me."

The two CIC agents came into the sitting room. Both were in their early thirties. He recognized both of them from his days at the XXIInd CIC Detachment in Marburg.

He knew they were enlisted men because they had not been billeted with the officers. He also knew that they were "real" CIC agents, as opposed to Special Agent (2nd Lt) J. D. Cronley Jr., who had been sort of a joke CIC special agent, whose only qualification for the job was his fluent German.

What the hell is going on?

What are these two guys doing here?

With packages? And letters?

What kind of packages?

Letters from whom?

"How you been, Lieutenant?" the heavier of the two agents asked of Cronley.

Cronley now remembered—or thought he did—that the man's name was Hammersmith. And that he was a master sergeant.

"Okay," Cronley replied. "How's things in Marburg?"

"About the same. What is this place?"

"If there is no objection from anyone, I'll ask the questions," Dunwiddie said.

The CIC agent displayed his credentials.

"No offense, Captain," Special Agent Hammersmith said, "but this is a CIC matter. I'll handle it from here."

Dunwiddie pulled his own CIC credentials from his jacket and displayed them.

"As I was saying, I'll ask the questions," Dunwiddie said.

"Sorry, sir," Hammersmith said. "I didn't know."

"You've got packages for Cronley?" Dunwiddie asked. "And letters?"

"Yes, sir," Hammersmith said. He took two letter-sized envelopes from his Ike jacket and extended them to Dunwiddie.

"They're addressed to Special Agent Cronley, sir."

"Then give them to him," Dunwiddie ordered. "Packages?"

"Four, sir. They're in our car. They're addressed to Lieutenant Cronley."

"One of you go get the packages. Ostrowski, help him."

"Yes, sir," Hammersmith and Ostrowski said on top of one another. Then Hammersmith gestured to the other CIC agent to get the packages.

"Now, who sent you here?" Dunwiddie asked.

"Major Connell, who's the Twenty-second CIC's exec, sent us to General Greene's office in the Farben Building. Then Colonel Mattingly sent us here."

"Hessinger, did we get a heads-up about this?" Dunwiddie asked.

"No, sir."

Dunwiddie looked at Cronley, who had just finished reading one of the letters.

He extended it to Dunwiddie.

"When you're finished, give it to El Jefe," he said.

Robert M. Mattingly

Colonel, Armor

2 January 1946

Special Agent J. D. Cronley, Jr., CIC
C/O XXIIIrd CIC Detachment
Munich
BY HAND
CC: Rear Admiral Sidney W. Souers
Lt Col Maxwell Ashton III

Dear Jim:

Vis-à-vis the packages addressed to you at the XXIInd CIC Detachment, and which were opened and seized as contraband by agents of the Postal Section, Frankfurt Military Post Provost Marshal Criminal Investigation Division.

I have assured both Major John Connell, of the XXIInd CIC Detachment, and the FMP DCI that the cigarettes, coffee, Hershey Bars, and canned hams were being introduced into Occupied Germany in connection with your official duties. The four packages of same were released and will be delivered to you with this letter.

May I suggest that you notify General Greene, or myself, the next time you feel it necessary to directly import such materials, so that we may inform the DCI and avoid a recurrence of what happened here?

With best personal regards, I am,

Sincerely,

Robert M. Mattingly

Robert M. Mattingly

Colonel, Armor

When Dunwiddie had read the first letter, he passed it to Schultz and then looked at Cronley. Cronley was not finished with what looked like a very long handwritten letter.

It was.

F-Bar-Z Ranch

Box 21, Rural Route 3

Midland, Texas

Christmas Eve 1945

Dear Jim,

I really hate to burden you with this, but there is no other option.

We have — your mother has — heard from her family in Strasbourg. This came as a surprise to us, as the only time we have ever heard from them was a few years before the war when they notified us that your mother's mother — your grandmother — had passed on.

That obviously needs an explanation, so herewith.

In early November of 1918, I was a very young (twenty-six), just promoted major. Colonel Bill Donovan sent me to Strasbourg to get the facts concerning rumors that he (and General Pershing) had heard about the Communists wanting to establish a "Soviet Government" there.

After the abdication of the German Emperor, Wilhelm, the Communists had done so in Munich, and were trying to do in Berlin and elsewhere.

Our little convoy (I had with me four officers and a half dozen sergeants traveling in half a dozen Army Model T Fords) arrived in Strasbourg on November sixth and found very nice accommodations in the Maison Rouge Hotel.

I immediately sent one of the officers and one of the sergeants back to Col. Donovan's HQ with the news we were in Strasbourg and prepared to carry out our orders to report daily on the situation.

I was by then already convinced I had been given the best assignment of my military career. It had nothing to do with the Communists, but rather with a member of the staff of the Maison Rouge, a strikingly beautiful blond young woman who had, blushing charmingly as she did so, told me her name was Wilhelmina.

Right. I had met your mother.

She had also told me that she could not possibly have dinner, or even a cup of coffee, with me, else her father would kill her.

Nothing would dissuade her from this, but over the next few days, I managed to spend enough time with her at the front desk to conclude that she was not immune to my charm and manly good looks, and it was only her father's hate of all things American that kept her from permitting our relationship to blossom.

The Communists solved the problem for us. on November 11, 1918 — Armistice Day — they started trying to take over the city. There was resistance, of course, and a good deal of bloodshed. Citizens were ordered by the French military government to stay off the streets, and to remain where they were.

The threat was real. Two of my officers and one of my sergeants were beaten nearly to death by the Communists.

Your mother's family lived on the outskirts of town and it would have been impossible for her to even try to get home. The Maison Rouge installed her (and other employees) in rooms in the hotel.

She was there for almost two weeks, during which time our relationship had the opportunity to bloom.

Finally, on November 22, General Henri Gouraud, the French military governor, had enough of the Communists. Troops, including Moroccan Goumiers, moved into the city and restored order. Brutally.

The next morning, I loaded your mother into a Model T and drove her home. I had the naïve hope that her father would be grateful that I had protected his daughter during the trouble and would be at least amenable to my taking her to dinner, if not becoming her suitor.

Instead, when he saw us pull up outside your mother's home, he erupted from the house and began to berate her for bringing shame on the family. I managed to keep my mouth shut during this, but when she indignantly denied — with every right to do so — that anything improper had happened between us, this served only to further enrage him.

I would say he slapped her, but the word is inadequate to describe the blow he delivered, which knocked her off her feet. At this point, I lost control and took him on. He wound up on the ground with a bloody nose and some lost teeth.

I loaded your mother, who was by then hysterical, back into the Model T and returned to the Maison Rouge.

When we got there, we found Colonel Donovan and a company of infantry. They had come to rescue us from the Communists. The French had already done that, of course.

When I explained my personal problems to Donovan, he said there was one sure way to convince your mother's father that my intentions were honorable, and that was to marry her.

To my delight and surprise, your mother agreed. We drove that same morning to Paris, armed with two letters from Donovan, one to the American ambassador, the other to the manager of the Hotel Intercontinental on rue de Castiglione.

The ambassador married us late that afternoon, and issued your mother an American passport. We spent the night in the Intercontinental and then drove back to Strasbourg as man and wife.

There was a black wreath on the door of your mother's house when we got there. Her father had suffered a fatal heart attack during the night.

Your mother's mother and other relatives attributed this to the thrashing I'd given him. While obviously there was a connection, I have to point out that your mother told me he had had three previous heart attacks.

Your mother was told she would not be welcome at the funeral services.

I managed to get myself assigned to the Army of Occupation, and your mother and I moved to Baden-Baden, where I served as liaison officer to the French authorities.

We were there nearly six months, during which she made numerous attempts to open a dialogue with her family, all of which they rejected.

Then, on a beautiful day in June, we boarded the Mauretania *at Le Havre. Eleven days later, we were in New York, a week after that I was relieved from active duty, and four days after that we got off the Texas & Pacific RR "Plains Flyer" in Midland.*

There was no more communication between your mother and her family until May (June?) of 1938, when she received a letter (since they had our address, it was proof they had received your mother's letters) from a Frau Ingebord Stauffer, who identified herself as the wife of Luther Stauffer, and he (Luther) as the son of Hans-Karl Stauffer, your mother's brother.

That would make Luther your first cousin. In this letter, Frau Stauffer told your mother that her mother — your grandmother — had died of complications following surgery.

When your mother replied to this letter, there was no reply.

We next heard from Frau Stauffer the day of Marjie's funeral. That night, your mother told me that she had received a letter begging for help for her literally starving family. I asked to see it, and she replied, "I tore it up. We have enough of our own sad stories around here."

That was good enough for me, and I didn't press her.

A week or so later, however, she asked me if I had the address from the 1938 letter, that she had thought things over and decided she could not turn her back on your Cousin Luther, his wife and children.

I was surprised, until I thought it over, that she didn't remember the address, Hachelweg 675, as it was that of her home where I had the run-in with your grandfather. Your mother said she intended to send a "small package or two" to your Cousin Luther's family.

The next development came when the postmaster told her they could neither guarantee nor insure packages to Strasbourg as they seemed to disappear in the French postal system.

Your mother then asked me if she "dared" to ask you to help. I told her you would be happy to do anything for her that was within your power.

Now, between us, man-to-man.

What this woman has asked for is cigarettes, coffee, chocolate, and canned ham. According to the Dallas Morning News, these things are the real currency in Germany these days, as they were after the First World War.

There are four large packages of same en route to you.

This woman also asked for dollars. I told your mother not to send money, as that would be illegal and certainly get you in trouble.

If you can deliver the packages to this woman without getting yourself in trouble, please do so.

Knowing these people as I do, however, I suspect that if this pull on the teat of your mother's incredible kindness is successful, it will not be their last attempt to get as much as they can from her.

Do whatever you think is necessary to keep them from starving, and let me know what that costs. But don't let them make a fool of you, me, or — most important — your mother.

As I wrote this, I realized that while I have always been proud of you, knowing that I could rely on your mature judgment to deal with this made me even more proud to be your father.

Love,
Dad

Cronley was still reading the long letter when Ostrowski and the CIC agent came back with two heavy packages and announced there were two more. Dunwiddie waited until they had returned with these before reaching for the letter Cronley, finally finished reading it, was now holding thoughtfully.

"It's personal," Cronley said. "From my father."

"Sorry," Dunwiddie said.

Cronley changed his mind. He handed Dunwiddie the letter, and then went to one of the boxes—all of which had white tape with "Evidence" printed on it stuck all over them—and, using a knife, opened it.

He pulled out an enormous canned ham.

"Anyone for a ham sandwich?" he asked.

"Does that about conclude your business here?" Dunwiddie asked Special Agent Hammersmith.

"Sir, could I get a receipt?" Hammersmith asked.

"Hessinger, type up a receipt for the special agent," Dunwiddie ordered. "Get his name. 'I acknowledge receipt from Special Agent . . .'"

"Hammersmith," Hammersmith furnished.

"'. . . of one official letter, one personal letter, and four cartons, contents unknown.' For Captain Cronley's signature."

"Yes, sir."

"*Captain* Cronley?" Hammersmith asked.

Dunwiddie did not respond to the question, instead saying, "Special Agent Hessinger can arrange rooms for the night for you, if you'd like, in the Vier Jahreszeiten hotel in Munich."

"I'd appreciate that," Hammersmith said, adding, "Captain, can I ask what's going on around here?"

"No, you can't," Dunwiddie said simply.

Hessinger came back into the sitting room with the announcement that the two CIC agents had gone.

"Jim, you knew those guys when you first came to Germany, right?" El Jefe asked.

Cronley nodded.

"In Marburg," he said. "And the first thing they're going to do when they get back there is tell Major Connell—"

"Who is he?" El Jefe asked.

"The Twenty-second's executive officer. But he really runs the outfit. 'Major, you're not going to believe this, but that wet-behind-the-ears second lieutenant you put on the road block? He's now a captain, and . . .'"

"That can't be helped," Dunwiddie said. "You are now a captain. And if this Major Connell is curious enough to ask Mattingly, Mattingly will either tell him how you got promoted or that it's none of his business."

"Or tell him," Hessinger said, "just between them, that for reasons he doesn't understand, Jim was transferred to the DCI. Where . . . witness the black market goodies . . . he has already shown he's absolutely way over his head and a petty crook to boot."

"You don't like Colonel Mattingly much, do you, Freddy?" El Jefe asked.

"He is a man of low principle," Hessinger announced righteously.

Cronley laughed.

"Don't laugh," Hessinger said. "He's determined to get you out of chief, DCI-Europe, and himself in. You noticed he sent copies of that letter to the admiral and Ashton? Showing what a really nice guy he is and what an incompetent *dummkopf* black marketeer you are."

"Where is Ashton, by the way?" Cronley asked.

"He asked for a car to take him into the PX in Munich," Hessinger began.

"Christ, Freddy, we could have sent somebody shopping for him," Cronley said. "I don't want him breaking his other leg staggering around the PX on crutches."

"I offered that," Hessinger said. "He refused. But don't worry."

"Why the hell not?"

"Because he really went to the orthopedic ward of the 98th General Hospital in Schwabing. I told Sergeant Miller—"

"Who?"

"Taddeus Miller. Staff sergeant. One of my guys," Dunwiddie furnished.

". . . to (a) not let him out of his sight, and (b) to call me and let me know where he really was."

"You didn't think he was going to the PX?"

"He was lying when he told me that. I could see that."

"You could see that he was lying?"

"I could see that he was lying. I always know."

"You always know?"

"Just about all the time, I know. You and General Gehlen are the only ones I can't always tell."

"Thank you very much," Cronley said.

"I have to know why you think so," El Jefe said.

"You don't want to know. He knows," Hessinger said. "It's not a criticism, it's a statement of fact."

Which means he didn't suspect a thing about Rachel until I fessed up.

Which makes me wonder how low I've fallen in his estimation?

Or Tiny's?

How far is all the way down?

"Quickly changing the subject," Dunwiddie said. "What are you going to do with your black market goodies, Captain, sir?"

"I'm tempted to burn them, give them to the Red Cross . . ."

"But you can't, right, because of your mother?" Hessinger asked. "Your parents?"

Cronley gave him an icy look, but didn't immediately reply. Finally he said, "I don't have the time to just run off to Strasbourg to play the Good Samaritan, do I?"

"You might. You never know."

"Freddy, you are aware that we're waiting to hear from Seven-K?" Cronley asked.

"Of course I am. What I am suggesting is that I don't think she's going to say 'Meet me at the Café Weitz tomorrow at noon.' There will probably be four or five days between her message and the meeting. Perhaps there will be time then. Or perhaps our trip to Vienna can be tied in with your trip to Strasbourg."

"Got it all figured out, have you, Freddy?" El Jefe said.

"Not all figured out. I learned about Jim's family just now, when you did. But by the time we hear from Rahil, I will probably have a workable plan."

"The thing I like about him is his immodesty," El Jefe said.

"When one is a genius, one finds it hard to be modest," Hessinger said solemnly.

"Jesus Christ, Freddy!" Cronley said, laughing.

"My own modesty compels me to admit that I didn't make that up," Hessinger said. "Frank Lloyd Wright, the architect, said it to a *Chicago Tribune* reporter."

[TWO]

Quarters of the U.S. Military Government Liaison Officer
The South German Industrial Development
Organization Compound
Pullach, Bavaria
The American Zone of Occupied Germany
1625 8 January 1946

When the door closed on Lieutenant Colonel George H. Parsons and Major Warren W. Ashley, Cronley looked around the table at General Gehlen, Mannberg, El Jefe, Hessinger, and Tiny and said, "Why does it worry me that they were so charming?"

Gehlen chuckled.

"I would say that it has something to do with a 'well done' message General Magruder sent Colonel Parsons," Hessinger said. "For the time being it is in their interest to be charming."

"What are you talking about?" Dunwiddie asked.

"What 'well done' message?" Cronley asked.

"The Pentagon sent a request for an update on Russian troop strength, especially tanks, in Silesia. You knew that, right?"

"And the general got it for us. Them."

"The general already had that intelligence on his Order of Battle. So the Pentagon asked for it one day, and the next day it was in Washington. Then General Magruder sent Colonel Parsons a 'well done' message. I am suggesting that if being charming to us produces 'well done' messages from General Magruder, Colonel Parsons is happy to polish our brass balls."

"I don't think you have that metaphor down perfectly, Freddy," Tiny said, chuckling, "but I take your point."

"How do you know Magruder sent the 'well done' message?" Cronley asked.

It took Hessinger a moment to frame his reply.

"I thought it would be in our interest to know what General Magruder and Colonel Parsons were saying to each other," he said finally. "So I established a sort of sub-rosa arrangement with Technical Sergeant Colbert of the ASA."

"This I have to hear," El Jefe said. "A sub-rosa arrangement to do what?"

"Give us copies of every message back and forth."

"In exchange for what?" El Jefe asked.

"You told me, when I told you we didn't have enough people to do what we're supposed to do, you said that I should keep my eyes open for people we could use, that you—we—now had the authority to recruit people from wherever for the DCI."

"So?"

"Sergeant Colbert has ambitions to be a professional intelligence officer. She thinks the next step for her would be to get out of the ASA and join the DCI."

"And you told him you could arrange that?" Cronley asked. "And then, 'she'? 'Her'?"

Hessinger nodded.

"I told her—her name is Claudette Colbert, like the movie actress—"

"Like the movie actress? Fascinating!" Cronley said. "Is there another one? Sergeant Betty Grable, maybe?"

"—that I would bring the subject up with you at the first opportunity. And I suggested to her that you would be favorably impressed if she could continue to get us all messages between the Pentagon and Colonel Parsons without getting caught."

"Jesus!" Cronley exclaimed. "Freddy, I'm sure that you considered that if we had this movie star sergeant transferred to us, she would no longer be in a position to read Parsons's messages."

"I did. She tells me that it will not pose a problem."

"Did *Claudette Colbert* tell you why not?" El Jefe asked.

"As a gentleman, I did not press her for details," Hessinger said. "But I suspect it has something to do with her blond hair, blue eyes, and magnificent bosoms. Women so endowed generally get whatever they want from men."

"Is that so?"

"That is so. When Claudette looked at me with those blue eyes and asked me for help in getting into the DCI, I was tempted for a moment to shoot you and offer her the chief, DCI-Europe, job."

"Thinking with your dick again, were you?" Cronley asked.

"That was a joke," Hessinger said. "I don't do that. We all have seen what damage thinking with your dick can do."

As Cronley thought, *That was a shot at me for fucking Rachel Schumann*, he simultaneously felt anger sweep through him, and sensed Tiny's and General Gehlen's eyes on him.

I can't just take that. Friends or not, I'm still his commanding officer.

So what do I do?

Stand him at attention and demand an apology?

Royally eat his ass out?

His mouth went on automatic and he heard himself say,

"The damage that thinking with one's male appendage can cause is usually proportional to the size of the organ, wouldn't you agree, Professor Hessinger? In other words, it is three times more of a problem for me than it is for you?"

Dunwiddie chuckled nervously.

El Jefe smiled and shook his head.

Cronley realized that he was now standing up, legs spread, with his hands on his hips, glaring down at Hessinger, who was still in his chair.

"Okay, Sergeant Hessinger," Cronley snapped. "The amusing repartee is over. Let's hear exactly what I've done to so piss you off that you felt justified in going off half-cocked to enlist the services of a large-breasted ASA female non-com in a smart-ass scheme that could have caused—may still cause—enormous trouble for us without one goddamn word to me or Captain Dunwiddie?"

Hessinger got to his feet.

"I asked you a question, Sergeant!"

Hessinger's eyes showed he was frightened, even terrified.

"I was out of line, Captain. I'm sorry."

"Sorry's not good enough, fish!"

Where the hell did that come from? "Fish"?

College Station.

The last time I stood with my hands on my hips screaming at a terrified kid, a fish, scaring the shit out of him, I was an eighteen-year-old corporal in the Corps . . .

He saw the kid, the fish, standing at rigid attention, staring straight ahead, as he was abusing him, reciting, "Sir, not being in-

formed to the highest degree of accuracy, I hesitate to articulate for fear that I may deviate from the true course of rectitude. In short, sir, I am a very dumb fish, and do not know, sir."

I didn't like abusing a helpless guy then, and I don't like doing it here.

"Sit down, Freddy," Cronley said, putting his hand on Hessinger's shoulder. "Just kidding."

Hessinger sat—collapsed—back into his chair.

"But you will admit, I hope, that going off that way to corrupt the blue-eyed nicely teated blond without telling either Tiny or me was pretty stupid."

"Yes, sir. I can see that now."

"So what were you pissed off about?"

Hessinger met his eyes for a moment, then averted them, then met them again.

"You really want me to tell you?"

"Yeah, Freddy, I really do."

And I really do. I didn't say that to Freddy to make nice.

"My skills are underutilized around here," Hessinger said.

"Freddy," Tiny said, "this place would collapse without you. And we all know it."

"You mean, I am very good at such things as making hotel reservations, getting vehicles and other things from supply depots, et cetera?"

"And getting us paid," Tiny said. "Don't forget that."

"Those are the things a company clerk does. So what you're saying is that I am a very good company clerk and supply sergeant."

"Actually, Freddy, I think of you as our adjutant, our administrative officer."

"Sergeants—and that's what I am, a pay grade E-4 sergeant—can't be adjutants or administrative officers."

"You're also a special agent of the CIC," Cronley argued.

"Nobody here is a bona fide CIC agent," Hessinger said. "You just kept the badges so you can get away with doing things you shouldn't be doing."

Jesus, he's pissed off because I promoted Tedworth to first sergeant!

Or, that's part of it.

"Sergeant Hessinger," Cronley said, "at your earliest convenience, cut a promotion order promoting you to master sergeant."

"You can't do that," Hessinger said.

"Why not? You told me I had the authority to promote Sergeant Tedworth."

"Sergeant Tedworth was a technical sergeant, pay grade E-6. You had the authority to promote him one grade, to first sergeant pay grade E-7. You can't skip grades when you promote people. People can be promoted not more than one pay grade at a time, and not more often than once a month."

"Okay. Problem solved," Tiny said. "Cut an order today, promoting you to staff sergeant. Then, a month from today, cut another one making you a technical sergeant. And a month after that . . . getting the picture?"

"That would work. Thank you."

"Happy now, Freddy?" Cronley asked.

"That I will get my overdue promotions, yes, but that does not deal with the basic problem of my being underutilized in the past, and will continue to be underutilized in the DCI."

"And how, Staff Sergeant Hessinger," Cronley asked, "would you suggest I deal with that?"

"If you would transfer Sergeant Miller to me—right now I am borrowing him from First Sergeant Tedworth—that would free me to spend more time doing more important things than making hotel reservations and stocking the bar here."

"Presumably, Captain Dunwiddie, you are aware that Sergeant Hessinger has been borrowing Sergeant Miller from Sergeant Tedworth?" Cronley asked.

Dunwiddie nodded.

"It's okay with Tedworth. He said we've been overworking Freddy. Miller's a good man."

"That raises the question in my mind whether Sergeant Miller is anxious to solve our personnel problem, or whether Abraham Lincoln Tedworth pointed his finger at him and said, 'Get your ass over to Hessinger's office and do what you're told.'"

"He came to me asking if I could use him," Hessinger said.

"I would like to hear that he's a volunteer from his lips," Cronley said. "And now that I think about it, I would like to hear from Claudette Colbert's ruby-red lips that she, too, is really a volunteer. But Sergeant Miller first. Where is he, Freddy?"

"Outside, in the ambulance."

"Outside, in the ambulance"? What the hell is that all about?

"Go get him."

When the door had closed on Hessinger, Dunwiddie said, "Don't let this go to your head, Captain, sir, but I thought you handled that pretty well."

"Me, too," El Jefe said.

The door opened and one of Gehlen's men, a tall, gaunt blond man whose name Cronley couldn't recall but he remembered had been a major, came in.

He marched up to Mannberg, came to attention, clicked his heels, and handed him a sheet of paper. Mannberg read it, handed it to General Gehlen, and then ordered, "There will probably be a reply. Wait outside."

The former major bobbed his head, clicked his heels again, turned on his heels, and marched out of the room.

"We have heard from Seven-K," Gehlen said. "Quote, 'Herr Weitz expects his friend to pay him not later than the fourteenth.' End quote."

"Today's the eighth," Cronley said. "That gives us six days to get to Vienna."

"Vienna's not the other side of the world," Dunwiddie said. "That shouldn't be a problem."

The door opened again.

Hessinger and Staff Sergeant Miller came in.

Miller was as coal black as Tiny Dunwiddie, but where Dunwiddie was massive, Miller was thin, almost gaunt. He towered over Hessinger.

Christ, Tiny's six-four and this guy is six, seven inches taller than that. He has to be close to seven feet tall.

Sergeant Miller marched up to Cronley, came to attention, and crisply saluted.

"Sir, Staff Sergeant Miller, Taddeus L., reporting to the captain as ordered, sir!"

Cronley returned the salute.

"At ease, Sergeant," Cronley ordered.

"Captain Cronley," Gehlen said. "Excuse me?"

"Sir?"

"Before we get into this, I think we should reply to Seven-K."

"Sure."

"And what should I say?"

"Say 'Ludwig always pays his debts on time,'" Hessinger said.

Gehlen looked at him in mingled disbelief and annoyance.

"Freddy," Cronley said, annoyance—even anger—in his tone, "shut up. No one asked you."

"I know. That's what I meant before when I said I was underutilized around here."

"Let's hear what he has to say," El Jefe said. "Starting with who's Ludwig?"

"Colonel Mannberg's Christian name is Ludwig. We can safely presume they know that. So they will not be surprised when he, and not the general, shows up at the Café Weitz."

"What makes you think I will not be going to the Café Weitz?" Gehlen asked.

He tried, but failed, to keep an icy tone out of his voice.

"I would be very surprised, General," Hessinger replied, "if Captain Cronley would expose you to that risk. I am extremely reluctant to expose Colonel Mannberg to that risk, but I can see no alternative."

"*You* are 'extremely reluctant,' are you, Freddy?" Cronley asked sarcastically. "You've given our little problem a great deal of thought, I gather? And come up with the solutions?"

"Our problems, plural. Yes, I have."

"'Problems, plural'?" Cronley parroted. "And the others are?"

"The other is you dealing with your family in Strasbourg."

"That's a personal problem that I will deal with myself, thank you just the same," Cronley said.

"No. The chief, DCI-Europe, doesn't have personal problems."

"What are you suggesting, Freddy?"

"That it is entirely possible that when you knock on your cousin Luther's door, bearing the black market Hershey bars and canned ham, he will smile gratefully at you and ask you in. Maybe he will even embrace you and kiss your cheek. And the next we will hear of you is when the new Rachel sends us a message saying we can have you back just as soon as we send Colonel Likharev into the Russian Zone of Berlin. Or maybe Vienna."

"My God!" Gehlen breathed. "That possibility never entered my mind."

After a very long moment, Cronley said, "Sergeant Miller, you never should have heard any of this."

"Mr. Hessinger has made me aware of the situation, sir."

"Okay. I'm not surprised. But I have to ask this. Are you a volunteer? Or did Tedworth, or for that matter Captain Dunwiddie, volunteer your services for you?"

"Sir, I went to Mr. Hessinger and told him I thought I could be more useful working for him, for DCI, than I could as just one more sergeant of the guard."

"Okay. With the caveat that I think you may—hell, certainly will—come to regret doing that, you're in."

"Thank you, sir."

"Okay, Freddy," Cronley ordered. "Let's hear your solutions to our problems, plural."

"Right now?"

"Right now."

"Taddeus, please get my briefcase from the ambulance," Hessinger said. "And while you're doing that, I will get started by talking about the death and resurrection of the 711th MKRC."

"Why don't you get started talking about something important?" Cronley challenged.

"A unit called the 711th Quartermaster Mess Kit Repair Company is a sophomoric joke . . ."

"So you have been saying," Cronley said.

"Shut up, Jim," El Jefe said. "Let's hear what he has to say."

Cronley recognized the tone of command in Schultz's voice and shut up.

". . . but within Captain Cronley's original idea, which was to provide a cover for our vehicles, there is a good deal that can be saved.

"For example," Hessinger began his lecture, "while there is obviously no such organization as a Quartermaster Mess Kit Repair Company, I don't think anyone would smile at, or question, a Quartermaster Mobile Kitchen Renovation Company.

"What does the 711th QM Mobile Kitchen Renovation Company do? It renovates the mobile kitchens of the European Command, each company-sized unit of which has a mobile kitchen. That means that no one would question our vehicles—our former ambulances—being anywhere in Occupied Germany or Liberated Austria where there might be an Army mobile kitchen in need of renovation.

". . . Personnel assigned to the 711th might be authorized a three-day pass from their labors, so that they might visit such cultural centers as Strasbourg . . ."

What later became known as "Hessinger's First Lecture" lasted an hour and fifteen minutes, and covered every detail of both problems facing the DCI. It recommended the reassignment of more of Tiny's Troopers to DCI duties, and replacing them with Ostrowski's Poles. And the designation of Kloster Grünau as home station for the 711th, with signs announcing that status being placed on the fence surrounding the monastery.

But finally it was over.

"All of this needs polishing," Hessinger concluded.

"Everything always needs polishing, as we say in the Navy," El Jefe said.

"We had a similar saying, oddly enough, in the Wehrmacht," General Gehlen said.

"So what do you want me to do now?" Hessinger asked.

"Get me an ambulance driver, and a road map to Strasbourg," Cronley said. "I want to go there either tomorrow or the day after and get that out of the way before I go to Vienna."

"I will drive, and I don't need a road map," Hessinger replied.

"You're going with me to Strasbourg?"

"Me and four of Tiny's Troopers. Them in an ambulance, you and me—Second Lieutenant Cronley and Sergeant Hessinger of the 711th Quartermaster Mobile Kitchen Renovation Company—in the Ford with the three hundred–odd miles on the odometer."

"Do I have any say in this?"

"I wouldn't think so, Second Lieutenant Cronley," El Jefe said. "It looks to me that Professor Hessinger has things well in hand."

"There is one little problem we haven't discussed," Cronley said.

"Which is?"

"How do we get Mannberg, Ostrowski, and that fifty thousand dollars to Vienna?"

"Yeah," Hessinger said thoughtfully.

"I'd like to send them on the Blue Danube, but we can't get them on the Blue Danube because they're not American."

"Yeah," Hessinger repeated thoughtfully.

"I have a brilliant idea," Cronley said. "Inasmuch as I am exhausted after dealing with Lieutenant Colonel Parsons, Major Ashley, and Staff Sergeant Hessinger, why don't we put off solving that until tomorrow morning?"

"Yeah," Hessinger said thoughtfully, for the third time.

[ONE]
Quarters of the U.S. Military Government Liaison Officer
The South German Industrial Development
Organization Compound
Pullach, Bavaria
The American Zone of Occupied Germany
0755 9 January 1946

"Sign this, please," Hessinger said, laying a sheet of paper on the table.

"What is it?" Cronley asked, and then read. "I'll be damned, 'Special Orders No. 1, Headquarters, Military Detachment, Directorate of Central Intelligence-Europe. Subject: Promotion of Enlisted Personnel.' What took you so long, Freddy? Or should I say 'Staff Sergeant Hessinger'?"

"I didn't know how to do it, so I called Sergeant Major Thorne."

"Who?"

"General Greene's sergeant major."

"And he told you how?"

"Correct."

"I was hoping that you had spent the night thinking about how we're going to get Mannberg, Ostrowski, and the fifty thousand to Vienna."

"I came up with several ideas, all of which are probably illegal," Hessinger said.

"Save them until the general and Mannberg get here."

General Gehlen, in another of his ill-fitting, ragged suits, and Colonel Mannberg, in his usual Wehrmacht uniform stripped of all insignia but a red stripe down the trouser legs, came in almost precisely at eight.

Cronley wasn't sure if he was impressed with their Teutonic punctuality or annoyed by it. He rose as Gehlen approached the table, as a gesture of courtesy, and Gehlen waved him back into his seat, shaking his head to suggest he didn't think the gesture was necessary.

By quarter after eight, the others—Dunwiddie, Schultz, Ostrowski, and Tedworth—had taken their places and begun their breakfast, and Cronley had finished his.

"What we left hanging last night," Cronley said, "was the question of getting Mannberg, Ostrowski, and the fifty thousand dollars to Vienna. The problem is that neither of them can get on the Blue Danube because they're not Americans. And the one solution I see for the problem is predictably illegal."

"What's your solution?"

"Give both of them DCI-Europe identity cards."

"You're right," Dunwiddie said. "That would be illegal. And it wouldn't be long before Colonel Mattingly heard about it. And he's just waiting for you to screw up."

"Your suggestion?"

"Put Colonel Mannberg in a Provisional Security Organization uniform and give him a PSO identity card. No one would question you having two Wachmann—Mannberg and Ostrowski—with you."

"That would work," Mannberg said.

No, mein lieber Oberst, it wouldn't.

"No, it would not," Cronley said. "I don't think this officers' hotel . . . what's it called?"

"The Bristol," Hessinger furnished. "And it's not just an officers' hotel. Majors and up."

". . . this majors-and-up officers' hotel is going to accommodate two DP watchmen," Cronley finished.

"So what's your solution?" Dunwiddie asked.

"I'm going to give both Mannberg and Ostrowski DCI identity cards."

"I don't think that would be smart," Schultz said.

"Well, then the choice is yours, Jefe," Cronley said. "Relieve me and you figure this out. Or let me do what I think is best. And giving Mannberg and Ostrowski DCI identity cards is what I think is best."

It took thirty seconds—which seemed much longer—for El Jefe to reply.

"When I think about it," he said finally, "I still think it's risky as hell, but I don't think it would be illegal. You're the chief, DCI-Europe. You can do just about anything you want."

"Until somebody catches him doing something we all know he shouldn't be doing, you mean," Dunwiddie said.

"Discussion over, Captain Dunwiddie," Cronley said. "How are you with a tape measure?"

"Excuse me?"

"While we're getting the DCI credentials filled out and sealed in plastic, we need somebody who knows how to determine sizes to take the colonel's and Ostrowski's measurements. Are you our man to do that?"

"What for?"

"So that you can go to the QM officers' clothing sales store and get Colonel Mannberg a couple of sets of ODs and a set of pinks and greens."

"I didn't think about that," Hessinger said.

"And get Ostrowski a set of pinks and greens while you're at it," Cronley said. "We don't want anyone to look out of place in this majors-and-up hotel in Vienna, do we?"

"I have one more thing to say, and then I'll shut up," Dunwiddie said.

"Say it."

"I can see the look—'I've got the sonofabitch now'—on Colonel Mattingly's face when he hears about this."

Cronley looked as if he was about to reply, but then changed his mind.

"I'd much prefer to put the colonel—and Max, too—in civilian clothing," he said. "Suits and ties. But that's out of the question, isn't it?" Cronley asked.

"I have civilian clothing," Mannberg said. "Or my sister does."

"Your sister?"

"And I think Max could wear some of it," Mannberg said.

"Your sister has your civilian clothing?" Cronley asked.

Mannberg nodded.

"I sent it to her when the general and I went to the East," he said.

"And she still has it?" Cronley asked. "Where?"

"We have a farm near Hanover," Mannberg said. "In the British Zone."

"Pay attention," Cronley said. "The chief, DCI-Europe, is about to lay out our plans. While General Gehlen's documents people are doing their thing with the DCI credentials, and Captain Dunwiddie is measuring Mannberg and Ostrowski and then going shopping for them, First Sergeant Tedworth is going to get in one of our new Fords and drive to Hanover to reclaim Colonel Mannberg's wardrobe. Any questions?"

[TWO]
Hachelweg 675
Strasbourg, Département Bas-Rhin, France
1255 10 January 1946

The olive-drab 1943 Ford Deluxe pulled to the curb and stopped. The driver, yet another enormous black sergeant, this one Sergeant Albert Finney, got out from behind the wheel and ran around the back of the car to open the rear passenger door.

Cronley got out. He was wearing an OD woolen uniform. His shoulder insignia, a modification of the wartime insignia of Supreme Headquarters, Allied Expeditionary Force (SHAEF), identified him as being assigned to the European Command (EUCOM). The gold bars of a second lieutenant were pinned to his epaulets, and the insignia of the Quartermaster Corps to his lapels.

Hessinger got out of the front seat. He was also wearing an OD Ike jacket and trousers. The first time Cronley had ever seen him not wearing his pinks and greens was that morning. His uniform now was adorned with staff sergeant's chevrons, QMC lapel insignia, and the EUCOM shoulder patch.

Two other of Tiny's Troopers and the ambulance were parked down the street just within sight of Hachelweg 675. The fourth had made his way to the back of Hachelweg 675, with orders from Sergeant Hessinger to "follow anyone who comes out the back door when we knock at the front."

Staff Sergeant Hessinger had orders for Second Lieutenant Cronley and Sergeant Finney, as well. "Remember," he said in German, "the only German either of you knows is *'Noch ein Bier, bitte'* and *'Wo ist die Toilette?'*"

"*Jawohl*, Herr Feldmarschall," Cronley had replied.

"You already told us that, Freddy," Sergeant Finney said in German.

He opened the trunk of the Ford and took out an open cardboard box. Four cartons of Chesterfield cigarettes, on their ends, were visible. So was an enormous canned ham.

Hessinger opened a gate in a stone wall and walked up to the house, with Cronley and Finney following him. The tile-roofed two-story building looked very much like Cronley's house in the Pullach compound, except that it desperately needed a paint job, several new windows, and roof repairs.

Cronley and Finney had been given a lecture by Professor Hessinger on the history of Strasbourg on the way from Pullach. He told them that over the years it had gone back and forth between being French and German so often that Strasbourgers never really knew to whom they owed their allegiance.

Cronley was surprised, even a little ashamed, that he had never given the subject much thought before. His mother spoke German; she had taught him to speak German from the time he was an infant. He had naturally presumed that she was a German. Or had been before his father had brought her to Midland, after which she was an American.

But when they had crossed the border today, it had been into France. Strasbourg was in France.

Hessinger told them it had been French until after the Franco-

Prussian War, when, in 1871, the Treaty of Frankfurt had given it to the newly formed German Empire. The Germans had promptly "Germanified" the area, and surrounded it with a line of massive forts, named after distinguished Germans, such as von Moltke, Bismarck, and Crown Prince von Sachsen.

After World War I, Hessinger had lectured, the area was given back to the French by the Treaty of Versailles. The French, after renaming the forts—Fort Kronprinz von Sachsen, for example, became Fort Joffre, after the famous French general, and Fort Bismarck became Fort Kléber—held Strasbourg until June of 1940, when the Germans invaded France and promptly reclaimed Strasbourg for the Thousand-Year Reich.

Four years later, Hessinger said, the French 2nd Armored Division rolled into Strasbourg and hoisted the French tricolor on every flagpole they could find.

"Strasbourgers," Hessinger said, and Cronley couldn't tell if his leg was being pulled or not, "keep German and French flags in their closets, so they can hang the right one out of their windows depending on who they're being invaded by this week."

There was a large door knocker, a brass lion's head, on the door. Freddy banged it twice.

Jesus, this is my mother's house, Cronley thought. *She went through this door as a little girl.*

And where we got out of the car is where Dad punched her father's—my grandfather's—lights out.

The door was opened—just a crack.

Cronley could see a woman. She had blond hair, brushed tight against her skull. She looked to be in her thirties, and she didn't look as if she was close to starvation.

"We are looking for Herr Luther Stauffer," Hessinger announced in German.

The woman shook her head, but otherwise didn't reply.

"Then Frau Stauffer," Hessinger said. "Frau Ingebord Stauffer."

The woman tried to close the door. She couldn't. After a moment, Cronley saw why: Hessinger had his foot in the doorjamb.

He also saw the fear in the woman's face.

It grew worse when Hessinger snapped, like a movie Nazi in a third-rate film, *"Papiere, bitte!"*

The woman, her face now showing even more fear, stepped back from the door.

And then the door opened.

A man appeared. He was blond, needed a shave, appeared to be in his middle to late thirties, and looked strangely familiar.

Why do I think my cousin Luther has been hiding behind the door?

"Oh, you're American," the man said in German, and then turned and said, "It's all right, dear, they're Americans."

Then the man asked, "How can I help you, Sergeant?"

"We're looking for Herr Luther Stauffer," Freddy said.

"May I ask why?"

"It's a family matter, not official," Freddy said.

"A family matter?" the man asked, taking a close look at Cronley.

"A family matter," Freddy repeated.

"I am Luther Stauffer."

"Lieutenant," Freddy said in English, "I think we found your cousin."

Hessinger, Cronley, and Finney all decided, judging by the

man's reaction to Freddy's question, that Luther Stauffer spoke—or at least understood—English.

"Tell him, Sergeant, please, that I have some things for him from his aunt, Wilhelmina Stauffer Cronley," Cronley said.

Freddy did so.

"Give him the box, Sergeant Finney," Cronley ordered.

As Finney extended the box, Stauffer pulled the door fully open and said, gesturing, "Please come in."

"What did he say?" Cronley asked.

Hessinger made the translation.

"Then go in," Cronley ordered.

"Yes, sir."

They found themselves in a small living room.

Finney extended the box to Stauffer again.

"This is for me?" Stauffer asked.

"From your aunt, Wilhelmina Stauffer Cronley," Hessinger said. "You are that Luther Stauffer, right? Frau Cronley is your aunt?"

"Yes," Stauffer said, as he put the box on the table.

"If that's so," Hessinger said, "then Lieutenant Cronley is your cousin."

Stauffer and Cronley looked at each other. Stauffer put out his hand, and Cronley took it.

Stauffer turned to his wife and quite unnecessarily announced, "The officer is my cousin." Then he turned to Cronley and said, "I'm sorry, I didn't get your name."

Cronley almost told him, but at the last second caught himself, and instead asked, "What's he asking?"

"He wants to know your name," Hessinger said.

"James. James D. Cronley Junior."

Stauffer took his hand again and said, "James. *Ich bin Luther.*"

Frau Stauffer took a look in the box.

"Oh, so much," she said.

"Tell her my mother got a letter from them, and then wrote me, and here we are," Cronley ordered.

Hessinger made the translation.

Frau Stauffer pulled out a drawer in a massive chest of drawers, came out with a photo album, laid it on the table and began to page through it. Finally, she found what she wanted, and motioned for Cronley to look.

It was an old photograph. Husband, wife, and two young children, a boy of maybe ten and a girl who looked to be several years younger.

"Luther's Papa," Frau Stauffer said, laying her finger on the boy, and then moving it to the girl. *"Dein mutter."*

"She says the girl in the picture is your mother," Hessinger translated.

"Ask him," Frau Stauffer asked, "if he has a picture of his mother now."

Hessinger translated.

As a matter of fact, I have two of her. Right here in my wallet.

Let me show you.

The first one was taken at College Park, the day I graduated from A&M. That's Mom, the lady in the mink coat with the two pounds of pearls hanging around her neck. The girl sitting on the fender of the custom-bodied Packard 280 is our neighbor's kid. Sort of my little sister. I called her "the Squirt."

In this picture, that's my mom standing next to President Truman.

That's my dad, pinning on my captain's bars. This was taken the day after I married the Squirt, and the day she got herself killed.

"Tell her, 'Sorry. I have a couple, but I left them back at the Kloster.'"

Hessinger made the translation, but, picking up on Cronley's slip, said, *"kaserne,"* not "Kloster."

Cronley saw on Luther's face that the translation was unnecessary.

Why is Cousin Luther pretending he doesn't speak English?

"Kloster?" Luther asked.

And he picked up on that, too.

"The lieutenant's little joke," Hessinger said. "Our *kaserne* is in the middle of nowhere, twenty miles outside Munich. The lieutenant jokes that we're all monks, kept in a *kloster* far from the sins of the city."

Luther smiled and then asked, "What exactly do you do in the Army?"

"Lieutenant, he wants to know exactly what you do in the Army."

"Tell him the 711th is responsible for making sure that the equipment in every mess hall in the European Command—and for that matter, in U.S. Forces in Austria—meets Army standards."

Hessinger made the translation. Luther confessed he didn't completely understand. Hessinger made that translation, too.

"You tell him what we do, Sergeant," Cronley ordered.

Hessinger rose to the challenge. He delivered a two-minute lecture detailing the responsibility the 711th QM Mobile Kitchen Repair Company had with regard to maintaining the stoves, ovens, refrigerators, dishwashers, and other electromechanical devices to be found in U.S. Army kitchens.

He explained that there were three teams who roamed Germany, Austria, and France inspecting and repairing such devices. Team 2 was commanded by Lieutenant Cronley. A dishwasher had broken down in Salzburg, and Team 2 had been dispatched to get it running.

Lieutenant Cronley had decided, Hessinger told Luther, that since Strasbourg was more or less on their way to the malfunctioning dishwasher, it was an opportunity for him to drop off the things his mother had sent to her family.

Cronley wasn't sure whether Hessinger had prepared this yarn before they got to Strasbourg or was making it up on the spot. But it sounded credible, and Cousin Luther seemed to be swallowing it whole.

"So you're going to Salzburg?" Luther asked.

Hessinger nodded.

"And from there?"

Why don't I think that's idle curiosity?

Before Hessinger could reply, Cronley said, "Ask him what he does."

"The lieutenant asks what your profession is," Hessinger said.

"I'm an automobile mechanic," Luther replied. "Or I was before the war. Now there are very few automobiles."

Hessinger translated.

"Ask him what he did in the war," Cronley ordered.

As Hessinger translated, Cronley saw that not only had Cousin Luther understood the question as he had asked it, but that he didn't like it, and was searching his mind for a proper response.

What the hell is this all about?

"Do you understand about Strasbourg?" Luther asked. "How over the years it has passed back and forth between French and German control?"

"Not really," said Hessinger, who had delivered a ten-minute lecture on the subject on the way to Strasbourg.

"Well . . ." Luther began.

Hessinger shut him off with a raised hand.

"Lieutenant, your cousin says Strasbourg has been under German and French control for years."

"Really?"

"Go on, Herr Stauffer," Hessinger ordered.

"Well, before the war, we were French," Luther explained. "And then when the Germans came, we were Germans again."

Hessinger translated.

"So what?"

"The lieutenant says he doesn't understand," Hessinger said to Luther.

"When the Germans came, they said I was now a German, and in 1941 I was conscripted into the German Army," Luther said.

There's something fishy about that.

When Hessinger had made the translation, Cronley said, "Ask him what he did in the German Army."

"The lieutenant wants to know what you did in the German Army."

"I was a common soldier, a grenadier, and then I escaped and hid out until the war was over."

Cousin Luther, that is not the truth, the whole truth, and nothing but.

What the hell are you up to?

Hessinger made the translation.

"Tell him I'm glad he made it through the war," Cronley said, and then asked, "How are we fixed for time, Sergeant?"

Hessinger looked at his watch.

"Sir, we're going to have to get on the road," Hessinger replied, and then told Luther the lieutenant was glad that he had made it through the war.

"Tell him we have to leave," Cronley ordered.

When Hessinger had done so, and Luther had replied, he made that unnecessary translation:

"He said he's sorry to hear that, but understands. He says he's very happy with your mother's gifts, and that he hopes this will not be the last time you come to Strasbourg."

"Tell him that if my mother sends some more things, I'll see that he gets them," Cronley said, and put out his hand to Luther.

"And where will you go from Salzburg?" Luther asked.

Hessinger looked to Cronley for permission to answer. Cronley nodded, hoping Luther didn't see him.

"Vienna," Hessinger said, and then, "He wanted to know where we're going from Salzburg. I told him. I hope that's all right."

"Sure. Why not?"

Frau Stauffer said *"Danke schön"* when she shook Cronley's hand, and looked as if she wanted to kiss him.

He smiled at her and walked to and out the door.

The Stauffers waved as they drove off.

[THREE]

When Sergeant Finney pulled the Ford up behind the ambulance, another of Tiny's Troopers—this one a corporal—got out of it and walked to the car.

Finney rolled the window down.

"We're through here. Go get Sergeant Graham," he ordered. "He's somewhere behind the house."

"You got it, Sarge," the corporal said, and took off at a trot.

"Tell me, Sergeant Finney," Cronley said, "now that you are a member of DCI-Europe, what is your professional assessment of Herr Stauffer?"

Finney thought it over for a moment, and then said, "That Kraut is one lying motherfucker."

Cronley didn't reply for a moment, then, coldly furious, said softly, "Sergeant, if you ever say that—or something like that—in my hearing again, you'll spend the rest of your time in Germany as a private walking around Kloster Grünau with a Garand on your shoulder."

"Yes, sir," Finney said, and then, "Captain, I'm sorry. I guess I just forgot he's your cousin."

"That's not what I'm talking about," Cronley said. "My lying Kraut kinsman doubtless has many faults, but I don't think we have any reason to suspect that he ever had incestuous relations with his mother."

"Sorry, Captain."

"You might want to pass the word around that that phrase is *strengstens verboten*. It turns my stomach."

"*Jawohl*, Herr Kapitän."

"And your take on Luther Stauffer, Mr. Hessinger?"

"The question is not whether he was lying to us, but why," Hessinger said. "I think we should find out why."

"How are we going to do that?"

"I think the first thing to do is see if we can find the Strasbourg office of the DST."

"The what?"

"The Direction de la Surveillance du Territoire," Hessinger said. "It's sort of the French CIC, except that it's run by the French National Police, not the army. They may have something on Cousin Luther."

"Okay."

"And before we do that, I suggest we change out of our Quartermaster Corps uniforms," Hessinger said. "I think we'll get more cooperation from our French Allies as CIC agents than we would as dishwasher machine repairmen."

"Why don't we go whole hog and dazzle them with our DCI credentials?"

"Because (a) I would be surprised if word of the DCI's establishment has worked its way through the French bureaucracy, and (b) even if it has, we want to make discreet inquiries."

[FOUR]
Office of the Chief
Direction de la Surveillance du Territoire
Département Bas-Rhin
Strasbourg, France
1335 10 January 1946

When his sergeant showed Cronley, Hessinger, and Finney into his office, Commandant Jean-Paul Fortin of the Strasbourg office of the DST rose behind his desk.

He was a natty man in his early thirties with a trim mustache. He was wearing U.S. Army ODs with French insignia. There were shoulder boards with four gold stripes attached to the epaulets, and a brass representation of a flaming bomb pinned to his left breast pocket. On his desk, in what Cronley thought of as an in-basket, was his uniform cap.

Cronley thought the hat was called a "kepi." It had a flat circular top and what looked like a patent leather visor. The top was red. There were four gold stripes on a dark blue crown, and in the center of the top was another flaming bomb.

Cronley remembered what Luther had said about his being conscripted into the German grenadiers. A flaming bomb was a grenade.

"Thank you for seeing us, Commandant," Cronley said.

He offered his CIC credentials. Commandant Fortin examined them and then looked questioningly at Hessinger and Finney.

They produced their credentials and Fortin examined them carefully.

"Bon," he said. "I regret that I have not much the English."

Oh, shit!

"It is to be hoped that you have the French?"

"Unfortunately, no," Hessinger said.

"Is possible German?"

"We all speak German, Major," Cronley said.

"Wunderbar!" Fortin said. "But of course, being in the CIC, you would. Now, how may the DST be of service to the CIC?"

"We're interested in a man named Luther Stauffer," Cronley said. "We've heard he was originally from Strasbourg, and we're wondering if the DST has anything on him."

"Herr Cronley, if you don't mind me saying so, you sound like a Strasbourger yourself."

"My mother, Commandant Fortin, was a Strasbourgerin. I learned my German from her."

"So was mine, a Strasbourgerin, I mean."

"Mine married an American right after the First World War," Cronley said. "And if you don't mind my asking, I've always been led to believe the DST was a police organization."

"It is. I've been seconded to it," Fortin said, and then bellowed, "Sergeant!"

When the sergeant appeared, Fortin said, "Check in the files for a man named . . ." He looked at Cronley.

"Stauffer," Hessinger furnished. "Luther Stauffer."

"Oui, mon Commandant."

"What is this Stauffer fellow wanted for?" Fortin asked.

"We didn't mean to give that impression," Hessinger said. "His name came up in an investigation of black market activities, that's all. We'd just like to know who he is."

"I thought your Criminal Investigation, DCI, did those sort of investigations."

"Most of the time, they do," Hessinger said.

Commandant Fortin is good. Is this going to blow up in our faces?

"To return to your earlier question," Fortin said, "there were . . . how do I say this delicately? . . . certain *awkward* problems here in Strasbourg. When the Germans came in 1940, there were some policemen, including senior officers, who were not too terribly unhappy."

"'Better Hitler than Blum'?" Hessinger said.

"Exactly," Fortin said. "I'm glad you understand."

"I don't," Cronley blurted, and immediately regretted it.

Fortin looked at Hessinger and signaled that Hessinger should make the explanation.

"He was premier of France for a while," Hessinger began. "A Jew, an anti-fascist, and a socialist, who thought the state should control the banks and industry. This enraged the bankers and businessmen in general, and they began to say, 'Better Hitler than Blum.' He was forced out of office before the war. After 1940, he was imprisoned by the Vichy government, and then by the Germans. We liberated him from a concentration camp, and he returned to France."

"I'm glad you understand," Fortin said. "The only thing I would add to that is that when he returned to France, Blum immediately re-divided the Fourth Republic into those who love him, and those who think he should have been shot in 1939."

"May I ask where you stand on Monsieur Blum?" Hessinger asked.

"A career officer such as myself would never dream of saying that a senior French official should be shot. Or fed to the savage beasts."

"I appreciate your candor, Commandant," Cronley said. "And I apologize for my ignorance."

Fortin waved his hand, to signal *No apology was necessary.*

"As I was saying, when the Germans came, many senior police officers were willing to collaborate with them. Many, perhaps most, of the junior policemen were not. The Germans hauled them off to Germany as slave laborers. Many of them died in Germany.

"When we—I had the honor of serving with General Philippe Leclerc's Free French Second Armored Division—tore down the swastika and raised the Tricolor over the Strasbourg Cathedral again, some of the senior police officers who had collaborated with the Boche were shot trying to escape, and the rest were imprisoned for later trial.

"That left Strasbourg without a police force worthy of the name. General Leclerc established an ad hoc force from the Second Armored and named me as its chief. He knew I was a Strasbourger. I have been here since, trying to establish a police force. That has proved difficult, as there are very few men in Strasbourg from whom to recruit. And policemen from elsewhere in France are reluctant to transfer here—"

He was interrupted when his sergeant came back into the office.

"I found two in the files, *mon Commandant,*" he announced. "A Stauffer, Karl, and a Stauffer, Luther."

He laid the files on Fortin's desk, as Cronley wondered, *Do I have another cousin?*

Fortin examined the folders.

"I believe you said 'Stauffer, Luther'?"

"That's the name we have, Commandant," Hessinger said.

"I thought it rang a bell," Fortin said. "Very interesting man. You're not the only one, Herr Cronley, who'd like to talk to him."

"You want him?" Cronley asked.

"That's why he's interesting," Fortin said. "We've been looking for him, but so, I've come to believe, was the Schutzstaffel."

He offered the file to Cronley, who overcame his curiosity and handed it to Hessinger with the explanation, "Mr. Hessinger is my expert in reading dossiers."

"I mentioned before," Fortin went on, "that when the Germans came in 1940, some of our fellow Strasbourgers, Herr Cronley, were not unhappy to see them. Some of them, in fact, were so convinced that Hitler was the savior of Europe, and National Socialism the wave of the future, that they joined the Légion des Volontaires Français.

"Luther Stauffer was one of them. He joined the LVF as a *feldwebel*—sergeant—and went off to Germany for training."

"So he was a collaborator?"

"So it would appear," Fortin said. "The LVF, after training, was sent to what the Boche called 'the East,' as the Wehrmacht approached Moscow. They fought the Russians there, and whether through bravery or ineptitude, suffered severe losses and were returned to Germany."

"You seem to know quite a bit about this volunteer legion," Cronley said.

"Keeping up with them became sort of a hobby with me while we were in England. And as I had been assigned to military intelligence, it wasn't difficult."

"How'd you get to England?"

"I was with Général de Brigade de Gaulle at Montcornet, and I was one of the officers he selected to accompany him to England when he flew there on June seventeenth, 1940."

"I don't know what that means," Cronley confessed.

"There are those, including me," Hessinger chimed in, "who believe the only battle the Germans lost in France in 1940 was Montcornet."

"You know about it?"

"De Gaulle attacked with two hundred tanks and drove the Germans back to Caumont," Hessinger replied.

"Where most of our tanks were destroyed by Stukas," Fortin said. "Who attacked us at their leisure because our fighter aircraft were deployed elsewhere," Fortin said. "Anyway, to answer Herr Cronley's question, a month to the day after Montcornet, I flew to England with Général de Gaulle."

If de Gaulle flew you to England with him, and you were with Leclerc when he liberated Strasbourg, and then became the Strasbourg chief of police, how come you're still a major?

Answer: You're not. You just want people to think you're not as important as you really are.

Colonel Sergei Likharev of the NKGB didn't want people to think he was as important as he is, so he called himself Major Konstantin Orlovsky.

I wonder if your real name is Fortin, Commandant—probably Colonel—Fortin?

"What was left of the Légion des Volontaires Français," Fortin went on, "was assigned relatively unimportant duties in Germany—guarding supply depots, that sort of thing."

"And Stauffer was among them?" Cronley asked.

"Oh, yes. The Boche liked him. He'd been awarded the Iron Cross and promoted to *leutnant* for his service in the East. Then, in September 1944, a month after Général Leclerc and the French Second Armored Division liberated Paris, the Germans merged all French military collaborators into what they called the 'Waffen-Grenadier-Brigade der SS Charlemagne.'"

"'*All* French military collaborators'?" Cronley parroted.

"The Boche had also formed the Horst Wessel brigade of young Frenchmen. Other collaborators had had a quasi-military role in Organisation Todt, which built the defenses in Normandy and elsewhere—the defenses that had failed to stop the Allied invasion. Then there was the collaborationist version of the Secret State Police, the Geheime Staatspolizei, which was known as the Milice. And there were others who fled as the Allies marched across France.

"The Germans didn't trust many of them, but they apparently did trust Leutnant Stauffer. He was taken into the SS as a *sturmführer*—a captain—and put to work training the newcomers."

"And here is Sturmführer Stauffer," Hessinger said, as he handed Cronley the dossier.

Cronley looked at the photograph of a young man in uniform.

I'll be a sonofabitch, Cousin Luther was an SS officer.

Fortin extended his hand for the dossier, looked at it, and said, "Forgive me for saying this, Mr. Cronley, but he looks very much like you."

"I noticed," Cronley said.

"In February 1945," Fortin went on, "the brigade was renamed 'the Thirty-third Waffen-Grenadier-Division der SS Charlemagne,' then loaded on a train and sent to fight the Red Army in Poland. On February twenty-fifth it was attacked by troops of the Soviet First Belorussian Front and scattered. What was left of them retreated to the Baltic coast, were evacuated by sea to Denmark, and later sent to Neustretlitz, in Germany, for refitting.

"The last time anyone saw Sturmführer Stauffer was when he went on a three-day leave immediately after getting off the ship in Germany," Fortin said matter-of-factly. "We think it reasonable to believe he deserted the SS at that time, even before his comrades reached Neustretlitz. It is possible, even likely, that he made his way here to Strasbourg and went into hiding."

"You think he deserted because he could see the war was lost?" Cronley asked.

"I'm sure he knew that, but I think it more likely that he heard somehow—he was an SS officer—what the Boche had in mind for them."

"Berlin?" Hessinger asked.

Fortin nodded.

"The remaining collaborators," Fortin amplified, "about seven hundred of them, went to Berlin in late April, just before the Red Army surrounded the city. A week later, when the Battle for Berlin was over, what few were left of them—thirty—surrendered to the Russians.

"According to the Russians, they fought bravely, literally until they had fired their last round of ammunition. I'd like to believe that. But on the other hand, what other option did they have?"

"Desertion?" Cronley asked.

"Desertion was more dangerous than fighting the Russians, as those thirty survivors learned. Of the seven hundred men who went to Berlin, seventy-two died at the hands of the SS for attempting to desert. They were hung from lamp poles *pour encourager les autres*."

"You have no idea where Luther Stauffer is?" Cronley asked.

"I have not been entirely truthful with you, Mr. Cronley," Fortin said. "I wouldn't be surprised if at this moment he's at Hachelweg 675 here in Strasbourg."

They locked eyes for a moment.

"And I have not been entirely truthful with you, either, Commandant Fortin," Cronley said.

He took his Directorate of Central Intelligence identification from his Ike jacket and handed it to Fortin.

Fortin examined it carefully and then handed it back.

"I'm impressed," he said. "The DCI has only been in business since the first of January, and here you are—what? a week and two days later?—already hard at work."

"And I'm surprised that the Strasbourg chief of police has even heard about the DCI."

"I'm just a simple policeman," Fortin said, with a straight face, "but I try to stay abreast of what's going on in the world. Are you going to tell me what your real interest in Luther Stauffer is, Mr. Cronley?"

"He's my cousin. I should lead off with that. He—actually his wife—wrote my mother begging for help, saying they were starving. She sent food—canned hams, coffee, cigarettes, et cetera—to me and asked that I deliver them to him."

"And?"

"When we were in his house, all three of us sensed that he wasn't telling us the truth. He said he was conscripted into the German Army . . ."

"Where he served as a common soldier, a grenadier," Hessinger injected.

". . . which sounded fishy to us, so Mr. Hessinger suggested that the police might be able to tell us something about him."

"I'm disappointed," Fortin said. "Frankly, I was hoping the DCI was working on the Odessa Organization. I'm almost as interested in that as I am in dealing with our collaborators."

"I'm sorry, I don't know what you're talking about."

"It stands for the Organisation der ehemaligen SS-Angehörigen," Hessinger said. "Organization of Former German SS Officers."

"Sort of a VFW for Nazis?" Cronley asked.

"'VFW'?" Fortin parroted.

"Veterans of Foreign Wars," Cronley explained. "An American veterans organization. My father has been president of VFW Post 9900 in Midland as long as I can remember."

"Your father was in the First War?" Fortin asked.

"He was. And he was here in Strasbourg when the Communists tried to take over the city. That's where he met my mother."

"Which you said is why you speak German like a Strasbourger," Fortin said. "And your mother, I gather, maintained a close relationship with her family here?"

"No. Quite the opposite. Once she married my father, her family wanted nothing to do with her. The only contact she ever had with them was a letter before the war saying her mother had died. And then the letter asking for help."

"What would your reaction be if I told you that once I get what I want to know from Luther Stauffer about Odessa, I'm going to arrest him and charge him with collaboration?"

"Why is Odessa so important?"

"The purpose of Odessa is to help SS officers get out of Germany so they can't be tried for war crimes. I like SS officers only slightly more than I like collaborators."

"What I have heard of Odessa," Hessinger said, "is that it's more fancy than fact."

"Then, Herr Hessinger, you have heard wrong," Fortin said simply.

"I can ask General Greene what he knows about Odessa," Cronley said to Hessinger.

"And what is your relationship with the chief of CIC of the European Command?" Fortin asked.

So he knows who Greene is. Commandant Fortin does get around, doesn't he?

"He tells me what I want to know," Cronley said.

"I'm just a simple policeman," Fortin repeated. "So when I look at you, Mr. Cronley, I see a young man. Logic tells me you are either a junior civilian, or a junior officer. And that makes me wonder why the chief of CIC, European Command, would tell you anything he didn't want to tell you."

When you can't think of anything else, tell the truth.

"Actually, I'm a captain seconded to DCI," Cronley said. "The reason General Greene will tell me everything I want to know is because he has been ordered to do so by Admiral Souers, who speaks with the authority of President Truman."

"And who do you work directly for, Captain Cronley?"

Army captains are rarely, if ever, directly subordinate to Navy admirals. And "Commandant" Fortin knows that. So the truth—that I work directly under Admiral Souers—won't work here.

"We have a phrase, Commandant, 'Need to Know.' With respect, I don't think you have the need to know that."

"I'm familiar with the phrase, Captain."

"If you don't mind, Commandant, I prefer 'Mr. Cronley.'"

"Of course," Fortin said. "I asked you before, Mr. Cronley, what your reaction would be if I told you I sooner or later intend to arrest your cousin Luther and see that he's tried as a collaborator?"

Cronley very carefully considered his reply before deciding again that when all else fails, tell the truth.

"I don't think I'd like the effect that would have on my mother."

"But you just told me she's had no contact with him since she married."

"He's her nephew. She's a woman. A kind, gentle, loving, Christian woman."

"And that would stop you from helping me to put him in prison?"

"The way you were talking, I thought you meant you were going to put a blindfold on him and stand him against a wall."

"If I had caught him when we liberated Strasbourg, I would have. But Général de Gaulle says that we must reunite France, not exacerbate its wounds, and as an officer, I must obey that order. The best I can hope for is that when I finally go to arrest him, he will resist and I will be justified in shooting him. If he doesn't, he'll probably be sentenced to twenty years. Answer the question."

"I have no problem with your trying him as a collaborator," Cronley said. And then, he thought aloud: "I could tell my mother I knew nothing about him, or his arrest."

"But you would be reluctant to lie to your mother?" Fortin challenged.

Cronley didn't reply.

"Because she is, what did you say, 'a kind, gentle, loving, Christian woman'?"

Again Cronley didn't reply.

"Allow me to tell you about the kind, gentle, and loving Christian women in my life, Mr. Cronley. There have been two. One was my mother, and the second my wife. When the Mobilization came in March of 1939, I was stationed at Saumur, the cavalry school. I telephoned my mother and told her I had rented a house in Argenton, near Saint-Martin-de-Sanzay, near Saumur, and that I wanted her to come there and care for my wife, who was pregnant, and my son while I was on active service.

"She would hear nothing about it. She said that she had no intention of leaving her home to live in the country. She said what I should do is send my family to my home in Strasbourg.

"I reminded her that we seemed about to go to war, and if that happened, there was a chance—however slim—that the Germans would occupy Strasbourg as they had done before. Mother replied that it had happened before and she'd really had no trouble with the Germans.

"So my wife went to stay with my mother.

"About six months after I went to England with Général de

Gaulle, the Milice and the SS appeared at her door and took my mother, my wife, and my children away for interrogation. They apparently believed that I hadn't gone to England, but was instead here, in Strasbourg, organizing the resistance.

"That was the last anyone saw of my mother, my wife, or my children. I heard what had happened from the resistance, so the first thing I did when I got back to Strasbourg with Général Leclerc was go to the headquarters of the Milice. The collaborators, my French countrymen, had done a very good job of destroying all their records.

"I have heard, but would rather not believe, that when the Milice, my countrymen, were through with their interrogation of my mother, my wife, and my children, their bodies were thrown into the Rhine."

"My God!" Cronley said.

"Your kids, too? Those miserable motherfuckers!" Sergeant Finney exclaimed bitterly in English.

Cronley saw on Fortin's face that he had heard the expression before.

Which means he speaks English far better than he wanted us to think.

Of course he speaks English, stupid! He spent almost four years in England.

Both Hessinger and Finney looked at Cronley, who had his tongue pushing against his lower lip, visibly deep in thought.

Finally he said, very softly, "My sentiments exactly, Sergeant Finney."

He turned to Fortin.

"Commandant, I really don't know what to say."

"I don't expect you to say anything, Mr. Cronley," Fortin said. "I just wanted you to understand my deep interest in your cousin, and in Odessa."

"Just as soon as we get back, I'll find out what General Greene knows about it, and get back to you with whatever he tells me."

I will also go to General Gehlen, who probably knows more about Odessa than anyone else.

But I can't tell you about Gehlen, can I, Commandant?

Even if Gehlen's never mentioned it to me.

And why hasn't he?

"I would be grateful to you if you did that."

"Is there anything else I can do for you?"

"Possibly."

"Anything."

"You didn't tell your cousin you're an intelligence officer?"

"Of course not."

"What did you tell him you do?"

"Repair dishwashing machines," Cronley said, chuckling.

"Excuse me?"

"Freddy, tell Commandant Fortin all about the 711th QM Mobile Kitchen Repair Company."

Hessinger did so.

"I wondered," Fortin said, when Hessinger had finished his little lecture. "The European Command has no record of the 711th anything. When you parked your car in front of Hachelweg 675 and the ambulance with the red crosses painted over down the street, it piqued my curiosity, and I had Sergeant Deladier"—he pointed to the outer office—"call Frankfurt and ask about it."

"I hope Frankfurt . . . I presume you mean EUCOM . . . didn't have its curiosity piqued," Cronley said.

Fortin shook his head.

"Deladier's a professional. He's been with me a long time," Fortin said. "And you would say your cousin accepted this?"

"I think he did."

"You would think so. What about you, Sergeant? Do you think Herr Stauffer thinks you're dishwashing machine repairmen?"

"Yes, sir. We had our act pretty much together. I think Stauffer believed us."

"Your act pretty much together?"

"We were all . . . not just me . . . in uniform. Mr. Cronley as a Quartermaster Corps second lieutenant, Mr. Hessinger as a staff sergeant. Stauffer had no reason not to believe what we told him."

"In addition to you being dishwashing machine repairmen, what else did you tell him?"

"We told him our next stop was Salzburg," Hessinger answered for him. "He seemed to find that very interesting."

"Because it would take you across the border into U.S. Forces Austria from EUCOM," Fortin said. "Crossing borders is a major problem for Odessa. Tell me, Sergeant, how much talking did you do when you were in the house?"

Finney thought it over for a moment before replying, "Commandant, I don't think I opened my mouth when I was in the house. All I did was carry the black market stuff."

"In other words, all you were was the driver of the staff car?"

"Yes, sir."

"Let me offer a hypothetical," Fortin said. "Let us suppose you were too busy, Second Lieutenant Cronley, to yourself deliver more cigarettes, coffee, et cetera, to your cousin Luther and instead sent Sergeant Finney to do it for you.

"Do you think your cousin might either prevail upon Sergeant Finney to take something—maybe a few cartons of cigarettes, or a canned ham—to, say, Salzburg as either a goodwill gesture, or because he could make a little easy money doing so?"

"I see where you're going, Commandant," Hessinger said.

"Start out more or less innocently, and then as Sergeant Finney slid down the slippery slope of corruption, move him onto other things such as moving a couple of men—'going home, they don't have papers'—across the border. *Und so weiter.*"

"Yeah," Cronley said.

"These people routinely murder people who get in their way. With that in mind, would you be willing to have Sergeant Finney do something like this?"

"That's up to Sergeant Finney," Cronley said.

"Hell yes, I'll do it. I'd like to burn as many of these moth—sonsofbitches as I can," Finney said.

"Thank you for cleaning up your language, Sergeant Finney," Cronley said. "I really would have hated to have had to order Mr. Hessinger to wash your mouth out with soap."

Finney smiled at him.

"I would suggest that in, say, a week Sergeant Finney deliver another package to Herr Stauffer," Fortin said. "How does that fit into your schedule?"

"Not a problem," Cronley said. "We have to be in Vienna on the fourteenth."

"Vienna?" Fortin asked.

"So we can be back at the monastery on the sixteenth. Finney could deliver a second package the next day, the seventeenth. That's a week from today."

"Why do I think you're not going to tell me what you're going to do in Vienna?"

"Because you understand that there are some things simple policemen just don't have the need to know," Cronley said.

"That's cruel," Fortin said, smiling, and put out his hand. "I'm perfectly willing to believe you're a second lieutenant of the Quartermaster Corps."

"It's been a pleasure meeting you, Simple Policeman," Cronley said. "I look forward to seeing you soon again."

[FIVE]
Suite 307
The Bristol Hotel
Kaerntner Ring 1
Vienna, Austria
1600 14 January 1946

It was time to go to what everybody hoped would be a meeting with Rahil, A/K/A Seven-K, at the Café Weitz, and Cronley and Schultz had just finished putting the fifty thousand dollars intended for her in former Oberst Ludwig Mannberg's Glen plaid suit when there came a knock at the door.

Putting the money into Mannberg's suit had proved more difficult than anyone had thought it would be. It had come from the

States packed in $5,000 packets, each containing one hundred fifty-dollar bills. There were ten such packets, each about a half-inch thick.

Mannberg's suit was sort of a souvenir of happier times, when young Major Mannberg had not only been an assistant military attaché at the German embassy in London, but in a position to pay for "bespoke" clothing from Anderson & Sheppard of Savile Row.

Cronley had not ever heard the term "bespoke" until today, but now he understood that it meant "custom-tailored" and that custom-tailored meant that it had been constructed about the wearer's body, and that meant room had been provided for a handkerchief, wallet, and maybe car keys, but not to accommodate twenty packets of fifty $50-dollar bills, each half an inch thick and eight inches long.

When they had finished, Mannberg literally had packs of money in every pocket in the suit jacket, and every pocket in his trousers. He also had a $2,500 packet in each sock. The vest that came with the suit was on the bed.

Ostrowski was larger than Mannberg and just barely fit into one of Mannberg's suits, providing he did not button the buttons of the double-breasted jacket. But to conceal the .45 pistol he was carrying in one of the holsters Hessinger had had made, he was going to have to keep his hand in the suit jacket pocket to make sure the pistol was covered.

"Who the hell is that?" Cronley asked, when the knock on the door came.

"There's one way to find out," El Jefe said, and went to the door and opened it. Ostrowski hurriedly shoved his pistol under one of the cushions of the couch he was sitting on.

There were three men at the door, all wearing ODs with U.S. triangles.

The elder of them politely asked, "Mr. Schultz?"

El Jefe nodded.

"If you don't mind, I'd like to ask you a few questions," the man said, and produced a set of CIC credentials. "May we come in?"

El Jefe backed away from the door and waved them in.

The three of them looked suspiciously around the room.

"What's the nature of your business in Vienna, Mr. Schultz, if you don't mind my asking?"

"What's this all about?" Schultz asked.

"Please, just answer the question."

"Why don't you have a look at this?" Schultz said, extending his DCI identification. "It will explain why I don't answer a lot of questions."

"Don't I know you?" one of them, the youngest one, asked of Cronley.

"You look familiar," Cronley said, and found, or thought he did, the name. "Surgeon, right?"

"Spurgeon," the man corrected him.

"I never saw one of these before," the CIC agent said, after examining El Jefe's DCI credentials.

"I'm not surprised," El Jefe said.

"Major, I knew this fellow at Holabird," the younger agent said.

"What?"

"We took Surveillance together," the younger agent said. "Right?"

"Under Major Derwin," Cronley confirmed.

"Terrible Tommy Derwin," Agent Spurgeon said. He put out his hand. "Cronley, right?"

"James D., Junior."

"Are you working?"

Cronley nodded.

"Doing what?"

"I'm sort of an aide-de-camp to Mr. Schultz."

"You're CIC?" the older agent asked.

Cronley produced his CIC credentials.

"I should have known it would be something like this," the older agent said.

"What would be something like this?" Schultz asked.

"Well, we encourage the people in the hotel to report suspicious activity, and one of the assistant managers did."

"Did he tell you what I did that was suspicious?" El Jefe asked.

"Well, he said he heard your men speaking Russian."

"Guilty as charged," Ostrowski said. "He must have overheard Ludwig and me."

He nodded toward Mannberg.

"You sound English," the older CIC agent said.

"Guilty as charged," Max repeated, and showed him his DCI credentials.

"Gentlemen, I'm sorry," the older agent said, "but you're in the business, and you know how these things happen."

"Not a problem," Schultz said. "You were just doing your job."

"You going to be in town for a while, Cronley?" Agent Spurgeon asked.

"We're leaving tomorrow," Schultz answered for him.

"Pity," Spurgeon said. "I was hoping we could have a drink and swap tales about Terrible Tommy Derwin and other strange members of the faculty of Holabird High."

"Sorry, we have to go," Schultz said.

"I guess you know that Derwin is here," Cronley said.

"He's here?"

"He's the new CIC/ASA inspector general for EUCOM," Cronley said.

"Oh, yeah," the senior agent said. "The old one, Colonel Schumann, blew himself up, didn't he?"

"Him and his wife," Cronley confirmed.

"Well, we'll get out of here," the senior agent said. "I'm really sorry about this, Mr. Schultz."

"You were just doing your job," El Jefe repeated.

"If there's ever anything we can do for you, just give us a yell."

"Can't think of a thing, but thanks."

Hands were shaken all around, and the Vienna CIC team left.

When they had, Cronley asked, "What the hell was that all about?"

El Jefe shrugged, then looked at his wristwatch and said, "We'd better get going."

[SIX]
Café Weitz
Gumpendorferstrasse 74
Vienna, Austria
1650 14 January 1946

When Cronley, El Jefe, and Finney walked into the Café Weitz, several of the waiters were drawing heavy curtains over the large windows looking out on the street. This would keep people on Gumpendorferstrasse, and on the trolley cars running down it, from looking into the café.

The curtains were drawn every night as darkness fell. During the day, the curtains were open, so Café Weitz patrons could look out onto Gumpendorferstrasse and the trolley cars.

But drawing the curtains did something else. During the day, looking out from the café gave the patrons a look at the empty windows of the bombed-out, roofless five-story apartment buildings across the street. With the curtains drawn, they were no longer visible.

And with the drawn curtains shutting out any light from the street, the only light in the café came from small bulbs in wall fixtures and in three chandeliers and small candles burning in tiny lamps on all the tables. This served to hide the shabbiness of the café's curtains and walls and everything else, and to offer at least a suggestion of its prewar elegance.

In one corner of the room, a string quartet (or quintet or sextet, it varied with the hour) of elderly musicians in formal clothing played continuously, mostly Strauss, but sometimes tunes from Hungarian light opera.

Cronley knew all this because he had come to the café three times before. So had everybody else. Cronley thought of it as reconnaissance, but Schultz called it "casing the joint."

After the first visit, they had gone back to the hotel, then, at Mannberg's suggestion, drawn maps of the café from memory. Very few of the first maps drawn agreed on any of the details except the location of the doors and the musicians, but the third, final maps drawn were pretty much identical.

It was decided that Cronley, El Jefe, and Sergeant Finney, who were all wearing OD Ike jackets with civilian insignia, would enter the café first and take the closest table they could find to the musicians. This would give them a pretty good view of most of the interior. Then Mannberg would enter, alone, and take a table that would be in clear view of anyone coming into the café. On his heels, but not with him, would be Maksymilian Ostrowski, who would take the closest table he could find to the door of the vestibule outside the restrooms, which, they were guessing, would be where, presuming she showed up, Seven-K/Rahil would take the money from Mannberg.

Or where agents of the NKGB would attempt to steal the fifty thousand dollars from Mannberg. Ostrowski's job was to see that didn't happen.

Cronley pointed to a table near the musicians, and a waiter who looked like he was in his mid-eighties led them to it and pulled out chairs for them.

A dog yipped at Cronley and he turned to see a tiny hot dog, as they called dachshunds back in Midland, in the lap of an old lady. About half the old women in the place had dogs of all sizes with them.

Cronley barked back at the tiny dachshund, wondering if it was a puppy or whether there was such a thing as a miniature dachshund.

Then he ordered a pilsner, the same for Finney, and El Jefe said he would have a pilsner and a Slivovitz.

"What the hell is that?"

"Hungarian plum brandy. Got a kick like a mule."

Cronley was tempted, but resisted. If they were going to meet a top-level agent of both the NKGB and the Mossad, he obviously should not be drinking anything that had a kick like a mule.

"And ask him if they have any peanuts," El Jefe said.

"I brought some, when they didn't have any last night," Finney said, and produced a tin can of Planters peanuts, opened it, and put it on the table.

The tiny dachshund barked.

Cronley looked at him.

"Franz Josef," the old lady said in English, "likes peanuts."

Cronley offered Franz Josef a peanut, which he quickly devoured.

"Is that a full-sized dog, or is he a puppy?" Cronley asked in German.

He felt Finney's knee signal him under the table, and saw that Mannberg had come into the café.

"Franz Josef is four," she said, this time in German.

"He's so small," Cronley said, and fed the dog another peanut.

He took a closer look at the woman. She wasn't as old as he had originally thought, maybe fifty-something, or sixty-something, but not really old. She had rouged cheeks and wore surprisingly red lipstick.

"Good things come in small packages," the old lady said.

"So they say," Cronley said. "Would you like a peanut? A handful of peanuts?"

"You are very kind," the old lady said in English. "A *kavalier*."

Cronley offered her the can of peanuts.

"A what?" he asked.

"You know, a man in armor on a horse. Thank you for the peanuts."

"My pleasure," Cronley said, and fed Franz Josef another peanut.

Finney's knee signaled him again, and he saw Max Ostrowski walk across the room, take a table near the door to the restroom vestibule. Then he leaned a chair against the table to show it was taken and walked into the restroom vestibule.

Cronley saw an old woman wearing an absurd hat and two pounds of costume jewelry march regally across the room and enter the restroom vestibule.

Shit!

Whatever is going to happen in there is now going to have to be put on hold until the old lady finishes taking her leak.

"Let me taste that," Cronley said, pointing to Schultz's Slivovitz.

El Jefe handed him the glass, and Cronley took a small sip.

His throat immediately started burning, and he reached quickly for his beer.

"Don't say I didn't warn you," El Jefe said, chuckling.

Five long minutes later, Cronley asked rhetorically, "What the hell's taking that old woman so long?"

Three minutes after that, the old woman finally came out and marched regally back across the café to her table.

"How long have you been in Vienna?" the old lady with the dog asked.

"This is the fourth day. We leave tomorrow."

"You're in the Army?"

"I work for the Army. I work with kitchen equipment."

"You Americans do everything with a machine."

"Yes, ma'am. We try to."

Finney's knee signaled him again and he saw Mannberg stand up and walk into the restroom vestibule. A moment later, Ostrowski followed him.

The waiter delivered the beer and the Slivovitz.

Finney paid for it.

Ostrowski came out of the restroom vestibule and sat at his table.

A minute or so later, Mannberg came out of the vestibule, laid money on his table, and, standing, drank what was left of his pilsner.

Then he walked out of the Café Weitz.

Ostrowski got to his feet a minute later and did the same thing.

I don't know what the hell went on in the bathroom, but obviously Mannberg somehow found out Rahil/Seven-K wasn't coming.

Shit!

I wonder what spooked her?

El Jefe had obviously come to much the same conclusion.

"I don't know about you two, but I'm going to go back to the hotel," he said.

"Yeah," Cronley said. "So long, Franz Josef."

The dog yipped at him again.

Cronley gave the can of peanuts to the woman.

"It was nice talking to you," he said.

"Yes, it was," she said. "And I thank you and Franz Josef thanks you for the peanuts."

"My pleasure. *Auf wiedersehen.*"

Cronley, Finney, and El Jefe had gone to the Café Weitz in the Ford staff car. Mannberg had taken the streetcar from Ringstrasse, and Ostrowski had walked.

They returned to the Hotel Bristol the same way.

When Ostrowski walked into the lobby of the hotel, Cronley, Finney, and Schultz were in the dining room.

When they saw him, Schultz asked, very concerned, "Where the hell is Ludwig? We should have brought everybody back here."

He stopped when he saw Mannberg come through the revolving doors into the lobby.

Mannberg walked to them and sat down.

"So what do we do now?" Cronley asked.

"Flag down the waiter so I can get one of those," Mannberg said, indicating Cronley's glass of whisky.

"That's not what I meant," Cronley said.

"Oh," Mannberg said, thinking he now understood the question. "We go back to Pullach. We're through here."

"Jesus Christ!" Cronley flared. "What do we do about getting the money to Seven-K?"

"By now, I'm sure she has it," Mannberg said. "I gave it to her man—actually her woman—in the restroom vestibule."

"Seven-K was there?"

"Yes, Jim, she was," Mannberg said, smiling broadly.

"She was in the café? Where?"

"Sitting next to you while you were feeding her and her dog peanuts."

[ONE]

Quarters of the U.S. Military Government Liaison Officer
The South German Industrial Development
Organization Compound
Pullach, Bavaria
The American Zone of Occupied Germany
1735 15 January 1946

It had taken Cronley, Hessinger, and Finney nine hours to drive the 270 miles from Vienna to Pullach in the Ford staff car. Schultz, Ostrowski, and Mannberg, who had left Vienna later on the Blue Danube, were already "home"—and sitting at the bar—when the three walked in. Captain Chauncey L. Dunwiddie, Major Maxwell Ashton III, and First Sergeant Abraham L. Tedworth were sitting at a table.

As Cronley headed for the toilet, Dunwiddie called, "My guys with you?"

He referred to the men who had gone to Strasbourg and then Vienna with Cronley in one of the ambulances and those in the two ambulances who had gone directly to Vienna.

"Very quickly, as my back teeth are floating," Cronley replied. "They left when we did, but since there is an MP checkpoint every other mile on the road, God only knows when they'll get here."

He then disappeared into the toilet, emerged a few minutes later, and went to the bar.

"Wait a minute before you get into that," Hessinger said, indicating the bottle of Haig & Haig Cronley had taken from behind the bar and was opening.

"With all due respect, Staff Sergeant Hessinger, I have earned this," Cronley said, and gave him the finger.

Hessinger appeared about to reply, and then went into the toilet. He came out two minutes later, and as Sergeant Finney went in, announced, "I have been thinking of something for the past two hours that will probably make me very unpopular when I bring it up."

"Then don't bring it up," Cronley said.

"We have to make a record, a report, of what we have been doing," Hessinger said. "And we have to do it before we start drinking."

When Cronley didn't immediately reply, Hessinger went on: "Sooner or later, somebody is going to want to know what we've been doing. Somebody is going to want to look at our records. And when that happens, saying 'We haven't been keeping any records' is not going to be an acceptable answer."

"Jesus!" Cronley said.

"He's right, Jim," El Jefe said. "We at least need to keep after-action reports."

"And who do we report to?" Cronley asked.

El Jefe didn't immediately reply, and Cronley saw on his face that he was giving the subject very serious consideration.

"I don't know why I didn't think of this," El Jefe said, after a long moment, and then answered his own question. "Because Cletus didn't do after-action reports. But that was then and in Argentina. This is now and you're in Germany. Cletus didn't have two different groups of people looking over his shoulder to find something, anything, proving he was incompetent. You do, Jim."

"Two groups?"

"Colonel Mattingly. And the two from the Pentagon . . ."

"Lieutenant Colonel Parsons and Major Ashley," Hessinger furnished.

"And then there's the problem of how do we keep the wrong people from getting their hands on the after-action reports Freddy is right in saying we have to make," Schultz went on.

"Classify them Top Secret–Presidential and Top Secret–Lindbergh," Cronley suggested.

"How do we keep the wrong people who hold Top Secret–Presidential and Top Secret–Lindbergh clearances from seeing them? Like Mattingly? And Whatsisname? McClung, the ASA guy?"

"And Dick Tracy," Cronley said.

"Who?" Ashton asked.

"Major Thomas G. Derwin, the new CIC/ASA inspector general. He's got all the clearances."

"Why do you call him 'Dick Tracy'?"

"He was more or less affectionately so known when he was teaching Techniques of Surveillance at Holabird High."

"You mean the CIC Center at Camp Holabird?" Ashton asked.

"Yes, I do," Cronley said. "One of the spooks who came to El Jefe's room in the Bristol was a fellow alumnus."

"What spooks who came to your room in the hotel?"

Cronley told him.

Ashton thought about that for a moment, and then said, "I know what we can do. About keeping the wrong people from seeing the after-action reports, I mean. Send them to me."

"I thought we were talking about the spooks who came to my room," El Jefe said.

Ashton ignored him and went on, "And once I get them, as chief, Operation Ost, I can decide who else should see them. I will decide nobody else should see them. That way, they would be on file in case, for example, the admiral wants to."

"That'd work," El Jefe said.

"Problem solved," Cronley said sarcastically. "Now all we have to do is write the after-action report—"

"Reports," Hessinger interrupted. "Plural. Starting, I suggest, with Tedworth grabbing Colonel Likharev."

"We need an after-action report on that?" Cronley asked, and as the words came out of his mouth, realized they would.

"On everything," Schultz confirmed.

"As I was about to say, I don't know how to write an after-action report," Cronley said.

"I do," Hessinger said.

"Congratulations. You are now our official after-action-report writer," Cronley said. "Have at it."

"I don't have the time," Hessinger said. "Since I am no longer the company clerk. We need somebody else to do it."

"You're talking about Staff Sergeant Miller? Your new deputy?"

"He can help, but I'm talking about Claudette Colbert," Hessinger said.

"Who?" Ashton asked.

"There are apparently two," Cronley said. "The movie star and Hessinger's. Hessinger's Claudette Colbert is an ASA tech sergeant who wants to be an intelligence officer," Cronley said.

"What about her?" El Jefe asked.

"She takes shorthand, and she types sixty words a minute," Hessinger said. "We could really use her."

"Not to mention, she intercepts for us what Parsons and Ashley are saying to the Pentagon. And vice versa," Cronley said.

"Then get her, Jim," Schultz said. "The admiral gave you authority to recruit people. Call Major McClung and tell him you want her."

"There's two problems with that," Cronley said. "I've never laid eyes on Sergeant Colbert, and until I—"

"You're recruiting her to push a typewriter, Jim, right? So what do you care what she looks like?"

"That's not what I meant. Freddy says she's a good-looking female. But I want to make sure she understands what she's letting herself in for."

"So send for her and ask her."

"Before he does that, he better find out if Major McClung is going to let her go," Hessinger said.

"Right," El Jefe said. "Get on the secure line and call Major McClung."

"How did you know we have a secure line to the ASA?"

"Because when I asked Sergeant Tedworth to show me your SIGABA installation, I saw how amateurishly the ASA—being Army—had set up your secure line and showed them the smart—Navy—way to do it," El Jefe said. "Sergeant Tedworth, would you please go in there and get the secure line phone for Mr. Cronley?"

"Yes, sir."

"Any questions, Mr. Cronley?"

Cronley shook his head.

"Not even about me calling you 'Mr. Cronley'?" El Jefe pursued.

"Okay. Why did you refer to me as 'Mr. Cronley'?"

"Because if when you call Major McClung you identify yourself as 'Captain Cronley,' he will be reminded that he outranks you. If you say you're 'Mr. Cronley,' that won't happen. 'Misters' don't have ranks, they have titles. For example, 'chief, DCI-Europe.'"

"But ol' Iron Lung knows I'm a captain. Also, I suspect he doesn't like me," Cronley argued. "Given those facts' bearing on the problem, my suggestion is that you call him."

"When I'm gone, Mr. Cronley, say tomorrow or the day after

tomorrow, you're going to have to deal with ol' Iron Lung—and others in the Farben Building—"

"You'll be gone tomorrow? Or the day—"

"I hadn't planned to get into this yet," El Jefe said. "But why not? This is as good a time as any.

"Freddy was not the only one having profound thoughts on the way back from Vienna," Schultz went on. "Okay, where to start? With my orders from the admiral. The admiral thinks that we don't—you don't—fully understand how potentially valuable an intelligence asset Colonel Likharev is—"

"But we've already turned him," Cronley argued.

"He's turned *for the moment*, for two reasons: You did a very good job, Jim, of selling him on his duty as a Christian, as a man, to do whatever he can to save his family from the attentions of the NKGB. You told him you would try to get his family out of Russia. And then the NKGB tried to kill him."

"I don't understand where you're trying to go with this," Cronley said.

"You know Colonel Sergei Likharev as well as anybody, Jim. What do you think he's doing practically every waking moment?"

Cronley thought a moment.

"Wondering if we can get his family out?" he asked finally.

"How about him wondering if you just said you were going to get his family out? Wondering if you never had any intention to do that? Wondering if you could be expected to try to hand him a line like that? In reversed circumstances, it's something he would have tried himself."

"But I wasn't lying!"

"I don't think he's convinced about that. I think every day he grows a little more convinced that he's been lied to. That one day, he'll be told, 'Sorry, we tried to get them out and it just didn't work.' And, frankly, one day we might have to do just that."

"Jesus!"

"And getting his family out is all he has to live for. If he loses that, I wouldn't be surprised if he tried to take himself out."

"Jesus!"

"And even if we kept him from doing that, and we're damned sure going to try to, he'll shut off the flow of intel. Either refuse to answer any more questions, or hand us some credible bullshit and send us on one wild-goose chase after another. And he'd be good at that.

"So what I thought on the way from Vienna is that Polo and I have to go to Argentina and look him in the eye and tell him everything that's happened and is happening. Everything. Including you loaning the DCI the hundred thousand of your own money, and meeting Rahil/Seven-K in the Café Weitz. Even you feeding her dog peanuts and not having a clue who she was."

"Why would he believe you? Or Polo?"

"Likharev, like many good intel officers, can look into somebody's eyes and intuit if they're lying. Or not. Freddy says he can do that. I believe him. I think Colonel Mannberg can do it. And I wouldn't be surprised if you could. Hell, I know you can. You wouldn't have been able to turn Likharev in the first place if you hadn't known in your gut when he was lying and when he was telling the truth."

"Okay," Cronley said. "I can do it. Let's say you're right and Likharev can do it. So he looked in my eyes and decided I wasn't lying about trying to get his family out. Doesn't that count?"

"That was then. Now he's had time to think his gut reaction was flawed."

"Okay. So now what?"

"I told you. Polo and I are on the next SAA flight to Buenos Aires. Leaving you here to deal with Major McClung and the others by your lonesome."

"Christ!"

"Hand Mr. Cronley the telephone, Sergeant Tedworth."

"My father could do that," Captain Dunwiddie said thoughtfully. "Look in my eyes and tell if I was lying."

"Thank you for sharing that with us, Captain Dunwiddie," Major Ashton said. "And now that I think about it, several young women I have known have had that ability."

The telephone was an ordinary handset and cradle mounted on an obviously "locally manufactured" wooden box about eight inches tall. There were three toggle switches on the top of the box, and a speaker was mounted on the side. A heavy, lead-shielded cable ran from it to the room in which the SIGABA system was installed.

"The left toggle switch turns the handset on," El Jefe said. "The one in the middle turns on the loudspeaker, and the one on the right turns on the microphone. I suggest you leave that one off."

"The line has been checked, and you're into the ASA control room in Frankfurt, Mr. Cronley," First Sergeant Tedworth said. "Just flick the left toggle."

"Is that the truth? Let me look into your eyes, First Sergeant," Cronley said, as he flipped the left toggle switch, and then the center one.

Almost immediately, there came a male voice.

"Control room, Sergeant Nesbit."

"J. D. Cronley for Major McClung."

"Hold one."

Thirty seconds later, the voice of Major "Iron Lung" boomed from the speaker.

"What can I do for you, Cronley?"

"I want to steal one of your people from you."

"I was afraid of that. General Greene showed me that *EUCOM will provide* letter."

"Actually, I want more than one of your people," Cronley said, and as the words came out he realized he was in "automatic mouth mode."

"I was afraid of that, too. Okay, who?"

"I've only got one name right now, somebody I know wants to come work for us."

"Okay, who?"

"One of your intercept operators, Tech Sergeant Colbert."

There was a just perceptible pause before McClung asked, "What do you want her for, besides intercepting messages between Colonel Parsons and the Pentagon?"

Christ, he knows!

Why am I surprised?

Because you forgot "to know your enemy," stupid.

So what do I do now?

I don't know, but lying to Major McClung isn't one of my options.

"That, too, but right now I want her because she can take shorthand and type sixty words a minute. Colonel Ashton has told me our record-keeping, especially after-action reports, is unacceptably in arrears."

"Meaning nonexistent?"

"That's what the colonel alleges."

"Welcome to the world of command," McClung said, chuckling. "Okay, you can have her. Who do I transfer her to?"

I don't have a fucking clue!

"Hold on," Cronley said.

Hessinger scribbled furiously on his clipboard and then handed it to Cronley.

Cronley read aloud what Hessinger had written:

"Military Detachment, Directorate of Central Intelligence, Europe, APO 907."

After a moment, McClung said, "Okay, who else?"

"Let me get back to you after I talk to them and ask if they want to come with us."

"Okay. Makes sense. I don't know what I would do if I were an ASA non-com and was asked to join the DCI."

"Why would you not want to?"

"Your DCI is a dangerous place to be. People, powerful people, don't like you. You ever hear of guilt by association?"

"How do you know that powerful people don't like me? Us?"

"I'm chief of ASA Europe. I listen to everybody's telephone calls and read all their messages."

"Well, I'll ask them anyway."

"Do that. When you find out, let me know."

"Will do."

"That all, Cronley?"

"I guess so."

"McClung out," he said, and Cronley sensed that the line was no longer operating. He hung up the handset and then flipped the toggle switches off.

"Now, that wasn't so hard, was it, Jim?" El Jefe asked.

"When I called McClung, I had him in the Enemies Column," Cronley said. "Now I don't think so."

"Why not? Something he said?"

"More the tone. Of the entire conversation, but especially in his voice."

"So, what we should do now is, while staring into the eyes of people we're talking to to see if they're lying, listen to the tone of their voices to see if they like us, or not?"

"May I say something?" Ludwig Mannberg asked.

"You don't have to ask permission to speak around here, Colonel," Cronley said.

"I had the same feeling about this officer, listening to his tone," Mannberg said. "I think Jim is right. But I also feel obliged to say that, in my experience, it is very dangerous to rely on intuition. And very easy to do so. Intuition can be often, perhaps most often, relied upon. But when you *want to rely* on intuition, don't. That's when it will fail you."

"I think I'm going to write that down," El Jefe said. "And I'm not being a wiseass." He paused and then went on. "No, I won't write it down. I don't have to. I won't forget 'when you want to rely on intuition, don't.' Thanks, Ludwig."

"Yeah, me too," Cronley said. "Thank you for that." He paused. "Now what do we do?"

"If you really can't think of anything else to do, why don't you get Sergeant Colbert in here?" Hessinger asked.

[TWO]

Office of the U.S. Military Government Liaison Officer
The South German Industrial Development Organization Compound
Pullach, Bavaria
The American Zone of Occupied Germany
1735 15 January 1946

Technical Sergeant Claudette Colbert knocked at the door, heard the command "Come," opened the door, marched into the office up to the desk of the liaison officer, came to attention, raised her hand in salute, and barked, "Technical Sergeant Colbert reporting to the commanding officer as ordered, sir."

In doing so, she shattered a belief Captain James D. Cronley Jr. had firmly held since his first days at Texas A&M, which was, *Unless you're some kind of a pervert, into kinky things like fetishes, a female in uniform is less sexually attractive than a spittoon.*

He would have thought this would be even more true if the uniform the female was wearing, as Sergeant Colbert was, was what the Army called "fatigues." Generously tailored to afford the wearer room to move while performing the hard labor causing the fatigue, "fatigues" conceal the delicate curvature of the female form at least as well as, say, a tarpaulin does when draped over a tank.

It was not true of Technical Sergeant Colbert now.

Cronley returned the salute in a Pavlovian reflex, and similarly ordered, "Stand at ease," and then, a moment later, added, "Have a seat, Sergeant," and pointed to the chair Hessinger had placed six feet from his desk.

Technical Sergeant Colbert sat down.

She found herself facing Captain Cronley, and on the left side of his desk, Lieutenant Colonel Ashton, Captain Dunwiddie, and Staff Sergeant Hessinger. Lieutenant Oscar Schultz, USN, Maksymilian Ostrowski, and former Colonel Ludwig Mannberg were seated to the right of Cronley's desk.

Only Colonel Ashton and Captain Dunwiddie were wearing the insignia of their ranks. Everyone else was wearing the blue triangles of civilian employees of the Army, including Ostrowski, whom Claudette knew to be a Pole and a DP guard. Ex-colonel Mannberg was wearing a very well-tailored suit.

Cronley, who was having thoughts he knew he should not be having about how Sergeant Colbert might look in the shower, forced them from his mind and asked himself,

How the hell do I handle this, now that she's here?

Shift into automatic mode and see what happens when I open my mouth?

In the absence of any better, or any other, idea . . .

"Sergeant, Sergeant Hessinger tells me that you would like to move to the DCI from the ASA. True?"

"Yes, sir."

"Why?"

"I've been on the fringes of the intelligence business, sir, since I came into the ASA. And the more I've learned about it, the more I realized I'd like to be in it. As more than an ASA intercept sergeant. As an intelligence officer."

"What would you like to do in what you call the intelligence business?"

"I don't know, sir. Once I get into the DCI, something will come up."

"What if I told you that what you would do if you came to DCI is typing and taking shorthand?"

"Sir, I would have my foot in the door. So long as you understood that I don't want to be a secretary, starting out taking shorthand and typing would be okay with me."

"DCI inherited from the OSS the notion that the best qualified person for the job gets the job and the authority that goes with it. You understand that? It means you would be working for Hessinger, although you outrank him. Would you be all right with that?"

"Yes, sir."

"Has anyone else got any questions for Sergeant Colbert?" Cronley asked.

There came shaken heads, a chorus of no's and uh-uhs.

"Okay, Sergeant Colbert, let's give it a try," Cronley said. "You can consider yourself a member of DCI from right now. What is that officially, Freddy?"

"Military Detachment, Directorate of Central Intelligence, Europe, APO 907," Hessinger furnished.

"Sir?" Sergeant Colbert said.

"Yes?"

"Sir, with respect, I have conditions. Before I'll agree to be transferred to DCI."

Now, what the hell?

"Conditions, Sergeant?" Cronley asked unpleasantly. "Before you 'agree to be transferred'? You don't have to agree to being transferred. I decide whether or not that will happen."

"Sir, with respect. Would you want me in DCI if I didn't want to be here?"

Turn off the automatic mouth or you really will say something stupid.

"What sort of conditions, Sergeant?" Lieutenant Colonel Ashton asked.

Cronley saw Schultz flash Ashton a withering look, and then he said, "She has a point, Jim."

"What sort of conditions, Sergeant?" Cronley asked.

"Just two things, sir. I'd like permission to wear civilian triangles. And if you're issuing what I guess could be called special IDs, I'd like one of those, too. I suppose what I'm saying—"

"That will not pose a problem," Cronley said. "We're all aware that it's easier to get things done if you're not wearing rank insignia. And that ties in with what I said before that in the DCI authority is based on your job, not your rank."

"Yes, sir. Thank you, sir."

"You said 'two things,' Sergeant."

"Yes, sir. I'd like to bring three of my girls with me."

What?

Her girls?

Jesus Christ, she's a dyke!

"Excuse me, Sergeant?"

"They want to get out of the ASA house . . ."

That she was queer never entered my mind!

Until just now.

So much for that intuition bullshit we were just talking about!

". . . and not only will they be useful here, but they'll be able to keep an eye on anything going to or from Washington," Sergeant Colbert went on, and then stopped, and then went on again, "It's not what you're thinking, sir."

So what do I say now?

Ask her what she thinks I'm thinking?

Cronley was literally struck dumb.

"Sir, I'm no more interested in other women—that way—than you are in other men."

"Sergeant, I hope I didn't say anything to suggest—"

"May I continue, sir?" she interrupted.

How could I possibly say no?

"Certainly," Cronley said.

"I'm glad this came up," she began. "To clear the air. One of the reasons I want to get out of the WAC is because I'm really tired of being suspected of being a dyke. And I've learned that every man, officer or enlisted, who looks at me thinks there is no other explanation for an attractive, unmarried woman being in the WAC except that she's a lesbian."

Cronley thought: *That's true. It may not be fair, but it's true.*

But he remained struck dumb.

"I'm heterosexual," Sergeant Colbert said. "And so are the women I want to bring with me into DCI. Is that clear?"

Cronley found his voice.

"Perfectly clear," he said. "And I appreciate your candor, Sergeant Colbert. Hessinger, get the names of the women Sergeant Colbert wants to bring with her, and see that they're transferred."

"Yes, sir," Hessinger said.

Sergeant Colbert stood up, came to attention, and looked at Cronley.

What the hell is that all about?

"Permission to withdraw, sir?" she asked.

Oh!

"Granted," Cronley said.

Sergeant Colbert saluted. Cronley returned it. Sergeant Colbert executed a snappy "left turn" movement and marched toward the door.

Cronley's automatic mouth switched on.

"Colbert! Just a minute, please."

She stopped, did a snappy "about face" movement, and stood at attention.

"Sir?"

"First of all, at ease," Cronley said. "You can knock off just about all the military courtesy, Colbert. For one thing, this isn't the Farben Building. For another, I'm wearing triangles, not bars. Pass that word to your girls."

"Yes, sir."

"Welcome to DCI, Claudette. Freddy will see that you have everything you need."

"Thank you."

She smiled and left the room.

Hessinger started to follow her, but stopped halfway to the door and asked, "Where do I put them?"

"To live, you mean? I hadn't thought about that," Cronley admitted.

"I think it would be a good idea if you did," Hessinger said.

"And I'm sure you have already given the subject some thought and are going to share those thoughts with me."

"I think it would be a good idea to get the three women she's bringing with her out of the ASA building, where they are now. With half a dozen other women, who are probably very curious about what's going on over here."

"So?"

"So I suggest you take the 'Guesthouse' sign off the guesthouse and put up one that says 'Female Quarters, Off Limits to Male Personnel.'"

"Do it."

"And I suggest that as soon as I can get Sergeant Colbert into blue triangles, you put her in one of our rooms in the Vier Jahreszeiten. She'll be working there."

"And what is Major Wallace going to think about that?"

"You'll have to think of something to tell him, and I think you should count on Major McClung telling him by this time tomorrow that you stole her from him."

Shit, I didn't think about that. McClung will certainly tell Wallace . . .

Or will he?

Now that I think about it, I don't think he will.

But this is probably one of those times that Mannberg talked about, when you really want to trust your gut feeling, and therefore shouldn't.

"As soon as you get Sergeant Colbert into blue triangles, put her in the Vier Jahreszeiten," Cronley said. "What she's doing there is none of Major Wallace's business."

Hessinger nodded and left the room.

"Don't let it go to your head, Jim," El Jefe said, "but you handled the sergeant well. Finally. For a while, I thought she was going to eat you alive."

"'Formidable' describes her well, doesn't it?"

"So does 'well-stacked.' Is that going to be a problem, now that she's made it so plain she's not a dyke?"

"Not for me. Ostrowski may have to watch himself."

That got the expected chuckles.

"So what do we do now?" Cronley asked.

"You get on the phone and get Polo and me seats on the next SAA flight to Buenos Aires. If they're sold out, tell them they're going to have to bump two people."

"What makes you think they'd do that?"

"Because, for the moment, at least until Juan Perón takes it away from us, South American Airways is a DCI asset and you're chief, DCI-Europe."

"But do they know that?"

"I told Cletus to make sure they know."

There he goes again.

"I told Cletus . . ."

El Jefe is a lot more—and probably was for a long time—more than just Clete's communications expert.

And the admiral sent him here. And not to take care of Polo.

So how do I find out what he's really up to?

Ask him?

Why not?

The worst that could happen would be for him to pretend he doesn't know what I'm talking about.

So I'll ask him.

But not now. In private, when the moment is right.

Cronley reached for the telephone, dialed "O," and told the Pullach compound operator to get him South American Airways at the Rhine-Main Air Force Base.

Five minutes later, he put the phone in its cradle and turned to Schultz.

"You're on SAA Flight 233, departing Rhine-Main at 1700 tomorrow."

"Which means we'll have to be there at 1600," Schultz replied.

"Which means we can have a late breakfast and leave here at ten, ten-thirty. Or even eleven," Cronley said. "That'll give us plenty of time for Ostrowski and me to fly you up there."

"No," Schultz said. "What that means is that so I can make my manners to Generals Smith and Greene, and the admiral would be very disappointed if I didn't, we have to get up in the dark so that we can leave at first light. And that means, of course, that you don't get anything more to drink tonight. Nor does Ostrowski."

It makes sense that he has to see Greene, but General Walter Bedell Smith, Eisenhower's deputy? I'm supposed to believe he's only a Navy lieutenant, the same as an Army captain, and he's going in for a social chat with General Smith? Even if the admiral sent him, there's something going on nobody's telling me.

Like there's something nobody's telling me about the appointment of Captain James D. Cronley Jr. as chief, Directorate of Central Intelligence, Europe. There's something very fishy about that, too. There's at least a platoon of ex-OSS colonels and light birds, now unemployed, better qualified than I am who should be sitting here.

My gut tells me—and screw Ludwig's theory that when you really want to trust your intuition, don't—that El Jefe has the answers to all of this.

So how do I get him to tell me?

I don't have a fucking clue.

"Or I could stay here and drink my supper and have Kurt Schröder fly you to Frankfurt."

"No."

"He's a much better Storch pilot than I am, El Jefe," Cronley said. "He flew General Gehlen and Ludwig Mannberg all over Russia."

"You're going to fly me to Frankfurt. Period."

"Yes, sir."

[THREE]
Office of the Chief, Counterintelligence Corps
Headquarters, European Command
The I.G. Farben Building
Frankfurt am Main
American Zone of Occupation, Germany
1135 16 January 1946

"Well, Colonel Ashton," General Greene said, coming from behind his desk as Cronley pushed Ashton's wheelchair into his office, "I'm really glad to see you. I was getting a little worried."

"Sir?"

Greene looked at his wristwatch.

"In twenty-five minutes, we're having lunch with General Smith. He is big on punctuality. You cut it pretty short."

"I didn't know about the lunch," Ashton said.

"You must be Lieutenant Schultz," Greene said, offering his hand. "Admiral Souers speaks very highly of you."

"That's very kind of the admiral," Schultz said.

Greene looked at Cronley, said, "Cronley," but did not offer his hand.

"This is Colonel Mattingly, my deputy," Greene said.

Schultz, Ashton, and Mattingly shook hands. Mattingly ignored Cronley.

"I understand that you met my CIC chief in Vienna," Greene said. "Colonel Stevens?"

Cronley thought, *Well, it didn't take Greene long to hear about that, did it?*

"We had a visit from the CIC in Vienna, but I didn't get his name," Schultz said.

"What was that about?"

"Apparently one of the hotel managers heard two of my people speaking Russian, and turned us in as suspicious characters."

"He didn't say what you were doing in Vienna."

"I didn't tell him," Schultz said.

"So he said. He also said that one of his agents knew Cronley."

"As I understand that," Schultz said, "they were apparently in CIC school together."

"Where they were students in Major Derwin's class on Techniques of Surveillance," General Greene said. "Which brings us, Cronley, to Major Derwin."

"Sir?"

"Major Derwin wants to talk to you."

What the hell for?

"Yes, sir?"

"He didn't tell me why, but he said he'd like to do so as soon as possible. What about today?"

"Not today, sir. As soon as I load these gentlemen onto the Buenos Aires flight, I have to get back to Munich."

"Well, when can I tell the major you will have time for him?"

"Sir, just about anytime after I get back to Munich. Anytime tomorrow."

"What's so important, Cronley," Colonel Mattingly demanded, "that you have to get back to Munich today? You don't actually expect Major Derwin to come to Munich to ask you what he wants to ask you, do you?"

"Colonel, if Major Derwin wants to ask me anything, I'll be in Munich," Cronley said.

General Greene, before Mattingly could reply to that, said, "Why don't we head for the generals' mess? It's always wiser to be earlier for an appointment with a general than late."

"Colonel Ashton," Cronley asked, "would it be all right if I waited for you and Lieutenant Schultz here after I get a sandwich in the snack bar?"

"Certainly."

"The guest list I got from General Smith's aide has you on it, Cronley," General Greene said. "You, Colonel Ashton, Lieutenant Schultz, and me."

Oh, so that's why Mattingly's pissed. He didn't get invited to break bread with Beetle Smith and I did.

That should delight me. But it doesn't.

I suppose I really am afraid of Colonel Robert Mattingly.

[FOUR]

The General Officers' Mess

The I.G. Farben Building

Frankfurt am Main

American Zone of Occupation, Germany

1159 16 January 1946

General Walter Bedell Smith, trailed by his aide-de-camp, a full colonel, marched into the general officers' mess, where General Greene, Ashton, Schultz, and Cronley were standing waiting for him just inside the door.

"Homer, why don't you check inside and see everything's set up, and then catch a sandwich or something while we eat? This is one of those top secret lunches behind a curtain one hears about, and you're not invited."

"Not a problem, General," the aide said, smiling, and went into the dining room.

"How are you, Paul?" Smith asked General Greene.

"Holding up under difficult circumstances, General."

"Welcome to the club, General."

Smith turned to Cronley.

"How are you, son? And how's our midget friend holding up?"

He means Tiny.

"Very well, sir. Tiny's holding the fort up in Munich."

"I'm Walter Smith, Colonel," Smith said to Ashton. "I guess you're the one I should have asked how he's holding up."

"I'm all right, sir. Thank you."

"And you," Smith said to Schultz, "by the process of elimination, must be 'the chief'?"

"Some people still call me that, General," Schultz said.

"Including Admiral Souers," Smith said. "He tells me you two are old shipmates?"

Cronley had never heard that before.

Why not?

"Yes, sir. That's true."

"Actually, when he told me he was sending you to Europe, I thought I heard an implication that there is more to your relationship than just being old shipmates."

Schultz seemed to be framing his reply when he saw he didn't have to. General Smith's aide was walking quickly back across the room to them.

"All set up, sir."

"Thanks, Homer. See you in forty-five minutes. Wait a minute. You're going to Buenos Aires today, right? How are you going to get out to Rhine-Main?"

From the look on General Greene's face, this was news—surprising news—to him, but he reacted quickly to it:

"I'll send them in one of my cars, General," he said.

"Homer, lay on a Packard for these gentlemen," General Smith said. "If there's no spare, use mine."

"Yes, sir."

"General, that's not necessary," Schultz said.

"I understand that chiefs feel free to argue with admirals,

Chief, but please don't argue with a general. A wounded warrior and the executive assistant to the director of Central Intelligence deserve no less than one of our Packards. Do it, Homer."

"Yes, sir."

What did he call El Jefe? "The executive assistant to the director of Central Intelligence"?

And Greene's face showed he had never heard that before, either.

Smith took El Jefe's arm and led him across the dining room.

"We'll be in Ike's dining room," he said. "Ike's in Berlin."

Ike's dining room turned out to be an alcove off the main room, the windows of which provided a panoramic view of the bombed-out ruins of buildings as far as the eye could see.

There was a table, now set at one end for five, but capable, Cronley guessed, of seating ten, maybe a dozen people comfortably.

Smith stood behind the chair at the head of the table, and indicated where the others were to sit. El Jefe and General Greene were seated close to Smith, and Cronley found himself seated across from Ashton.

A waiter in a starched white jacket appeared. Cronley guessed he was a sergeant.

"There will be no menus today," General Smith announced. "I'm really pressed for time. Anybody who doesn't like a steak, medium rare, a baked potato, and green beans is out of luck. Charley, serve the food and then draw the curtain and make sure we're not interrupted."

"Yes, sir," the waiter said.

Serving the food and putting two silver coffee services on the table took very little time.

"Okay," General Smith said. "General Eisenhower really

wanted to be here today, but our Russian friends in Berlin are being difficult. And the reason he wanted to be here—and the reason he asked Admiral Souers to send someone senior over here—is because he wanted to hear from someone who knows what's really going on with Operation Ost. More precisely, he's concerned about the level of threat of exposure. And since there is, I devoutly hope, no paper trail, that will have to be word of mouth. And I think we should start by hearing the opinion of the junior officer involved. Captain Cronley."

Shit!

Cronley stood up.

"Sir—"

"Sit down, please," General Smith said, "and tell me the first thing that comes to your mind vis-à-vis Operation Ost being compromised."

Oh, what the hell. When in doubt, tell the truth.

"Sir, the first thing that comes to my mind is that we just started to make a paper trail."

"That's very interesting," Smith said softly. "And whose idea was that?"

"My . . . I guess he could be called my administrative officer. Staff Sergeant Hessinger."

"And you thought this idea of your *staff sergeant* was a good idea?"

"Sir, Hessinger said something to the effect that eventually somebody is going to want to look at our records. And if that happens, and we say, 'We haven't been keeping any records,' that's not going to be an acceptable answer."

"And I agreed, General," Schultz said. "And told Cronley to

start making after-action reports on everything of significance that's happened at Kloster Grünau—"

"Where?" Smith interrupted.

"The monastery," Schultz furnished.

General Smith nodded his understanding.

"And at the Pullach compound. And about everything else he's done of significance anywhere."

"And who gets these after-action reports?" Smith asked.

"Colonel Ashton," Cronley said. "As responsible officer for Operation Ost. And he sits on them, hoping that no one will ever want to see them."

General Smith considered that for a full thirty seconds.

"Your sergeant was right, Cronley," he said. "Napoleon said, 'An army travels on its stomach,' but the U.S. Army travels on its paper trails. If this thing blows up in our faces, and we didn't have any kind of a paper trail, (a) they wouldn't believe it, and (b) in the absence of a paper trail, we could be accused of anything. I think General Eisenhower would agree. I also think it would be a good idea if I had a look at them, in case they needed . . . what shall I say? . . . a little editing."

"Yes, sir," Cronley said.

"Not your decision to make," Smith said. "Chief, what about it?"

After a moment, Schultz said, "Hand-carry them to General Smith personally. Either you or Tiny."

"Yes, sir."

"Back to the basic question, Cronley: What is your assessment of the risk of exposure of Operation Ost? Increased, diminished, or no change?"

"Greatly diminished, sir."

"Why?"

"Sir, just about all of General Gehlen's Nazis are already in Argentina. There's a dozen, maybe twenty, still unaccounted for in Eastern Europe. If we can get them out, either to West Germany or Italy, we'll use the Vatican to get them to Argentina. I mean, we're no longer going to use SAA to transport them."

"If you're right, and I have no reason to doubt that you are, that's good news," General Smith said. "Colonel Ashton, what's your assessment of the same thing, this blowing up in our faces in Argentina?"

"Sir, I'll probably regret saying this, but I don't think it's much of a problem, and the chances diminish by the day."

"Why do you say that?"

Schultz answered for him: "General, the only people looking for Nazis in Argentina are the FBI. And since Juan Domingo Perón and the Catholic Church don't want any Nazis found, the FBI is going to have a very hard time finding any."

"You don't sound as if you're rooting for the FBI," Smith said. "Doesn't that make you uncomfortable?"

"No, sir, it doesn't. President Truman and General Eisenhower getting burned by J. Edgar Hoover over Operation Ost is what makes me, and Admiral Souers, uncomfortable."

"I'd forgotten that you have spent so much time in South America," General Smith said, but it was a question, and everybody at the table knew it.

When Schultz didn't reply immediately, Smith made a statement that was clearly another question: "Chief, in the lobby just now, I said that I thought, when he told me he was sending you to

Europe, that Admiral Souers was implying there's more to your relationship than being old shipmates. Then Homer appeared before you could reply. Or saved you from having to reply."

"You sure you want me to get into that, General?"

"Only if you're comfortable telling me."

"Comfortable, no, but the admiral trusts you, which means I do, and I think you have the right to know," Schultz said. "So okay. The admiral and I were shipmates on battleship USS *Utah* in 1938. He was then a lieutenant commander and I had just made chief signalman. About the time he made commander, and went to work for the chief of Naval Intelligence, the Navy sent me to Fort Monmouth, in New Jersey, to see what the Army Signal Corps was up to. My contact in ONI was Commander Souers. I kept him up to speed about what the Army was developing—radar, for one thing—and, more important, what became the SIGABA system."

"It's an amazing system," General Smith said. "You were involved in its development?"

"Yes, sir, I was. In 1943, I installed a SIGABA system on a destroyer, the USS *Alfred Thomas*, DD-107, which then sailed to the South Atlantic to see what kind of range we could get out of it. To keep SIGABA secret, only her captain and two white hats I had with me knew what the real purpose of that voyage was.

"We called at Buenos Aires, official story 'courtesy visit' to Argentina, which was then neutral. Actual purpose, so that I could get some SIGABA parts from Collins Radio, which were flown down there in the embassy's diplomatic pouch.

"A Marine captain comes on board, in a crisp khaki uniform, wearing naval aviator's wings, the Navy Cross, the Distinguished Flying Cross, and the third award of the Purple Heart . . ."

"Cletus?" Cronley asked.

"Who else? Anyway, he tells the skipper he understands that he has a SIGABA expert on board and he wants to talk to him. Cletus Frade is a formidable guy. The skipper brings Captain Frade to the radio shack.

"He says he's heard I'm a SIGABA expert. I deny I ever heard of SIGABA. 'What is it?'

"He says, 'Chief, if you ever lie to me again, I'll have you shot. Now, are you a capable SIGABA repairman or not?'

"I tell him I am. He asks me if I know anything about the RCA 103 Radar—which was also classified Top Secret at the time—and I tell him yes. He says, 'Pack your sea bag, Chief, orders will soon come detaching you from this tin can and assigning you to me.'

"I don't know what the hell's going on, but I'm not worried. The skipper's not going to let anybody take me off the *Alfred Thomas*. Who the hell does this crazy Marine think he is? The chief of Naval Operations?

"At 0600 the next morning, so help me God, there is an Urgent message over the SIGABA. Very short message. Classified Top Secret–Tango, which security classification I'd never heard of until that morning. 'Chief Signalman Oscar J. Schultz detached USS *Alfred Thomas*, DD-107, assigned personal staff Captain Cletus Frade, USMCR, with immediate effect. Ernest J. King, Admiral, USN, Chief of Naval Operations.'

"At 0800, Cletus is waiting for me on the wharf. In civvies, driving his Horch convertible, with a good-looking blond sitting next to him. It's Dorotea, his Anglo-Argentine wife. He says we're going out to the ranch, and should be there in time for lunch.

"'Sir,' I say, 'what's going on here?'

"'Congratulations, Chief, you are now a member of Team Turtle of the Office of Strategic Services. The team's out at the ranch. What we do, among other things, is look for German submarines, supposedly neutral ships that supply German submarines, and then we sink them or blow them up or arrange for the Navy to do that for us. We use the RCA 103 Radar to find them, and the SIGABA to pass the word to the Navy. So we need you to keep those technological marvels up and running.'"

"That's quite a story," General Smith said.

"Yeah. But let me finish, General, it gets better."

"I wouldn't miss it for the world," General Smith said.

"So we go out to the ranch. I found out later that it's about as big as Manhattan Island. Really. Cletus owns it. He inherited it, and a hell of a lot else, from his father, who was murdered at the orders, so the OSS guys told me, of Heinrich Himmler himself when it looked like El Coronel Frade was going to become president of Argentina.

"And I met the team. All a bunch of civilians in uniform. Well, maybe not in uniform. But not professional military men, if you know what I mean. No offense, Polo."

"None taken, El Jefe. That's what we were, civilians in uniform. On those rare occasions when we wore uniforms."

"Admiral Souers—by then he was Rear Admiral, Lower Half—finally learned that I'd been shanghaied off the USS *Alfred Thomas.* He got a message to me saying that he couldn't get me out of Argentina, but I could still be of use to the Office of Naval Intelligence by reporting everything I could learn about what Frade and Team Turtle were up to. The admiral said that it was very important to ONI.

"By then, I'd already heard about the trouble Clete was having with the naval attaché of our embassy—a real asshole—and the FBI and some other people supposed to be on our side, and I'd gotten to know the OSS guys. So first I told Clete what the admiral wanted, told him I wasn't going to do it, and then I got on the SIGABA and told the admiral I wasn't going to report to ONI on Team Turtle and why.

"I got a short message in reply. 'Fully understand. Let me know if I can ever help with anything Frade needs.'"

"And then one thing led to another, General," Ashton said. "First, El Jefe became de facto chief of staff to Frade, and then de jure. Or more or less de jure. Without telling El Jefe that he was going to, Clete got on the horn—the SIGABA—to Admiral Souers and told him he was going to ask the Navy to commission El Jefe and was the admiral going to help or get in the way?"

"Two weeks later," El Jefe picked up the story, "the naval attaché was forced to swear me in as a lieutenant, USNR. The attaché couldn't say anything, of course, but that really ruined his day, which is why I asked Clete to have him ordered to do it."

General Smith chuckled.

"The reason I look so spiffy in my uniform is that it's practically brand-new," El Jefe said. "I don't think it's got two weeks' wear on it."

"You didn't wear it because you were too cheap to buy more gold stripes when you were made a lieutenant commander," Ashton said. "Or when Clete got you promoted to commander so you'd outrank me and could take command of what was still the OSS, Southern Cone, when he took off his uniform."

Schultz gave him the finger.

"Clete thought—and he was right—that it looked better if people thought I was a chief, rather than an officer," Schultz said. "So we kept my change of status quiet."

"You're a full commander, Oscar?" Cronley asked.

"I retired a couple of weeks ago as a commander, U.S. Naval Reserve, Jim," Schultz said. "What I am now is a member of what they call the Senior Executive Service of the Directorate of Central Intelligence. My title is executive assistant to the director."

When Cronley didn't reply, Schultz said, "Why are you so surprised? You've been around the spook business long enough to know that nothing is ever what it looks like."

"Like the chief, DCI-Europe, isn't what he looks like?"

"Meaning what?"

"Meaning that I'm very young, wholly inexperienced in the spook business, and pretty slow, so it took me a long time to figure out that there's something very fishy about a very junior captain being chief, DCI -Europe, and that no one wants to tell him what's really going on."

"Well, Jim, now that you have figured that out, I guess we'll have to tell you. I will on the way to the airport."

"Why don't you tell him now?" General Smith said. "I think General Greene should be privy to this."

"Yes, sir," Schultz said. "Okay. Where to start? Okay. When President Truman was talked into disbanding the OSS—largely by J. Edgar Hoover, but with a large assist by the Army, no offense, General—"

"Tell it like it is, Chief," General Smith said.

"He first realized that he couldn't turn off everything the OSS was doing—especially Operation Ost, but some other operations, too—like a lightbulb. So he turned to his old friend Admiral Souers to run them until they could be turned over to somebody else.

"Admiral Souers convinced him—I think Truman had figured this out by himself, so I probably should have said, the admiral convinced the President that the President was right in maybe thinking he had made a mistake by shutting down the OSS.

"The admiral didn't know much about Operation Ost, except that it existed. Truman told him what it was. The admiral knew I was involved with it in Argentina, so he sent for me to see what I thought should be done with it.

"The President trusted his old friend the admiral, and the admiral trusted his old shipmate. Okay? The President was learning how few people he could trust, and learning how many people he could not trust, starting with J. Edgar Hoover.

"So Truman decided a new OSS was needed. Who to run it? The admiral.

"So what to do about Operation Ost, which was important for two reasons—for the intel it had about the Russians, and because if it came out we'd made the deal with Gehlen and were smuggling Nazis out of Germany, Truman would be impeached, Eisenhower would be court-martialed, and we'd lose the German intelligence about our pal Joe Stalin.

"So how do we hide Operation Ost from J. Edgar Hoover, the Army, the Navy, the State Department, the *Washington Post*, et cetera, et cetera? We try to make it look unimportant. How do we do that? We pick some obscure bird colonel to run it. Which bird colonel could we trust? For that matter, which light bird, which major, could we trust?

"And if we found one, that would raise the question, which full colonel, which light bird would General Gehlen trust? I mean really trust, so that he'd really keep up his end of the deal?

"The President says, 'What about Captain Cronley?'"

"You were there, Chief?" General Smith asked. "You heard him say that?"

"I was there. I heard him say that. The admiral said, 'Harry, that's ridiculous!' and the President said, 'Who would think anything important would be handed to a captain?'

"The admiral said, 'Who would think *anything* in the intelligence business would be handed over to a captain?'

"And the President said, 'There are captains and then there are captains. I know. I was one. This one, Cronley, has just been given the DSM and a promotion to captain by the commander in chief for unspecified services connected with intelligence. J. Edgar knows it was because Cronley found the submarine with the uranium oxide on it. J. Edgar would not think there was anything funny if Captain Cronley were given some unimportant job in intelligence that might get him promoted.'

"The admiral said something about giving Cronley Operation Ost because no one would think Operation Ost was important if a captain was running it, and the President said, 'For that reason, I think we should name Captain Cronley chief, DCI-Europe, and let that leak.'

"'Harry,' the admiral said, "'General Gehlen is an old-school Kraut officer. I don't think he'll stand still for taking orders from a captain.'

"And the President said, 'Why don't we ask him?'

"So we asked General Gehlen. So there you sit, Mr. Chief, DCI-Europe. Okay? Any questions?"

"How soon can I expect to be relieved when you find some bird colonel you can trust, who's acceptable to General Gehlen and should have this job?"

"The job is yours until you screw up—or one of your people does—and Operation Ost is blown."

"Then I get thrown to the wolves?"

"Then you get thrown to the wolves. If that happens, try to take as few people down with you as you can. Any questions?"

"No, sir," Cronley said, and a moment later, "Thanks, Oscar."

[FIVE]
Suite 507
Hotel Vier Jahreszeiten
Maximilianstrasse 178
Munich, American Zone of Occupation, Germany
2010 16 January 1946

There had been a delay in the departure of SAA flight 233, so Cronley had told Max Ostrowski, "Head home. That way, if I have to go to Munich instead of Kloster Grünau, there will be only one Storch parked in the transient area to arouse curiosity, not two."

When Schultz and Ashton finally got off the ground, he knew there was no chance of his making it to the monastery strip before dark, so he went to the snack bar in the terminal and had a greasy hamburger, fries, and a Coke before leaving Rhine-Main.

He had another—much better—hamburger at Schleissheim, the Munich military post airfield, when he landed, and then got a ride to the hotel.

As he walked down the corridor to his room, he saw light under the door to 507, which was where Fat Freddy held court, and he pushed the huge door handle down and walked in.

I will tell Freddy everything Schultz said in the generals' mess and see what he has to say.

Hessinger was not behind the desk. Technical Sergeant Claudette Colbert was.

She rose from behind the desk at which she was typing when she saw him.

She was wearing a "pink" as in pinks-and-greens officer's skirt and a khaki shirt, and he saw an officer's green tunic on the coat-rack.

Well, it didn't take much time for her to get in triangles, did it?

"Good evening, sir."

"Now that you're a civilian, you can drop the 'sir,' Claudette."

"Sorry, I forgot."

"Where's Freddy?"

"He said he was going to visit a friend."

"Yeah."

"He left a number, shall I call him for you?"

"I try not to call Freddy when he's visiting friends. He sulks."

She smiled.

"Is Mr. Ostrowski with you?"

"He's at Kloster Grünau. I had to wait until Schultz and Ashton took off, which meant it was too dark for me to land there. So I came here."

"Major Derwin called. He said he'd like to see you at ten hundred tomorrow."

What does that sonofabitch want?

"Wonderful!"

"Can I get you anything?"

"No, thank you. I'm going to go to my room, have a stiff drink, and go to bed."

"How did things go with General Greene?"

"It was interesting, Claudette, but not worthy of an after-action report."

Subject: Screw Up and Get Thrown to the Wolves.

"That's what I've been doing," she said, nodding at the typewriter. "After-action reports."

"Claudette—"

"My friends call me 'Dette,'" she said.

"Because if they shortened it the other way, it would be 'Claude'?"

"And I don't want to be called 'Claude.'"

"Well, Dette, as I was about to say, Freddy will push you around if you let him. Don't let him. It's quarter after eight. Knock off. The after actions aren't that important."

"Okay, I'll finish this one and knock off," she said. "Thank you."

"Good night, Dette."

"Good night . . . What should I call you?"

"Good question. When no one's around, call me Jim. Otherwise, Mr. Cronley."

"Got it. Good night, Jim."

"Good night," Cronley said, and walked out.

Cronley went to his room, which was actually a suite, found a bottle of scotch, poured himself a stiff drink, and then decided he would first have a shower and then have the drink, catch the 2100 news broadcast on the American Forces Network Munich radio station, and then go to bed.

Ten minutes later, as he pulled on the terrycloth bathrobe that came with the suite, he heard over AFN Munich that he was just in time for the news. It was always preceded by a solemn voice proclaiming, "Remember, soldier! VD walks the streets tonight! And penicillin fails once in seven times!"

And he wondered again, as he often did, how Daddy or Mommy explained the commercial to nine-year-old Jane or Bobby when they asked, "Daddy, what's that man talking about?"

When he came out of the bathroom, Technical Sergeant Colbert was sitting in an armchair.

"You almost got a look at something you don't want to see," he snapped. "What the hell are you doing in here?"

"Well, I finished the first after-action report, and thought you might want to see it. Wrong guess?"

"I don't think being in my room is smart," he said.

"Since Freddy gave me the master key, I thought coming in made more sense than waiting in the hall for you to finish your shower," she said. "Shall I leave?"

"Let me see the after action," he said.

She got out of the chair, walked to him, and handed him some typewritten sheets of paper. He glanced at the title: "Likharev, Sergei, Colonel NKGB, Capture Of."

He became aware that she was still standing close to him.

He looked at her.

"We cleared up one misunderstanding between us yesterday," she said. "Why don't we clear up this one?"

"Which one is that?"

"Officers, and you're a good one, don't fool around with enlisted women, right?"

"I'm glad you understand that."

"And everyone knows that a recently widowed officer would have absolutely no interest in becoming romantically involved with another woman, especially a subordinate enlisted woman seven years older than he is, right?"

She must have really gone through my personal files.

"Right again. Is there going to be a written test on this?"

"But you would agree that there is a great difference between a continuing romantic involvement and an every-once-in-a-while-as-needed purely physical relationship, if both parties are (a) aware of the difference, and (b) have been forced into the strangest perversion of them all?"

"What the hell would that be?"

"Oscar Wilde said it was celibacy," she said.

"I don't think I like this conversation, Sergeant Colbert."

She laughed deep in her throat, and then pointed at his midsection.

His erect penis had escaped his bathrobe.

Her right hand reached for it, and with her left she pulled his face down to hers.

She encountered little, virtually no, resistance.

VIII

[ONE]

Suite 507
Hotel Vier Jahreszeiten
Maximilianstrasse 178
Munich, American Zone of Occupation, Germany
0955 16 January 1946

Knowing that Major Thomas G. "Dick Tracy" Derwin was either already behind the door or would be there shortly triggered many thoughts in Cronley's mind as he put his hand on the enormous door lever and pushed down.

He remembered being with Derwin at the officers' club bar in Camp Holabird when the Squirt came in.

He remembered why his fellow spooks in training had called Derwin "Dick Tracy," and that it had not been rooted in admiration.

What the hell does he want from me?

He had dressed to meet him. That is, in triangled pinks and greens, not in his captain's tunic, as that would have established the captain/major relationship between them.

While he was putting on the triangled pinks and greens, he had thought about Ludwig Mannberg's elegant wardrobe, now shared with Max Ostrowski. He thought it would be a good idea to get some civvies for himself. There were a lot of bona fide U.S. civilians around wearing civvies, so why not?

The problem there was, where could he get some? He had two Brooks Brothers suits in Midland—two because his mother said he could be counted upon to spill soup on the first one he put on—and he didn't think they would fit anyway.

And, of course, he was concerned, deeply concerned, about what was going to happen when he faced Sergeant Claudette Colbert after their most-of-the-night romp in the sheets, which was probably the dumbest thing he'd done since he started screwing Rachel Schumann. Or more accurately, had allowed Rachel Schumann to play him for the three-star naïve fool he could not deny being.

There were only two good things he could think of concerning his new relationship with Sergeant Colbert. He was willing to bet she wasn't an NKGB agent, and she sure knew how to romp.

And he wondered about not if, but how soon Fat Freddy would pick up on what was going on between him and good ol' Sergeant Colbert.

He pushed open the door and entered the room.

Fat Freddy was behind his desk and Dette behind hers, hammering furiously at her typewriter. The door to Major Harold Wallace's office was open. He was chatting with Major Thomas G. Derwin, who sat in front of his desk with a briefcase on his lap. Both looked out at him.

"Good morning, sir," Freddy said. "Major Derwin is here to see you. He's in with Major Wallace."

"Sir," Dette said, "General Gehlen said that he'd like to see you as soon as it's convenient."

When Cronley looked at Colbert, she met his eyes. She smiled warmly, but it was just that, nothing more or less.

"Did he say where he was?"

"At the compound, sir."

"Please call him back and tell him I'll come out there as soon as Major Derwin and I have finished talking about whatever he wants to talk about."

"Yes, sir. I'll make sure a car is available."

Cronley walked to Wallace's office door.

"Good morning, gentlemen."

"Major Derwin has been waiting to see you, Jim," Wallace said.

"Captain Cronley," Derwin said.

"I'm sorry to have kept you waiting, Major," Cronley said. "What's on your mind?"

"It would be better, I think, if we discussed that privately."

What the hell does he want?

"Sounds ominous. Did one of Tiny's Troopers complain I've been mean to him?"

Derwin didn't reply.

"Why don't we go in my office?" Cronley asked.

Derwin got to his feet and walked to the door. As they walked across the outer office, Dette asked, "Can I get you and the major coffee, sir?"

"That would be very nice, Dette, thank you," Cronley said. He turned to Major Derwin. "Should I ask Miss Colbert to bring her book?"

"No. That won't be necessary," Derwin said firmly.

The office, now that of the chief, DCI-Europe, had formerly

been the office of Colonel Robert Mattingly and reflected both the colonel's good taste and his opinion of his own importance in the scheme of things. It therefore was larger and more elegantly furnished than Wallace's office, and he saw that Derwin had picked up on that.

"Have a seat, please, Major," Cronley said. "And when Miss Colbert has gotten us some coffee, you can tell me what's on your mind."

Derwin took a seat, holding his briefcase on his lap, but said nothing.

Dette came into the office, laid a coffee set on the table, poured, and then left.

"Okay, Major. Let's have it," Cronley said.

"Something has come to my attention, Cronley, that I thought, in the interest of fairness, I would ask you about before I go any further with my investigation."

There he goes again, playing Dick Tracy. "My investigation."

What the hell's going on?

"Which is?"

"What would you care to tell me about your relationship with my predecessor, the late Lieutenant Colonel Anthony Schumann?"

"Excuse me?"

"And with Colonel Schumann's wife, Mrs. Rachel Schumann?"

"Why are you asking?"

"Please, Captain Cronley, just answer the question."

"Okay. I knew both of them."

"How well?"

"Slightly."

"So you're telling me there's nothing to the story that you tried to kill Colonel Schumann?"

"Oh, for Christ's sake!"

"Once again, Cronley, please answer my question."

Cronley leaned forward and depressed the intercom lever.

"Dette, would you ask Major Wallace to come in here, please? Right now?"

"Yes, sir."

"At the moment, Cronley, I have nothing to say to Major Wallace," Derwin said.

Wallace put his head in the door sixty seconds later.

"What's up?"

"Come on in and close the door," Cronley said. "And then, when no one else can hear us, please tell Major Derwin what you know about my attempt to murder the late Colonel Schumann. He's investigating that."

"What?" Wallace asked incredulously, chuckling. "Seriously?"

"He sounds very serious to me."

"This is a serious matter," Derwin said.

"What should I tell him, Jim?" Wallace asked.

"Everything . . . well, maybe not *everything*. And make sure he understands that whatever you tell him is classified Top Secret–Presidential."

"What I am about to tell you, Major Derwin," Wallace said, with a smile, "is classified Top Secret–Presidential."

Derwin didn't reply.

"The penalty for divulging Top Secret–Presidential material to anyone not authorized access to same is castration with a dull bayonet, followed by the firing squad, as I'm sure you know."

"I have to tell you, Major, I don't find anything humorous in this," Derwin said.

"Stick around, it gets much funnier," Wallace said. "Well, one day Colonel Schumann—and a dozen associates—found himself on a back road not from here—I've always wondered what he was doing out in the boonies . . ."

"Me, too," Cronley said.

Now I know, of course, what the sonofabitch was doing there. He was looking for it. He wanted to find out what was going on at Kloster Grünau so he could tell his handler in the NKGB.

". . . but anyway, there he was, and he comes up on a monastery, or what had been a monastery, Kloster Grünau, surrounded by fences and concertina barbed wire. On the fence were signs, 'Twenty-third CIC' and, in English and German, 'Absolutely No Admittance.'

"Colonel Schumann had never heard of the Twenty-third CIC, and he thought as IG for CIC Europe he should have heard of it."

"What was this place?" Derwin asked.

"You don't have the need to know that, Major," Cronley said.

"You're not in a position to tell me what I need to know, Cronley," Derwin snapped.

"Yeah, he is," Major Wallace said. "But anyway, Schumann, being the zealous inspector general he was . . . I shouldn't be making fun of him, the poor bastard got himself blown up. Sorry. Anyway, Schumann drives up the road and is immediately stopped by two jeeps, each of which has a pedestal-mounted .50 caliber Browning machine gun and four enormous soldiers, all black, in it.

"He tells them he wants in, and they tell him to wait.

"A second lieutenant wearing cowboy boots shows up. He's the security officer for Kloster Grünau. His name is James D. Cronley Junior."

"A second lieutenant named Cronley?" Major Derwin asked.

"This was before he got promoted."

"I'd like to hear about that, too," Derwin said.

"That's also classified Top Secret–Presidential," Wallace said. "Anyway, Second Lieutenant Cronley politely tells Lieutenant Colonel Schumann that nobody gets into Kloster Grünau unless they have written permission from either General Greene or Colonel Robert Mattingly.

"Lieutenant Colonel Schumann, somewhat less politely, tells Second Lieutenant Cronley that second lieutenants don't get to tell lieutenant colonels, especially when he is the CIC IG, what he can't do. And tells his driver to 'drive on.'

"Second Lieutenant Cronley issues an order to stop the staff car.

"One of the .50s fires one round.

"Bang.

"Right into the engine block of Colonel Schumann's staff car. It stops.

"At that point, Colonel Schumann decides that since he's outgunned, the smart thing to do is make a retrograde movement and report the incident to General Greene. He does so just as soon as he can get back to Frankfurt, dragging the disabled staff car behind one of his remaining vehicles.

"General Greene tells him Second Lieutenant Cronley was just carrying out his orders, and for Colonel Schumann not only not to try again to get into Kloster Grünau, but also not to ask questions about it, and finally to forget he was ever there.

"End of story," Wallace concluded. "Did I leave anything out, Jim?"

"No. That was fine. Thank you."

"Any questions, Major?"

"That story poses more questions than it answers," Derwin said. "What exactly is going on at this monastery?"

"I told you before, Major, you don't have the need to know that," Cronley said.

"And I'm more than a little curious, Cronley, how you became a captain so . . . suddenly."

"I'm sure you are," Cronley said, and then: "Oh, hell, let's shut this off once and for all."

He went to a door and opened it. Behind it was a safe. He worked the combination, opened the door, took out a manila envelope, and then took two 8×10-inch photographs from it.

"These are classified Top Secret–Presidential, Major," he said, as he handed them to Major Derwin.

"Do I get to look, Jim?" Major Wallace asked.

"Who's the fellow pinning on the bars?" Wallace asked a moment later. "I recognize the guy wearing the bow tie, of course."

"My father."

"Why is President Truman giving you a decoration?" Derwin asked. "What is that?"

Wallace answered for him: "It's the Distinguished Service Medal."

"What did Cronley do to earn the DSM?"

"The citation is also classified," Cronley said.

He took the photographs back, put them back in the envelope, put the envelope back in the safe, closed the door, spun the combination dial, and then closed the door that concealed the safe.

"Are we now through playing Twenty Questions, Major Derwin?" Cronley asked.

"For the moment."

"I want to play," Major Wallace said.

"Excuse me?" Major Derwin said.

"I want to play Twenty Questions, too. What the hell is this all about, Derwin? You're not a CIC special agent, you're the CIC IG—without any authority whatever over the DCI—so why are you asking Cronley all these questions?"

"That, as Cronley has said so often today, is something you don't have the need to know."

"I'm making it my business," Wallace said. "My first question is, who told you Cronley shot up Schumann's staff car? No, who told you he tried to murder the poor bastard?"

"I learned that from a confidential source."

"What confidential source?"

"You don't have the need to know, Major Wallace."

"Do you want me to get on the horn to General Greene, tell him what you've been doing, and have him order you to tell me all about your confidential source?"

"Why would you want to do that?"

"For a number of reasons, including Colonel Tony Schumann was a friend of mine, but primarily because the Army has handed me a CIC supervisory special agent's credentials and told me to look into things I think smell fishy."

"You're interfering with my investigation, Major," Derwin said.

Wallace reached for the telephone on Cronley's desk, dialed "O," and said, "Get me General Greene."

"That won't be necessary," Derwin said.

"Cancel that," Wallace said, and put the handset into its cradle.

Derwin went into his briefcase and pulled out a business envelope that he handed to Wallace.

"This was hand-delivered to me at my quarters in the Park Hotel," he said.

"Hand-delivered by whom?" Wallace asked, as he took a sheet of paper from the envelope.

"I mean, it was left at the desk of the Park, and put in my box there, not mailed."

"I never would have guessed," Wallace said sarcastically, "since there's no address on the envelope, only your name."

A moment later, he said, his voice dripping with disgust, "Jesus H. Christ!"

He handed the sheet of paper to Cronley.

DEAR MAJOR DERWIN:

THERE ARE THOSE WHO BELIEVE THE EXPLOSION WHICH TOOK THE LIVES OF YOUR PREDECESSOR, LIEUTENANT COLONEL ANTHONY SCHUMANN, AND HIS WIFE WAS NOT ACCIDENTAL, AND FURTHER THAT THE PROVOST MARSHAL'S INVESTIGATION OF THE INCIDENT WAS SUSPICIOUSLY SUPERFICIAL.

THERE ARE THOSE WHO WONDER WHY CAPTAIN JAMES D. CRONLEY JR., OF THE XXIIIRD CIC DETACHMENT, WAS

NOT QUESTIONED BY THE CRIMINAL INVESTIGATION DIVISION IN THE MATTER, OR, FOR THAT MATTER, BY THE CIC, IN VIEW OF THE SEVERAL RUMORS CIRCULATING CONCERNING CRONLEY:

THAT HIS RELATIONSHIP WITH MRS. SCHUMANN WAS FAR MORE INTIMATE THAN APPROPRIATE.

THAT COLONEL SCHUMANN NARROWLY AVOIDED BEING MURDERED BY CRONLEY AT THE SECRET INSTALLATION, A FORMER MONASTERY, CRONLEY RUNS IN SCHOLLBRUNN.

THAT AMONG THE MANY SECRETS OF THIS INSTALLATION, KLOSTER GRÜNAU, ARE A NUMBER OF RECENTLY DUG UNMARKED GRAVES.

It took Cronley about fifteen seconds to decide the author of the letter had NKGB somewhere in his title, or—considering the other Rahil—*her* title.

"I have determined both that this letter was typed on an Underwood typewriter, and the paper on which this is typed is government issue," Major Derwin said.

"You're a regular Dick Tracy, aren't you, Derwin?" Wallace said.

"Excuse me?"

"I mean, that really narrows it down, doesn't it? There are probably twenty Underwood typewriters here in the Vier Jahreszeiten and twenty reams of GI paper. I wonder how many Underwoods there are in the Farben Building, but I'd guess four, five hundred and three or four supply rooms full of GI typewriter paper."

"I was suggesting that it suggests this was written by an American."

"You're a regular Sherlock Holmes, aren't you, Derwin?"

"There's no call for sarcasm, Major Wallace," Derwin said.

"That's coming to me very naturally, Major Derwin," Wallace said. "Permit me to go through this letter one item at a time.

"Item one: The explosion which killed my friend Tony Schumann and his wife was thoroughly—not superficially—investigated, not only by the DCI, but also by the Frankfurt military post engineer and by me. And I was there before the DCI was even called in. The gas line leading to his water heater developed a leak. The fucking thing blew up. Tony and his wife were in the wrong place at the wrong time. Period. End of that story.

"So far as Cronley's 'intimate' relationship is concerned, I was here when Cronley was ordered, *ordered*, to take Mrs. Schumann to dinner. He was as enthusiastic about doing so as he would have been . . . I don't know what . . . about going to the dentist for a tooth-yanking.

"I've already dealt with that nonsensical allegation that Cronley attempted to murder Colonel Schumann at Kloster Grünau. That brings us to the unmarked graves at the monastery. What about that, Cronley? Have you been burying people out there in unmarked graves?"

Truth to tell, which I obviously can't, there are three I know about, those of the three men, almost certainly NKGB agents, that Max Ostrowski killed when they damn near killed Sergeant Abraham Lincoln Tedworth.

And then I suspect, but don't know—and I don't want to know—that former Oberstleutnant Gunther von Plat and former Major Kurt Boss are looking up at the grass in the cloister cemetery. They disappeared shortly after Clete turned Colonel Sergei Likharev in Argentina, and he told Clete, and Clete told me to tell General Gehlen, that they had been the bad apples in Gehlen's basket who had given him the rosters of Gehlen's people Tedworth found on Likharev.

"Every Friday afternoon," Cronley said. "We call it 'the Kloster Grünau Memorial Gardens Friday Afternoon Burial Services and Chicken Fry.'"

Wallace laughed, then turned to Major Derwin.

"What have you done with this thing, Derwin? Have you shown it to anybody else? The DCI, maybe? Anybody else?"

"I was not at that point in my investigation—"

"Your investigation?" Wallace asked, heavily sarcastic. "Derwin, were you ever a CIC agent in the field?"

"Of course I was."

"Where?"

"What has that got to do with anything?"

"I can check your records."

"I was the special agent in charge of the Des Moines office."

"That's all?"

"And then I was transferred to CIC Headquarters."

"You mean the CIC School?"

"The school is part of CIC Headquarters."

"And since I don't think there were many members of the Japanese Kempei Tai, or of Abwehr Intelligence, running around Des Moines, Iowa, what you were doing was ringing doorbells, doing background investigations? 'Mrs. Jones, your neighbor Joe Glutz, now in the Army, is being considered for a position in which he will have access to classified information. We are checking to see if he can be trusted with it. Which of his sexual deviations would you like to tell me about?'"

"I don't have to put up with this . . . this being mocked and insulted."

"The first thing that comes to my mind is for me to go to General Greene and give him my take on you, which is that you saw when you were being sent to replace my good friend Tony Schumann, you decided it was going to give you a chance to be a real CIC agent. And then when whatever miserable sonofabitch in our ranks decided to stick it to Cronley sent you that letter, you saw it as your chance to be a hotshot.

"But if I did that, and he shipped your ass to the Aleutian Islands to count snowballs, which he would do, and which you would deserve for your Dick Tracy bullshit, the prick in our midst who tried to stab Cronley in the back would hear about it and crawl back into his hole.

"And I am determined to find that bastard and nail him to the wall.

"So what you are going to do, Major Derwin, is put that goddamn letter back in your briefcase and then drop your quote investigation unquote. And forget investigations, period. You will keep that letter so that you take it out from time to time to remind you how close you came to getting shipped to the Aleutians. If you get another letter, or if there is any other contact with Cronley's buddy the letter writer, I want to hear about it.

"Now, if this is satisfactory to you, get out of here and get in your car, and go to Frankfurt or anywhere else and do what an IG is supposed to do. If this is not satisfactory to you, I am going to get on the horn and call General Greene and tell him what a bad boy you have been. Which is it to be?"

"I really don't understand your attitude—"

"Which is it to be?" Wallace snapped.

"I don't seem to have much choice in the matter, do I?" Derwin said, mustering what little dignity he could. Then he turned to Cronley: "Captain Cronley, I assure you it wasn't my intention to accuse you of any wrongdoing. I was just . . ."

"If that's intended as an apology, Major Derwin. Accepted."

Christ, I actually feel sorry for him.

Derwin nodded at Wallace and walked out of the office.

"Jesus Christ, Jim," Wallace said. "Do you believe that?"

"I don't know what to think," Cronley said.

"Think about candidates for the letter writer," Wallace said. "I think we can safely remove Colonel Mattingly and myself from the list of suspects . . ."

I'll be goddamned. Maybe it wasn't the Russians. Maybe it was Mattingly. Wallace, no. Mattingly, maybe.

". . . but who else can you think of who is green with jealousy that you're now the chief, DCI-Europe?"

Cronley shook his head, and then his mouth went on automatic.

"Be glad they didn't give you the job," he said.

Wallace looked at him curiously.

What the hell, why not tell him?

Screw Ludwig, I'm going with my gut feeling about Wallace.

Wallace's one of the good guys.

"I had lunch with General Smith yesterday," Cronley said.

"And General Greene. And Lieutenant Colonel Ashton. And Lieutenant Schultz, who is really not Lieutenant Schultz, by the way, or even Commander Schultz, which is what he really was when he was working for Cletus Frade, but executive assistant to the director, Directorate of Central Intelligence."

"Interesting."

"And I raised the subject of why was I named chief, DCI-Europe, when there were so many fully qualified people of appropriate rank and experience around. And Schultz told me."

"Like Bob Mattingly, you mean?"

"And you."

"And what did Schultz tell you?"

"Mattingly, first. Schultz didn't come right out and say this . . ."

"But?"

"I got the feeling the admiral thinks Mattingly is more interested in his Army career than the DCI."

"Explain that."

"That since he's thinking of his Army career, he'd be more chummy with the assistant chief of staff for intelligence—with the Pentagon generally, and ONI, and the FBI—than the admiral wants his people to be. He was in ONI, and he knows how unhappy they were when Truman started up the DCI to replace the OSS, which they thought they'd buried once and for all."

Wallace didn't reply to that immediately, but Cronley thought he saw him nod just perceptibly, as if accepting what Cronley had told him.

Then Wallace asked, "And that applies to me, too?"

"I was given the job, the title, because no one is going to think that something important like Operation Ost is going to be handed to a very junior captain. Or the corollary of that, DCI-Europe—and Operation Ost—can't be very important if they gave it to a very junior captain."

"That makes a perverse kind of sense, I suppose."

"Which brings us to you."

"Oh?"

"Nobody told me this either, but if—more than likely when—this blows up and I get thrown to the wolves—and they did tell me to expect getting thrown to the wolves—somebody's going to have to take over from me."

"You mean me?" Wallace asked dubiously.

"Think about it. You're only a major, not a full-bull colonel. You've got an unimportant job running a small—actually phony—CIC detachment close to DCI-Europe. It would seem natural to give you something unimportant like DCI-Europe when the young incompetent running it, as predicted, FUBAR . . ."

"'Fucked Up Beyond Any Repair.'" Wallace chuckled as he made the translation.

"The executive assistant to the director of the Directorate of Central Intelligence shows up here," Cronley said. "He says, 'I guess you heard how Cronley blew it.' You say, 'Yes, sir.' El Jefe says, 'Wallace, you're ex-OSS. I would be very surprised if while you were sitting here with your thumb in your ass running this phony CIC detachment, you didn't snoop around and learn a hell of a lot about what Cronley was doing.'

"Then he says, 'We were counting on this. So tell me what you know, or suspect, and I will fill in the blanks before I have you transferred to DCI, and you take over as chief, DCI-Europe.'"

"Jesus Christ!"

"Yeah. Anyway, that's my take."

"If you're right, why wouldn't Schultz have told you to keep me up to speed on what you're doing?"

"Because he's being careful. He knows you were Mattingly's Number Two in the OSS. He didn't tell me to tell you anything. This is my scenario."

"Schultz doesn't know we're having this little chat?"

"I thought about asking him if I could, and decided not to because he probably would have said, 'Hell, no!'"

"But you're going to tell me anyhow?"

"I'll tell you as much as I can, but there's a lot going on you neither have the need to know, nor want to know."

"Like what?"

"Next question?"

"So what are you going to tell me? And for that matter, why?"

"Despite Ludwig Mannberg's theory that when you really want to trust a gut feeling, don't—my gut tells me I can trust you."

"I realize I'm expected to say, 'Of course you can.' But I'll say it anyway."

"There are two operations I think you should know about. One involves my cousin Luther . . ."

"Your *cousin* Luther?" Wallace asked incredulously.

"My cousin Luther and Odessa," Cronley confirmed, and proceeded to relate that story.

When he had finished, Wallace asked, "You realize that Odessa is the CIC's business, and none of yours?"

"I'm making it mine," Cronley said. "And the second operation I think you should know about is our getting Colonel Likharev's family out of Russia."

"Whose family out of Russia?"

"The NKGB major Sergeant Tedworth caught sneaking out of Kloster Grünau turned out to be an NKGB colonel by the name of Sergei Likharev. We shipped him to Argentina, where Clete and Schultz turned him . . ."

He went on to tell Wallace the details of that, finishing, "That's what we were doing in Vienna, giving a Russian female NKGB agent, who also works for Mossad, a hell of a lot of expense money.

"And just before our little chat with Dick Tracy Derwin, Claudette Colbert—"

"Hessinger's new, and I must say, very-well-put-together assistant? Is her first name really Claudette, like the movie star?"

"Yes, but she prefers to be called 'Dette.'"

"And is Freddy dallying with her?"

"No. Freddy sees her as his way out of being what he calls 'the company clerk,' and he's not going to screw that up by fooling around with her."

"She makes me really sorry there's that sacred rule forbidding officers to fool around with enlisted women," Wallace said, and then quickly added, "Just kidding, just kidding."

"Anyway, Dette told me just before we had our chat with Derwin that General Gehlen wants to see me as soon as possible. I think that's because he's heard from Seven-K . . ."

"His Soviet asset?"

Cronley nodded. "A/K/A Rahil. And I've started to think of her as our asset. So far we've given her a hundred thousand dollars."

"One hundred thousand?" Wallace parroted incredulously.

Cronley nodded again. "And she'll be worth every dime if she can get Likharev's family out and he stays turned."

"You think he will stay turned?"

"Yeah," Cronley said thoughtfully after a moment.

"Gratitude?"

"A little of that, but primarily because . . . he's smart . . . he will realize that once we get his family to Argentina, that's not the end of it. The NKGB will know that he's alive and turned and has his family with him. And the NKGB can't just quit. Likharev knows they'll really be looking for him to make an example, *pour encourager les autres*, of what happens to senior NKGB officers who turn, and we're the only protection he has."

"Yeah," Wallace said.

"So, instead of going out to Schleissheim and removing the Storch from curious eyes, I'm going to have to go to Pullach."

"Can I ask about that?"

"Ask about what?"

"You and the Storchs. Now that EUCOM has been told to give DCI-Europe anything it wants, why don't you get a couple, or three or four, L-4s and get rid of the Storchs? And all the problems having them brings with it?"

"The Storch is a better airplane than the Piper Cub. And only Army aviators are allowed to fly Army airplanes, and I'm not an Army aviator . . ."

"I'd forgotten that."

". . . and I don't want two, three, or four Army aviators out here, or at the Pullach compound, seeing a lot of interesting things that are none of their business."

"Understood," Wallace said, then added, "You're good, Jim. You really try to think of everything, don't you?"

"Yes, I do. And one time in say, fifty times, I do think of everything. The other forty-nine times something I didn't think of bites me in the ass."

Wallace chuckled.

"Or something comes out of the woodwork, like Dick Tracy?"

"Like Dick Tracy," Cronley agreed. "Do you think you turned him off for good?"

"Yeah. I think the more he thinks about it, the more he will decide the best way to cover his ass is to stop playing Dick Tracy."

"Jesus, I hope so," Cronley said, and then stood up and walked out of his office.

[TWO]

"Where's the car?" Cronley asked Hessinger.

"Wait one, please," Hessinger said, and then, raising his voice, called, "Colbert, are you about finished in there?"

"Be right there," she called, and came out of the supply room.

"Claudette has finished four of the after-action reports," Hessinger said. "I need you to look at them as soon as possible."

"Not now, Freddy. I have to see General Gehlen. Maybe after that."

"I propose to have Claudette drive you out to Pullach. She drives, you read the after actions, and tell her what, if anything, needs to be fixed. Okay?"

Cronley didn't immediately reply.

"And then," Hessinger said, "she drives you wherever you have to go, Schleissheim, or back here, or even out to Kloster Grünau, when you're through with the general."

"Don't look so worried, Mr. Cronley," Claudette said. "I'm a pretty good driver, for a woman, if that's what's worrying you."

"Let's go. Where's the car?"

"By now it should be out front," she said. "Let me get my purse and a briefcase for the after actions."

"'Individuals in possession of documents classified Top Secret or above must be suitably armed when such documents are being transported outside a secure area,'" Hessinger said.

Obviously quoting verbatim whatever Army regulation that is from memory.

"I've got my snub-nosed .38 in my purse," Claudette announced.

"Where did you get a snub-nosed .38?" Cronley asked.

"I brought mine from the ASA," Claudette said. "I thought I'd need it here. 'The officer or non-commissioned officer in charge of an ASA communications facility where Top Secret or above material is being handled, or may be handled, shall be suitably armed.'"

And that, too, was quoted verbatim from memory.

Then she added, "Don't worry, Mr. Cronley, I know how to use it. Actually, I shot Expert with it the last time I was on the range."

"And where is your .45, Mr. Cronley?" Hessinger asked.

"In my room."

"You should go get it, and not only because of the classified documents, if you take my meaning, as I am sure you do."

"I stand chastised," Cronley said. "I'll go get my pistol and meet you out front, Dette."

"Yes, sir."

Five minutes later, when he walked through the revolving door onto Maximilianstrasse, the Opel Kapitän was at the curb, with the rear door open and Claudette at the wheel.

He looked at the door, then closed it and got in the front seat beside Claudette.

She didn't say anything at first, but when they were away from the curb, she said, "I was trying to make it easy for you. Opening the rear door, I mean."

"How so?"

"Officers ride in the backseat, when enlisted women are driving."

"But we are not an officer and an enlisted woman, Miss Colbert. We are dressed as two civilian employees of the Army are dressed, and hoping the people think we work for the PX."

She chuckled.

"And I wanted to be sure that you didn't think I was trying to get cozy when I shouldn't."

"Never entered my mind. What you should be worried about—what *we* should be worried about—is Freddy, who is twice as smart as he looks, and he looks like Albert Einstein. Do you think . . . ?"

"I don't think he thinks anything. Read the after actions. That's what's on his mind."

He opened her briefcase and took out the after-action reports. There were four:

LIKHAREV, SERGEI, COLONEL NKGB, CAPTURE OF
LIKHAREV, SERGEI, COLONEL NKGB, RESULTS OF
CAPTAIN CRONLEY'S INTERROGATION OF
LIKHAREV, SERGEI, COLONEL NKGB, TRANSPORT TO
ARGENTINA OF
TEDWORTH, ABRAHAM L., FIRST SERGEANT, ATTEMPTED
NKGB MURDER OF

Cronley read all of them carefully, decided they were better than he expected they would be, and then made a few minor changes to each so that Freddy would know he had read them.

"Very nice, Dette," Cronley said, putting them back in her briefcase.

"I got the details of Tedworth grabbing the Russian from Tedworth," she said. "And the details of Ostrowski saving him from getting garroted from him and Ostrowski. The interrogation and transport stuff I got from Freddy."

"These are first class," Cronley said. "I moved a couple of commas around so Freddy would see I'd really read them, but they were fine as done. You're really good at this sort of thing."

"I'm also very good at Gregg shorthand," she said. "Which is really causing me an awful problem right now."

What the hell is she talking about?

"The reason Freddy wanted you to come to us from the ASA is because you can take shorthand. How is that a problem?"

"You remember when you came out of your office, Freddy had to call me out of the supply closet?"

Cronley nodded.

"What I was doing in there was taking shorthand."

"Of what?"

"What was being said in your office. What went on between you and Major Derwin and Major Wallace."

"What?"

"As soon as I reported to Freddy, he told me about Colonel Mattingly, who he said absolutely could not be trusted, and that while he thought Major Wallace could be trusted, he wasn't sure."

Freddy really brought her on board, didn't he?

"He's right about Mattingly, but I can tell you Major Wallace is one of the good guys."

"So I learned when I was in the supply closet."

"I still don't understand what you being in the closet has to do with you . . ." He stopped. "Jesus, Freddy bugged Mattingly's office? My office?"

"Actually, that's how I met him," she said.

"Find someplace to pull off the road," Cronley said. "We're almost to Pullach, and I want to finish this conversation before we get there."

"Yes, sir."

"Sir"?

She turned onto a dirt road and drove far enough down it so the Kapitän could not be seen from the paved road.

"You're not supposed to sit with the engine idling in a Kapitän," she said, almost as if to herself. "But it's as cold as that witch's teat we hear so much about, so to hell with it. I'll leave it running."

"You were telling me how you met Freddy," Cronley said.

"Before you moved the ASA Munich station into the Pullach

compound, Freddy started hanging out around it. Around me. I thought he wanted to get into my pants. I knew who he was—that he was in the mysterious, not-on-the-books CIC detachment—and I thought just maybe he could help me to get out of the ASA at least into his branch of the CIC, so I didn't run him off.

"Finally, when he thought it was safe, he took me to the movies. After the movie—it was *They Were Expendable.* You know, Robert Montgomery and John Wayne? About PT boats in the Philippines?"

"I remember the movie," Cronley said.

"So after the movie, when Freddy was driving me back to my *kaserne*—in this car, by the way—he pulls off onto a dark street, and I thought, here it comes, and started asking myself how much I really wanted out of the ASA and into the intelligence business.

"But what he whipped out was his CIC credentials. He said what he was going to say to me was classified. Then he said he had reason to want to bug two offices, and he didn't want anyone to know he was doing it."

"Why did he go to you for that?" Cronley asked.

"The ASA—Army Security Agency—started out making sure nobody was tapping Army telephones. It went from that to making sure nobody was bugging Army offices, and finally to intercepting radio signals. Freddy knew that. You didn't?"

"I must have slept through that lecture at the CIC School. Or chalk it up to my all-around naïveté, innocence, about things I ought to know."

"Oddly enough, some women find naïveté and innocence to be charming, even erotic, characteristics in younger men. But to fill in the blanks in your education, the ASA teaches ASAers courses in how to find bugs. It therefore follows if you know how to take them out, you know how to put them in. *Verstehen Sie?*"

Actually, she should have said du. Du *is the intimate form of* Sie. *And God knows we have been intimate.*

This is not the time for language lessons.

"Okay, so where did you get the bugs you put in for Freddy?"

"There's a rumor going around that the ASA sometimes installs bugs, too. Anyway, I got half a dozen bugs from the supply room. And installed them in what was then Mattingly's office, now yours, and in Wallace's. And Freddy promised to see what he could do about getting me transferred out of ASA."

"When did you put these bugs in?"

"A long time ago. Or what seems like a long time ago. You were then a second lieutenant in charge of the guards at the mysterious Kloster Grünau."

"That does seem like a long time ago, doesn't it?" Cronley said. "Which means Freddy regularly bugged both Mattingly and Wallace."

"He did. You didn't know this?"

Cronley shook his head.

"And today he ordered you to . . . what's the word, transcribe? . . ."

Colbert nodded.

". . . my conversation with Major Derwin?"

"Right. Which is the original source of my loyalty dilemma. And it gets worse."

"Explain that to me, now that we've already established that I'm naïve and innocent."

"When Freddy said, 'Derwin worries me. Get in there and get

a record of what's said, and don't let Cronley know,' that put me in a hell of a spot. Freddy lived up to his end of his deal with me—there I was in triangles—and I obviously owed my loyalty to him.

"On the other hand—and this has nothing, well, *almost* nothing, to do with you sweeping me off my feet with that innocence and naïveté I find so erotic—you got me out of the ASA, you're my boss and Freddy's boss . . . Getting the picture? So what do I do? Who gets my loyalty?"

"You did the right thing to tell me about this," he said.

"Even if that was betraying Freddy's trust in me? Even if that means you will no longer trust him?"

"Pay attention. Freddy didn't tell me about the bugs because if he got caught, he could pass a lie-detector test saying I knew nothing about the bugs. And he told you not to let me know you were listening to the bugs because he had a good idea, was worried about, Derwin's interest in me. And he really didn't want me to know you heard either what Derwin asked me, or what my answers were."

"You mean you were fooling around with Colonel Schumann's wife?"

And here we are at decision time. Do I tell her everything, or not?

I don't have any choice.

She's either part of this team, or she's not.

And I can't send her back to the ASA because (a) she's already learned too much about Freddy, and now about me, and (b) I believe what they say about hell having no fury like a pissed-off female, and (c) she would have every right to be thoroughly pissed off because she's done nothing wrong.

So once again, it's fuck Ludwig Mannberg's firm belief that if you really want to trust your intuition, don't.

"Turn that around, Dette. Rachel Schumann was fooling around with me. More accurately, she was making a three-star fool of me."

"She was into the erotic attraction of your innocence and naïveté, is that what you're saying?"

"In hindsight, I don't think she liked me at all. I think she held me in great contempt . . . and, from her viewpoint, rightly so. She was playing me like a violin, to coin a phrase."

"Her viewpoint?"

"That of an NKGB operative. And for all I know, an NKGB officer. Probably an NKGB officer."

"You're telling me this colonel's wife was a Russian spy?"

"Him, too."

"My God!"

"Welcome to the wonderful world of intelligence."

"What information did she want from you?"

"Whatever she could get about Kloster Grünau and Operation Ost generally, and whatever she could get about Likharev specifically."

"You're implying she got it. From you."

"She got what she wanted to know about Likharev. From me."

"Like what?"

"Like the fact that he wasn't buried in an unmarked grave at Kloster Grünau, despite an elaborate burial we conducted for him in the middle of the night. That he was in fact on his way to Argentina. And because I gave her that information, people died and were seriously wounded—Americans and Argentines—in Argentina, and the NKGB damned near managed to take out Likharev."

"You're sure about all this?"

"I'm sure about all this."

"Then there was something fishy about the explosion that killed this woman? Her and her husband?"

"Listen carefully. The only thing I *know* is that there was an explosion. That said explosion was investigated by everybody and his brother, including Major Wallace, who thought, still thinks, which we had better not forget, that Schumann was a fine officer and a good friend—and nothing fishy was uncovered."

"But you have your suspicions, right?"

"Next question?"

"So what do I do with my Gregg notes?"

"Transcribe them accurately and in full, give them to Freddy, who already knows everything, and don't tell Freddy we had this little chat. Questions?"

"No, sir," she said, then, "Yes, one. A big one. Where the hell did I get the idea you're naïve and innocent?"

"Does that mean I've lost the erotic appeal that went along with that?"

"Perish the thought! I meant nothing of the kind!"

"Put the car in gear, please, Miss Colbert. Before we get in trouble, we better go see the general."

She did so, and then parroted, "'*We* better go see the general'?"

"Yeah. I think it's important that you get to know one another. And when we finish, you can bring Freddy up to speed on what he had to say. Thereby sparing me from having to do so."

[THREE]
Office of the U.S. Military Government Liaison Officer
The South German Industrial Development
Organization Compound
Pullach, Bavaria
The American Zone of Occupied Germany
1205 16 January 1946

As they were passing through the final roadblock and into the inner compound, the massive sergeant manning it, when he was sure Colbert was concentrating on the striped barrier pole as it rose, winked at Cronley and gave him a thumbs-up in appreciation of her physical attributes. Cronley winked back.

When they went into the "Military Government" building, they found General Reinhard Gehlen, Colonel Ludwig Mannberg, Major Konrad Bischoff, and Captain Chauncey Dunwiddie sitting around a coffee table.

"Oh, I'm so glad you could finally find time for us in your busy schedule," Dunwiddie greeted Cronley sarcastically. "Where the hell were you?"

Cronley's mouth went on automatic: "'Where the hell were you, *sir*?' is the way you ask that question, Captain Dunwiddie," he snapped.

His anger dissipated as quickly as it had arisen. "What the hell's the matter with you, Tiny? You got out of the wrong side of the bed?" He turned to Gehlen and the others. "Sorry to be late. Couldn't be helped. I was being interrogated by Major Derwin."

"The CIC IG?" Tiny asked incredulously. "What was that about?"

"This is getting out of hand," Cronley said. "Time out." He made the *Time out* signal with his hands.

"This meeting is called to order by the chief, DCI-Europe, who yields to himself the floor. First order of business: Gentlemen, this is Miss Claudette Colbert. She is now Mr. Hessinger's deputy for administration. She comes to us from the ASA, where she held all the proper security clearances. You already know Colonel Mannberg, Dette, and you may know Captain Dunwiddie. That's former Major Konrad Bischoff, of General Gehlen's staff, and this, of course, is General Gehlen."

"Mannberg has been telling me about you, Fraulein," Gehlen said, and bobbed his head. "Welcome!"

"Your call, General," Cronley said. "Do you want to start with why you wanted to see me, or why I was delayed getting out here?"

"Actually, I'm curious about the major," Gehlen said. "Derwin, you said?"

"Yes, sir. Major Thomas G. Derwin. When Colonel Schumann died, Major Derwin was sent from the CIC School to replace him as the CIC/ASA inspector general. When I was a student at the CIC School, I was in Major Derwin's classes on the Techniques of Surveillance. Major Derwin was known to me and my fellow students as 'Dick Tracy.'"

"I gather he is not one of your favorite people," Gehlen said drily. "What did he want?"

"He said he wanted to ask me about credible rumors he'd heard about (a) my having an 'inappropriate relationship' with the late Mrs. Schumann, and (b) that I had attempted to murder Colonel Schumann at Kloster Grünau."

"And what did you tell him, Jim?" Mannberg asked.

"I asked Major Wallace to join us. He explained to Major Derwin what had happened at Kloster Grünau when Colonel Schumann had insisted on going in, and told Major Derwin that the idea I had had an inappropriate relationship with Mrs. Schumann was absurd."

"Jim," Tiny said, "are you sure you want Sergeant Colbert to hear this?"

"She already has. And since she's wearing triangles, why don't you stop calling her 'Sergeant'?"

"And then?" General Gehlen asked.

"Major Wallace asked Major Derwin from whom he'd heard the rumors, and after some resistance, Derwin produced a typewritten letter he said had been put in his box at the Park Hotel, where he lives."

"Who was the letter from?" Gehlen asked.

Cronley held up his hand in a *Wait* gesture.

"It began by saying the water heater explosion was suspicious, and the investigation 'superficial.' That set Wallace off. He said that he personally investigated the explosion, that he got there before the CID did, and there was nothing suspicious about it.

"He really lost his temper. He said the only reason he wasn't getting on the telephone to General Greene, to tell him what an asshole Derwin was—"

"He used that word?"

"Did he, Dette?"

"Words to that effect, sir," Claudette said.

"How would she know?" Tiny challenged. "She was in there with you?"

"Let me finish, please, Tiny, then I'll get to that," Cronley said. "Wallace said the only reason he wasn't going to General Greene, who would almost certainly relieve Derwin, was because he was determined to find out who wrote the letter to Derwin, and if Derwin was relieved, whoever wrote it would crawl back in his hole, or words to that effect, and he'd never catch him. He also told Derwin to call off his 'investigation' of the allegations in the letter as of that moment."

"Did Major Wallace have any idea who wrote the letter?" Mannberg asked.

"He thinks it's someone, one of us, who doesn't think I should have been named chief, DCI-Europe."

"That's what it sounds like to me," Gehlen said. "And you think Major Derwin will cease his investigation?"

"Yes, sir. I don't think he wants to cross Major Wallace. You knew Wallace was a Jedburgh?"

"Yes, I did."

"Did I leave anything out, Dette?"

"Sir, you didn't get into the tail end of your conversation with Major Wallace."

"I asked before, was Serg— Miss Colbert in there with you?" Tiny said.

"Fat Freddy put bugs in what was Mattingly's office, and Wallace's. Or, actually, Miss Colbert did, when Freddy asked her to."

"You knew about that?" Tiny asked.

Cronley shook his head.

"I think, when Freddy thinks the moment is right, he'll tell me."

"Then how did you find out?" Tiny asked.

"With your permission, sir?" Claudette said, before Cronley could open his mouth. "When Mr. Hessinger ordered me to transcribe what would be said between Mr. Cronley and Major Derwin, I realized I could not do that without Mr. Cronley's knowledge, so I told him."

"Afterward?" Mannberg asked.

"Yes, sir."

"Why?"

"There is no question in my mind that I owe Mr. Cronley my primary loyalty, sir."

"What was 'the tail end' of your conversation with Wallace?" Tiny asked.

"I told him what I learned from El Jefe in the Farben Building. Why I'm chief, DCI-Europe. And I told him that Lieutenant Schultz hasn't been a lieutenant for some time, and that he retired a little while ago as a commander, and is now executive assistant to the director of the Directorate of Central Intelligence. A few little things like that."

"Why? He doesn't have the need to know about little things like that," Tiny said.

"Because I've come to understand that unless I want to be tossed to the wolves—did I mention El Jefe told me that was a distinct possibility?—I'm going to need all the friends I can get that I can trust. And after carefully considering Ludwig's theory that when you really want to trust your intuition, that's when you shouldn't, I decided, Fuck it . . . Sorry, Dette."

She gave a deprecating gesture with her left hand.

". . . I decided (a) Wallace can be trusted, and (b) I need him. And the more time I've had to think it over, the more I think I made the right decision."

"Even though Wallace was Mattingly's Number Two in the OSS?" Tiny challenged.

"Mattingly was a politician in the OSS. The only time he ever served behind the enemy lines, if you want to put it like that, is when he flew over Berlin in a Piper Cub to see what he could see for General White. Wallace jumped into France three times. And into Norway once with a lieutenant named Colby. My gut feeling is that he's one of us."

"One of us? I was never behind enemy lines, or jumped anywhere. Where do I fit into 'us'?"

"I'm tempted to say you get a pass because you're a retard," Cronley said. "But you're one of us because you got a Silver Star, two Purple Hearts, and promotion to first sergeant in the Battle of the Bulge. You've heard more shots fired in anger than I ever heard. Mattingly never heard one. Not one. Do you take my point, Captain Dunwiddie?"

"I take your point, Captain Cronley," General Gehlen said, and then added, "Tiny, he's right, and you know it."

Dunwiddie threw up his hands in a gesture of surrender.

"Is this where someone tells me that we've heard from the lady with the dachshund?" Cronley asked innocently.

"It is," Mannberg said, chuckling. "Go ahead, Konrad."

"It is Seven-K's opinion," former Major Konrad Bischoff began, "that the exfiltration of Mrs. Likharev and her children from their present location—which I believe is in Poland, although I was not told that, and Seven-K's man in Berlin said he doesn't know—"

"Seven-K's man in Berlin?" Cronley interrupted.

A look of colossal annoyance flashed across Bischoff's face at the interruption.

Fuck you, I don't like you, either, you sadistic, arrogant sonofabitch!

"Answer the question, Konrad," Mannberg said softly, in German. The softness of his tone did not at all soften the tone of command.

"NKGB Major Anatole Loskutnikov," Bischoff said.

"We've worked with him before," Gehlen said. "We suspect he also has a Mossad connection."

"And you sent Bischoff to Berlin to meet with him?"

"Correct."

"And what did Loskutnikov tell you?" Cronley asked.

"That Seven-K believes it would be too dangerous to try to exfiltrate the Likharev woman and her children . . ."

Not "Mrs. Likharev"? She's a colonel's wife. You wouldn't refer to Mannberg's wife as "the Mannberg woman," would you? You really do think all Russians are the untermensch, *don't you?*

". . . through either Berlin or Vienna."

"So what does she suggest?"

Bischoff ignored the question.

"According to Loskutnikov, Seven-K says the exfiltration problem is exacerbated by the mental condition of the woman and the children—"

"Meaning what?" Cronley interrupted. "They're afraid? Or crazy?"

Bischoff ignored him again.

"—which is such that travel by train or bus is dangerous."

"I asked you two questions, Bischoff, and you answered neither."

"Sorry," he said, visibly insincere. "What were they?"

"Since Bischoff is having such difficulty telling you, Jim, what he told me," General Gehlen said, "let me tell you what he told me."

"Please," Cronley said.

"A lot of this, you will understand, is what I am inferring from what Bischoff told me and what I know of this, and other, situations."

"Yes, sir."

"Understandably, Mrs. Likharev is upset—perhaps terrified—by the situation in which she now finds herself. She has been taken from the security of her Nevsky Prospekt apartment in Leningrad and now is on the run. I agree with Bischoff that she and the children are probably in Poland. She knows what will happen if the NKGB finds them. Children sense when their mother is terrified, and it terrifies them.

"Seven-K knows that if they travel by train or bus, the odds are that a terrified woman will attract the attention of railroad or bus station police, who will start asking questions. Even with good spurious documents, which I'm sure Seven-K has provided, travel by bus or train is dangerous.

"So that means travel by car, or perhaps truck. By car, providing that they have credible identification documents, would be safer than travel by truck. What is an obviously upper-class Russian woman doing riding around in a truck in Poland with two children?"

"I get it."

"To use your charming phrase, Jim, 'cutting to the chase,' what Seven-K proposes is that the Likharevs be transported to Thuringia . . ."

"My massive ignorance has just raised its head."

"The German state, the East German state, which borders on Hesse in the Kassel-Hersfeld area. Do you know that area?"

"I've been to both Hersfeld and Kassel. When I first came to Germany, I was assigned to the Twenty-second CIC Detachment in Marburg. But do I know the area? No."

Gehlen nodded.

"And then be turned over to us and then taken across the border."

"Turned over to us?"

"Preferably to Americans, but if that is not possible, to us. Seven-K says Mrs. Likharev cannot be trusted to have control of her emotions to the point that she could cross the border with her children alone."

"Turned over to whomever in East Germany?"

Gehlen nodded.

"I can see it now," Cronley said, "Fat Freddy, Tiny, and me sneaking across the border."

"Not to mention what the lady and her kids would do when they saw the Big Black Guy," Tiny said. "If Tedworth and I terrified Likharev, what would she do when she saw me?"

"We could use the Storchs to get them," Cronley said thoughtfully. "If we had someplace to land . . ."

"Could you do that?" Gehlen asked.

"I don't know, but I know where to get an expert opinion."

"From whom?" Tiny asked, and then he understood. "If you ask Colonel Wilson about this, he'll get right on the horn to Mattingly."

"We don't know that," Cronley said. "We'll have to see how much I can dazzle him with my DCI credentials."

"It's a lousy idea, Jim," Tiny said.

"It's a better idea than you and me trying to sneak back and forth across the border with a woman on the edge of hysteria and two frightened kids. Saddle up, Dette, I need a ride to the airport. I'm off to see Hotshot Billy Wilson."

[FOUR]
En Route to Schleissheim Army Airfield
1255 16 January 1946

"Is there anything I should know about this Colonel Wilson you're going to see?" Claudette asked.

"Aside from the fact that he's twenty-five years old, you mean?"

"Twenty-five and a lieutenant colonel? You're pulling my leg."

"No, I'm not. Do you remember seeing that newsreel of General Mark Clark landing in a Piper Cub on the plaza by the Colosseum in the middle of Rome when he took the city?"

She nodded.

"Hotshot Billy was flying the Cub. And I guess you know that General Gehlen surrendered to the OSS on a back road here in Bavaria?"

"I heard that story."

"Wilson flew our own Major Harold Wallace, then Mattingly's deputy, there to accept the surrender. And Mattingly got Wilson to turn over his Storchs to me when the Air Force didn't like the Army having any. Wilson is the aviation officer of the Constabulary. As soon as he gets here, which may be very soon, any day, Major General I.D. White, whom Tiny refers to as 'Uncle Isaac,' because White is his godfather, will assume command of the Constabulary. And before he went into the OSS, Mattingly was sort of a fair-haired boy in White's Second Armored Division."

"That's a lot of disjointed facts."

"That occurred to me as I sat here thinking about it. So, thinking aloud: Presuming we can find someplace to land in Thuringia, someplace being defined as a small field—the Storch can land on about fifty feet of any kind of a runway, and get off the ground in about a hundred fifty feet—near a country road, getting Mrs. Likharev and her kids out in our Storchs makes a lot more sense than sending people into East Germany on foot to try to, first, find them, and then try to walk them back across the border."

"Storchs, plural? Who's going to fly them?"

"I'll fly one, and maybe Max Ostrowski the other one."

"Maybe?"

"I won't know if he'll be willing to take the chance until I ask him," Cronley said simply. "So the question is, where can I find, just over the Hesse/Thuringia border, a suitable field near a suitable country road? I don't have a clue, but I think Colonel Wilson will not only be able to get this information for me, but have other helpful suggestions to make.

"Or he may not. He may decide to pick up the phone and call

Mattingly and say, 'You won't believe what Loose Cannon Cronley's up to.'

"You're going to take that risk?"

Cronley didn't reply directly, instead replying, "Mannberg has a saying, 'Whenever you really want to trust your intuition, don't.' In this case, I'm going to trust my intuition about Colonel Wilson. I don't see where I have any choice."

"Where is this Colonel Wilson? At Sonthofen?"

"Yeah. It's about a hundred miles, a hundred and fifty kilometers, from Munich. Take me about an hour to get there."

"And then you're coming back here?"

"If there's enough time, I'll go out to Kloster Grünau. I want to keep the Storch out of sight as much as possible."

"Well, if you need anything, you know where to find me."

Fifteen minutes later, as he began his climb-out from Schleissheim, he realized that as he climbed into the Storch, Miss Colbert had repeated the same words she had said to him in the Kapitän.

And he concluded that the repetition had not been either coincidental or innocent.

[ONE]
U.S. Army Airfield B-6
Sonthofen, Bavaria
American Zone of Occupation, Germany
1320 16 January 1946

Ground Control had ordered Army Seven-Oh-Seven—Cronley's Storch—to take Taxiway Three Left to the Transient parking area, but before he got there, a checkerboard-painted *Follow me* jeep pulled in front of him, and the driver frantically gestured for Cronley to follow him.

He did so and was led to a hangar, where a sergeant signaled him to cut his engine, and then half a dozen GIs pushed the Storch into the hangar and closed the doors once it was inside.

Lieutenant Colonel William W. Wilson appeared, and stood, hands on his hips, looking at the Storch.

Cronley climbed down from the airplane.

"Good afternoon, Colonel," he said.

"You're not going to salute?"

"I'm a civilian today," Cronley said, pointing to the triangles. "Civilians don't salute."

"They're not supposed to fly around in aircraft the Air Corps has grounded as unsafe, either," Wilson said.

"Are you going to turn me in?"

"No, but I am going to ask what the hell you're doing here?"

"I need a large favor and some advice."

"You picked a lousy time."

"I saw all the frantic activity. What's up, an IG inspection?"

"Worse, much worse," Wilson said. "Well, let's go somewhere where no one will be able to see me talking to you."

He led Cronley to a small office he'd been to before, the day Wilson had turned the Storchs over to him, and then waved him into a chair.

"Okay. What sort of advice are you looking for?"

Cronley didn't reply, instead handing Wilson his DCI credentials.

"Okay," Wilson said, after examining them and handing them back. "Colonel Mattingly told me about this, but I am nevertheless touched that you're sharing this with me. And, of course, am suitably impressed with your new importance."

"I'm not important, but what I need your advice about is very important."

"And highly classified? I shouldn't tell anybody about this little chat?"

"Especially not Colonel Robert Mattingly."

"Sorry, Cronley. I can't permit you to tell me to whom I may or may not tell anything I want. And that especially includes Colonel Robert Mattingly, who is, you may recall, both a friend and the deputy chief of CIC-Europe. Is our conversation over?"

"No. I'll have to take a chance on your good judgment."

"*You'll* have to take a chance on *my* good judgment?" Wilson parroted softly.

"Right."

"I can't wait to hear this."

"I am in the process of getting the wife and children of NKGB Colonel Sergei Likharev out of Russia and to Argentina."

"That must be an interesting task. Who is Colonel Whatsisname and why are you being so nice to him?"

"One of Tiny's Troopers caught him sneaking out of Kloster Grünau . . ." Cronley began the story, and finished up, ". . . whom we have reason to believe are now in Poland."

"And how much of this does good ol' Bob Mattingly know?"

"More, I'm sure, than I like. But not everything."

"And Hank Wallace?"

"He knows just about everything."

"And you don't think he's going to share it with ol' Bob?"

"I don't think he will."

"Did you tell him not to? *Ask* him not to?"

"I did."

"And he agreed?"

"Yes, he did."

"Now how do you envision my role in this cloak-and-dagger enterprise?"

Cronley told him.

When he had finished, Wilson said, "Oddly enough, I was up there several days ago. What used to be the Fourteenth Armored Cavalry Regiment and is now the Fourteenth Constabulary Regiment is stationed in Fritzlar. While I was there, very carefully avoiding any intrusion into the air space of Thuringia State, I flew the border. I wasn't looking for them, of course, but I saw a number of places into which I believe one could put an aircraft such as a Storch."

"Could you mark them on a map for me?"

"I'll do better than that," Wilson said. "At first light tomorrow, an L-4 aircraft attached to the Fourteenth Constab will fly the border and take pictures of fields in Thuringia which look suitable for what you propose."

"Thank you," Cronley said.

"Always willing to do what I can for a noble cause," Wilson said.

"And will you tell me, teach me, what you know about doing something like this?"

"That will depend on whether General White tells me whether I can or not."

"Isn't he in the States? At Fort Leavenworth?"

"He *was* in the States at Fort *Riley*, the Cavalry School. Right now, he's somewhere en route here—the route being Washington-Gander, Newfoundland-Prestwick, Scotland-Rhine-Main—where he is tentatively scheduled to land at ten tomorrow morning."

"I didn't know that."

"Not many people do. I didn't even tell good ol' Bob Mattingly when my spies told me. What is important is the moment General White sets foot in Germany, he becomes commanding general of the United States Constabulary. When that happens, I don't do anything without his specific permission. Especially something like this."

"When is he coming here?"

"First, he has to make his manners to General Eisenhower, or

General Smith, or General Clay—or all three. When that's done, he can get on his train and come to Sonthofen."

"His train? He's coming here by train? When does he get here? Can you get me in to see him?"

"Tranquillity, reflection, and great patience, I am told, are the hallmarks of the successful intelligence officer," Wilson said. "Slow down."

"Yes, sir."

"Better."

"Yes, he's coming by train. When Generals Eisenhower, Smith, Clay, and other senior brass were assigned private trains, it looked like the rest of the private trains would be doled out to other deserving general officers before General White returned from Fort Riley to assume command of the Constab and he wouldn't get one.

"That, of course, was an unacceptable situation for those of us who devotedly serve General White. So one of the as-yet-unassigned private trains was spirited away to Bad Nauheim and parked on the protected siding where Hitler used to park his private train. It was suitably decorated with Constabulary insignia, but kept out of sight until now. It is scheduled to leave Bad Nauheim at 0700 tomorrow for the Frankfurt Hauptbahnhof, where it will be ready for him when the aforementioned senior officers are through with him."

"Then he is coming here. Back to my question, when he gets here, can you get me in to see him?"

"Simple answer, no. In addition to his pals and cronies who will meet the plane at Rhine-Main, all of the senior officers of the Constabulary, and its most senior non-commissioned officers, will be lining the corridors here to make their manners to General White."

"I've got to get him to tell you you can help me."

"You are aware of the relationship between Captain Dunwiddie and the general?"

"I am."

"My suggestion: Load Captain Dunwiddie on a Storch and fly him to Rhine-Main first thing in the morning. General White will be delighted to see him, and the odds are he will invite Captain Dunwiddie to ride the train with him from Frankfurt here. Although it will be crowded by many of General White's legion of admirers, including me, I'm sure there would still be room for the pilot who had flown Tiny to meet his Uncle Isaac. And if you get lucky, maybe you could get the general's undivided attention for a half hour or so to make your pitch. How much of this does Tiny know?"

"Everything."

"Smart move."

"Thank you," Cronley said. "I don't mean for that, for everything."

"Mr. Cronley, Hotshot Billy Wilson is really not the unmitigated three-star sonofabitch most would have you believe he is."

[TWO]
Suite 507
Hotel Vier Jahreszeiten
Maximilianstrasse 178
Munich, American Zone of Occupation, Germany
1735 16 January 1946

"Twenty-third CIC, Miss Colbert speaking."

"Miss Colbert, this is Captain Cronley."

"Yes, sir?"

"Is Mr. Hessinger or Major Wallace there?"

"No, sir. They left about five minutes ago. There's a Tex-Mex dinner dance at the Munich Engineer Officers' Club. They won't be back until very late. Is there anything I can do for you?"

"It looks like you're going to have to, Miss Colbert. Get on the horn to Captain Dunwiddie and tell him (a) this is not a suggestion, then (b) he's to get out to Kloster Grünau right away. He is to tell Max Ostrowski to fly him and Kurt Schröder—"

"Excuse me, sir. I want to get this right. Kurt Schröder is the other Storch pilot, correct?"

"Correct. Tell him to fly here—I'm at Schleissheim, just landed here—at first light, and I will explain things when they're here."

"Yes, sir. I'll get right on it."

"Oh, almost forgot. Tell Captain Dunwiddie to wear pinks and greens and to bring a change of uniform."

"Yes, sir, pinks and greens. Is there anything else you need, sir?"

"I think you know what that is. Do you suppose you could bring it to my room? I'll be there in about twenty minutes."

"It will be waiting for you, sir."

[THREE]
Suite 527
Hotel Vier Jahreszeiten
Maximilianstrasse 178
Munich, American Zone of Occupation, Germany
1935 16 January 1946

"As much as I would like to continue this discussion of office business with you, Miss Colbert," Cronley said, "I haven't had anything to eat since breakfast and need sustenance. Let's go downstairs and get some dinner."

"And while I can think of nothing I'd rather do than continue to discuss office business with you like this, Captain Cronley . . ."

"You mean in a horizontal position, and unencumbered by clothing?"

". . . and seem to have somehow worked up an appetite myself, I keep hearing this small, still voice of reason crying out, 'Not smart! Not smart!'"

"I infer that you would react negatively to my suggestion that we get some dinner and then come back and resume our discussion of office business?"

"Not smart! Not smart!"

"Oddly enough, I have given the subject some thought. Actually, a good deal of thought."

"And?"

"It seems to me that the best way to deal with our problem is for me to treat you like one of the boys. By that I mean while I don't discuss office business with them as we do, if I'm here at lunchtime, or dinnertime, and Freddy is here, or Major Wallace, or for that matter, General Gehlen, I sometimes have lunch or dinner with them. Not every time, but often. I'm suggesting that having an infrequent dinner—or even a frequent dinner—with you would be less suspicious than conspicuously not doing so. Take my point?"

"I don't know, Jim."

"Additionally, I think if we listen to your small, still voice of reason when it pipes up, as I suspect it frequently will, and do most of the things it suggests, we can maintain the secret of our forbidden passion."

"It will be a disaster for both of us if we can't."

"I know."

After a moment, she shrugged and said, "I am hungry. Put your clothes on."

"With great reluctance."

"Yeah."

Lieutenant Colonel George H. Parsons and Major Warren W. Ashley were at the headwaiter's table just inside the door to the dining room when Cronley and Colbert walked in.

"Oh, Cronley," Parsons said, "in for dinner, are you?"

Actually I'm here to steal some silverware and a couple of napkins.

"Right. Good evening, Colonel. Major."

The headwaiter appeared.

"Table for four, gentlemen?"

"Two," Cronley said quickly. "We're not together."

"But I think we should be," Parsons said. "I would much rather look at this charming young woman over my soup than at Major Ashley."

The headwaiter took that as an order.

"If you'll follow me, please?"

They followed him to a table.

"You are, I presume, going to introduce your charming companion?" Colonel Parsons said, as a waiter distributed menus.

"Miss Colbert, may I introduce Lieutenant Colonel Parsons and Major Ashley?"

"We've met," Claudette said. "At the Pullach compound."

"I thought you looked familiar," Ashley said. "You're the ASA sergeant, right?"

"She was," Cronley answered for her. "Now she's a CIC special agent of the Twenty-third CIC, on indefinite temporary duty with DCI."

"I see," Parsons said.

"But, as I'm sure you'll understand, we don't like to talk much about that," Cronley said.

"Of course," Parsons said. "Well, let me say I'll miss seeing you at the Pullach compound." He turned to Cronley. "Sergeant . . . I suppose I should say 'Miss' . . . ?"

"Yes, I think you should," Cronley said.

"*Miss* Colbert handled our classified traffic with Washington," Parsons went on. "Which now causes me to wonder how secure they have been."

"I'm sure, Colonel, that they were, they are, as secure as the ASA can make them," Cronley said. "Or was that some sort of an accusation?"

"Certainly not," Parsons said.

Cronley chuckled.

"Did I miss something, Mr. Cronley?"

"What I was thinking, Colonel, was 'Eyes Only.'"

"Excuse me?"

"Way back from the time I was a second lieutenant, every time I saw that I wondered, 'Do they really believe that?' Actually, 'They can't really believe that.'"

"I don't think I follow you," Parsons said.

"I know I don't," Ashley said.

"Okay. Let's say General Eisenhower in Frankfurt wants to send a secret message to General Clay in Berlin. He doesn't want anybody else to see it, so he makes it 'Eyes Only, General Clay.'"

"Which means only General Clay gets to see it," Ashley said. "What's funny about that?"

"I'll tell you. Eisenhower doesn't write, or type, the message himself. He dictates it to his secretary or whatever. He or she thus gets to see the message. Then it goes to the message center, where the message center sergeant gets to read it. Then it goes to the ASA for encryption, and the encryption officer and encryption sergeant get to read it. Then it's transmitted to Berlin, where the ASA people get it and read it, and decrypt it, then it goes to the message center, where they read it, and finally it goes to General Clay's office, where his secretary or his aide reads it, and then says, 'General, sir, there is an Eyes Only for you from General

Eisenhower. He wants to know . . .' So how many pairs of eyes is that, six, eight, ten?"

"You have a point, Cronley," Colonel Parsons said. "Frankly, I never thought about that. But that obviously can't be helped. The typists, cryptographers, et cetera, are an integral part of the message transmission process. All you can do is make sure that all of them have the appropriate security clearances."

"That's it. But why 'Eyes only'?"

"I have no answer for that," Parsons said. "But how do you feel about someone, say, the cryptographer, sharing what he—or she—has read in an Eyes Only, or any classified message, with someone not in the transmission process?"

"Do you remember, Colonel, what Secretary of State Henry Stimson said when he shut down the State Department's cryptanalytic office?"

"Yes, I do. 'Gentlemen don't read other gentlemen's mail.' I think that was a bit naïve."

"You know what I thought when I heard that?" Cronley asked rhetorically. "And I think it applies here."

"I don't know what you're talking about," Major Ashley said.

"I wondered, 'How can I be sure you're a gentleman whose mail I shouldn't read unless I read your mail?'"

"How does this apply here?" Ashley asked sarcastically.

"Hypothetically?"

"Hypothetically or any other way."

"Okay. Let's say, hypothetically, that when Miss Colbert here was in charge of encrypting one of your messages to the Pentagon, and had to read it in the proper discharge of her duties, she reads

'If things go well, the bomb I placed in the Pentagon PX will go off at 1330. Signature Ashley.'"

"This is ridiculous!" Ashley snapped.

"You asked how it applies," Cronley said. "Let me finish."

Ashley didn't reply.

"What is she supposed to do? Pretend she hasn't read it? Decide on her own that it's some sort of sick joke and can be safely ignored? Decide that it's real, but she can't say anything because she's not supposed to read what she's encrypting? In which case the bomb will go off as scheduled. Or go to a superior officer—one with all the proper security clearances—and tell him?"

"This is absurd," Ashley said.

"It's thought-provoking," Colonel Parsons said, and then turned to Colbert.

"See anything you like on the menu, Miss Colbert?"

"My problem, Colonel, is that I don't see anything on the menu I don't like."

"Shall we have a little wine with our dinner?" Colonel Parsons asked. "Where's the wine list?"

[FOUR]
Suite 527
Hotel Vier Jahreszeiten
Maximilianstrasse 178
Munich, American Zone of Occupation, Germany
2105 16 January 1946

"Stop that," Claudette said. "I didn't come here for that."

"I thought you'd changed your mind."

"Are you crazy?"

"I don't know about crazy," Cronley said. "How about 'overcome with lust'?"

"You just about admitted to Colonel Parsons that I've been feeding you his messages to the Pentagon."

"The moment he saw you with me, he figured that out himself," Cronley said. "I never thought he was slow."

"And that doesn't bother you?"

"He would have heard sooner or later that you defected to DCI."

"Jimmy, please don't do that. You know what it does to me."

"That's why I'm doing it."

"So what's going to happen now?"

"Well, after I get your tunic off, I'll start working on your shirt."

"What's Parsons going to do now?"

"Spend an uncomfortable thirty minutes or so with Ashley,

wondering what incriminating things they said in the messages you turned over to Hessinger and me."

"Jimmy, I told you to stop that."

"Yeah, but you didn't sound as if you really meant it."

"And then what's he going to do?"

"See about getting another communications route to the Pentagon. Which will probably be hard, as he would first have to explain what's wrong with the one he has, and then if he did that, said he had good reason to believe I was reading his correspondence, he would then have to explain to Greene, or ol' Iron Lung, what it was he wanted to tell the Pentagon he didn't want me to know.

"Oh, there they are! I knew they had to be in there somewhere!"

"Are you listening to me? What if Freddy comes back and comes in here? . . . Oh, God, Jimmy! . . . Jimmy, let me do that, before you tear something!"

[FIVE]
Schleissheim Army Airfield
Munich, American Zone of Occupation, Germany
0545 17 January 1946

Captain Chauncey L. Dunwiddie squeezed himself out of the Storch, and a moment later, Max Ostrowski followed him. Kurt Schröder started to follow Ostrowski.

"Stay in there, Kurt," Cronley called to him, "we're leaving right away." And then asked, "Have you enough fuel to make Eschborn?"

Schröder gave him a thumbs-up.

"Why are we going to Frankfurt?" Dunwiddie asked.

"Actually, we're going to Rhine-Main," Cronley said, directing his answer to Ostrowski.

"Rhine-Main or Eschborn?"

"Rhine-Main, and we have to be there by nine-thirty."

"Got it," Ostrowski said, and headed back for the Storch.

"Why are we going to Frankfurt?" Tiny asked.

"Get in the airplane, I'll tell you on the way."

"I've got things to do in Pullach."

"Not as important as this. Get in the goddamn airplane."

"Yes, *sir*," Tiny replied sarcastically.

"Schleissheim departure control, Army Seven-Oh-Seven, a flight of two aircraft, request taxi and takeoff."

"Army Seven-Oh-Seven, take Taxiway Three to threshold of Two Seven."

"Schleissheim departure control, Army Seven-Oh-Seven, on the threshold of Two Seven. Direct, VFR to Rhine-Main. Request takeoff."

"Army Seven-Oh-Seven, you are number one on Two Seven."

"Schleissheim, Oh-Seven rolling."

"Why are we going to Frankfurt?"

"For Christ's sake, Tiny, put a fucking cork in it."

"Army Seven-Oh-Seven. Schleissheim. Say again?"

"You had something you wished to ask me, Captain Dunwiddie?"

"Why are we going to Frankfurt?"

"We are going to see your beloved Uncle Isaac."

"You're referring to General White?"

"Unless you have another godfather you call Uncle Isaac."

"You're saying General White is in Frankfurt?"

"ETA Rhine-Main ten hundred."

"How do you know that?"

"Hotshot Billy Wilson told me."

"You're referring to Lieutenant Colonel Wilson?"

"Who else, for Christ's sake, is known as 'Hotshot Billy'?"

"And why are you taking me to Frankfurt?"

"Because I need ten minutes, maybe a little more, of White's time, just as soon as I can get it, and you're going to arrange it."

"I'll do no such thing."

"What?"

"My personal relationship with General White is exactly that, personal. And if you don't mind, please refer to him as '*General* White.'"

"Are you constipated, or what?"

Dunwiddie did not reply.

"Just for the record, Captain Dunwiddie, I do not wish to intrude on your personal relationship with General White. I'm not going to ask him, for example, if he has any pictures of you as a bare-ass infant on a bearskin rug he'd be willing to share with me. This is business."

"Official?"

"Yes, official."

"Then I suggest that if you need to see General White that you contact his aide-de-camp and ask for an appointment."

"If I had the time, maybe I would. But I don't have the time."

"Would you care to explain that?"

"Hotshot Billy told me he can't do anything more for me to get Mrs. Likharev and the kids across the border than he already has, unless he gets permission from White."

"Can you tell me what Colonel Wilson has done for you so far?"

"He told me that when, a couple of days ago, he flew the East/West German border around Fritzlar, he thinks he saw places, fields, roads, right across the border in Thuringia where we could get the Storchs in and out.

"And as we speak, at least one and maybe more than one Piper Cub of the Fourteenth Constab—"

"The nomenclature is L-4," Dunwiddie interrupted.

"—which is stationed in Fritzlar, is flying the border taking aerial photographs of these possible landing sites. He has promised to give me what they bring back. But when I asked him to teach me and Ostrowski and Schröder what he knows about snatch operations—and Hotshot Billy knows a lot—he said he couldn't do anything more, now that White has returned to Germany, without White's permission."

"That's the way things are done in the Army."

"Fuck you, Tiny."

"You might as well turn the airplane around, Jim. Because I

flatly refuse to be in any way involved with getting General White involved in one of your loose-cannon schemes."

"Before I respond to that, I think I should tell you the reason I know White will be in Frankfurt is because Wilson told me. And it was Wilson who suggested that the quickest way for me to get permission from White for him to help me was to get you to Frankfurt to meet your Uncle Isaac when he gets off the plane. Wilson says he's sure White will invite you to ride on his private train, and if you get on it, so will I. How could they do less for the man who flew Chauncey to meet his Uncle Isaac?"

"You're not listening, Jim. I refuse to become involved."

"You're not listening, I told you this was important. And a word to the wise: I've had about all of your West Point bullshit I can handle, Tiny."

"I went to Norwich, not West Point. So did General White."

"Well, pardon me all to hell. I forgot that Wilson's the West Pointer, not you and your Uncle Isaac. Same comment, I've had enough of this bullshit. Grow the fuck up, you're in the intelligence business, not on the parade ground of some college. That *I will not lie, cheat, or steal, or tolerate those who do* philosophy doesn't work here."

"I beg to disagree."

"You will get me on that fucking train, Tiny, because this isn't a suggestion, or a request, it's what you proper soldiers call a direct order. Once I'm in with the general, you can tell him you're there against your will, or even—shit, why not?—that I threatened to shoot you if you wouldn't go along."

"Now you're being sophomoric."

"Am I? You saw how little the assassination option upset me

when it was necessary. I will do whatever is necessary to get Mrs. Likharev and her two kids out of the East. If I thought I had to shoot you because you were getting in the way of my getting them out, I would."

"You're crazy."

"Or dedicated. Now take off your headset. I have no further interest in hearing anything you might wish to say."

[SIX]
Rhine-Main USAF Air Base
Frankfurt am Main
American Zone of Occupation, Germany
0955 17 January 1946

As Cronley trailed a *Follow me* jeep down a taxiway to a remote area of the Rhine-Main airfield, he saw there was an unusual number of Piper Cubs parked on the grass beside the taxiway. And then he saw that just about all of them bore U.S. Constabulary markings.

There were a number of vehicles lined up beside a mobile stairway where the general's plane was expected to stop. Three buses, one of them bearing Constabulary insignia, three 6x6 trucks, a dozen staff cars, and two Packard Clippers.

He hand-signaled Tiny first to look where he was pointing, and then for him to put on his headset.

"There's a welcoming party," he said. "Jesus, there's even a band."

Dunwiddie did not reply.

"I don't know how long it's going to take for General White to get off his plane and into one of those Packards, but it won't take long, and I can't afford you giving me any trouble. Got it?"

Dunwiddie did not reply.

When the *Follow me* had led Cronley to where he wanted him to park the Storch on the grass—maybe a quarter-mile from the cars and buses—an Air Force major wearing an Airfield Officer of the Day brassard drove up.

Oh, shit!

More trouble about the Storchs.

Cronley got out of the airplane as the major got out of his jeep.

"Interesting airplane, Captain," the major said.

Christ, I forgot I'm wearing my bars!

Belatedly, Cronley saluted.

"They're great airplanes," Cronley agreed. "Plural," he added, pointing to the Storch with Ostrowski and Schröder in it.

"I also understand the Air Force has grounded them."

Cronley took his DCI credentials from his pocket and handed them to the major.

"Not all of them. I hope I won't break your heart when I tell you the Air Force really doesn't own the skies or everything that flies."

"Those are the first credentials like that I ever saw," the major said.

"There's not very many of them around," Cronley said.

"How can I be of service to the Directorate of Central Intelligence?"

"Don't say that out loud, for one thing," Cronley said, smiling.

"Okay," the major said, returning the smile. "And aside from that?"

"I need to get the Storchs fueled and on their way as soon as possible."

"On their way and out of sight?" the major asked.

"That, too."

"That I can do. I'll have a fuel truck come out here."

"And then I have to be in that crowd welcoming General White back to Germany."

"Quite a crowd," the major said, gesturing around the field at all the L-4s. "I would say that every other colonel and lieutenant colonel in the Constabulary is here to watch General White get off the plane."

"So I see. But the skies will fall and the world as we know it will end if we're not standing there when the general gets off the plane."

He pointed to Dunwiddie in the Storch.

"Well, I wouldn't want that on my conscience. I'll make you a deal. I've never been close to a Storch before. If you can arrange a tour for me of one of those airplanes, I'll take you over there in my jeep."

"Deal," Cronley said.

He waved at Max Ostrowski to get out of his Storch, and then called, "Captain Dunwiddie, you may deplane."

"Yes, sir?" Ostrowski asked.

"The major is going to take Captain Dunwiddie and me over there. He's also going to get a fuel truck sent here. When he comes back, show him around the Storch. Then as soon as you're fueled, you and Kurt head for home. I'll get word to you there what happens next."

"Yes, sir."

Cronley saw the major had picked up on Ostrowski's British accent. But he didn't say anything.

The major motioned for Cronley to get in the jeep. Cronley motioned for Dunwiddie to get in the jeep.

"After thinking it over," Dunwiddie said, "I've decided you're entitled to the benefit of the doubt."

Cronley nodded, but didn't say anything.

Almost as soon as the jeep started moving, the radio in the jeep went off:

"Attention, all concerned personnel. The VIP bird has landed."

"I'm not surprised," Cronley said. "I am famous for my ability to make the world follow my schedule."

The major laughed.

As they got close to where the VIP bird would apparently be, they were waved to a stop by a sergeant of the U.S. Constabulary. He was wearing a glossily painted helmet liner bearing the Constabulary "Circle C" insignia, and glistening leather accoutrements, a Sam Browne belt, to which was attached a glistening pistol holster, and spare magazine holsters.

"End of the line," the major said.

"Thanks," Cronley said, offering his hand.

When he got out of the jeep, he remembered to salute.

A lieutenant and a sergeant marched up to them. They, too, wore the natty Constabulary dress uniform, and the sergeant held a clipboard.

The lieutenant saluted crisply.

"Good morning, gentlemen," he said. "May I have your names, please?"

"If that's a roster of some kind," Cronley said, "I don't think we're on it."

"Excuse me, sir," the lieutenant said. "I didn't see the patch."

What the hell is he talking about?

"'Hell on Wheels' comrades are in the rear rank of those greeting General White," the lieutenant said. "Senior officers and personal friends are in the first rank. If you'll follow the sergeant, please?"

Aha! He saw the 2nd Armored patch on Tiny's shoulder. That's what he's talking about!

They followed the sergeant with the clipboard toward the reception area.

There they were met by a Constabulary major.

They exchanged salutes.

"Hell on Wheels comrades in the rear rank, by rank," the major said, pointing to two ranks of people lined up.

"Yes, sir," Tiny said. "Thank you, sir."

I think I have this ceremony figured out.

Majors and up and personal friends are in the front row.

Anybody who served under General White in the 2nd "Hell on Wheels" Armored Division is a "comrade"—which, considering our relationship with the Soviet Union, seems to be an unfortunate choice of words—and is in the rear row.

Tiny belongs in the front row, and I don't belong here at all, but this is not the time to bring that up.

What I'll try to do is pass myself off as a comrade.

They found themselves about three-quarters of the way down the rear rank, between a major wearing a 2nd Armored Division patch and a first sergeant. Cronley guessed there were forty-odd, maybe fifty-odd, people in each rank.

They had just taken their positions when a Douglas C-54 transport with MILITARY AIR TRANSPORT SERVICE lettered along its fuselage taxied up. In the side window of the cockpit was a red plate with two silver stars on it.

The band started playing.

That's "Garry Owen." The song of the 7th Cavalry Regiment.

I know that because I was trained to be a cavalry officer and they played it often enough at College Station to make us aware of our cavalry heritage.

And where I learned that the 7th Cavalry, Brevet Brigadier General George Armstrong Custer commanding, got wiped out to the last man at the Battle of the Little Big Horn.

I've never quite figured out how getting his regiment wiped out to the last man made Custer a hero.

The mobile stairs were rolled up to the rear door of the C-54.

The door opened.

A woman with a babe in arms appeared in the doorway, and then started down the stairs.

She was followed by fifteen more women, and about that many officers and non-coms, who were quickly ushered into the buses waiting for them.

Clever intelligence officer that I am, I deduce that the airplane's primary purpose was to fly dependents over here. Dependents and officers and non-coms who were needed here as soon as possible. General White was just one more passenger.

Is there a first-class compartment on Air Force transports?

The procession came to an end.

The band stopped playing.

A stocky, muscular officer in woolen ODs appeared in the aircraft door. There were two stars pinned to his "overseas cap."

The band started playing "Garry Owen" again.

People in the ranks began to applaud.

Someone bellowed "Atten-hut!"

Cronley saw that it was a full colonel standing facing the two ranks of greeters.

When the applause died, the colonel did a crisp about-face movement and saluted.

The major general at the head of the stairs returned it crisply.

That is one tough sonofabitch.

The tough sonofabitch turned and then with great care helped a motherly-looking woman down the stairs.

They then disappeared from sight.

Three minutes later, the general appeared, now shaking hands with the major standing ahead of Cronley in the comrades and personal friends rank. He was trailed by the woman and a handful of aides.

They disappeared again to reappear sixty seconds or so later, now in front of Captain Dunwiddie.

"Chauncey, I'm delighted to see you!" the general said. "Honey, look who's here! Chauncey!"

The woman stood on her toes and kissed Captain Dunwiddie.

Major General I.D. White looked at Captain Cronley.

"You are, Captain?"

"Cronley, sir. James D. Junior."

"You hear that, Paul?"

"Yes, sir."

"Bingo!"

"Yes, sir."

"Correct me if I'm wrong. What's next is that I go to make my manners to General Eisenhower . . ."

"To General Smith, sir. General Eisenhower is in Berlin."

"Okay. And Mrs. White goes to the *bahnhof* to get on my train?"

"Yes, sir."

"Put these two in the car with her," General White ordered.

"Yes, sir."

General White stepped in front of the first sergeant standing next to Cronley.

"How are you, Charley?" he asked. "Good to see you."

[SEVEN]
Dining Compartment, Car #1
Personal Train of the Commanding General,
U.S. Constabulary
Track 3, Hauptbahnhof
Frankfurt am Main
American Zone of Occupation, Germany
1305 17 January 1946

Captains Cronley and Dunwiddie rose when Major General White walked into the dining compartment trailed by two aides.

"Sit," he said.

He walked to his wife, bent and kissed her, and then sat down.

The train began, with a gentle jerking motion, to get under way.

"Tim!" General White called.

"Yes, sir?" a captain wearing the insignia of an aide-de-camp replied.

"Find the booze, and make me a stiff one."

"Bourbon or scotch, sir?"

"Scotch," he said. "Georgie always drank scotch."

"I.D.," Mrs. White said, "it's one o'clock in the afternoon."

"And make Mrs. White one," the general said. "She's going to need it. Hell, bring the bottle, ice, everything. We'll all have a drink to Georgie."

"I have no idea what you're talking about," Mrs. White said.

"General Smith was kind enough to fill me in on the last days of General George Smith Patton Junior," White said. "He knew I would be interested."

"Oh," she said.

"Would you like Captain Cronley and myself to withdraw, sir?" Tiny asked.

White considered that a moment.

"No, Chauncey, you stay. You can write your dad and tell him what General Smith told me. Then I won't have to. So far as Captain Cronley is concerned, I would be surprised if he doesn't already know. Do you?"

"Yes, sir. I believe I've heard."

"Besides, I have business with Captain Cronley I'd like to get out of the way before we go into the dining car for our festive welcome-back-to-Germany luncheon."

"Sir?"

The aide appeared with whisky, ice, and glasses, and started pouring drinks.

"First of all, it was an accident. Georgie was not assassinated by the Russians. Or anyone else. To put all rumors about assassination to rest. It was a simple crash. Georgie's driver slammed on the brakes, Georgie slipped off the seat, and it got his spine.

"The car was hardly damaged. It's a 1939/40 Cadillac. General Smith asked me if I wanted it, and as I couldn't think of a polite way to say no, I said, 'Yes, thank you.'

"They knew from the moment they got him in the hospital—and Georgie knew, too—that he wasn't going to make it. But they decided no harm would be done if they tried 'desperate measures.' These were essentially stretching him out, with claws in his skin and muscles to relieve pressure on his injured spine, and administering sufficient morphine to deal with the pain the stretching caused.

"The Army then flew Beatrice over here. Little Georgie is at West Point. He was discouraged from coming with his mother.

"The morphine, or whatever the hell they were giving Georgie for the pain, pretty well knocked him out.

"So, after Beatrice arrived, Georgie stopped taking the morphine whenever Beatrice was with him. When she finally left his room to get some sleep, he got them to give him morphine. Then Beatrice ordered that a cot be brought into his room so she wouldn't have to leave him."

"Oh, my God!" Mrs. White said.

"So, he stopped taking the morphine. Period. And eventually, he died. Instead of getting killed by the last bullet fired in the last battle, Georgie went out in prolonged agony, stretched out like some heretic they were trying to get to confess in the Spanish Inquisition."

White's voice seemed to be on the cusp of breaking.

Mrs. White rose, and went to him and put her arms around him, and for a minute he rested his head against her bosom.

Then he straightened.

Cronley saw a tear run down his cheek.

Mrs. White leaned over and picked up a shot glass from the table.

"Gentlemen," she said, "if I may, I give you . . ."

Everyone scrambled for a glass and to get to their feet.

". . . the late General George Smith Patton Junior, distinguished officer and Christian gentleman," she finished.

And then she drained the shot glass.

The others followed suit. Somebody said, "Hear, hear."

"You may recall, Captain Cronley," White said, as he sat down, "that when you told me your name at Rhine-Main, I said, 'Bingo.'"

"Yes, sir."

"One of the first things I planned to do on arrival here was to send for you."

"Sir?"

"Got the briefcase, Paul?" General White asked.

Whatever this is about, the Patton business is apparently over.

Why was I on the edge of tears? The only time I ever saw him was in the newsreels. The last time, he was pissing in the Rhine.

"Sir, I've never let it out of my sight," White's senior aide-de-camp, a lieutenant colonel, said.

He then set a leather briefcase on the table, opened it, took out a sheet of paper, and handed it to Cronley.

"Please sign this, Captain," he said, and produced a fountain pen.

"What is that?" Dunwiddie asked.

"Although your curiosity seems to have overwhelmed your manners, Chauncey," General White said, "I'll tell you anyway. It's a briefcase full of money. One hundred thousand dollars, to be specific."

He turned to Cronley.

"Admiral Souers asked me to bring that to you, Captain," he said. "And to say 'thank you.'"

"What's that all about?" Mrs. White asked.

"You heard what I just said to Chauncey? About curiosity?"

"What's that all about?" she repeated.

"I won't tell her, Captain. You may if you wish."

"Ma'am, it's a replenishment of my—the DCI's—operating funds."

"In other words, you're not going to tell me?"

"He just did. Told you all he can," General White said. "And while we're on the subject of Admiral Souers, Captain Cronley, he told me of your role in getting done what Colonel Mattingly was unable to do—get Chauncey his commission. Thank you."

"No thanks necessary, sir."

"And on that subject, where is Bob Mattingly?"

No one replied.

White looked at Cronley.

"What is it about Colonel Mattingly that you're not telling me, Captain?"

"I don't know where he is, sir. I presume he's in his office in the Farben Building."

"But he wasn't at Rhine-Main, and he's not on the train. Is he, Paul?"

"Not so far as I know, General."

"Okay. Chauncey, who told you to be at Rhine-Main?"

"Captain Cronley."

"Captain Cronley—and you are warned, I'm already weary of playing Twenty Questions—who told you when we were arriving at Rhine-Main?"

"Colonel Wilson, sir."

"And why do you suppose he told you that?"

"Sir, I told Colonel Wilson I needed ten minutes of your time, and he suggested that if Tiny . . . Captain Dunwiddie and I met your plane, I might be able to get it."

"There's a protocol for getting ten minutes of my time. You get in touch with my aide-de-camp and ask for an appointment, whereupon he schedules one. Is there some reason you couldn't do that?"

Cronley didn't immediately respond.

"And Colonel Wilson is damned well aware of that protocol."

He looked at his watch.

"There's no time now. I'm due at my festive lunch. But as soon as that's over, get Hotshot Billy in here, and we'll get to the bottom of this."

"Yes, sir," his senior aide said.

"What this looks like to me, Captain Cronley, is that you tried to use my personal relationship with Captain Dunwiddie to get around established procedures. I find that despicable. And, so far as you're concerned, Chauncey . . ."

"Uncle Isaac, Cronley doesn't have time for your established procedures," Dunwiddie said.

"What did you say?" White demanded.

"I said, 'Uncle Isaac, Cronley doesn't have time—'"

White silenced him with a raised hand.

"My festive lunch will just have to wait," he said. "Tim, my compliments to Colonel Wilson. Please inform him I would be pleased if he could attend me at his earliest convenience."

The junior aide-de-camp said, "Yes, sir," and headed for the door.

He slid it open, went through it, and slid it closed.

Thirty seconds later, the door slid open again.

Lieutenant Colonel William W. Wilson came through it,

marched up to General White, saluted, and holding it, barked, "Sir, Lieutenant Colonel Wilson reporting to the commanding general as ordered, sir."

White returned the salute with a casual wave of his hand in the general direction of his forehead.

"Waiting for me in the vestibule, were you, Bill?"

"Yes, sir. I hoped to get a minute or two of the general's time."

"How modest of you! Captain Cronley hoped to get ten minutes."

Wilson didn't reply.

"Where to start?" General White asked rhetorically. "Bill, Captain Cronley tells me you suggested he bring Chauncey to Rhine-Main because he wanted the aforementioned ten minutes of my valuable time, and you thought his bringing Chauncey would help him achieve that goal. True?"

"Yes, sir."

"And you are going to tell me why this is so important, right?"

"Sir, I suggest that Captain Cronley could do that better than I can."

White looked at Cronley, and when Cronley didn't immediately open his mouth, said, "You heard the colonel, Captain. Cat got your tongue?"

"General, the subject is classified Top Secret–Presidential . . ." Cronley said uneasily.

"And these people, so far as you know, might be Russian spies?" General White said, waving his hand at his aides and his wife.

"Sir—"

"Actually, I'm not sure about her, so throughout our twenty-nine years of married bliss, I have never shared so much as a memorandum classified 'confidential' with her. As far as Colonel Davidson and Captain Wayne are concerned, if you say anything I think they should not have heard, I'll have them shot and have their bodies thrown off the train. You may proceed."

"Yes, sir. Sir, we have turned a Russian, NKGB Colonel Sergei Likharev—"

"Who is 'we'? Are you referring to Colonel Mattingly? Is that why he's among the missing?"

"No, sir. Colonel Mattingly had nothing to do with turning Colonel Likharev. Tiny and I turned him."

"You and Chauncey turned an NKGB colonel?" White asked incredulously.

"Uncle Isaac, please give Jim, and me, the benefit of the doubt," Tiny said.

"I.D.," Mrs. White ordered, "get off your high horse and hear the captain out."

"You may proceed, Captain Cronley," General White said.

"Yes, sir. Sir, one of the reasons Colonel Likharev turned was because we promised him—"

"'We' being you and Chauncey?"

"Yes, sir."

"Promised him what?"

"You'll never find out if you keep interrupting him," Mrs. White said. "Put a cork in it!"

"Sir, we, Tiny and me, promised Likharev we would try to get his family—his wife, Natalia, and their sons, Sergei and Pavel, out of Russia. This is important because Mr. Schultz believes, and he's right, that by now Likharev is starting to think that we lied to him about trying to get his family out—"

"Excuse me, Captain," Mrs. White interrupted. "Mr. Schultz? You mean Lieutenant Schultz? The old CPO?"

"Yes, ma'am."

"Now the admiral's Number Two," General White said. "You met him the first time Admiral Souers came to Fort Riley."

"Pardon the interruption. Please go on, Captain," Mrs. White said.

"Yes, ma'am. Well, we've gotten them—I should say, General Gehlen's agents in Russia have gotten them—out of Leningrad as far as Poland. That's what that hundred thousand is all about. It went to General Gehlen's agents. Now we have to get them . . .

". . . So when Colonel Wilson said he couldn't help us any more without your permission, I decided I had to get your permission. And here we are."

General White locked his fingers together and rocked his hands back and forth for a full thirty seconds.

Finally, he asked, "Bill, what are the odds Cronley could pull this off?"

"Sir, I would estimate the odds at just about fifty-fifty," Wilson said.

General and Mrs. White exchanged a long look, after which White resumed rocking his finger-locked hands together, for about fifteen seconds.

"George Patton was always saying we're going to have to fight the Russians sooner or later," he said finally.

He looked at his wife again. She nodded.

"Try to not let this be the lighting of the fuse that does that," General White said.

"Sir, does that mean . . . ?" Colonel Wilson began.

"It means, Bill, that while you are providing Captain Cronley with whatever he needs, you will try very hard not to light the fuse that starts World War Three."

"Yes, sir."

[ONE]

Conference Compartment, Car #2

Personal Train of the Commanding General, U.S. Constabulary

Approaching Hauptbahnhof

Munich, American Zone of Occupation, Germany

1615 17 January 1946

The sliding door from the corridor opened and Captain Chauncey L. Dunwiddie stepped inside.

The commanding general, United States Constabulary, was sitting at a twenty-foot-long highly polished wooden conference table around which were also seated more than a dozen officers, the junior of them a lieutenant colonel.

General I.D. White's eyebrows rose in disbelief.

"What?" General White asked.

Captain James D. Cronley Jr. slid into the room.

"Oh, I now understand," General White said. "You two decided the red Conference in Session light was actually advertising a brothel."

Mrs. White slipped into the room.

"I didn't hear that," she said.

"Hear what, my love?"

"I insisted they make their manners," she announced. "So that I would not have to hear you complaining that they hadn't."

"Why are they making their manners? We're nowhere near Sonthofen."

"They're getting off in Munich."

"I've seen Chauncey a total of twenty minutes," he protested.

"Duty calls, apparently," she said.

Tiny came to attention.

"Permission to withdraw, sir?"

"Granted."

Tiny saluted, followed a half second later by Cronley.

The general returned them.

Cronley started to follow Mrs. White out of the conference compartment.

"Cronley!"

Captain Cronley froze in mid-step and then turned to face General White.

"Yes, sir?"

"The next time you want to talk to me, seek an appointment. I've told Colonel Davidson to put you ahead of everybody but my wife."

"Yes, sir. Thank you, sir."

[TWO]

The Hauptbahnhof
Munich, American Zone of Occupation, Germany
1635 17 January 1946

The private train of the commanding general, U.S. Constabulary, rolled into what little was left of the *bahnhof*—it had been nearly destroyed during the war, and the recently started reconstruction had taken down what little had remained after the bombing—and stopped.

The door to the first car of the train slid open.

Two Constabulary troopers stepped onto the platform. One of them came to attention to the left of the door and the other to the right.

As first Captain James D. Cronley Jr. and then Captain Chauncey L. Dunwiddie came through the door, the troopers saluted crisply.

Captains Cronley and Dunwiddie returned the salute.

One of the troopers put a glistening brass whistle—which had been hanging from his epaulet on a white cord—to his lips and blew twice.

The train immediately began to move. The troopers went quickly through the door and it slid closed.

Captain Cronley addressed those waiting on the platform, Mr. Friedrich Hessinger and Miss Claudette Colbert.

"How nice of you to meet us. And now that you have seen the

evidence of the high regard in which Captain Dunwiddie and myself are held by the U.S. Constabulary, I am sure we will be treated with greater respect and deference than you have shown in the past."

"Well, I'm awed," Miss Colbert said.

"You got us to come down here to watch you get off the train?" Mr. Hessinger asked incredulously.

"What happened," Tiny said, "is that Colonel Wilson was showing us the communications on the train, and asked if there was anyone we wanted to call. Our leader said, 'Let's get Freddy on the phone, and have him pick us up at the *bahnhof.* Save the price of a taxicab.' So he did."

"A cab would have cost you fifty cents!" Hessinger complained.

"'A penny saved is a penny earned,'" Cronley quoted piously. "Isn't that true, Miss Colbert?"

"And 'A fool and his money are soon parted,'" she replied.

Their eyes met momentarily.

He forced the mental image this produced of Miss Colbert in her birthday suit from his mind.

Nose to the grindstone, Cronley!

"Is Major Wallace in the office?" he asked.

"Probably for the next five minutes," Freddy said. "He really hates missing Happy Hour at the Engineer O Club, and that starts at five o'clock."

"I may have to ruin his evening," Cronley said. "We've got a lot to do and we're going to need him."

"For instance?" Freddy asked.

"I'll tell you at the office," Cronley said, "when I tell him."

"For instance," Tiny said, "we've got to get the Storchs to Sonthofen first thing in the morning, which means I'm going to have to go out to Kloster Grünau and set that, and some other things, up. Do I just take the Kapitän?"

"I can drive you out there," Claudette said.

"Do it. We'll need the Kapitän in the morning," Cronley ordered.

[THREE]
Hotel Vier Jahreszeiten
Maximilianstrasse 178
Munich, American Zone of Occupation, Germany
1705 17 January 1946

Major Harold Wallace was checking to ensure the door to Suite 507 was securely locked when Cronley and Hessinger came down the aisle.

"What would it take to get you to miss Happy Hour at the Engineer O Club?"

"Not much, as I have something to tell you," Wallace said. "I didn't know if you were coming back here today or not."

He unlocked the door and waved Cronley and Hessinger into the office.

As soon as Cronley was in the office, he said, "Maybe I can save us both time. What would you say if I told you I need your help with getting Mrs. Likharev and offspring over the border?"

"The first thing that pops into my mind is that you have FUBAR something somehow."

"Not yet. But that's probably inevitable."

"And the second thing is that you don't want me to mention this to Colonel Mattingly. True?"

"True."

"One of the things I thought you might be interested in hearing is that Colonel Mattingly was on the horn a couple of hours ago—"

"You haven't answered my question. Can I tell you what problems I have without Mattingly hearing about any of them?"

"I thought that question had arisen and been disposed of," Wallace said, just a little sharply.

"Sorry," Cronley said, and a moment later, added: "I apologize."

Wallace nodded, then said, "The officer in question was on the horn a couple of hours ago. It has come to his attention that General White has returned to Germany, specifically, that he flew into Rhine-Main, where a large number of friends and others met him, and then, after making his manners to General Smith, set off for Sonthofen on his private train. He was curious as to why he was not (a) informed of this, and (b) was not invited to the arrival at Rhine-Main or to ride on the train."

"And he thought you might know?"

"That, and he wondered if Tiny, because of his relationship with the general, knew about this, and didn't think he would be interested."

"Tiny knew about it because I told him. I don't know if he would have told Mattingly or not . . . he probably would have, being the good soldier he is . . . but he didn't have the time."

"And who told you?"

"Hotshot Billy Wilson."

"The plot thickens. What the fuck is going on?"

Cronley told him all that had happened.

During the recitation, Cronley saw that Hessinger was unable to keep his face from registering surprise, concern, alarm, and disbelief. Or various combinations of the foregoing.

"But, I just thought of this," Cronley concluded. "Mattingly not getting invited may be innocent. I mean, nobody consciously decided, 'Let's not tell Mattingly.'"

"Explain that."

"General Smith, who knew he was coming, either presumed Mattingly knew, or more than likely, didn't give a damn about who was going to be at Rhine-Main or on the train. Anyway, after he told Hotshot Billy—"

"Why would Smith tell Hotshot Billy?"

"They were coconspirators in the Let's Save a Train for General White business. Wilson told me Smith was disgusted with all the three stars fighting like ten-year-olds over who gets a train, and decided they would get the proper message if two-star White showed up with one.

"Try to follow my reasoning: Smith told Wilson, expecting that Wilson would . . . as he did . . . spread the word around in the Constabulary. He didn't tell Mattingly because he figured Mattingly was in the Farben Building and would know. Did Smith tell Greene? I don't know. Probably not. So if Greene didn't know, he couldn't tell Mattingly. And if he did know, he didn't tell him because he thought he would already have heard."

Wallace grunted.

"General White asked where Mattingly was."

"How do you know that?"

"Because he asked me where he was."

"You were on the train?"

"Tiny and I just got off it."

"As soon as Bob Mattingly hears that you and Tiny were on that train—and he will—you're the villains, you know that? The master politician will decide he's been out-politicked by two captains he doesn't much like anyway. And he's one ruthless sonofabitch. I've seen him in action. Christ, I actually wondered if he wrote that *Cronley's been fucking Mrs. Rachel Schumann* letter to Dick Tracy."

"If I'm putting you on the spot now, asking for help and don't tell Mattingly . . ."

"You are. But after our little chat the other day, I did some thinking of my own."

"About what?"

"About why I'm here running what you so accurately describe as a 'phony CIC Detachment.'"

"I shouldn't have said that."

"Why not? It's true. So why am I here doing it? Two reasons, the most important probably being that ol' Bob can throw me to the wolves you mentioned. 'I'm really surprised that Major Wallace didn't learn that Cronley was doing black masses, running a brothel, making bootleg whisky, and burying people in unmarked graves at Kloster Grünau. Maybe being a Jedburgh doesn't really qualify someone to be an intelligence officer.'"

He looked at Cronley as if expecting a reply, and when none

came, went on: "Reason two: If I was in the Farben Building doing what I should be doing . . ."

"Which is?"

"Intelligence. Advising Greene. Or maybe General Clay. This may come as a shock to you, but when I was not being a heroic Jedburgh, parachuting behind enemy lines à la Errol Flynn or Alan Ladd, I was a pretty good intelligence officer. A better one than Bob Mattingly. And, while I was wallowing in self-pity, I wondered why I never got a silver leaf, or an eagle. And wondered if it was because good ol' Bob Mattingly liked me where I was, as a major. I did the work, and he got the credit."

Cronley's mouth went on automatic.

"If you were good in the OSS, you can bet your ass El Jefe knows it. Which is why—"

"I'm here running a phony CIC outfit, so that I can step in and replace you when you FUBAR everything?"

"Yeah."

"Well, I thought about that, too, and what I decided to do, Captain Cronley, is make goddamn sure you don't FUBAR anything. So tell me your problems vis-à-vis getting Mrs. Likharev and her children across a border. I have a little experience in that sort of thing."

"Thank you."

"Which brings us to Friend Freddy," Wallace said. "Who has been sitting there like a sponge, soaking all this in."

"Sir?"

"Are you willing to deceive Colonel Mattingly and anyone else who gets in our way? Or are you thinking of some way you can cover your ass?"

"You have no right to think that about me!" Freddy flared.

"Correct answer," Wallace said. "Fortunately for you. I always hate to use the assassination option, even when it's called for."

"So do Cronley and I," Hessinger said.

Wallace's eyebrows rose.

"One day we'll have to exchange secrets," he said. "But not now. Before Brunhilde walks in from wherever she is . . ."

It took Cronley a moment to realize he was talking about Claudette Colbert.

"She's driving Tiny out to Kloster Grünau," he said.

". . . we have to decide about her. Do we bring her into this? Yes or no. If yes, how far? Only so far as needed? Or total immersion? Freddy, you first, you're junior. If I ask Jim first, you're liable to go along with whatever he says."

"What did you say, 'total immersion'?" Hessinger said. "Yes. All the way."

"May I ask why you have such confidence in the lady?"

"She has ambitions. We can help her achieve them."

"And you don't think she'd expose us?"

"No. But even if she did, we'd still have that option you mentioned."

"Jim?" Wallace asked.

"I agree with Freddy."

"Tiny, I presume, is a given?" Wallace asked.

"Captain Dunwiddie has one weakness for our line of work," Freddy said. "His family, his education at Norwich, has inculcated in him the officer's honor code."

"You're saying that's bad?"

"I'm saying that he might not be able to do some of the things we may have to do."

"I'd say we might have to explain to him the necessity of doing some of the things we may have to do," Cronley said.

"Well, what's your call?" Wallace said. "In or out?"

"In. With that caveat," Freddy said.

After a just perceptible hesitation, Cronley said, "In."

"That brings us to Ostrowski and Schröder," Wallace said. "What makes you think that both—or either—are going to volunteer to go along with this?"

"I think both will, but we need only one volunteer."

"You're not thinking you can carry this off, moving the woman and the two kids, using just one Storch, are you?"

"No. Two Storchs. One of which I will fly."

"And what does Billy Wilson think of that idea?"

"I think I overcame most of his objections. Most of which centered around both Max and Schröder being more experienced pilots than me."

"And?"

"Tomorrow, I go back to flight school at Sonthofen."

"Are you willing to listen to further argument, from other people with experience in this sort of thing?"

"Who do you have in mind?"

"Me, for one. And General Gehlen and Colonel Mannberg. I was about to suggest that we invite the general for dinner. By the time he could get here, Brunhilde should be back."

"Freddy," Cronley ordered, "get on the phone and ask General Gehlen if he and Colonel Mannberg will join us for dinner."

Hessinger picked up the secure telephone.

"This brings back many memories," Wallace said. "Most of them unpleasant, of planning operations like this in London. Specifically, one of the first lessons we learned. Painfully. And that is, unless everyone with a role in an operation knows everything about it, it will almost certainly go wrong."

[FOUR]
Office of the Chief, DCI-Europe
Hotel Vier Jahreszeiten
Maximilianstrasse 178
Munich, American Zone of Occupation, Germany
1745 17 January 1946

When Claudette Colbert returned from driving Dunwiddie to Kloster Grünau, Cronley greeted her the moment she closed the door. "Dette, we're going to have a meeting. I want it to be formal. Set it up in my office. I'll be at the head of the table. Put General Gehlen at the other end . . ."

"I get the idea."

"Major Wallace will be joining us."

"Got it."

"And, for the future, as soon as you can, arrange with your former buddies in the ASA to make absolutely sure it's not bugged, with emphasis on my office."

"Done," she said. "I mean, already done. I arranged for that when I came here. It was last swept just before we went to pick you up at the *bahnhof*, and they'll sweep it again at 0500 tomorrow."

"Great! You are a woman of amazing talents."

"Of all kinds," she said.

She looked around the room to make sure no one was looking at her, and then, smiling, stuck her tongue out at him in a manner which she intended to be, and which he interpreted to be, somewhere between naughty and lascivious.

When General Gehlen and Colonel Mannberg arrived ten minutes later, the conference table was already set. There was a lined pad, three pencils, and a water glass before each chair. There was a water pitcher in the center of the table, and a small canvas sack, which was stenciled all over, in bright yellow, "BURN." In front of Cronley's chair was a secure telephone.

Gehlen had brought former Major Konrad Bischoff with him.

Mannberg and Bischoff were in well-tailored suits and looked like successful businessmen. Cronley thought, for the umpteenth time, that Gehlen looked like an unsuccessful black marketeer.

I guess Bischoff saw Mannberg in his nice suit and figured, what the hell, if he can do it, why not me?

Claudette, who was sitting to Cronley's side with her shorthand notebook in front of her, looked at Cronley questioningly.

"Miss Colbert, will you set a place for Major Bischoff? Konrad, this is Miss Colbert, our new administrative officer."

Bischoff nodded at her curtly and sat down. Claudette got a lined pad, three pencils, and a water glass and set them before him.

"Before we get started, General," Cronley said, "I know you've met Major Wallace, but I don't know how much you know about him."

"Actually, Jim," Gehlen replied, "the three of us, Ludwig, Konrad, and I, were very much aware of the irony when Major Wallace flew into Elendsalm to accept our surrender. We'd been hoping to . . . have a chat . . . with him for years. We almost succeeded twice, once in Norway and again in Moravia. But failed. And now there he is, all smiles, coming to chat with us."

"You didn't mention that, General, either at Elendsalm or here," Wallace said, smiling.

"At the time, Major, it didn't seem to be the appropriate thing to do."

"And here?"

"Jim never shared with me what you're really doing here, and I thought it was best . . ."

"To let the sleeping dog lie?"

"Sleeping tiger, perhaps. We always thought you were far more dangerous than a dog."

"I'm flattered."

"And are you now going to tell us what you've been really doing here?"

"I don't expect you to believe this, General, but nothing. What I'm doing now is working for Jim. But we don't want that to get around."

"Understood."

"That out of the way," Cronley said, "let's get started. First things first. Major Wallace was telling me earlier that the OSS learned . . . painfully, he said . . . that if all parties to an operation are not involved in all aspects of its planning, the operation goes wrong."

Cronley saw Gehlen and Mannberg nod just perceptibly in agreement.

"So to make sure that doesn't happen here, how do we handle that?"

Hessinger raised his hand.

Resisting with effort the temptation to say, "Yes, Freddy, you may. But don't dawdle in the restroom, and remember to wash your hands," Cronley asked, simply, "Hessinger?"

Hessinger stood up.

"Since Major Wallace brought that up, I have given the matter some thought," he said. "What I suggest is the following: That we have a . . . how do I describe this? I will rephrase. I suggest that Miss Colbert take minutes of this meeting. Every member of this group . . . which brings us to that. What is the group? I suggest the group consists of those present, plus, of course, Captain Dunwiddie. And either or both Max Ostrowski and Kurt Schröder, presuming they volunteer for this operation."

"Tiny is in the process of finding that out," Cronley interrupted. "I think they both will."

"Very well," Hessinger said. "We define the group as those present, plus Captain Dunwiddie, and possibly, to be determined, Schröder and Ostrowski. When Miss Colbert types the minutes of this meeting—in one copy only—she will append at the end the names of the group . . . every member of the group, including those who were not present. Every member of the group will sign by his name, acknowledging that he is familiar with the contents.

"Then, tomorrow, when Captain Dunwiddie comes here, he will read the minutes—which will be, twenty-four hours a day, in the custody of Miss Colbert or myself—and sign them, acknowledging that he is familiar with everything.

"If he has something to add—hypothetically, that Ostrowski

does not wish to participate—Miss Colbert or I will type this up as Annex 1 to the minutes, again appending the names of all members of the group, who, when then they read Annex 1, will sign again to acknowledge they are familiar with the added information. *Und so weiter* through what I suspect will be Annex 404."

Hessinger looked as if he had something else to say, but decided against saying it. He sat down.

After twenty seconds, Wallace said, "That'd work."

Gehlen said, chuckling, "Freddy—Feldmarschal von Moltke—where were you when I needed a really smart general staff officer to find a simple solution to answer a complex problem, and all I had was Ludwig?"

Mannberg smiled, then applauded, and a moment later, so did Bischoff, Wallace, and Cronley.

My God, Fat Freddy is actually blushing!

"Miss Colbert," Cronley said, "item one, in your transcript of these proceedings, will be the adoption of Mr. Hessinger's 'How to Keep Everybody Who Needs to Know Up to Speed' plan."

"Yes, sir," Claudette said.

"May I suggest, Jim," Gehlen said, "that item two be a report of your trip to Frankfurt?"

"Yes, sir. But I think I'd better begin that with a report of my meeting with Colonel Wilson. As I think everybody knows . . ."

"And when do you think you'll have these aerial photographs of places where the Storchs could touch down?" Major Wallace asked.

"I didn't ask, which was stupid of me," Cronley replied. "But

I would guess that a Piper Cub with the film aboard—I told you at least two Constabulary Cubs from the Fourteenth would be used?—was at Sonthofen before the train got there. And I wouldn't be surprised if when Wilson picks me up at Schleissheim in the morning, he has prints with him."

"I'd like a look at them," Bischoff said. "Actually, what I'd like to do is get copies of them to Seven-K."

"And if they were intercepted some way, don't you think the Russians would thereafter wonder why the Americans were so interested in obscure Thuringian fields and back roads that they shot aerials of them?" Wallace asked sarcastically.

"Good point," Gehlen said.

"You have common maps, presumably?" Wallace asked.

What the hell is a common map?

Oh. Seven-K and Bischoff have identical maps.

"Yes, of course we do."

"Presumably with . . . imaginative . . . coordinates?"

Gehlen chuckled.

What the hell does that mean?

"Of course," Bischoff said tightly.

"Then I suggest that the thing to do is get the pilots who shot the aerials to match them to a standard map, and then we change those coordinates to the imaginative ones. Would that be the thing to do, General?"

"Presuming the imaginative coordinates have not been compromised."

"You think it's worth taking the chance?"

"I don't think we have much choice."

"Okay with you, Jim?"

He's asking my permission to do something, and I don't have a fucking clue what that something is.

"Absolutely."

Wallace reached for the secure telephone.

"Major Wallace," he said. "Authorization Baker Niner Three Seven. I say again, Baker Niner Three Seven. Get me Lieutenant Colonel Wilson at Constab headquarters in Sonthofen.

"Colonel, this is the Bavarian office of the German-American Tourist Bureau. It has come to our attention that you have been taking pictures which might be suitable for our next 'Visit Beautiful Occupied Bavaria' brochure . . .

"Well, that would depend on who you might think it is . . .

"Congratulations, Hotshot! You have just won the cement bicycle and an all-expenses-paid tour of the beautiful Bavarian village of Pullach . . .

"No. I haven't, actually. I'm parched. But as soon as I get off the phone, in other words, after you answer, truthfully, a couple of questions, I intend to quickly remedy that situation . . .

"The first is, I need to know, presuming they came out and you have them, if you've thought of matching the photos taken this morning to a GI map? My boss has been wondering . . .

"Yes, as a matter of fact I am talking about him. But I thought you were the one everyone calls 'the Boy Wonder.'"

Wallace turned to Cronley.

"Colonel Wilson wishes me to remind you that he's done this sort of thing before, and knows what's required. He will bring what's required when he picks you up in the morning."

He turned back. "Final question, Bill. On a scale of one to ten, what's our chances of carrying this off . . . ?"

"That bad, huh? Well, it's been nice chatting with you. Green Valley out."

Cronley's mouth went on automatic. He parroted, "'Green Valley'? What the hell is that?"

"A code name from another time," Wallace said. "*My* code name."

"I had the feeling you knew one another," General Gehlen said. "You said 'that bad.' Colonel Wilson doesn't think much of our chances?"

"Colonel Wilson said I should know better than to try to estimate the chances of an operation being successful."

"What did he mean by that?" Cronley asked. "Why not?"

"The only pertinent question to be asked is, 'Is it necessary?' And you've already made that decision, haven't you?"

"Yeah, I have," Cronley said, as much to himself as in response to Wallace's question.

"Konrad," General Gehlen asked, "once we get them, how long is it going to take to get the coordinates of possible pickup sites to Seven-K?"

"That would depend, Herr General, on whether we send them by messenger—"

"Which would be slower in any event than by radio, even if we knew where Rahil is," Mannberg interrupted.

"But would present less of a risk of interception," Bischoff argued.

"It would take too much time," Gehlen said. "The time element here is critical. Rahil is greatly exposed moving around Poland or Bohemia, Moravia—"

"General," Wallace interrupted, smiling, "that's Czechoslovakia again. The Protectorate of Bohemia and Moravia is history. You lost the war."

"Indeed, we did. What I meant to say, Green Valley, was that Seven-K is greatly exposed moving around that *part of the world* with a Russian woman and two Russian children with the NKGB looking for them."

"Well, if you think they're in what used to be Moravia, people other people are looking for are sometimes very hard to find in Moravia. Even by . . ."

Gehlen shook his head, and smiled.

"Searchers directed by Major Konrad Bischoff of Abwehr Ost," he said.

"We heard you were personally directing the searchers," Wallace said.

"Perhaps if I had, we would have met sooner than we did," Gehlen said. "What happened was that my man normally in charge of important searches, Oberst Otto Niedermeyer, wasn't available, so Kon—"

"You're talking about the guy I met in Argentina?" Cronley blurted.

"I'm sure we are, Jim," Gehlen said.

Jesus, this intelligence business is really a small world, isn't it?

"So Konrad got the job of . . . trying to arrange a conversation with Green Valley," Gehlen concluded.

"And damned near succeeded," Wallace said. "There I was, all by my lonesome in a muddy field in picturesque Králický Sněžník. I could actually hear your motorcycles coming up the valley, and no sign of anything in the sky to get me the hell out of there. I was about to kiss my . . . rear end . . . goodbye, when there was Billy

Wilson coming down the valley in his puddle jumper, about ten feet off the ground."

"We saw him," Bischoff said. "We were looking for a Lysander—"

"A what?" Cronley asked.

"A British ground cooperation aircraft, Jim," Gehlen explained. "With short field capability. The OSS used them often in situations like Major Wallace's."

"Which we expected to land, and then get stuck in the muddy fields," Bischoff explained.

"But instead you got Hotshot Billy in an L-4, with oversized tires," Wallace said. "He touched down and I got in and away we went."

"We were amazed when you got off the ground," Bischoff said. "You flew right over us."

"Which brings us to that," Wallace said.

"Excuse me?" Gehlen said.

"Once Bill Wilson landed that Piper Cub, I was in it in about twenty seconds, tops, and we took off," Wallace said. "That's not going to happen with Mrs. Likharev and her two kids."

"Point well taken," Gehlen said.

And now these guys are sitting around, cheerfully remembering the day Wallace almost, but not quite, got caught behind enemy lines.

Almost like friends.

Almost, hell, really like friends.

Thank God that I got Wallace involved in this.

"It's entirely possible, even likely," Gehlen said, "that the Likharev children, and perhaps even Mrs. Likharev herself, have never been in an airplane before."

"And the children will see they are about to be separated from their mother and handed over to strangers," Mannberg added.

Cronley actually felt a chill as the epiphany began to form.

Oh, shit, it took me a long time even to start figuring this out.

I never even questioned how come an OSS veteran, a major, a Jedburgh, who had been Mattingly's Number Two, got himself demoted to commanding officer of a CIC detachment with no mission except to cover DCI.

Jesus, there were three majors in the XXIInd CIC in Marburg. It would have made much more sense to send any one of them to a bullshit job in Munich, and it makes no sense at all for them to have sent somebody like Wallace, who—what did he say that he should be doing, "advising Greene or maybe General Clay"?

Who is "them" who sent Wallace here?

"The obvious corollary of that is that Mrs. Likharev, already distressed by her situation," Gehlen said, "will be even more distressed at the prospect of her being separated from her children."

Mattingly?

Wallace knows (a) that what he was ordered to do here is a bullshit job, and (b) who ordered him here.

So why did he put up with it?

Because what he's really doing here is keeping an eye on me and Gehlen and company.

And Gehlen knows that. That's why he told El Jefe he'd rather not have either Mattingly or Wallace at DCI. He'd rather have me. So El Jefe had Wallace assigned to the bullshit job.

Why?

To keep Gehlen happy.

And to put Wallace in a place where he'd have plenty of time and opportunity to keep an eye on both Gehlen and me.

And since Wallace has to know this, that means he's working for Schultz, has been working for Schultz all along.

"They, the Likharev woman and the children, will have to be tranquilized," Bischoff said matter-of-factly.

"I can see that now," Wallace said sarcastically, "the Boy Wonder here, hypodermic needle in hand, chasing Russian kids all over some Thuringian field, while your agent tries to defend him from their mother."

So that's what you think of me, "the Boy Wonder"?

Why not?

You know what a fool I am.

"There are other ways to sedate people," Gehlen said, chuckling. "But getting the Likharevs onto, into, the airplanes is a matter of concern. I suggest we think about—not talk about—the problem while we have our dinner."

"I suggest," Wallace said, "that until we get the aerials, and their coordinates, from Bill Wilson tomorrow, there's nothing much to talk or think about. One step at a time, in other words."

"Concur," Gehlen said, and stood up.

"I should have my notes typed up by the time you get back," Claudette Colbert said.

"While I appreciate your devotion to duty, Claudette," Wallace said, "that'll wait until tomorrow, too. You stick your notes in the safe and come to dinner with us."

And what's your real role in this, Claudette?

Did my innocence and naïveté really cause you to throw your maidenly modesty to the winds?

Or did someone tell you that I tell females with whom I am cavorting sexually everything they want to know?

And if so, who told you that? Is Fat Freddy part of this?

Or have you been working for Wallace all along, and he told you to get to me through Hessinger?

[FIVE]
Suite 527
Hotel Vier Jahreszeiten
Maximilianstrasse 178
Munich, American Zone of Occupation, Germany
0310 18 January 1946

"Fuck it," Captain James D. Cronley Jr. announced and swung his legs out of bed.

He was in his underwear. He found the shirt he had discarded when he went to bed, and then his uniform trousers. He pulled on socks, made a decision between Shoes, Men's Low Quarter, Brown in Color, and Uribe Boots, San Antonio, Texas, choosing to jam his feet into the latter.

Then he walked to his door, unlocked it, and went down the corridor to Suite 522, where he both pushed the doorbell and knocked at the door.

A full ninety seconds later, Major Harold Wallace, attired in his underwear, opened the door.

"If you're looking for Brunhilde, Romeo, she's in 533," Major Wallace said.

"I'm looking for you, Colonel," Cronley said.

"Colonel? How much have you had to drink, Jim?"

"Not a drop. Not a goddamn drop."

"What's on your mind at this obscene hour?"

"I have some questions I need to have answered."

"Such as?"

"How long have you been working for Schultz?"

"How long have I what?"

"I think you heard me, Colonel."

"I think you better go back down the corridor and jump in your little bed."

"I'm not going to do that until I get some answers," Cronley said.

Cronley gestured with his hand around the room. "And to put your mind at rest, Colonel, about the wrong people hearing those answers, I told Brunhilde to have the ASA guys sweep your suite for bugs after dinner and again at midnight."

"And if I don't choose to answer your questions?"

"Then we're going to have trouble."

"You're threatening me?"

"I'm making a statement of fact."

"Your pal Cletus warned me not to underestimate you," Wallace said, and waved him into the room.

Wallace sat in an armchair, and motioned for Cronley to sit on a couch.

"Okay. What questions have you for me?"

"Let's start with how long you've been a colonel."

"What makes you think I am a colonel? Where the hell did you come up with that?"

"If you're going to play games with me, Colonel, we'll be here a long time."

Wallace looked at him for a long thirty seconds before replying.

"Why are you asking?"

"I figure if I get a straight answer to that, straight answers to my other questions will follow."

"And if I give you a straight answer, then what? You tell the world?"

"You know me better than that."

"I guess I knew this conversation was coming, but I didn't think it would be this soon. Been doing a lot of thinking, have you?"

"Since just before we went to dinner. I'm sorry I didn't start a lot earlier. So, what's your answer?"

"I was promoted to colonel the day after Bill Wilson pulled me out of Králický Sněžník. It was April Fools' Day, 1945. I guess that's why I remember the exact date. Is that what tipped you off?"

"Wilson's a starchy West Pointer. You called him 'Hotshot.' He doesn't like to be called Hotshot. So how were you getting away with it? Maybe because you outrank him? And if that's true . . ."

"You figured that out, did you, you clever fellow?"

"It started me thinking about what else I didn't know."

"For example?"

"You brought up 'my pal Cletus.' Does he know what's going on here?"

"What do you think?" Wallace said sarcastically.

"You met him before—him and El Jefe—before the day you came to Marburg with him and Mattingly, to pick up Frau von Wachtstein?"

Wallace nodded.

"In—the middle of 1943, I forget exactly when—Wild Bill Donovan decided that David Bruce, the OSS station chief in London, should be brought up to speed on what was happening in Argentina. Things that could not be written down.

"Bruce couldn't leave London, so he sent me, as sort of a walking notebook. I spent three weeks there with Cletus and El Jefe. Which is how, since we are laying all our secrets on the table, you got in the spook business."

"I don't understand."

"When we got back to OSS Forward—the Schlosshotel Kronberg in Taunus—that night, after picking up Frau von Wachtstein, we—Mattingly, Frade, and I—had a private dinner. Toward the end of it, Mattingly mentioned the trouble we were having finding an officer to command Tiny's Troopers, who were going to provide security not only for Kloster Grünau, but for the Pullach compound when we got that up and running."

"Why didn't you just get Tiny a commission?"

"All I knew about Tiny at the time was that he was a first sergeant who'd got himself a Silver Star in the Battle of the Bulge. I didn't know he'd almost graduated from Norwich. And I certainly didn't know he called General White 'Uncle Isaac.' I'm now sure Mattingly did, and knew that Lieutenant Dunwiddie would ask questions First Sergeant Dunwiddie couldn't ask. Mattingly likes to be in control."

"You don't like him much, do you?"

"Mattingly is a very good politician. You need people like that. I was telling you how you got in the spook business."

"Sorry."

"So Cletus said, what about Jim Cronley? What they've got him doing is sitting at an unimportant roadblock in the boonies, or words to that effect, to which Mattingly replied, that wouldn't work. You'd need a Top Secret–OSS clearance to work at Kloster Grünau. You didn't have one, and he couldn't imagine anyone giving you one. Mattingly said he was surprised that you even had a Top Secret–CIC clearance, or words to that effect.

"This seemed to piss ol' Cletus off. I don't think he likes Mattingly much anyway. Cletus said, 'Well, I'll bet you his Uncle Bill would give him one.' And Mattingly bit. 'His Uncle Bill? Who the hell is his Uncle Bill?'

"He's not really his uncle. But Jimmy calls him that.

"And Mattingly bit again.

"What's Cronley's Uncle Bill got to do with Top Secret–OSS clearances?

"'Just about everything,' Cletus said. 'I'm talking about General Donovan. He and Jimmy's father won World War One together.'

"I was looking at Mattingly. I could see on his face that he was weighing the advantages of having Wild Bill's nephew under his thumb against the risks of having Wild Bill's nephew under his thumb, and as usual was having trouble making a major decision like that. So he looks at me for a decision, and since I had already decided—wrong decision, as it turned out—that you couldn't cause much trouble at Kloster Grünau, I nodded. And that is how you became a spook."

"Did Cletus know you were a colonel?"

"Sure."

"So why were you pretending to be a major?"

"When David Bruce set up OSS Forward, he knew it would be facing two enemies, the Germans and the U.S. Army. Colonel Mattingly is very good at dealing with U.S. Army bureaucrats, if properly supervised. I provided that supervision and dealt with the enemy. It was easier to do that if people thought I was a major."

"And then, when DCI came along . . ."

"The admiral thought that I was the guy who should keep an eye on Gehlen."

"And the chief, DCI-Europe?"

"And the chief, DCI-Europe, and Schultz thought I could do that better if everybody thought I was a major. It never entered anybody's mind that Little Jimmy Cronley would be the one to figure this out, and then Little Jimmy does. Or figures out most of it. And tells me, touching the cockles of my heart, that he has decided to trust me and needs my help. So I confess to him what I think needs to be confessed, and hope that's the end of it.

"And then you appear, in the middle of the goddamn night, and tell me you've been thinking. As I said, Clete warned me not to underestimate you, but I did. And, this taking place in the middle of the night, I told you more than I should have. Frankly, the assassination option occurred to me."

"You wouldn't tell me that if you planned to use it."

"At least not until after we get Mrs. Likharev and kiddies across the border," Wallace said. "Any more questions?"

"Where does Claudette fit in all this?"

"I haven't quite figured that out myself," Wallace said. "I'm tempted to take her and Freddy's version, that she wanted out of the ASA . . ."

"She's not working for you?"

Wallace shook his head.

". . . and was willing to let Freddy into her pants as the price to be paid to get out."

"Freddy's not fucking her," Cronley said.

"He said with a certainty I find fascinating."

Cronley didn't reply.

"One possibility that occurs to me is that you know Freddy has not been bedding Brunhilde because you are."

Again, Cronley didn't reply.

"Well, that went right over my head," Wallace said. "You're a regular fucking Casanova, aren't you, Boy Wonder? Fucking Brunhilde is pretty goddamn stupid for a number of reasons."

Then Wallace saw the look on Cronley's face.

"Okay. So what else is there that you don't want to tell me?"

Cronley remained silent.

"Goddammit, Jim. Answer the question. What else do you know that I should?"

Cronley exhaled audibly.

"You're not going to like this," he said.

"Understood. That's why I insist you tell me."

"I suspect—suspect, not know—that Gehlen was responsible for that gas water heater explosion."

"Gehlen had Tony Schumann and his wife killed, is that what you're saying?"

Cronley nodded.

"Why would he order that?"

"Because the Schumanns were NKGB agents."

"That's preposterous!"

"It's true."

"How could you possibly know that?"

"You know that the NKGB was waiting for Likharev when he went to Buenos Aires?"

"Yes. So what? The Soviet Trade Mission to the Republic of Argentina knew we had him, they knew we were sending people to Argentina, so they started watching the airport. That's what Cletus thinks, and I agree with him."

"They knew exactly when he would arrive in Buenos Aires," Cronley said. "They probably had six, eight, maybe ten hours to set up that ambush. The ambush involved a lot of people, at least a dozen. They even used Panzerfausts. A lot of planning had to be involved. They weren't just keeping an eye on the airport on the off chance that Likharev would show up."

Wallace considered that a moment.

"How could they possibly know exactly when he would arrive?"

"Because I told Rachel Schumann and she told her—their—handler."

"What the hell are you talking about?"

"After we loaded him on the plane at Rhine-Main, I went to the Park Hotel . . . next to the *bahnhof*?"

"I know where it is."

"And Rachel came to see me there."

"Why would she do that?"

"Because the Boy Wonder called her. The Boy Wonder had just loaded an NKGB major—this was before Clete turned him, and we learned Likharev's really a colonel—on an airplane, and the Boy Wonder thought he was entitled to a little prize for all his good work. Like some good whisky and a piece of ass."

"You were fucking Rachel Schumann?" Wallace asked incredulously.

"In hindsight, in a non-sexual sense, Rachel was fucking me. At the time, I thought it was my masculine charm. And I thought all her questions about Kloster Grünau were simply feminine curiosity. So, when she showed up at the Park Hotel for fun and games, I proudly told her what I had just done. And thirty minutes later, she left. She had to go home, she said, to her husband."

"So when we heard what had happened in Buenos Aires, I put two and two together. The only way the Russians in Buenos Aires could have heard the precise details of when Likharev would get there was because they had gotten them from Rachel. And I'd given them to Rachel. The only other people who knew the details were Tiny and Hessinger, and I didn't think either one of them would have tipped the NKGB. So I finally gathered my courage and fessed up."

"To Gehlen?"

"Gehlen, Tiny, and Hessinger. Gehlen wasn't as surprised, or as contemptuous, as I thought he would be. He said that he'd always wondered what Colonel Schumann was doing on that obscure back road in Schollbrunn, the day I shot up his car, why he had been so determined to get inside Kloster Grünau right then."

"That's all?"

"Well, he talked me out of my solution to the problem."

"Which was?"

"I wanted to shoot both of them and then tell General Greene why I had. General Gehlen said the damage was done, and my going to the stockade, or the gallows, would accomplish nothing. And so, coward that I am, I accepted his advice."

After a long moment, Wallace said, "We joke about the assassination option, but sometimes . . ."

"So I've learned."

"You're sure . . . ?"

"The other thing I've learned is never to be sure about anything."

"And Tiny? And Hessinger? Are you sure they can be . . ."

"Trusted? As sure as I am of anything."

"What does Brunhilde know about this?"

"I don't *know* what she knows, but I'm presuming she knows everything."

"And do you think she might somehow try to use this knowledge to further her intelligence career?"

"I don't *know* she wouldn't, but how could I be sure?"

"You can't. Have you told her what you've been thinking?"

"No."

"You ever hear that the bedroom is usually where the most important secrets are compromised?"

"I guess I'm proof of that, aren't I?"

"That argument could be reasonably made," Wallace said drily.

"Colonel," Cronley began, and stopped.

"What, Cronley?"

"Sir, the only thing I can say in my defense is that I very seldom make the same mistake twice."

"I'm glad you said that," Wallace said. "Both things."

"Sir? Both things?"

"I'm glad you seldom make the same mistake twice, and I'm glad you said 'Colonel.'"

"Sir?"

"For one thing, you are hereby cautioned not to say it out loud again," Wallace said. "But don't forget it. Now that my secret—that I'm the senior officer of the DCI present for duty—is no longer a secret to you, remember that when you have the urge to go off half-cocked. Get my permission before you do just about anything. For example, like forming an alliance with Commandant Jean-Paul Fortin of the Strasbourg office of the DST to investigate Odessa. I have a gut feeling that somehow that's going to wind up biting you in the ass. And if your ass gets bitten, so does mine."

"You want me to try to get out of that?"

"To coin a phrase, that cow is already out of the barn. But I want to hear everything that comes your way about that operation."

"Yes, sir."

"So long as you don't FUBAR anything that would necessitate your being relieved, the longer, in other words, everybody but you—correction: you, Hessinger, and Dunwiddie—believes you to be the chief, DCI-Europe, the better. So conduct yourself accordingly, Captain Cronley."

"Yes, sir. Sir, you didn't mention Gehlen."

"An inadvertent omission. Gehlen knows. But let's keep him in the dark a little. He's smarter than both of us, but I don't think he should be the tail wagging our dog. And unless we're very careful, that's what'll happen. That which-tail-should-wag-whose-dog analogy, by the way, came from the admiral, via Schultz."

"Yes, sir."

"Anything else?"

"Can't think of anything, sir."

"Then go to bed, Captain Cronley."

[ONE]
U.S. Army Airfield B-6
Sonthofen, Bavaria
American Zone of Occupation, Germany
1125 18 January 1946

The olive-drab Stinson L-5, which had large "Circle C" Constabulary insignia painted on the engine nacelle, came in very low and very slow and touched down no more than fifty feet from the end of the runway. The pilot then quickly got the tail wheel on the ground and braked hard. The airplane stopped.

The pilot, Captain James D. Cronley Jr., looked over his shoulder at his instructor pilot, Lieutenant Colonel William W. Wilson, and inquired, "Again?"

"If you went around again, could you improve on that landing?"

"I don't think I could."

"Neither do I. Actually, that wasn't too bad for someone who isn't even an Army aviator."

Cronley didn't reply.

"How many tries is that?" Williams said.

"I've lost count."

"Well, whatever the number, I think I have put my life at enormous risk sufficiently for one day. Call the tower and get taxi instructions to Hangar Three."

Cronley did so.

When he had finished talking to the tower, and they were approaching Hangar Three, Lieutenant Colonel Wilson said, "I didn't hear the proper response, which would have been, 'Yes, sir,' when I told you to call the tower."

"Sorry."

"And the proper response to my last observation should have been, 'Sorry, sir. No excuse, sir.'"

"With all possible respect, go fuck yourself, Colonel, sir."

Wilson laughed delightedly.

"I wondered how long it would take before you said something like that," he said. "Your patience with your IP during this phase of your training has been both commendable and unexpected."

Cronley, smiling, shook his head and said, "Jesus Christ!"

Wilson asked innocently, "Yes, my son?"

A sergeant wanded them to a parking space on the tarmac between another L-5 and a Piper L-4.

They got out of the Stinson. Wilson watched as Cronley put wheel chocks in place and tied it down.

"Now comes the hard part," Wilson said. "Making decisions. Deciding what to do is always harder than actually doing it."

He waved Cronley toward a small door in the left of Hanger Three's large sliding doors.

Inside, as Cronley expected them to be, were both of what he thought of as "his Storchs." They had been flown from Kloster Grünau, with a stop in Munich, to Sonthofen that morning by Kurt Schröder and Max Ostrowski.

They were being painted. Perhaps more accurately, "unpainted." Wilson had told him what was planned for the aircraft: Since it might be decided—Wilson had emphasized "might"—to use the Storchs to pick up Likharev's family in East Germany, the planes would have to go in "black," which meant all markings that could connect the planes with the U.S. government would have to be removed.

That would have to be done now. There would not be time for the process if they waited for a decision about which airplanes would be used.

This meant the XXIIIrd CIC identification Cronley had painted on the vertical stabilizer after he'd gotten the planes from Wilson had to be removed—not painted over. Similarly, so did the Constabulary insignia Wilson had painted over when he gave the planes to Cronley. And the Star and Bar insignia of a U.S. military aircraft painted on the fuselage had to go, too. Removed, not overpainted. And when that was done, both would have to be painted non-glossy black.

When Cronley stepped into the hangar through the small door, Schröder and Ostrowski were sitting, Ostrowski backwards, on folding metal chairs watching soldier mechanics spray-painting the vertical stabilizer on one of the Storchs.

When Cronley started for them, Wilson touched his arm and pointed toward the hangar office.

"Our little chat first. You can chat with them later."

Cronley was surprised when he entered Wilson's office to see Major Harold Wallace and former Oberst Ludwig Mannberg. Wallace was standing next to a corkboard to which an aerial chart, a standard Corps of Engineers map, and a great many aerial photos were pinned. Mannberg was sitting at Wilson's desk.

Wilson was apparently as surprised to see them as Cronley was.

"To what do I owe this unexpected pleasure?" Wilson asked.

Wallace gestured at the corkboard.

"I decided the best place to do this was here."

"How'd you get here?"

"You see that C-45 parked on the tarmac?"

"Yes, I saw it."

"I wouldn't want this to get around, but I have friends in the Air Corps," Wallace said. "I borrowed that."

"The Air Corps loaned you a C-45?"

"I thought we might need one."

"Which means two Air Corps pilots get to know a lot more than I'm comfortable with?" Wilson said. "Or at the very least will ask questions we can't have them asking."

"Oddly enough, Colonel," Wallace said, "those thoughts occurred to me, too. So as soon as we landed here . . ."

He sounds like a colonel dealing with a lieutenant colonel who has annoyed him.

". . . I loaded the C-45 pilots into two of your puddle jumpers and had them flown back to Fürstenfeldbruck. You can fly C-45s, right?"

Wilson nodded.

"So can I," Cronley blurted.

Wallace looked at him.

"I find that very interesting. If true, it may solve one of our problems. But first things first. How did he do in flight school?"

"He's almost as good a pilot as he thinks he is."

"In other words, in your professional judgment, he could safely land an L-5—or an L-4 or one of those newly painted airplanes out there in the hangar—on some remote field or back road in Thuringia, load someone who probably won't want to go flying aboard, and take off again?"

"Yes, he could," Wilson said.

"I'm really sorry to hear that," Wallace said. "It would have been better if I could have told him, 'Sorry, you flunked flight school. I can't let you risk getting either Mrs. Likharev or the kiddies killed.'"

"If I didn't think I could do it, I wouldn't insist on flying one of the Storchs," Cronley said.

"You wouldn't *insist*, Captain Cronley?" Wallace asked sarcastically.

I am being put in my place.

In a normal situation, he would be right, and I would be wrong.

But whatever this situation is, it's not normal.

In this Through-the-Looking-Glass world, allowing myself to be put in my place—just do what you're told, Cronley—would be dereliction of duty.

"Yes, sir. Sir, while I really appreciate the assistance and expert advice you and Colonel Wilson are giving me, the last I heard, I was still chief, DCI-Europe, and the decisions to do, or not do, something are mine to make."

"You've considered, I'm sure, that you could be relieved as chief, DCI-Europe?" Wallace asked icily.

"I think of that all the time, sir. As I'm sure you do. But, until that happens . . ."

"I realize you don't have much time in the Army, Captain, but certainly somewhere along the way the term 'insubordinate' must have come to your attention."

"Yes, sir. I know what it means. Willful disobedience of a superior officer. My immediate superior officer is the director of the Directorate of Central Intelligence, Admiral Souers. Isn't that your understanding of my situation?"

Wallace glowered at him for a long fifteen seconds.

"We are now going to change the subject," he said finally. "Which is not, as I am sure both you and Colonel Wilson understand, the same thing as dropping the subject. We will return to it in due course."

Wallace looked at him expectantly.

He's waiting for me to say, "Yes, sir."

But since I have just challenged his authority to give me orders, I can't do that.

So what do I do?

His mouth went on automatic.

"Sure. Why not?" he said.

Cronley saw Wallace's face tighten, but he didn't respond directly.

But he will eventually.

"Why are you so determined to use the Storchs?" Wallace asked.

"Why don't you think it's a good idea?"

"Okay. Worst-case scenario. Assuming you are flying an L-4 or an L-5. You land but can't, for any one of a dozen reasons that pop into my mind, take off. There you are with a dozen Mongolians aiming their PPShs at you. Getting the picture?"

"What's a—what you said?"

"A Russian submachine gun. The Pistolet Pulyemet Shpagin. It comes with a seventy-five-round drum magazine."

"Okay. What was the question?"

"They are probably going to ask what you are doing on that back road. My theory is that it would be best to be naïve and innocent. I suggest you would look far more naïve and innocent if you were wearing ODs, with second lieutenant's gold bars on your epaulets and flying a Piper or a Stinson than you would wearing anything and flying a Storch with no markings.

"You could say you were a liaison pilot with the Fourteenth Constabulary Regiment in Fritzlar, flying from there to, say, Wetzlar, and got lost and then had engine trouble and had to land."

Cronley didn't reply.

After a moment, Wallace said, "Please feel free to comment on my worst-case scenario."

"You mean I can ask why it didn't mention Mrs. Likharev and the boys? I thought they were the sole reason for this exercise. Where are they in your scenario when the Russians are aiming their PP-whatevers at me?"

"You insolent sonofabitch, you!" Wallace flared, and immediately added: "Sorry. You pushed me over the edge."

Cronley didn't reply.

"Okay, smart-ass. Let's hear your scenario. Your best-case scenario," Wallace said.

"Okay. We—Ostrowski, Schröder, me, both Storchs, and a couple of ASA radio guys—are in a hangar in Fritzlar. If they don't have a hangar, we'll build one like the one we built at Kloster Grünau, out of tents. We're hiding the Storchs is the idea.

"We hear from Seven-K, who tells us at which of the possible pickup points she and the Likharevs will be and when. We tell her, 'Okay.'

"Ostrowski and I get in one Storch, Schröder in the other. We fly across the border, pick up Mrs. Likharev and the boys and bring them back to Fritzlar. I haven't quite figured out how to get them from Fritzlar to Rhine-Main yet. Maybe in that C-45 you borrowed from the Air Force."

"And where in your best-case scenario are the Russians with the PPShs in my worst-case scenario?" Wallace asked, softly but sarcastically.

"We are going to be in and out so fast that unless they're following Seven-K down those remote roads, the Russians probably won't even know we were there."

"Isn't that wishful thinking?" Wallace asked.

"What was it Patton said, 'Do not take counsel of your fears'?"

"He also said," Oberst Mannberg interjected, "'In war, nothing is impossible provided you use audacity.'"

"Now that we understand the military philosophy behind this operation," Wallace snapped, "let's talk specifics. Starting with why the Storchs?"

"It's a much better airplane than either the L-4 or the L-5."

"And you feel qualified to fly one of them onto what's almost sure to be a snow-covered and/or icy back road? Or onto a snow-covered field?"

"Well, Schröder has a lot of experience doing just that. I think

Colonel Mannberg will vouch for that. And I have a little experience doing that myself."

"The snow-covered pastures around Midland, Texas?" Wallace challenged.

"I never flew a Storch in the States," Cronley said. "But I did fly one off of and onto the ice around the mouth of the Magellan Strait in Patagonia. Trust me, there is more snow and ice there than there is anywhere in Texas or Germany."

"You flew a Storch down to the mouth of the Strait of Magellan?" Wallace asked dubiously.

"No. Actually I flew a Lockheed Lodestar down there. I flew Cletus's Storch *while* I was down there. I also flew a Piper Cub when I was down there." He paused and looked at Wallace. "Look, Colonel Wilson told you I'm competent to fly this mission. Isn't that enough?"

"I'll decide what's—"

"Jim," Mannberg interrupted, "you said, I think, that you and Ostrowski would fly in one Storch?"

It was a bona fide question, but everyone understood it served to prevent another angry exchange between Cronley and Wallace.

Cronley looked at Wallace.

"Answer the man," Wallace said.

"We land. Me first," Cronley said. "Ostrowski gets out and goes to Seven-K, or whoever is with Mrs. Likharev and the boys. He says, 'Mrs. Likharev, we'll have you over the border—'"

"Ostrowski speaks Russian?" Wallace challenged.

"He does, and better than Schröder," Cronley said. "Let me finish. Ostrowski says, 'Mrs. Likharev, we'll have you and the boys over the border in just a few minutes. And the way we're going to do that is put you and him'—he points to the smaller boy—'in that airplane'—pointing to the Storch Schröder has by now landed—'and I will take this one in that airplane'—he points to the Storch I'm flying.

"He leads Mrs. Likharev to Schröder's Storch . . ."

"What if she doesn't want to go? What if she's hysterical? What if Seven-K has already tranquilized her?" Wallace challenged.

". . . where Schröder says, in Russian, with a big smile, 'Hi! Let's go flying.' They get in Schröder's plane and he takes off. Ostrowski and the older boy get in my airplane, and I take off," Cronley finished.

"What if she doesn't want to go? What if she's hysterical? What if Seven-K has already tranquilized her?" Wallace repeated.

"I thought you wanted my *best*-case scenario?" Cronley replied, and then went on before Wallace could reply. "But, okay. Let's say she's been tranquilized—let's say they've all been tranquilized—then no problem getting them into the planes. If she's hysterical, then Ostrowski tranquilizes her, and the boys, too, if necessary."

"And how are you going to get all of them into the planes?"

"The boys are small."

"How do you know that?"

"Because when Tiny and I were working on Likharev, he told us his son was too young to get in the Young Pioneers. That makes him less than twelve."

"There are two boys . . ."

"If one of them was old enough to be a Young Pioneer, he would have said so. That makes both of the boys less than twelve." He paused, then added: "Feel free to shoot holes in my scenario."

Wallace looked as if he was about to reply, but before he could, Mannberg said, "Not a hole, but an observation: When we were doing this sort of thing in the East, whenever possible, we tried to arrange some sort of diversion."

Wallace looked at him for a moment, considered that, but did not respond. Instead he said, "Tell me about you being able to fly a C-45."

"My father has one," Cronley said. "I've never been in a C-45, but I'm told it's a Beech D-18. What they call a 'Twin Beech.'"

"And Daddy let you fly his airplane?"

"Daddy did."

"How often?"

"The last I looked, often enough to give me about three hundred hours in one."

"You are *licensed* to fly this type aircraft?" Wallace asked dubiously.

Cronley felt anger well up within him, but controlled it.

"I've got a commercial ticket which allows me to fly Beech D-18 aircraft under instrument flight rules," Cronley said calmly.

"So why is it you're not an Army aviator?"

Cronley's anger flared, and his mouth went on automatic.

"I wanted to be an Army aviator, but my parents are married and that disqualified me."

As soon as the words were out of his mouth, he regretted them.

But the response he got from Army aviator Wilson was not what he expected.

Wilson smiled and shook his head, and said, "Harry, if his flying that C-45 is important, I can give him a quick check ride. To satisfy you. I'm willing to take his word. Actually, he has more time in the Twin Beech than I do."

"You're telling me, Cronley," Wallace said, "that if I told you to get in that C-45 and fly it to Fritzlar, you could do that?"

"I could, but I'd rather have the check ride Colonel Wilson offered first."

"Bill, how long would that take?"

"Thirty, forty minutes. No more than an hour."

"Do it," Wallace ordered. "I've got some phone calls to make."

"Now?"

"Now," Wallace said. "To coin a phrase, time is of the essence."

[TWO]
U.S. Air Force Base
Fritzlar, Hesse
American Zone of Occupation, Germany
1615 18 January 1946

"Fritzlar Army Airfield, Air Force Three Niner Niner, a C-45, at five thousand above Homberg, estimate ten miles south. Approach and landing, please," Cronley said into his microphone.

After a moment, there was a response.

"Air Force Three Niner Niner, this is Fritzlar U.S. Air Force Base. By any chance, are you calling me?"

"Shit," Cronley said, and then pressed the TALK button. "Fritzlar, Niner Niner, affirmative. Approach and landing, please."

When he had received and acknowledged approach and landing instructions, Cronley replaced the microphone in the clip holder on the yoke.

Captain C. L. Dunwiddie, who was sitting in the copilot's seat, asked, "Why do I suspect your best-laid plans have gone agley?"

"I thought this was going to be a Constabulary landing strip. It's an Air Force base, and I think the Air Force is going to wonder what two cavalry officers are doing with one of their airplanes."

"Fritzlar, Three Niner Niner on the ground at fifteen past the hour. Close me out, please."

"Niner Niner, you are closed out. Take Taxiway Three Left and hold in position. You will be met."

"Niner Niner, Roger," Cronley said, and then turned to Tiny and pointed out the window. "Not only an Air Force base, but a big one."

There were three very large hangars, a control tower atop a base operations building, and other buildings. Too many to count, but at least twenty P-47 "Thunderbolt" fighters were on the tarmac or in one of the hangars.

"And one that seems to have avoided the war," Dunwiddie said. "I don't see any signs of damage—bomb or any other kind—at all."

"Here comes the welcoming committee," Cronley said, pointing at a jeep headed toward them down the taxiway.

The jeep drove right up to the nose of the C-45.

An Air Force major, who was wearing pilot's wings and had an AOD brassard on his arm, stood up in the jeep, pointed to the left engine, and then made a slashing motion across his throat, telling Cronley to shut down that engine. He then made gestures mimicking the opening of a door.

Cronley gave him a thumbs-up and started to shut down the left engine.

The jeep turned and drove around the left wing, obviously headed for the C-45's fuselage door.

"I don't suppose you know how to open the door?" Cronley asked Dunwiddie.

Dunwiddie got out of his seat and headed toward the door.

"Welcome to Fritzlar, Captain," the Air Force major said, as he stepped into the cockpit.

Well, if he's seen the railroad tracks, he's seen the cavalry sabers. And the blank spot on my tunic where pilot's wings are supposed to go.

Now what?

"Thank you," Cronley said.

"The word we got is to get you out of sight. And the way we're going to do that is have you taxi to the center one of those hangars"—he pointed to the row of three large hangars—"where we will push you inside, and where your people are waiting for you."

"Your people"? Who does he mean?

"Fine," Cronley said. "Actually, we don't care who sees the C-45. But very early tomorrow morning there will be two Storchs we really don't want anybody to see."

"We'll be ready for them," the Air Force major said.

Cronley advanced the throttle and began to taxi.

"I'm not supposed to ask questions . . ." the major said.

"But?"

"You just said 'Storchs,' didn't you?"

Cronley nodded.

"That funny-looking German light airplane?"

"There are those of us who love that funny-looking German light airplane."

"I've never actually seen one."

"Well, you'll have your chance in the morning. And I'll bet you could play I'll-show-you-mine-if-you-show-me-yours with the pilot of one of them. He used to fly Spitfires for the Free Polish Air Force, and I know he'd like a good look at one of those P-47s."

"Great!" the major said.

"Just don't talk about them being here to anybody, okay?"

"The word I got was 'Just give them what they ask for and don't ask questions.'"

"Major, I didn't hear you ask any questions."

"That's right. And I really wondered about the guys in the back."

"They're Special Service soldiers. We're going to put on a soldier show for the Constabulary troopers."

"The hell you are!"

"They sing gospel songs. You know, like 'What a Friend We Have in Jesus,' 'When the Roll Is Called Up Yonder,' songs like that."

"That's why they need those Thompson submachine guns, right? 'Repent, or else?'"

"No. They're for use on Air Force officers who can't resist the temptation to go in the O Club and say, 'Guys, you won't believe what just flew in here.'"

"My lips are sealed," the major said, and then added, "Really."

"Good," Cronley said.

A dozen or so Air Force mechanics in coveralls were waiting in front of the hangar. One of them, a tough-looking master sergeant, signaled for Cronley to cut his engine.

Cronley did so, and as soon as the propellers stopped turning, the men started to push the C-45 tailfirst into the hangar.

"I'll need this thing fueled," Cronley said to the Air Force major.

"Consider it done. When are you leaving?"

"I'm usually the last person they tell things like that. But I was a Boy Scout and like to be prepared."

Once they were inside the hangar, it seemed even larger than it did from the tarmac. Cronley saw three jeeps and two three-quarter-ton trucks lined up, all bearing Constabulary insignia. He asked the two questions on his mind:

"How come this place is intact? What did the Germans use it for?"

"The story I heard is that the Krauts used it to train night fighters, and to convert airplanes to night fighters. They ran out of material to convert airplanes, and then they ran out of fuel for the night fighter trainer planes they had. How it avoided being bombed—or even strafed—I don't know. Maybe, when our guys flew over it, there were no planes on the ground, so they looked elsewhere for something to shoot up. That's what I would have done. What's the point in shooting up a hangar when you can shoot up planes on the ground? Or locomotives? When you shoot up a locomotive, that's something. You get a great big cloud of escaping steam."

"Sounds like fun."

"It was, except when they were shooting back. And sometimes they did."

"The Constabulary is here on the airfield?"

"Yeah. The airbase and the *kaserne* are one and the same thing."

They were now inside the hangar. The left of the double doors closed, and the closing right door stopped, leaving a ten-foot opening.

So those Constabulary vehicles can get out, obviously.

The C-45 stopped moving.

The Air Force major rose from the copilot's seat and stood in the opening to the passenger section. Cronley remained seated until he saw the major stepping into the passenger section, and then he stood up.

When he looked down the aisle, he saw that Tiny and Tiny's Troopers and one of the two ASA sergeants had already gotten off the airplane. As soon as the second ASA sergeant had gone through the door, the Air Force major went through it.

Cronley looked out the door and saw there were maybe twenty Constabulary troopers in formation facing the aircraft. They wore glistening helmet liners, white parkas, and highly polished leather Sam Browne belts, and were carrying Thompson submachine guns slung over their shoulders.

He turned and went down the stair doors backwards.

Someone bellowed, "Ah-ten-hut!"

Oh, shit, some senior officer, maybe the Eleventh regimental commander, is here. That explains all the troopers lined up.

We're not the only people in this hangar.

Cronley turned from the stair doors for a look.

A massive Constabulary officer—almost as large as Tiny—marched up to Cronley, came to attention, and raised his hand crisply in salute. Cronley saw a second lieutenant's bar glistening on the front of his helmet liner.

"Sir," the second lieutenant barked, "welcome to the Eleventh Constabulary Regiment!"

Mutual recognition came simultaneously.

"Jimmy?" the second lieutenant inquired incredulously.

I'll be goddamned, Cronley thought, but did not say aloud, *that's Bonehead Moriarty!*

Second Lieutenant Bruce T. Moriarty and Captain James D. Cronley Jr. were not only close friends, but alumni and 1945 classmates of the Agricultural and Mechanical College of Texas, more popularly known as Texas A&M.

At College Station, Moriarty had experienced difficulty in his first month having his hair cut to the satisfaction of upperclassmen. He had solved the problem by shaving his skull, hence the sobriquet "Bonehead."

Captain C. L. Dunwiddie, who would have been Norwich '45 had he not dropped out so as not to miss actively participating in World War II, and who was standing in front of the line of eight of his troopers, saw the interchange between the Constab Second John and Cronley and had a perhaps Pavlovian response.

"Lieutenant!" he boomed.

He caught Lieutenant Moriarty's attention. When he saw that the command had come from Captain Dunwiddie and that the captain was beckoning to him with his index finger, he performed a right turn movement and marched over to him, wondering as he did, *Who the hell is he? I'm six-three-and-a-half and 255, and he's a lot bigger than me.*

Bonehead came to attention before Tiny, saluted, and inquired, "Yes, sir?"

"Listen to me carefully, Lieutenant," Captain Dunwiddie said to Second Lieutenant Moriarty. "You do not know Captain Cronley. You have never seen him ever before in your life. Any questions?"

"No, sir."

"Carry on, Lieutenant."

"Yes, sir."

Lieutenant Moriarty saluted. Captain Dunwiddie returned it. Lieutenant Moriarty did a precise about-face movement, and then marched back to Captain Cronley, where he executed a precise left turn movement.

"Sir, Colonel Fishburn's compliments. The colonel would be pleased to receive you, sir, at your earliest convenience. I have a jeep for you, sir. And men to guard your aircraft."

"Captain Dunwiddie and I also have men to guard my airplane," Cronley said. "And two other non-coms who'll need a place to sleep. I suggest we leave that for later, while Captain Dunwiddie and I make our manners to Colonel Fishburn. I presume Captain Dunwiddie is included in the colonel's invitation?"

"Yes, sir, I'm sure he is."

"Well, then, I suggest you leave one of your sergeants in charge of your men, I'll leave one of my sergeants in charge of mine, and we'll go see Colonel Fishburn."

"Yes, sir."

"Captain, can I have a word?"

Cronley turned and saw that he was being addressed by Technical Sergeant Jerry Mitchell of the ASA.

Mitchell, a lanky Kansan, was the senior of the ASA non-coms Major "Iron Lung" McClung had loaned to DCI-Europe.

"Anytime, Jerry."

"Did you see that control tower, or whatever it is?"

He pointed upward and to the rear of the hangar.

There was a control-tower-like four-story structure attached to the rear of Hangar Two. There was a second, free-standing six-story structure, painted in a yellow-and-black checkerboard pattern and bristling with antennae, across the field.

"Yes, I did."

"It looks like they have two," Mitchell said.

"Yeah. And you would like to use this one, right?"

"Yes, sir."

"Bonehead, who would we have to see to use the building in the back of the hangar? We need it for our radios."

"You'd have to ask the post engineer."

"What about Colonel Fishburn? Could he give us permission to use it?"

"Of course, but you're supposed to go through channels."

"Mitch, the building is yours," Cronley said to Sergeant Mitchell. Then he turned to Lieutenant Moriarty. "Take me to your leader, Bonehead."

[THREE]
Office of the Regimental Commander
11th Constabulary Regiment
U.S. Air Force Base, Fritzlar, Hesse
American Zone of Occupation, Germany
1705 18 January 1946

"Sir, the officers Lieutenant Moriarty met at the airport are here," the sergeant major said.

"Send them in, Sergeant Major," a deep voice called.

The sergeant major gestured to Cronley and Dunwiddie to pass through the colonel's portal. Cronley gestured to Lieutenant Moriarty to come along.

Cronley and Dunwiddie marched through the door, stopped, and came to attention six feet from the colonel's desk. Moriarty stopped behind Dunwiddie.

Cronley raised his hand in salute.

"Sir, Captains Cronley, J. D., and Dunwiddie, C. L., at your orders."

Colonel Richard L. Fishburn, Cavalry, a tall, lean, sharp-featured man, returned the salute crisply.

"You may stand at ease, gentlemen," he said, then went on, "Very nice, but I don't think that courteous 'at your orders' statement is accurate." He paused, then went on again: "I saw you on the train when you made your manners to General White. Correct?"

"Yes, sir."

"I have received my orders vis-à-vis your visit from General White," Colonel Fishburn said. "Not directly. Via Lieutenant Colonel Wilson. Who, while not a cavalryman, is at least a West Pointer, and therefore most likely would not say he was speaking for the general, if that were not the case. Wouldn't you agree?"

Dunwiddie and Cronley said, "Yes, sir," in chorus.

"I have a number of questions, but the orders I have are to provide you whatever you need and not ask questions of you. Colonel Wilson told me he will explain everything to me personally when he honors the regiment with his presence first thing in the morning. So, gentleman, what can I do for you between now and then?"

"Sir, we brought ten men with us," Cronley said. "They will need quarters."

"Not a problem. Lieutenant Moriarty, take care of that."

"Yes, sir."

"And, sir, we need a secure place where our radiomen can set up their equipment and erect an antenna. There's a sort of second control tower attached to Hangar Two that I'd like to use."

"That, of course, makes me wonder why you brought your own communications, but of course I can't ask. Moriarty, is letting these people use that building going to pose a problem?"

"No, sir."

"And I presume you would be pleased to ensure these gentlemen are fed and are given someplace to rest their weary heads tonight?"

"Yes, sir."

"Well, that would seem to cover everything. Unless you have something?"

"No, sir," Cronley and Dunwiddie said in chorus.

Colonel Fishburn looked at Cronley as if he expected him to say something.

After a moment, Cronley realized what Colonel Fishburn expected.

He raised his hand in salute.

"Permission to withdraw, sir?"

"Granted," Colonel Fishburn said, returning the salute.

"Atten-hut," Cronley ordered. "About-face. Forward, march."

Captain Dunwiddie and Lieutenant Moriarty obeyed the orders and the three officers marched out of the regimental commander's office.

The jeeps that had carried them from the hangar were waiting at the curb outside the headquarters building. Their drivers came to attention when they saw Cronley, Dunwiddie, and Moriarty come out of the building.

Cronley put his hand on Moriarty's arm when they were halfway between the building and the jeeps.

"Hold it a minute, Bonehead," he said.

"Can I infer now you know me?" Moriarty said.

"How could I ever forget you?"

"Are you going to tell me what the hell's going on?"

"If you have a bottle of decent whisky in your BOQ, I'll tell you what I can. And if you don't have a bottle of decent whisky, why don't we stop at the Class VI store on our way to your BOQ?"

Moriarty, after an awkward pause, said, "I don't have a BOQ, Jim."

"So where do you sleep?"

"Ginger and I are in Dependent Quarters."

After another awkward pause, Cronley replied, "That's right. You married Ginger, didn't you?"

"You were there, Jimmy. All dressed up in your brand-new second lieutenant's uniform, holding a saber over us as we came out of the chapel."

And if I wasn't the world's champion dumb fuck, that's what I should have done, married the Squirt the day after I graduated.

The Squirt was one of Ginger's bridesmaids, but I didn't pay any attention to her. I wanted to—and did—jump the bones of another bridesmaid, a blond from Hobbs whose name I can't even remember now. Probably couldn't remember the next day.

And look where I am now!

"I don't think my seeing Ginger—or Ginger seeing me—right now is a good idea, Bonehead."

"She knows I went to the airport to meet some big shot," Moriarty said. "She'll ask me how that went. And I don't lie to Ginger."

"Can she keep her mouth shut?"

"Fuck you!"

"Bonehead, what we're doing here is classified Top Secret–Presidential," Cronley said.

Moriarty looked at him for a long five seconds.

"So what do I tell my wife, Captain Cronley, sir?"

"Jim, I suggest you go see Mrs. Moriarty and play that by ear," Dunwiddie said.

"You work for him, Captain? I thought it was the other way around," Moriarty said to Dunwiddie.

"I work for him, Lieutenant."

"Why don't we all go make our manners to Mrs. Moriarty?" Cronley asked.

[FOUR]

Officer Dependent Quarters O-112
11th Constabulary Regiment
U.S. Air Force Base, Fritzlar, Hesse
American Zone of Occupation, Germany
1725 18 January 1946

Mrs. Virginia "Ginger" Adams Moriarty was red-headed, freckled, twenty-two years old, and conspicuously pregnant.

"Well, I'll be!" she greeted Cronley. "Look what the cat dragged in! I guess you're with the big shot Bruce met. Hey! What's with the captain's bars?"

A moment later, having seen the look on Cronley's face, she said, "Why don't we all pretend I didn't say what I just said. Let me start all over." She then did so: "Jim, what a pleasant surprise."

"Hey, Ginger."

"I think you know how devastated Bruce and I were when we heard about Marjie."

"Thank you. Ginger, this is Chauncey Dunwiddie, who is both my executive officer and my best friend."

"My friends, for reasons I can't imagine, Mrs. Moriarty, call me 'Tiny.' I hope you will."

"Welcome to our humble abode, Captain Tiny."

"Thank you. Mrs. Moriarty, I'd like to show—"

"If you want me to call you 'Captain Tiny,' you're going to have to call me 'Ginger.'"

"Deal. Ginger, I'd like to show you something."

"Will that hold until I give you something to cut the dust of the trail?"

"I'm afraid not," Tiny said, and extended his DCI credentials to her.

She studied them carefully.

"Wow!" she said. "Have you got one of these, Jim?"

"He does," Dunwiddie said, and put out his hand for the credentials.

"Tiny," Cronley said, and when Dunwiddie looked at him, he pointed to Moriarty.

Dunwiddie handed the credentials to Moriarty.

"Jesus!" Bonehead said, after he had examined them.

"Don't blaspheme," Ginger said.

"Sorry," he said.

"Well, Marjie always said Jimmy was going to be somebody special," Ginger said, and then added, "I guess I can't ask what's going on."

"You want to tell them, Jim, or should I?" Tiny asked.

Cronley pointed at Dunwiddie, mostly because his mind was flooded with images of the Squirt and he didn't trust himself to speak.

"Ginger, Bonehead, what I'm about to tell you is classified Top Secret–Presidential. And even if we succeed in doing what we're here to try doing, you are to tell no one at any time anything about it. Understood?"

Both nodded.

"In the next couple of days, we're going to try to pick up a woman, a Russian woman, and her two sons in Thuringia and bring them back across the border."

"Can I ask why?" Moriarty asked.

"I'm sorry, I don't think you have the need to know that. But I will tell you that it's important. Not just a mercy mission."

"Got it," Bonehead said.

"I understand," Ginger said.

"The only reason I've told you this much is so you won't go around asking questions. Any questions you would ask would attract attention to us. And we don't want to attract any attention at all. Understand?"

"Got it," Bonehead said again.

"I understand," Ginger said. "The rumors are already starting."

"What rumors are those?" Cronley asked.

"That you're the advance party for a secret—or at least not yet announced—visit by General White."

"Where'd you hear that?"

"This afternoon—fifteen minutes ago. In the checkout line at the commissary."

Cronley made a *Give me more* gesture with his hands.

"Well, one of the girls—one of the officers' wives—said that she had heard from a friend of hers in Sonthofen . . . you know what I mean?"

"I was there earlier today," Cronley said.

"Constabulary Headquarters," Ginger went on. "Anyway, the girl in line said she had heard from a friend of hers, whose husband is also a Constab officer, that they were preparing General White's train . . . You know he has a private train?"

"Colonel Fishburn said he saw them on the general's private train," Bonehead furnished.

"You do get around, don't you, Jimmy? Marjie would be so proud of you!"

"Ginger, do me a favor. Stop talking about the . . . Marjie. It's painful."

"Sorry," she said, and then considered what she had said, and went on, "Jimmy, I didn't think. I'm really sorry."

"It's okay, Ginger. Now what was the rumor in the commissary checkout line?"

"Well, she said her friend told her her husband had told her that they were getting General White's train ready for a secret—no, she said, 'unannounced'—for an *unannounced* visit to the Constab units up here. You know, Hersfeld, Wetzlar, Fulda, Kassel, and of course here. And then another lady said, 'He's coming here first. They already flew in the advance party. Just now. Special radios and everything.'"

"Jesus Christ!" Cronley said, shaking his head.

"Jimmy, you're as bad as Bruce. Please don't blaspheme. It's a sin."

"The OLIN is incredible if not always infallible, Jim," Tiny said. "I know. I grew up in it."

"The what?"

"The Officers' Ladies Intelligence Network."

"Well, is he, Jimmy? Is General White coming here?" Ginger asked.

"I have no idea, but having people think we're part of his advance party is even better than having them think we're a soldier show, which is what I told that Air Force officer."

"And even better than having them think we're from the 711th Mobile Kitchen Renovation Company," Tiny said, chuckling. "Ginger, did I hear you say something about something to cut the dust of the trail?"

"Why don't we go in the living room?" Ginger suggested.

There were a number of framed photographs on a side table in the living room, including one of the Adams-Moriarty wedding party.

"Tiny," Cronley said softly, and when Dunwiddie looked at him, pointed at it.

When Dunwiddie took a closer look, Cronley said, "Second from the left. The late Mrs. James D. Cronley."

"Nice-looking," Tiny said.

"Yeah," Cronley said.

"You never showed me a picture of her."

"I never had one."

Ginger, as she handed them drinks, saw they were looking at the picture.

"Are you married, Captain Tiny?"

"No, ma'am."

"What is it they say, 'Lieutenants should not marry, captains may, and majors must'?"

"My mother told me that," Tiny said. "As a matter of fact, keeps telling me that."

"You're from an Army family?"

"Yes, ma'am."

"Oh, is he from an Army family," Cronley said. "Not only did his grandfather, First Sergeant Dunwiddie of the legendary Tenth U.S. Cavalry Regiment, beat Teddy Roosevelt's Rough

Riders up San Juan Hill in the Spanish-American War, but his father, Colonel Dunwiddie, is a 1920 classmate of General White's at Norwich."

"Really?" Ginger asked.

"That's what he was doing on General White's train. Making his manners to his godfather."

"General White is your godfather?" Ginger asked incredulously.

"Yes, ma'am, he is," Tiny said, and glowered at Cronley.

"I would rather have that truth circulating among the ladies at the commissary checkout line than have them wonder what we were doing on the train," Cronley said.

Dunwiddie considered that for a moment, and then, grudgingly, said, "Okay, blabbermouth, point well taken."

"You mean I can tell the girls?"

"Only if the subject comes up, Ginger," Cronley said. "If, and only if, the subject comes up, then and only then, you can say, 'What I heard, girls, is that Captain Dunwiddie is General White's godson.' Okay, Ginger?"

"Got it," she said.

"And now, before we accept Captain Dunwiddie's kind offer to dine with him, at his expense, at the O Club, what else should we talk about?"

Bonehead took the question literally.

"A couple of weeks ago, we had a meeting of Aggies in Kassel. One of them was a classmate of your pal Cletus Frade, before Frade dropped out, I mean. He said he heard he became an ace with the Marines on Guadalcanal early in the war. But that was the last he heard. Did he come through the war all right, Jimmy, do you know?"

"I was about to say," Cronley said, "that it's a small world, isn't it?"

"And I was about to say the trouble with letting one worm out of the can is then the rest want out," Dunwiddie said.

"I don't understand," Ginger said.

"This doesn't get spread among the ladies in the checkout line or anywhere else, okay?"

"Understood."

"Colonel Cletus Frade, Navy Cross, United States Marine Corps . . ."

"He got to be a colonel?" Bonehead asked incredulously.

"A full-bull fire-breathing colonel," Cronley confirmed. "He spent most of the war running the OSS in Argentina. In his spare time, he got married—to a stunning Anglo-Argentine blond named Dorotea—and sired two sons. And one day, when he was visiting Germany . . ." He stopped in midsentence. "The look on Captain Dunwiddie's face tells me he's wondering why I'm telling you all this."

"You're very perceptive," Dunwiddie said.

"I have my reasons," Cronley said. "So let me go off on a tangent for a moment. Bonehead, what kind of a security clearance do you have?"

"Top Secret. As of about a month, six weeks ago."

"I think I know where you're going," Dunwiddie said.

"You're very perceptive. Should I stop?"

"Go on."

"Captain Dunwiddie and I have need, Bonehead, of a white company grade officer with a Top Secret security clearance to command Company C, 203rd Tank Destroyer Battalion, the enlisted men of which, some of whom you met today, are all of the African persuasion, and most of whom are as large as you are."

"Despite its name and distinguished heritage, Bonehead, Charley Company today has nothing to do with destroying tanks," Dunwiddie said.

"What it does these days is guard two classified installations we run in Bavaria," Cronley said.

"And also supervises Company 'A,' 7002nd Provisional Security Organization, which is a quasi-military organization whose members are almost entirely Polish displaced persons, which also guards these two classified installations," Dunwiddie furnished. "Would you be interested in assuming that responsibility?"

"You said 'company.' Companies are commanded by captains."

"Not always. In olden times, when I was a second lieutenant, I had the honor of commanding Charley Company," Cronley said.

"If you're not pulling my leg about this, Jimmy, Colonel Fishburn would never let me go. We're short of officers as it is."

"Well, then," Dunwiddie said, "let me rephrase: Presuming Colonel Fishburn would let you go, would you like to command two hundred thirty–odd Black American soldiers and a like number of Polish DPs?" Dunwiddie asked.

"Sir, I just told you, Colonel Fishburn wouldn't let me go."

"You call him 'sir' and refer to me by my nickname? Outrageous!"

"Answer the question, Lieutenant," Dunwiddie said.

Bonehead considered the question a moment, then asked, "Is there a good hospital in Munich?"

"That's a question, not an answer, Bonehead," Cronley said. "Why is a hospital important to— Oh."

"The 98th General Hospital in Munich, Lieutenant," Tiny said, "is one of the best in the U.S. Army. Apropos of nothing whatever, its obstetrical services are about the best to be found in Europe."

"No shit?" Bonehead asked.

"Bruce, you're not really thinking of going along with Jimmy, are you?"

"No shit, Bonehead," Cronley said. "It's a great hospital."

"Sweetheart . . ."

"The colonel would be furious if he even thought you're thinking of asking for a transfer."

"Then the both of you better be prepared to act really surprised when his orders come down," Cronley said.

"You're not going to ask Colonel Fishburn?" Ginger asked, but before Cronley could reply, she looked at Dunwiddie and asked, "Can he do that, Captain Tiny?"

"Yes, ma'am," Dunwiddie said. "He can."

"How soon?"

"Well, what we're here for shouldn't take more than three days. A couple of days to finish what we've started here. Say a week."

Presuming, of course, that I'm not strapped to a chair in an NKGB jail cell by then watching them pull my toenails out with pliers.

Or pushing up daisies in an unmarked Thuringian grave.

Or a blackened corpse sitting in the burned-out fuselage of a crashed or shot-down Storch.

"You seem very confident about this, Jimmy," Ginger said.

"Ginger, that's why my men call me 'Captain Confidence.' Isn't that so, Captain Dunwiddie?"

Dunwiddie shook his head.

"Why don't we go to the O Club?" he suggested. "I saw a sign in the headquarters saying tonight is steak night."

"They import the steak from Norway," Ginger said, then with great effort and some grunts, she pushed herself out of her chair.

[FIVE]
The Officers' Open Mess
11th Constabulary Regiment
Fritzlar, Hesse
American Zone of Occupation, Germany
1830 18 January 1946

Since all German restaurants and bars were off-limits, the officers of the 11th Constabulary Regiment had three choices for their evening meal: They could eat at home, or have a hamburger or a hot dog at the PX snack bar, or they could go to the officers' open mess. If they wanted a drink, or a beer, they had only their home or the O Club to choose between, as the PX did not serve intoxicants of any kind.

On special occasions, such as "Steak Night," the O Club was usually very crowded. When Cronley, Dunwiddie, and the Moriartys walked in, there was a crowd of people waiting to be seated.

Among them was a young woman who was just about as conspicuously in the family way as Mrs. Moriarty. When she saw Mrs. Moriarty, she went to her, called her by her first name, kissed the air near her cheek, and announced, "Tommy has a theory." She nodded in the direction of her husband. Cronley followed the nod and saw a rather slight lieutenant.

"Tommy says," the woman continued, "the way to get in here quickly is to tell the headwaiter you have a party of eight. Interested?"

Her meaning was clear to Ginger Moriarty. They should merge parties. But then Ginger did the arithmetic. "But there's only six of us."

"Tell them we're expecting two more. We can't be responsible if they don't show up, can we?"

Cronley went from *Oh, shit, the last thing I need is to sit next to another mother-to-be* to quite the opposite reaction in a split second when he saw on Lieutenant Tommy's chest the silver wings of a liaison aviator.

"Go get the lieutenant, Bonehead," he ordered. "His wife is right. He has a great theory."

He went to the headwaiter and said, "We're a party of eight. Colonel and Mrs. Frade will join us later. When the colonel comes, will you send him and his lady to our table, please?"

"Yes, sir, of course. And which is your table, Captain?"

"I thought you'd tell me," Cronley replied. "Whichever table you've reserved for Colonel Frade. Maybe that empty one over there?"

"If you and your party will follow me, sir?"

"Tom, this is Captain Jim Cronley," Bonehead said, when they were all at the table. "We were at Texas A&M together. And this is Captain . . . I didn't get your first name, sir?"

"My friends call me, for reasons I can't imagine, 'Tiny,'" Dunwiddie said.

". . . Dunwiddie."

"How do you do, sir?" Lieutenant Thomas G. Winters said to Dunwiddie and then to Cronley.

"Why don't you sit across from me, Lieutenant?" Cronley said. "And we'll seat Mrs. Moriarty next to your wife?"

"Yes, sir," Lieutenant Winters said.

"That way she won't get in Captain Dunwiddie's way when he reaches for the scotch bottle, which he will do again and again and probably again."

"Yes, sir."

"Where is the waiter?" Cronley asked. "Be advised, Lieutenant, that Captain Dunwiddie is picking up the tab tonight, so feel free to order anything."

"You seem to be in a very good mood," Dunwiddie said. "Ginger, how much did you give him to drink at your quarters?"

"Just that one," Ginger said.

The waiter appeared.

"You speak English, I hope?"

From the waiter's reply in English, it was clear he did not speak the language well.

"We'll start off with a bottle of Haig & Haig Pinch," he said in German. "And then bring us the menu."

"*Jawohl*, Herr Kapitän," the waiter said, and marched off.

"That's very kind of you, sir," Lieutenant Winters said. "But I'm not drinking."

"You don't drink?"

"Not tonight, sir. I'm flying in the morning."

"I thought the rule there was that you had to stop drinking eight hours before you flew."

"Sir, the Army rule is twelve hours before you fly."

Cronley looked at his watch.

"It's 1815," he said. "That means, if you took a drink now, you could take off tomorrow morning at, say, 0630 and still follow the rule. So what do you say?"

"Sir. Thank you, sir, but no thank you."

"You must take your flying very seriously."

"Yes, sir. I do."

"And exactly what kind of flying do you do?"

"Whatever I'm ordered to do, sir."

"Jimmy, what the hell are you up to?" Lieutenant Moriarty asked.

"Put a cork in it, Bonehead," Cronley said.

"Same question," Dunwiddie said. "Lieutenant, Captain Cronley is known for his unusual—some say sick—sense of humor. Don't take him seriously."

"Yes, sir," Winters said, visibly relieved.

"I'm dead serious right now," Cronley said. "Answer the question, Lieutenant. Exactly what kind of flying do you do?"

"Sir, I do whatever is expected of me as an Army aviator."

"Like flying the Hesse/Thuringia border?"

Winter's face tightened, but he did not reply.

"With a photographer in the backseat taking pictures of the picturesque Thuringian countryside?"

Winters stood up.

"The captain will understand that I am not at liberty to discuss the subject he mentions. The lieutenant begs the captain's permission to withdraw."

"Sit down, Lieutenant," Cronley ordered. When Winters remained standing, Cronley said, "That was not a suggestion."

Winters sat down.

"Clever fellow that I am, I suspected it was you the moment I saw the West Point ring. And, of course, the wings."

"Sir?"

"What the hell are you talking about, Jim?" Dunwiddie said, not at all pleasantly.

"You're an intelligence officer . . . and on that subject, show Lieutenant Winters your credentials. And that's not a suggestion, either."

"Jesus!" Tiny said, but handed Winters his credentials folder.

"You may show that to Mrs. Winters, Lieutenant, but you are cautioned not to tell anyone what you saw."

Mrs. Winters's eyes widened when she examined the credentials.

"Now, where were we?" Cronley asked rhetorically. "Oh, yeah. Tell me, Captain Dunwiddie, if you were a West Pointer, and a lieutenant colonel of artillery, and an aviator, and required the services of another aviator to fly a mission . . ."

"Along the border," Dunwiddie picked up. "That you didn't want anybody talking about . . ."

". . . wouldn't you turn first to another graduate of Hudson High who was also an artilleryman?"

Dunwiddie shook his head.

"I thought you were just being a pr— giving him a hard time."

"That thought never entered my mind," Cronley said. "Because if he turned out to be who I thought he was, I wanted to be very nice to him, because first thing tomorrow morning he's going to take me border-flying again. I want to see what he saw and photographed."

"Sir, I couldn't do that without authorization," Winters said.

"Did Colonel Fishburn authorize the flights you already made?"

"No, sir. But—"

"A certain lieutenant colonel, whose name we shall not mention, told you it was all right, right?"

"Yes, sir."

"Did he tell you why we were interested in the fields and back roads of Thuringia?"

"Yes, sir. He said that somebody was going to land a light airplane . . ."

"I'm one of them," Cronley said. "Now, we can go to Colonel Fishburn, which you will note Hot—the unnamed lieutenant colonel . . . did not do . . . and show him our credentials, following which I'm sure he will tell you to take me flying down the border. But if we do that, his sergeant major will hear about it, and so will his wife, and all the girls in what Captain Dunwiddie calls the Officers' Ladies Intelligence Network . . . which would not be a good thing."

Lieutenant Winters looked at Cronley, expressionlessly, for twenty seconds.

Then he said, "Sir, if you'll tell me where you're staying, I'll pick you up at 0530, which will give us time for a cup of coffee and an egg sandwich before we take off at first light."

XII

[ONE]

Hangar Two

U.S. Air Force Base, Fritzlar, Hesse

American Zone of Occupation, Germany

0840 19 January 1946

"What the hell is that?" Lieutenant Thomas Winters, Artillery, inquired of Captain James D. Cronley as they taxied up to the hangar in the L-5.

"I believe it is a C-47, which is the military version of the Douglas DC-3. I'm surprised you don't know that."

There was indeed a C-47 sitting in front of Hangar Two. It had the Constabulary insignia on the nose, which surprised Cronley.

"I mean that funny-looking black airplane they're pushing into the hangar," Winters said, in exasperation.

"I don't see a funny-looking black airplane," Cronley replied. "Possibly because I know that funny-looking black airplanes like that are used only in classified operations I'm not supposed to talk about."

As Winters parked the L-5 and shut it down, a lieutenant wearing Constabulary insignia and aviator's wings walked up to it and saluted.

Cronley got out of the Stinson and returned the salute.

"Colonel Wilson's compliments, gentlemen," the lieutenant announced. "The colonel would be pleased if you would join him aboard the general's aircraft."

"Lieutenant," Cronley asked, straight-faced, "is that the colonel some people call 'Hotshot Billy'?"

"Only full colonels or better can do that, sir," the lieutenant replied. "Anyone of lesser rank who uses that description can expect to die a slow and painful death."

"Lead on, Lieutenant," Cronley said.

A nattily turned-out Constabulary corporal, who looked as if he was several months short of his eighteenth birthday, was standing guard at the steps leading to the rear door of the aircraft. He saluted, then went quickly up the steps and opened the door, which was, Cronley noted, a "civilian" passenger door, rather than the much wider cargo door of C-47 aircraft.

The sergeant came down the steps and Cronley, followed by Winters, went up them.

The interior of the aircraft was not the bare-bones, exposed-ribs interior of a standard Gooney Bird. Nor even the insulation-covered ribs and rows of seats in the interior of a DC-3 in the service of, say, Eastern Airlines. There were eight leather-upholstered armchairs and two tables in the fuselage, making it look not unlike a living room.

General White was not in his aircraft, but Lieutenant Colonel William W. Wilson, Major Harold Wallace, and former Oberst Ludwig Mannberg were, sitting in the armchairs.

"Good morning, gentlemen," Cronley said.

"Where the hell have you been?" Wilson demanded.

Cronley saw on Lieutenant Winters's face that he was now questioning the wisdom of their flight.

"Lieutenant Winters was kind enough to give me a tour of the Thuringian-Hessian border." He turned to Winters. "I believe you know the colonel, Lieutenant," he said. "And this officer is Major Harold Wallace of the Twenty-third CIC Detachment, and this gentleman is Herr Ludwig Mannberg of the Süd-Deutsche Industrielle Entwicklungsorganisation."

Winters saluted and Wallace and Mannberg offered him their hands.

Wallace ordered Cronley and Winters, who were standing awkwardly on the slanted floor of the airplane, into armchairs with a pointed finger. Wilson waited impatiently until they were seated, and then asked, rather unpleasantly, "Cronley, you're not suggesting that Winters suggested this aerial tour of the border?"

"No, sir, I'm not. But I took one look at him and I could see that Lieutenant Winters is a fine pilot, a credit to the United States Military Academy and Army Aviation generally, and decided on the spot that I would recruit him for service with DCI-Europe. Then I asked him to give me an aerial tour of the area."

"You decided to recruit him for DCI?" Wilson asked incredulously.

"He can do it," Wallace said, smiling. "I think the phrase is 'drunk with newfound authority.'"

"I mention that now because I wanted you to know you can speak freely in his presence about our current enterprise," Cronley said. "He knows all about it. Well, maybe not *all* about it, but a good deal about it."

"And how much did you tell Colonel Fishburn about our current enterprise?" Wallace asked.

"Essentially nothing, sir. When Captain Dunwiddie and I made our manners to the colonel, he led us to believe that Colonel Wilson had told him that he would explain everything to him when he got here."

"So you didn't tell Colonel Fishburn that you wanted Lieutenant Winters to fly you up and down the border?" Wilson asked.

"When we made our manners to Colonel Fishburn, I hadn't met Lieutenant Winters. We met him at dinner last night."

"In other words, Colonel Fishburn doesn't know that you have been using one of his airplanes and one of his pilots to fly the border?"

"As far as I know, sir, he does not."

"And you didn't think you should tell him?"

"I thought he might object, and I wanted to make that tour."

"I will be damned!" Wilson said.

"Why do you want the lieutenant in DCI?" Wallace asked.

"I thought it would be nice if at least one of the pilots in the aviation section of DCI-Europe was a bona fide U.S. Army aviator."

"I didn't know there was an aviation section of DCI-Europe," Wallace said.

"As of today, there is. Or there will be as soon as I can sign the appropriate documents, which by now Fat Freddy and Brunhilde should have prepared."

"You're going to have an aviation section for the Storchs, is that what you're saying?"

"I'm going to have an aviation section in which I can *hide* the Storchs. There will also be other aircraft, two L-4s or L-5s and, if General Greene can pry one loose from the Air Force, a C-45. I'm going to tell him just as soon as I can get on the SIGABA, which I think should be up and running by now."

"He's unbelievable! My God, he's only a captain!" Colonel Wilson said. "A very young and junior captain! And he's going to *tell* a general officer what he wants?"

"What's that Jewish word, Billy?" Wallace asked.

Cronley saw on Winters's face that he had picked up on Major Wallace calling Lieutenant Colonel Wilson by the diminutive of his Christian name.

"'Chutzpah'?" Wallace went on, "Meaning audacity? Isn't that what Patton was always saying, '*L'audace, l'audace, toujours l'audace!*'?"

"It also means unmitigated effrontery or impudence," Wilson said.

"I remember when you were a captain, they said the same things about you," Wallace said. "And I remember your defense: 'I did what I believed to be the right thing to do.'"

Cronley now saw on Winters's face his expectation that Major Wallace would now suffer what a major could expect after speaking so disrespectfully to a lieutenant colonel.

"Tom," Cronley said, "now that you're in the intelligence business, you'll have to understand that nothing is ever what it looks like."

Winters looked at him, but did not reply.

"And look at you now, Billy," Wallace went on, "the youngest lieutenant colonel in the Army."

Wilson looked as if he was going to reply, but changed his mind.

"There's more," Cronley said. "Freddy did some research on how the OSS operated administratively, and found out they had people working for them they called 'civilian experts.'"

"So?" Wallace asked.

"So now DCI-Europe has two such civilian experts. They will be paid—I'm quoting what Freddy found out—'the equivalent of the pay of commissioned officers with similar responsibilities, plus a suitable bonus for voluntarily undertaking assignments involving great personal risk, plus a death benefit of ten thousand dollars should they lose their lives in the performance of their duties.'"

"We had a number of such people," Wallace confirmed.

Cronley saw in Winters's expression that he had picked up on the "we."

"And now DCI-Europe has two of them. Maksymilian Ostrowski, former captain, Free Polish Air Force, and Kurt Schröder, former *hauptmann*, Luftwaffe."

"I can't find fault with that," Wallace said. "What about you, Colonel?"

"I hate to admit it, but it makes sense."

"Anything else?"

"A couple of things. When I speak with General Greene, I'm going to ask him to transfer to DCI-Europe not only the six ASA guys he's loaned me, two of whom I brought here with me, but also to get Second Lieutenant Bruce Moriarty of the Eleventh Constabulary Regiment transferred to me. Us."

"Not 'us,' Cronley," Wallace said. "Transferred to *you*, in your role as chief, DCI-Europe. As you know, I have nothing to do with DCI-Europe."

"Sorry."

"But since the subject has come up, what's this all about? Start with the ASA men," Wallace ordered. "And the last time I looked, Brunhilde is not a guy."

"Freddy had already arranged for Brunhilde to be transferred to DCI. I'm talking about the radio guys. They're smart. Freddy told me that at the Reception Center, when they enlisted or get drafted, they all scored at least 110 on the Army General Classification Test and were given their choice of applying for Officer Candidate School or going into the ASA."

"And these guys didn't want to be officers?"

"They didn't want to serve four years if they could get out of the Army after two," Cronley said. "The point is, they're smart. That has its ups and downs. Because they're smart, they do their jobs well. That's the up. The down is that if somebody else needs them, and Greene transfers them, they'll walk away knowing too much about DCI-Europe, and that makes me uncomfortable."

"Okay. Point taken. But how do you know they want to leave the ASA?"

"Because I offered them an immediate one-stripe promotion if they did, and a second three months after that."

"You can do that?"

"According to Fat Freddy, I can. I promoted him to staff sergeant."

"Okay. What about the lieutenant? Who is he?"

"An A&M classmate of mine. He'll be given command of

Company C, 203rd Tank Destroyer Battalion and the Polish guards."

"That's a lot of responsibility for a second lieutenant," Wallace said.

"He can handle it. And we need somebody to handle it."

"Anything else?"

"I told Brunhilde to look for some clerical help among the WACs in ASA. We're going to need all kinds of help in that department."

"It looks like you're building quite an empire, Cronley," Wilson said. His tone suggested he didn't approve.

Cronley's temper flared and his mouth went on automatic, and as usual, he regretted the words as soon as they came out of his mouth.

"Sir, I'm doing what I believe to be the right thing to do. If my superiors in the DCI decide I'm not doing the right thing, or doing more than I should, they'll relieve me."

Not smart. Not smart. Rubbing what Wallace said to him in his face was not smart.

And that "my superiors" crack sounded as if I'm daring Wallace to relieve me. Not smart.

Stupid.

"I'm sure that would happen," Wallace said.

"We saw one of the black birds as we came in," Cronley said. "Are they both here?"

"The second came in just before you did. They're being serviced. I brought the mechanics I gave you with us."

"I should have thought of that, of servicing the Storchs."

"Yes, you should have," Wallace said, "but nobody's perfect, right?"

"Yes, sir."

"What do we hear from Seven-K?" Cronley asked.

"We have communication scheduled for noon," Mannberg said. It was the first time he opened his mouth. "We may get a schedule then."

"Then there's time for Winters to take Schröder on a tour of the border," Cronley said. "I think that's important. I saw a lot I didn't see in the photos."

"As you may have noticed, Tom," Wilson said, "Captain Cronley has a tendency to volunteer people for things they'd really rather not do. Are you comfortable with what's happening? Are you sure you want to get involved in something like this?"

"Sir, something like this is obviously more important than dropping bags of flour on M-8 armored cars, which is what I've been doing here."

"Tom, you wouldn't be here now if I hadn't asked you to make the first tour of the border, the one with a photographer in the backseat. Then Cronley, who is clever at that sort of thing, and knew about that mission, figured out that it was you who flew it, and then cleverly convinced you that flying the border again with him in the backseat was something I would approve, so you flew it. Correct?"

"Yes, sir."

"That being the case, I feel that I should say this: Intelligence, and especially black operations like this one, are indeed more exciting and important than dropping flour bags on M-8 armored cars. But there's a downside for someone like you. You're a West

Pointer, a professional soldier, the son of a general officer. You know there is little love between intelligence types and . . . the Army Establishment. If you go with Cronley, you will almost certainly be kissing your career goodbye. And any chance of pinning stars on your own epaulets one day. And if your father were here, I know he'd agree with me."

"Sir, I got the impression I didn't have any choice in the matter."

"Well, I'm going to give you that choice. Now, and think your answer over carefully before you reply. Let me add there's no need for you to fly the mission Captain Cronley suggests. He can fly Schröder down the border as well as you can. Here's the question: Would you like to just walk out of here and go back to your duties with the Eleventh Constabulary and forget anything like this ever happened? Colonel Fishburn doesn't know you flew this unauthorized mission, and I can see no reason that he should ever learn about it. Think it over carefully."

You sonofabitch! Cronley thought, as his mouth went on automatic.

"I've got something to say," he said.

"No, you don't, Captain Cronley," Wilson snapped. "This is between Lieutenant Winters and myself."

"No, Billy, it isn't," Wallace said. "Cronley's involved. Let's hear what he has to say."

"It's none of Cronley's goddamn business!"

"I disagree," Wallace said. "Go ahead, Jim."

I don't have a goddamn clue what to say, Cronley thought, and then his mouth went on automatic again:

"The first thing I thought when I heard Colonel Wilson just

now was that I wished he would keep his nose out of my business," Cronley said. "Then, I thought, well, he's actually a nice guy. Colonel Wallace—"

"Oops!" Wallace interrupted. "Another cow out of the barn. Watch yourself, Jim."

"—has made that clear, and I know it from personal experience."

"Why don't you tell *him* to keep *his* nose out of *my* business?" Wilson asked.

"Pray continue, Captain Cronley," Wallace said.

"And then I remembered another time Colonel Wilson had wisely counseled a junior officer. The day I met him. He knew that I had been promoted to captain from second lieutenant before I had enough time in grade to be a first lieutenant, and he was kind enough . . . as the youngest lieutenant colonel in the army . . . to explain to me what he believed that meant.

"I remember what he said. Word for word. I've thought of it a thousand times since then. And I even quoted it, and the source, when Captain Dunwiddie—another professional soldier like you, Tom—was uncomfortable with the direct commission as a captain I asked the admiral to arrange for him."

"How long do I have to listen to this?" Lieutenant Colonel Wilson protested.

"For however long it takes him to make his point. Put a cork in it, Billy."

"Quote," Cronley said, "'The advantages of getting rank, et cetera, means that you can do things for the good of the service that otherwise you could not do. And that's what we professional soldiers are supposed to do, isn't it? Make contributions to the good of the service?' End quote.

"What I'm suggesting, Tom," Cronley said, "is that you base your decision, as a professional soldier, on where you can make the greater contribution to the good of the service."

After a moment, Wallace said, "Colonel Wilson, in the opinion of the senior officer present, Captain Cronley has just nailed your scrotum to the wall."

"Or I nailed it there myself," Wilson said.

"Your call, Lieutenant Winters," Wallace said.

"Two things, sir," Winters said. "First, Colonel Wilson, sir, I really appreciate your concern. Second, Captain Cronley, sir, is there anything in particular you want me to show the Storch pilot?"

"Welcome to Lunatics Anonymous, Lieutenant," Wallace said.

"What I think we should do now is make our manners to Colonel Fishburn," Wilson said.

"Why don't you do that while I get on the SIGABA and have a chat with the Navy?" Wallace replied.

"I was afraid you'd say that."

"Mitchell has problems with the SIGABA?" Cronley asked.

"No," Wallace said. "According to Dunwiddie, Mitchell has been up and running since about nineteen hundred last night. Why do you ask?"

"I've been wondering why you didn't get on the SIGABA as soon as you got here. And why you're all sitting here in the Gooney Bird. There's a . . . I guess you could call it a 'lounge' in the building. Complete with a coffee machine."

"I was dissuaded from doing just that by Colonel Wilson," Wallace said. "May I tell the captain why, Colonel?"

"Why not? It may add to his professional knowledge."

"Colonel Wilson thought it was entirely likely that Colonel Fishburn would ask him if he'd seen you. And if he replied in the negative, that Colonel Fishburn would wonder why not."

"And if that happened," Wilson said, "and I think it would have, I would have had to tell him you were flying up and down the border in one of his airplanes, which I did not want to do, or profess innocence vis-à-vis knowledge of your whereabouts. Since I am (a) a West Pointer, and (b) not in the intelligence business, I do not knowingly make false statements to senior officers. Now when I make my manners, I can tell him truthfully, repeat, truthfully, that I came to see him immediately after getting off General White's aircraft. I don't expect either you or Major Wallace to understand that, but that's the way it is."

But deceiving him is okay, right?

"I understand, sir," Cronley said.

"And if that question is asked," Wilson said, "and I believe it will be, I can now reply that I had a brief word with you aboard the general's aircraft."

"Yes, sir," Cronley said.

[TWO]
Hangar Two
U.S. Air Force Base, Fritzlar, Hesse
American Zone of Occupation, Germany
1150 19 January 1946

Technical Sergeant Jerry Mitchell and Sergeant Pete Fortin of the ASA started to rise when Cronley, Wallace, Dunwiddie, Mannberg, Ostrowski, and Schröder filed into what looked like it had once been a control tower and now was the radio room.

"Sit," Wallace ordered with a smile.

"How we doing?" Cronley said.

"Waiting, sir," Mitchell said. "They're usually right on time. We've got about nine and a half minutes to wait."

"Which gives us time to run over what's going to happen," Wallace said, "so let's do that."

"Yes, sir. Seven-K initiates the contact. They will transmit, three times, a five-number block. Pete'll type it, and hand it to me. If it matches the number Colonel Mannberg gave us, we will reply with the five-block number he gave us. They'll check that against their list of numbers. Then we'll be open. Protocol is that they send, in the clear, a short phrase, a question to verify that Colonel Mannberg is on this end."

"For example?" Wallace asked.

"Middle name Ludwig," Mannberg said. "My middle name is Christian, so we would send that, for example."

"And then," Mitchell said, "they reply with what they want to send us. We acknowledge, and that's it."

"I hate to sound like a smart-ass," Cronley said.

"Hah!" Wallace said.

"But I think you forgot to turn the SIGABA on."

"It's off, Captain. I was afraid that there might be some interference with the eight slash ten from it."

"With the what?"

Mitchell pointed to three small, battered, black tin boxes. They were connected with cables, and what could be a telegraph key protruded from the side of one of them, and a headset—now on Sergeant Fortin's head—was plugged into one of the boxes.

"That's what we're using," he said. "It's German. The SE 108/10 transceiver."

"Seven-K has one just like it," Mannberg said. "We used them quite successfully from 1942. The slash ten means it's Model 10, based on the original model 108."

"I thought it was something you found in here," Cronley admitted. "And were fooling around with."

"No, sir, that's it. It's a hell of a little radio," Sergeant Fortin said. "Puts out ten watts."

"And that thing with the white button on it sticking out from the side is the telegraph key?" Cronley asked.

"Right," Fortin said.

"Where'd you get it, from Colonel Mannberg?"

"This one, I think, we got from Iron Lung . . . Major McClung. But Colonel Mannberg did give us a couple of them."

Sergeant Fortin, who had been sitting relaxed in his chair before his typewriter, suddenly straightened and began typing. It didn't take long. He ripped the paper from the machine and handed it to Mitchell as he fed a fresh sheet of paper into the typewriter.

Mitchell consulted a sheet of paper in his free hand.

"Send Seven Zero Two Zero Two," he ordered. "I repeat, Seven Zero Two Zero Two."

Fortin put his finger on "the thing with the white button on it" and tapped furiously.

"Seven Zero Two Zero Two sent," he reported.

Thirty seconds later, Fortin's fingers flew over his keyboard for a few seconds. He tore the sheet of paper from the machine, handed it to Mitchell, and then fed a fresh sheet of paper into the typewriter.

"Peanut dog," Mitchell said, and then looked at Colonel Mannberg.

"Franz Josef," Cronley ordered. "Send Franz Josef. I spell."

He then did so, using the Army phonetic alphabet.

Fortin typed what he had said, but did not put his finger on "the thing with the white button on it," instead looking at Sergeant Mitchell for guidance. Mitchell, in turn, looked at Mannberg.

"Send Franz Josef," he ordered.

"Spell again," Fortin ordered.

Cronley did so.

Fortin put his finger on "the thing" and tapped rapidly.

"Franz Josef sent," he reported.

And then, almost immediately, he began to type again. It took him a little longer this time, but less than five seconds had passed before he tore the sheet of paper from the machine and handed it to Mitchell.

"Able Seven," Mitchell read, using the Army phonetic for "A." Then he said, "Dog Tare Tare Fox One Six Oboe Oboe."

"Meaning what?" Wallace demanded impatiently.

"Sir, the protocol is coordinates first. So Able Seven is a place. Dog is D. Tare is T, and F is Fox, so DTTF, which means Date and Time To Follow. One Six is the time, 1600. Oboe is O, so OO, which means out."

"Acknowledge receipt of the message," Wallace ordered.

"Not necessary. When they sent OO, that meant they were off."

"Rahil is really clever," Mannberg said admiringly. "By asking for the dog's name, she ascertained that Cronley was here—it was very unlikely that anyone else would know the dog's name—and if Cronley was here, it was very likely that I was, too."

"And what if I didn't remember the dog's name?" Cronley asked.

"Then she would have given us one more opportunity to establish our bona fides. She would have posed another question, a difficult one, the answer to which would be known only to me. And if we didn't send the correct response to that, we would have had to start from the beginning."

"What's this Able Seven?" Wallace said. "How far from here is it? Where's the maps and the aerial photos?"

"I've set them up in the room downstairs, sir," Dunwiddie said.

"Why not in here?"

"There's not room for all of them in here, sir," Dunwiddie said.

"Dumb question," Wallace said. "Sorry, Tiny."

[THREE]
Hangar Two
U.S. Air Force Base, Fritzlar, Hesse
American Zone of Occupation, Germany
1225 19 January 1946

"The room downstairs" occupied all of the floor immediately below the radio room/control tower. Dunwiddie had acquired somewhere what looked like a Ping-Pong table, and it was now covered with aerial photographs. Two large maps, one of them topographical, had been taped to the walls.

Wallace first found Able Seven on the topographical map, and then went to the table and started examining the aerial photographs of the site.

Cronley looked at one of the photos and immediately recognized the site. It was a snow-covered field near a thick stand of pine trees. A narrow road ran alongside it.

He then went to the map and, using two fingers as a compass, determined that it was about thirty miles from the Fritzlar Airbase in a straight line, maybe thirty-five miles distant if he flew down the border for most of the way, and then made a ninety-degree turn to the left. Site Able Seven was about a mile, maybe a mile and a half, inside Thuringia.

He sensed that Schröder was looking over his shoulder, and turned and asked, "What do you think?"

"I think I'd like to know what the winds are going to be,"

Schröder replied. "If they're coming from the North, it means we could make a straight-in approach from our side of the border . . ."

"And if they're from the South, we'll have to fly another couple of miles into Thuringia," Cronley finished for him.

"Precisely."

"If the winds are from East or West, no problem."

"Correct."

"Well, there's no way we could set up a wind sock in that field. Seven-K is going to come down that road two minutes before, or a minute after, we land. She's not going to be able to park on that road and wait for us."

"So we pray for winds from the North," Schröder said, "will be satisfied with either easterly or westerly, and will hope for the best if they're from the South."

"Wait a minute," Cronley said. "Ludwig, could we get a message to Seven-K, asking her to park her car, or whatever she's driving, with the nose, the front, facing into the wind?"

Mannberg considered the question a moment.

"So you'll know the winds on the ground?" he asked. His tone suggested he already knew the answer. "Yes," he went on. "It'll . . . the encryption of the message . . . will take a little doing. But yes, it can be done. And I think it should. I'll get right on it. We don't have much time."

"How much time do you think we do have?" Cronley asked.

"If I had to guess, which I hate to do, I'd say Seven-K would probably want to make the transfer at first light tomorrow, or just before it gets dark tomorrow. Or—she's very cautious—at first light the day after tomorrow. Or just before sunset the day after tomorrow."

"Makes sense. Then, since I have nothing else to do between now and tomorrow morning, I am now going to the O Club and drink the hearty last meal to which condemned men are entitled. Would anyone care to join me?"

"Wrong," Wallace said.

"I don't get a hearty, liquid last meal?"

"You have plenty to do between now and tomorrow morning at the earliest."

"Such as?"

"Such as, presuming you can get Mrs. Likharev and the boys over the border, what are you going to do with them once they are here?"

Cronley actually felt a painful contraction in his stomach, as if he'd been kicked.

"Jesus H. Christ, that never entered my mind. How could I have been so stupid?"

"Because I have been almost that stupid myself, I'm resisting the temptation to say because being stupid comes to you naturally," Wallace said. "I thought about it, but didn't recognize how many problems we have until Hessinger started bringing them to my attention."

"Jesus H. Christ," Cronley repeated.

"You've already said that," Wallace said. "Now, what I suggest we do is send somebody to the PX snack bar for hamburgers, hot dogs, Coke, and potato chips, which we will consume as we sit at the Ping-Pong table and discuss solutions."

"Yes, sir," Cronley said.

"You are appointed Recorder of this meeting, Captain Cronley, which means you will write everything down on a lined pad as we speak. We can't afford forgetting anything again."

"Yes, sir," Cronley said.

He sat down at the table. Dunwiddie handed him a lined paper tablet and half a dozen pencils.

Wallace, Mannberg, and Dunwiddie sat down. Schröder and Ostrowski looked as if they didn't know what they should do.

"Please be seated, gentlemen," Wallace said. Then he turned to Cronley. "The floor is yours, Captain Cronley."

"Sir, I'd rather you run this. I don't even know where to start."

Wallace looked at him, then opened his mouth, and visibly changed his mind about saying what immediately came to him, and then said, "At the beginning would seem to be a good place.

"Presumption One," he began. "Both planes take off from Thuringia with everybody on board and make it back here.

"Unknowns: Condition of the aircraft and the people on board.

"Worst-case scenario: Airplanes are shot up and there are dead or wounded aboard.

"Medium-case scenario: Airplanes are not shot up and no wounded. But Mrs. Likharev and either or both boys are sedated.

"Best-case scenario: Airplanes are not shot up. Mrs. Likharev and the boys are wide awake.

"Any other scenario suggestions?"

There were none.

"It seems obvious that there should be two ambulances waiting when the planes land," Wallace said.

"Inside the hangar," Cronley said. "If they are parked outside, people will be curious."

"Point taken," Wallace said. "Recommended solution: We get Colonel Wilson to arrange with Colonel Fishburn for the ambulances and station them inside the hangar. Any objections?"

There were none.

"Comments?"

"Two," Cronley said.

"One at a time, please."

"What do we do if there are wounded in the ambulances?"

"They go first to the regimental aid station here for treatment. If they're in bad shape—where's the nearest field hospital?"

No one knew.

"Tiny," Wallace ordered, "get on the phone."

"And while he's doing that, what if there are dead on the planes?" Cronley asked.

"You, Max, and Kurt wouldn't be a problem."

"That's nice to know," Max said sarcastically.

"I meant, you've got DCI credentials," Wallace said. "They'd get you into the hospital, dead or alive."

"That's comforting," Max said.

"The Likharevs don't have DCI credentials," Cronley said.

"Army hospitals treat indigenous personnel requiring emergency medical attention," Wallace said.

"What's 'indigenous' mean?" Cronley asked.

"Native. German."

"The Likharevs are Russian," Cronley said.

"So we tell the aid station they're German," Wallace said impatiently.

"What if one or more of them are dead?" Cronley asked. "What do we do with the bodies?"

Wallace considered the question.

"More important, what do we tell Colonel Likharev?" Cronley asked.

"Whatever we tell him, he's not going to believe," Wallace said.

"We fly the bodies to Kloster Grünau," Max said. "Where we put them in caskets and bury them with the full rites of the Russian Orthodox Church. The ceremony, and the bodies in the caskets, are photographed. Photographs to be shown to Colonel Likharev."

"The nearest field hospital is the Fifty-seventh, in Giessen," Tiny reported. "There is an airstrip."

"Photographs to be taken to Argentina by Captain Dunwiddie," Wallace said.

"If Mrs. Likharev, or the oldest boy, survives, Dunwiddie takes her, or him, or both and the photographs of the funeral, to Argentina," Cronley said.

"Tiny," Wallace said, "have Colonel Wilson arrange for a Signal Corps photographer to be here from the moment the Storchs take off. When he shows up, put the fear of God in him about running his mouth."

"Yes, sir."

"Our story to Colonel Likharev," Cronley said, straight-faced, "would have more credibility if one of us—Max, Kurt, or me—got blown away and Tiny could show the colonel a dozen shots of our bloody, bullet-ridden corpses."

"You're insane, Cronley," Wallace said, but he was smiling.

Ostrowski, shaking his head, but also smiling, gave Cronley the finger.

Kurt Schröder's face showed he neither understood nor appreciated the humor.

"Moving right along," Wallace said. "Best scenario, everybody is standing intact on the hangar floor. Objective, to get them to Argentina. Question: How do we do that?"

"Simple answer. Load them in either the Twin Beech or the Gooney Bird, fly them to Rhine-Main, and load them aboard a South American Airways Constellation bound for Buenos Aires," Cronley said.

"Now let's break that down," Wallace said. "What are the problems there?"

"Well, we don't know when there will be an SAA airplane at Rhine-Main," Cronley said.

"Tiny, maybe—even probably—Hessinger has the SAA schedule. Find out."

"Yes, sir."

"Medium-bad scenario," Wallace went on. "The next SAA flight is not for three days."

"Can we fly them into Eschborn—and we can, in either airplane, I've seen Gooney Birds in there—and stash them at that hotel for the brass—the Schlosshotel Kronberg in Taunus?"

"Yeah," Wallace said.

"Even if one or more of them is 'walking wounded'?" Cronley asked.

"And what if Mrs. Likharev is on the edge of hysteria?" Ostrowski asked.

"And that, the walking wounded, and the possibility of Mother being hysterical, raises the question of how do we care for them while they're en route to either Rhine-Main or Eschborn?" Wallace asked.

"Get a nurse from the aid station here when we get the ambulances," Cronley said. "No. Get a nurse and a doctor."

"Why both?"

"Couple of reasons. The nurse, because the presence of a woman is likely to be comforting to Mrs. Likharev if she is hysterical, or looks like she's about to be, and the doctor to sedate her, or the kids, if that has to be done."

"I don't like the idea of taking a doctor—and that's presuming we can get one—and a nurse to either Rhine-Main or Eschborn," Wallace said.

No one said anything for a long moment.

"What about having Claudette Colbert go to Frankfurt, or Eschborn?" Dunwiddie asked. "Have her in either place when our plane gets there?"

"Permit me a suggestion," Ludwig Mannberg said. "Have both a doctor and a nurse in the hangar when the Storchs return, to take care of every contingency. If any of them are seriously injured, he could determine whether it would be safe to take them to the hospital in Giessen, or even to the Army hospital in Frankfurt . . . what is it?"

"The Ninety-seventh General Hospital," Dunwiddie furnished.

"Ideally, the latter," Mannberg went on. "Instead of the Schlosshotel Kronberg. I suggest that if any of the Likharevs require medical attention, the place to do that would be in Frankfurt, where the good offices of Generals Smith and Greene could be enlisted to discourage the curious.

"If necessary, the doctor or the nurse or both could go on the airplane with the Likharevs. If their services were not required, they wouldn't go. I agree with Cronley that the presence of a woman would be a calming influence on Mrs. Likharev, and suggest that Fraulein Colbert could fill that role."

"I agree with everything he just said," Cronley said.

"How could you not?" Wallace asked sarcastically. "Okay, we're in agreement that Brunhilde can make a contribution, right?"

Wallace looked around the table. Everybody nodded.

"My take on that is, if so, why not get her up here right now? How would we do that?"

"Going down that road," Cronley began, "we get Hotshot Billy to fly her up here."

[FOUR]
Hangar Two
U.S. Air Force Base, Fritzlar, Hesse
American Zone of Occupation, Germany
1450 19 January 1946

They went down that road, and many others, without interruption—not even to send someone to the PX snack bar for the hot dogs, hamburgers, Cokes, and potato chips Major Wallace had promised—until Sergeant Pete Fortin came into the room.

This stopped their discussion, which was then on how to get photographs of Mrs. Likharev and her sons to former Major Konrad Bischoff in Munich so they could be affixed to the Vatican passports they would need to leave the American Zone of Occupied Germany.

"What is it, Sergeant?" Major Wallace demanded, not very pleasantly.

"Two things, sir. Our next contact is at fifteen hundred . . ."

Wallace looked at his watch and shook his head in what was almost certainly disbelief that it was already that late.

". . . and Sergeant Mitchell says there's something funny going on at the Constab that maybe you want to have a look at it."

"Something funny?" Wallace asked. "Okay. We'll pick this up again just as soon as I finish taking a leak, seeing what's amusing Sergeant Mitchell, and having our chat with Seven-K."

He stood up and went directly to the restroom. There he stood in front of one of the two urinals. Captain Dunwiddie shouldered Captain Cronley out of the way and assumed a position in front of the adjacent urinal. Former Colonel Mannberg got in line behind Major Wallace, and Kurt Schröder got in line behind him as Max Ostrowski got behind Captain Cronley.

Minutes later, after climbing the stairs, they filed into the radio room in just about that order.

Cronley looked at where Dunwiddie was pointing, out one of the huge plate-glass windows. He saw what looked like three troops of Constabulary troopers lining up on a grassy area half covered with snow in front of the 11th Constabulary Regiment headquarters.

"Okay, I give up," Cronley said. "What's going on?"

"Beats me," Dunwiddie admitted. "It's too early for that to be a retreat formation."

"Jesus, there's even a band," Cronley said.

"Regiments don't have bands," Dunwiddie said.

"This one does," Cronley argued.

"Gentlemen, if you're going to be in the intelligence business, you're really going to have to remember to always look over your shoulder," Major Wallace said, and pointed out the plate-glass window to their immediate rear.

The window gave a panoramic view for miles over the countryside, and in particular of the road down a valley and ending at the air base.

And down it was coming a lengthy parade of vehicles. First came a dozen motorcycles, with police-type flashing lights, ridden side by side. Then a half-dozen M-8 armored cars, in line, and also equipped with flashing police-type lights.

The first thing Cronley thought was, having seen an almost identical parade up the road from Eschborn to the Schlosshotel Kronberg, that one carrying the supreme commander, Allied Powers Europe, to a golf game, *What the hell is Eisenhower doing in Fritzlar?*

Then he saw the car following the M-8s. Eisenhower had a 1942 Packard Clipper as a staff car. What was in line here was a 1939 Cadillac. Not any '39 Cadillac. A famous one, the one General George S. Patton had been riding in when he had his fatal accident.

"You will recall, I'm sure, Captain Cronley," Major Wallace said, "that Colonel Wilson said that he would speak to General White about some sort of diversion?"

Both of their heads snapped from the open window to the side of the room, where Sergeant Fortin was furiously pounding his typewriter keyboard.

"Seven-K," Wallace said. "Right on time."

Fortin ripped the sheet of paper in the typewriter from it and handed it to Mitchell.

"Jesus Christ!" Mitchell said when he read it.

"Do I acknowledge?" Fortin asked.

"You're sure this is all? You didn't miss anything?"

"That's it."

"What does it say?"

"One Six Zero Zero, Oboe Nan Easy How Oboe Uncle Roger. Repeat One Six Zero Zero, Oboe Nan Easy How."

"Sixteen hundred. One hour." Wallace made the translation.

"Right now?" Cronley asked incredulously. "Today?"

"They sent it twice, Captain," Fortin said.

"And added One Hour, to make sure we understood she meant today," Wallace said.

"Holy shit!" Cronley said.

"Do I acknowledge?" Fortin asked again.

"Jim, can you do it?" Wallace asked. "Can you be at Able Seven in an hour? In fifty-eight minutes?"

Cronley thought it over.

"God willing, and if the creek don't rise," he said.

"Acknowledge receipt, Sergeant Fortin," Wallace ordered.

"Nothing's in place," Cronley said. "No ambulances, no doctor, no nothing."

"Nothing at Able Seven to give us the winds on the ground," Ostrowski said.

"I know," Wallace said.

"Yeah," Cronley said.

"Seven-K wouldn't order this unless she thought she had to," Oberst Mannberg said.

"They just sent Oboe Oboe," Sergeant Fortin said. "They're off."

"Which means we can't ask her to reschedule," Wallace said.

"Kurt," Cronley said, "I guess we better go wind up the rubber bands."

Schröder's face showed he had no idea what Cronley meant.

"Didn't you have model airplanes when you were a kid?" Cronley asked.

Then he mimed winding the rubber bands in a model airplane by turning the propeller.

Schröder smiled, wanly, and then gestured for Cronley to precede him out the door of the radio room.

[FIVE]
Hangar Two
U.S. Air Force Base, Fritzlar, Hesse
American Zone of Occupation, Germany
1510 19 January 1946

"Well?" Wallace asked, when Cronley finished his walk around his Storch.

"I don't think anything important fell off," Cronley said. "Is Tiny in the control tower?"

Wallace nodded.

"Where he has dazzled the Air Force with his DCI credentials," Wallace said. "When you call, they will clear you—both of you—to taxi from the tarmac outside to Taxiway Two, then to the threshold of Runway One Six for immediate takeoff."

"I see the pushers are here," Cronley said, pointing to Tiny's Troopers, who were prepared to push the Storchs from the hangar. "So I guess I better get in, and then you get the doors open."

"I need a couple of minutes in private with you, Schröder, and Ostrowski first," Wallace said.

"What for?"

"Over there," Wallace said, pointing to a door in the rear wall of the hangar. "Now."

Oberst Mannberg was already in the room when Cronley, followed by Ostrowski and Schröder, entered. Wallace closed the door.

"If you're going to deliver some sort of pep talk," Cronley said, "I'd just as soon skip it, thank you just the same."

"Shut up for once, Jim," Wallace said, and then he said, "Okay, everybody extend your right hand, palm up. I'm going to give you something."

When the three had done so, Wallace dropped what looked like a brown pea into each palm.

"Pay close attention. Cronley, don't open your mouth before I finish. Got it?"

"Yes, sir."

"Those are L-pills," Wallace said. "Inside the protective rubber coating is a glass ampoule. When the ampoule is crushed by the molars of the mouth, sufficient potassium cyanide will be released to cause unconsciousness within three seconds, brain death within sixty seconds, and heart stoppage and death within three minutes. That process is irreversible once begun. Any questions?"

No one had any questions.

"I will not insult anyone's intelligence by asking if you understand the purpose of the L-pills."

"We had something like this in the East," Schröder said.

"Almost identical, Kurt," Mannberg said.

"Is this what Hitler and his mistress used?" Ostrowski asked. "What Magda Goebbels used to kill her children in the Führerbunker?"

Mannberg nodded.

"And what a number of captured agents on both sides chose to use rather than give up what they knew they should not give up," Wallace said. "Or to avoid interrogation by torture."

Cronley, Ostrowski, and Schröder looked at the brown peas in their hands, but made no other move.

"Aside from shirt pockets, the most common place to carry one of these is in one's handkerchief," Wallace said. "The place of concealment recommended by the OSS, to Jedburghs, was insertion in the anus."

"Really?" Cronley asked, and then began to laugh.

"What the hell can you possibly find amusing about this, Cronley?" Wallace demanded furiously.

"Excuse me, sir," Cronley replied, still laughing, as he moved his hand to his shirt pocket and dropped the L-pill in.

"Sometimes I really question your sanity," Wallace said furiously.

"What I was thinking, sir," Cronley said, stopped to get his laughter under some control, and then continued, "was that the OSS's recommendation for concealment of your pill really gave new meaning to the phrase 'stick it up your ass,' didn't it?"

Then he broke out laughing again.

A moment later, Ostrowski joined in. And then Mannberg. Then Wallace was laughing, and finally Schröder.

"You think 'stick it up your ass' is funny, huh, Kurt?" Cronley asked. "I finally said something that made you laugh!"

"You are out of your mind!" Schröder said, and then, still laughing, went to Cronley and embraced him.

They walked out of the room with their arms around each other and then got in the Storchs.

[SIX]
Hangar Two
U.S. Air Force Base, Fritzlar, Hesse
American Zone of Occupation, Germany
1525 19 January 1946

"Fritzlar clears Army Seven-Oh-Seven a flight of two aircraft as Number One to take off on One Six on a local flight."

Cronley shoved the throttle to takeoff power and then answered, "Fritzlar, Seven-Oh-Seven rolling."

As soon as he was off the ground, Cronley saw that his normal climb-out would take him directly over the three troops of Constabulary soldiers lined up in front of the 11th Constabulary Regiment headquarters.

That would obviously draw the attention of the Constabulary troopers to the two funny-looking black aircraft, which was not a good thing.

On the other hand, it would be a worse thing if he tried to use the amazing flight characteristics of the Storch to make a sharp, low-level turn to the right to avoid flying over the troops and didn't make it.

He pulled his flaps and flew straight.

As he flew over the troops, he saw General White, Colonel Fishburn, and Lieutenant Colonel Williams looking up at him.

[SEVEN]
Able Seven
(Off Unnamed Unpaved Road Near Eichsfeld,
Thuringia)
Russian Zone of Occupation, Germany
1555 19 January 1946

There was a small truck on the road.

As Cronley flew closer, he saw that it was an old—ancient—Ford stake body truck, and that red stars were painted on the doors.

He remembered seeing on *March of Time* newsreel trucks like that driving over the ice of a lake, or a river, to supply Stalingrad.

A stocky man in what looked like a Russian officer's uniform got out of the cab of the truck . . .

He's wearing a skirt?

That's not a man. That's Seven-K. Rahil.

. . . and went quickly to the back.

A boy jumped out of the truck.

Is that the old one, or the young one?

And then a woman.

Mrs. Likharev.

Mrs. Likharev turned and helped a smaller boy get out of the truck.

Seven-K pointed to the approaching Storchs, and then took the woman's arm and propelled her into the field beside the road.

Cronley signaled to Schröder, who was flying off Cronley's left wing, to land. Schröder nodded and immediately dropped the nose of his Storch.

Cronley slowed the Storch to just above stall speed so that he could watch Schröder land.

Schröder got his Storch safely on the ground, but watching him put Cronley so far down the field that he knew he couldn't—even in the Storch—get in. He would have to go around.

By the time he did so, Mrs. Likharev and the boys were standing alone in the field, making no move to go to Schröder's Storch.

Seven-K was getting into the truck. As soon as she did so, the truck drove off.

Cronley put his Storch on the ground. At the end of his landing roll, he was twenty feet from Schröder's Storch.

Ostrowski was out of Cronley's Storch the instant it stopped, and ran to Mrs. Likharev and the boys. He propelled them toward Schröder's Storch.

Christ, the little one has Franz Josef!

What the hell?

Christ, I've got to turn around.

Why the hell didn't I think about that?

Ostrowski hoisted Mrs. Likharev into Schröder's airplane, and then handed her the smaller boy and the dog.

Schröder's engine roared and he started his takeoff roll.

Ostrowski came to Cronley's Storch, hoisted the larger boy into it, and then got in himself.

Cronley turned the Storch, shoved the throttle to takeoff power, and started to roll.

When he had lifted off, he turned to look at Likharev's elder son, thinking he would reassure him.

He quickly looked away.

He had never before in his life seen absolute terror in anyone's eyes. He saw it now.

[EIGHT]
Hangar Two
U.S. Air Force Base, Fritzlar, Hesse
American Zone of Occupation, Germany
1630 19 January 1946

The hangar doors opened as Cronley taxied up to them. He stopped and killed the engine. Before that process was over, half a dozen of Tiny's Troopers appeared and pushed the Storch into the hangar. Then the doors closed.

Schröder's Storch was already in the hangar, and its passengers had gotten out of the aircraft.

There were two ambulances in the hangar, and what looked like two doctors and twice that many nurses. And someone Cronley really didn't expect to see. The general's wife.

Mrs. White was standing with her arm around Mrs. Likharev. The younger boy was standing beside them with a hot dog in one hand and a Hershey bar in the other. Captain Dunwiddie was holding Franz Josef.

Cronley felt his eyes water and his throat tighten.

"We have a problem with this one," Max Ostrowski said.

"What?"

"He crapped his pants. He pissed his pants and he crapped his pants. I'm soaked with piss from my navel to my knees."

Cronley failed to suppress a giggle. And the laughter that followed.

"Fuck you," Ostrowski said, and then he chuckled, which turned into a giggle.

Cronley put his mouth to the open window and bellowed, "Captain Dunwiddie!"

When Captain Dunwiddie appeared beside the plane, so did Mrs. White and Mrs. Likharev.

"Is there a problem?" Mrs. White inquired.

"Yes, ma'am," Cronley said. "This young man has had an accident, as my mother used to call it."

"Big or little?"

"Both. And Captain Ostrowski has suffered collateral damage."

Mrs. White managed to suppress all but a small giggle.

Then she said, "Captain, I understand you speak Russian?"

"Yes, ma'am, I do."

"Then tell Mrs. Likharev of the problem, and tell her not to worry, Captain Dunwiddie will deal with it."

"Yes, ma'am."

"What am I supposed to do about it?" Dunwiddie asked.

"You're a Cavalry officer, Chauncey, you'll think of something," Mrs. White said.

Captain Dunwiddie stood beside the Storch and told Cronley what he had thought of as a solution to the problem.

"I'll have my guys form a human shield around Max and the boy as they get out of the plane and then march them across the hangar to where we billeted the ASA guys. And while they're having a shower, I'll get them clothing from somewhere."

"Good thinking, Chauncey," Cronley said. "You're a credit to the U.S. Cavalry."

"Fuck you."

Cronley stayed in the plane until Max and the boy, shielded by eight very large, very black soldiers, had been marched across the hangar and into the building at the rear.

Then he climbed out of the Storch.

Mrs. White, Mrs. Likharev, the younger boy, and the dachshund were standing near the ambulances. The boy was feeding Franz Josef a piece of his hot dog.

Cronley exhaled.

Well, it's over. Really, completely over.

Or will be as soon as we get those two some clean clothes.

I feel sorry for the kid. He has to be embarrassed.

For himself.

And for what he did to Max.

And then his mind's eye was filled with the older kid's terror-frozen eyes in the airplane right after they'd taken off.

And then he felt a sudden chill.

And threw up. And then dropped to his knees and threw up again. And then once again.

Jesus H. Christ!

He got awkwardly to his feet.

He felt dizzy and another sudden chill.

Oh, no, not again!

He closed his eyes, put his hands on his hips, leaned his head back, and took a deep breath.

And was not nauseous again.

He opened his eyes and found himself looking at Major Harold Wallace.

"I must have eaten something . . ."

"You all right now, Jim?" Wallace asked.

"I'm fine. A little embarrassed."

"Don't be. It happens to all of us."

"Yes, it does," Lieutenant Colonel William Wilson said. Cronley hadn't been aware of his presence until he spoke. "When I picked the colonel up outside Králický Sněžník, he didn't even wait until we got home. He puked all over the L-4 before we got to two hundred feet."

"Thank you for sharing that, Billy," Wallace said.

"I thought I should. I thought Tex here should hear that."

"And, for once, you're right," Wallace said. "Tex, Schröder made it to the latrine just now before he tossed his cookies. But then he has more experience with this sort of thing than you do."

That's "Tex" twice.

Have I just been christened?

"So what happens now?"

"Odd that you should ask, Tex," Wallace said. "As I was just about to tell you."

[NINE]
Suite 507
Hotel Vier Jahreszeiten
Maximilianstrasse 178
Munich, American Zone of Occupation, Germany
1645 20 January 1946

"I didn't expect to see you until tomorrow, at the earliest," Miss Claudette Colbert said to Captain James D. Cronley Jr. when he walked into the office.

"Nice to see you, too, Miss Colbert."

"Are you going to bring me up to speed, sir?"

"When no one's around, you can call me 'Tex,' Miss Colbert."

"Tex?"

"I have been so dubbed by Major Wallace. Where's Freddy?"

"At the *bahnhof*, meeting General Greene and party."

"Greene is here? What the hell is that all about?"

"There was an unfortunate accident at the *bahnhof* yesterday afternoon."

"What kind of an accident?"

"Major Derwin apparently lost his balance and fell onto the tracks under a freight train as it was passing through. He had just gotten off the Blue Danube from Frankfurt, and was walking down the platform when this happened."

"Is Major Wallace aware of this?"

"'Tell Captain Cronley not to even think assassination option,' end quote."

"Jesus Christ!" Cronley said, and then asked, "And that's why Greene is here?"

"'General Greene is going to meet with the Munich provost marshal to offer the CIC's assistance in the investigation of this unfortunate accident,' end quote."

"What the hell was Derwin doing back here?"

"'He telephoned Lieutenant Colonel Parsons of the War Department's liaison mission to DCI-Europe and told him he had information regarding DCI-Europe that he felt Parsons should have' . . ."

"Jesus!"

". . . continuing the quote, 'which we of course do not know, as that was an ASA telephone intercept.' End quote."

"My God!"

"There was another intercept. General Greene called Colonel Parsons and asked him what he knew about what Derwin wanted to tell him. Parsons said he had no idea, that he had never even met Derwin."

"Is that another quote?"

"No."

"Then I won't ask where that came from."

"Thank you. Your turn, Tex."

"Okay. You know the Likharevs are in Sonthofen?"

"As guests of General and Mrs. White. And where they will remain until we can get them on the SAA flight to Buenos Aires the day after tomorrow."

"Right," Cronley said. "I didn't know about the day after tomorrow."

"Mrs. Likharev and the colonel have exchanged brief messages over the SIGABA."

"I didn't know that, either. I'm glad."

"Which resulted in this," Claudette said, and handed him a SIGABA printout.

```
PRIORITY

TOP SECRET LINDBERGH

DUPLICATION FORBIDDEN

FROM POLO

VIA VINT HILL TANGO NET

2210 GREENWICH 18 JANUARY 1946

EYES ONLY ALTARBOY

QUOTE MAY ALL OF GODS MANIFOLD BLESSINGS FALL ON
YOUR SHOULDERS STOP I WILL FOREVER BE IN YOUR
DEBT STOP YOUR LOVING FRIEND SERGEI ENDQUOTE

POLO

END

TOP SECRET LINDBERGH
```

"Well, you know what they say," Cronley said. "Russians sometimes get carried away."

"You're crying, Tex," Claudette said.

He shrugged.

"I know how to cure that," she said. "But I don't think this is the place to do it. Why don't we go to your room?"